ON THE LINE

"Another gripping tale, and her many fans will be delighted to return to Hidden Cove and see what's happened to their favorite characters."
—*Booklist*

"Ms. Shay is always worth reading and never fails . . . As usual, she has a compelling story with three-dimensional characters and situations."
—*Huntress Reviews*

"An exhilarating, fiery romance . . . Readers will appreciate this dynamic homage to real heroes."
—*Midwest Book Review*

AFTER THE FIRE

"This powerful, emotionally realistic book is the first of Shay's new trilogy about the men and women who put their lives on the line every day and how that dedication and commitment affect all those around them. Poignant and compelling, this novel reinforces Shay's well-earned reputation as a first-rate storyteller."
—*Booklist*

"Powerfully written . . . genuine . . . Shay pays homage to rescue workers with this exhilarating tale that demands a sequel."
—*Midwest Book Review*

"[With her] moving and action-filled romance, Ms. Shay begins a new series that will tug on readers' hearts. She deftly balances multiple story lines with characters you can recognize from real life and care about."
—*Huntress Reviews*

continued . . .

TRUST IN ME

"[This] powerful tale of redemption, friendship, trust, and forgiving shows once again that Shay knows how to pack an emotional wallop."
—*Booklist*

"An unusual and compelling tale . . . I don't know when I have become more involved in a novel's characters and story."
—*The Romance Reader*

"A master storyteller . . . Don't miss this book or you will be sorry you did."
—*Reader to Reader Reviews*

"Each one of [Shay's novels] is a moving tale of friendship, the truest form of love."
—*Huntress Reviews*

PROMISES TO KEEP

"A wonderful work of contemporary romance. With a plot ripped straight from the headlines, *Promises to Keep* evokes genuine people confronting a genuine crisis with all the moral, ethical, and emotional struggles in between."
—*New York Times* bestselling author Lisa Gardner

"Emotion, romance, realism, and intrigue. A love story that you'll never forget. *Promises to Keep* is romantic suspense at its very best, with a dynamic cast of characters, a plot that will hold you on the edge of your seat, and an ending that you'll remember long after you turn the last page."
—*USA Today* bestselling author Catherine Anderson

Titles by Kathryn Shay

PROMISES TO KEEP
TRUST IN ME
AFTER THE FIRE
ON THE LINE
NOTHING MORE TO LOSE
SOMEONE TO BELIEVE IN

SOMEONE TO BELIEVE IN

KATHRYN SHAY

BERKLEY SENSATION, NEW YORK

THE BERKLEY PUBLISHING GROUP
Published by the Penguin Group
Penguin Group (USA) Inc.
375 Hudson Street, New York, New York 10014, USA
Penguin Group (Canada), 90 Eglinton Avenue East, Suite 700, Toronto, Ontario M4P 2Y3, Canada
(a division of Pearson Penguin Canada Inc.)
Penguin Books Ltd., 80 Strand, London WC2R 0RL, England
Penguin Group Ireland, 25 St. Stephen's Green, Dublin 2, Ireland (a division of Penguin Books Ltd.)
Penguin Group (Australia), 250 Camberwell Road, Camberwell, Victoria 3124, Australia
(a division of Pearson Australia Group Pty. Ltd.)
Penguin Books India Pvt. Ltd., 11 Community Centre, Panchsheel Park, New Delhi—110 017, India
Penguin Group (NZ), Cnr. Airborne and Rosedale Roads, Albany, Auckland 1310, New Zealand
(a division of Pearson New Zealand Ltd.)
Penguin Books (South Africa) (Pty.) Ltd., 24 Sturdee Avenue, Rosebank, Johannesburg 2196, South Africa

Penguin Books Ltd., Registered Offices: 80 Strand, London WC2R 0RL, England

This is a work of fiction. Names, characters, places, and incidents either are the product of the author's imagination or are used fictitiously, and any resemblance to actual persons, living or dead, business establishments, events, or locales is entirely coincidental. The publisher does not have any control over and does not assume any responsibility for author or third-party websites or their content.

SOMEONE TO BELIEVE IN

A Berkley Sensation Book / published by arrangement with the author

PRINTING HISTORY
Berkley Sensation edition / September 2005

Copyright © 2005 by Mary Catherine Schaefer.
Excerpt from *Conflict of Interest* copyright © 2006 by Mary Catherine Schaefer.
Cover art by Franco Accornero.
Cover design by George Long.

ISBN: 0-425-20530-4

BERKLEY® SENSATION
Berkley Sensation Books are published by The Berkley Publishing Group,
a division of Penguin Group (USA) Inc.,
375 Hudson Street, New York, New York 10014.
BERKLEY SENSATION and the "B" design are trademarks belonging to Penguin Group (USA) Inc.

PRINTED IN THE UNITED STATES OF AMERICA

10 9 8 7 6 5 4 3 2 1

*For my sisters,
Joanie, Dee Dee, and Patty,
and for my brother Joe.
As shown in this book,
siblings are priceless.*

 PROLOGUE

"LADIES AND GENTLEMEN of the jury. Have you reached a verdict?"

"Yes, Your Honor, we have." His face somber, the foreman handed a paper to the bailiff.

As the court officer brought the findings to the judge, District Attorney Clayton Wainwright scanned the courtroom. It was like a morgue. And he just didn't get it. He'd proven his case, and he was sure the perpetrator would be convicted. So why was Sandra Jones, the judge, glaring at him, the jury looking as if it were about to sentence Christ to crucifixion, and even his own assistant acting like Clay had betrayed God?

He stole a glance at the defendant. Hell, she looked about sixteen, not twenty-five. Long dark hair, porcelain skin. Even a few freckles if you got up close. Her appearance just didn't fit with the image of the worldly anti–youth gang specialist that she'd made a name as. Maybe that was why, right from the start, this case had put a sour taste in everybody's mouth. Truthfully, Clay had had some moments of self-doubt himself. But it was his job to prosecute her, and was in keeping with his tough-on-crime, particularly juvenile crime, stance.

Her face blank, the judge handed the verdict back to the bailiff who returned it to the foreman. He read aloud, "The jury finds Bailey O'Neil guilty of Accessory After the Fact."

Clayton was far from elated, but she deserved the outcome. She was guilty as hell of harboring a criminal, in this case a teenager, knowing he'd committed murder.

He heard a gasp, and saw O'Neil grab on to her lawyer, her complexion ashen. A hush came over the courtroom.

Then the foreman spoke up. "The members of the jury have a statement I'd like to read, Judge Jones, if that's all right."

"I object," Clay said, bolting out of his chair. "This is clearly out of order."

"Objection overruled. Sit down, Mr. Wainwright. You got what you wanted." The judge turned her attention to the juror. "Go ahead, Mr. Foreman."

He read, "While we recognize the error committed by Ms. O'Neil, and acknowledge that the evidence is substantial, we strongly recommend a light sentence. Ms. O'Neil has kept kids out of gangs, as shown by the defense presented, and she's saved lives doing it. We applaud the good she's done, and believe she can do even more to stop youth gangs, given the chance. The requisite fine is acceptable, but the two-to-five-year imprisonment is not. We recommend a suspended sentence."

Clay was on his feet again, but before he could open his mouth, the judge held up her hand, palm out. "Mr. District Attorney. Do not object. I've heard your arguments. I will take the jury's wishes under consideration. The defendant is to remain in custody until Monday of next week, when I'll render the sentence. Court is adjourned." The slap of the gavel echoed like a gunshot in the too-silent courtroom.

What the hell was going on here? If the defendant received a suspended sentence, it would send the wrong message to people in general, and kids especially. To them, it would say, "Adults will protect you when you break the law." Clay snapped his briefcase shut. He noticed no one congratulated him, not even his assistant. He looked over to the defense table; O'Neil's attorney held her in his arms. She cried softly. Clay felt an unwarranted spurt of guilt.

But what else was he supposed to do? A young man had been murdered, and this newly convicted woman had harbored the killer. When the punk had been caught and questioned, it had slipped out that he'd hidden in the office of his "guardian angel," who was Bailey O'Neil, and that he'd told her what he'd done. Still, she'd lied to the police when they questioned her about his whereabouts. The boy later contended the murder was committed in self-defense, but that was yet to be determined.

As soon as Clay left the building, he was surrounded by reporters sticking microphones in his face and flashing cameras at him. Backdropped by busy traffic sounds on the street, a crowd had gathered on the courthouse steps. "Mr. Wainwright, does this case affect your throwing your hat into the ring for the Senate race this year?" one reporter asked.

Straightening his tie, Clay cleared his throat and swallowed his doubts. "Why would it?"

"It's no secret Bailey O'Neil has the sympathy of people in this town."

"The jury found her guilty. I did my part in upholding the law, which she broke. As you know, I'm running for the senate on a zero-tolerance-for-crime platform, in concert with the Republican Party's stance, particularly for teenagers. I believe the voters want a safer city, state, nation."

"Don't you think this is a little like Goliath attacking David?" another reporter shouted.

"No, I don't." And he didn't. He fully believed he was doing the right thing, even if watching Bailey O'Neil had been tough to take. In some ways, he bought the defense's theory that hers was a do-gooder's knee-jerk reaction to protect a kid. Her lawyer had called her a "street angel" in his closing statements.

Well, the Street Angel was going to be caged, he guessed. It was the right thing to do. He just hoped this case didn't haunt him the rest of his career.

ONE

ELEVEN YEARS LATER

CLAY WAINWRIGHT SLAPPED the morning's *New York Sun* down onto his desk after reading the inflammatory letter to the editor. "What the hell does that woman want from me?"

"Calm down, Senator." Usually as patient as Job, his press secretary, Mica Proust, sighed with weary exasperation.

"I'll calm down when our little Street Angel has her wings clipped once and for all." Hell, Bailey O'Neil was still using the name she'd gotten during the trial more than a decade ago when he'd prosecuted, and won, a case against her.

"Thorn's coming right up."

"Yeah, well, he won't like this one." Loosening his tie, Clay unbuttoned the collar of his light blue shirt. He'd already shed his suit coat; his temper had heated his body and caused his blood pressure to skyrocket.

Mica gave Clay an indulgent look, like the ones his string of nannies used to bestow on him. He didn't particularly appreciate the comparison. "I'm continually amazed at the effect that woman has on you. You face the Senate Majority Leader down without a qualm, and I've seen you handle angry constituents without breaking into a sweat. But her . . ."

He gave the older woman a self-effacing grin. "I know. She turns me into a raving maniac. Maybe because she got off practically scot-free for Accessory After the Fact."

"A year behind bars is not scot-free." Slick and tidy, Jack Thornton, his chief of staff, entered Clay's office, which was housed in the Russell Building on Capitol Hill. Thorn took a seat on one of the two leather couches in the mahogany-paneled room, propped his ankle on his knee, and shook his head. "The Street Angel's at it again, I take it."

While Mica filled Thorn in, Clay pushed back his chair, stood, and began to pace. He ran a frustrated hand through his thick crop of hair as he covered the carpet. When Mica finished, Clay started to rant again. "I have not lost my edge. I have not caved to politics. Who the hell does she think is, suggesting I should retire to a country home and play golf, for God's sake?"

"More than likely she's pissed at you now for blocking the funding for Guardian House in the Appropriations Committee." Thorn's voice was neutral as he studied his notes. "And for writing those memos to the governor and her local senators about that interactive network she's got up and running at ESCAPE."

"ESCAPE!" Her anti–youth gang operation. "I'd close it down completely if I could."

"And she knows you'd do that."

"It's a menace to society. The police should deal with gang intervention. Not a social agency that coddles young criminals."

This was an old debate, one they were all well-versed in.

Thorn said, "What happened eleven years ago also remains between you."

"That woman's only gotten worse in the last decade. Guardian needs to be stopped. The last thing we should be funding is a shelter for gang kids. The money from Stewart's new bill should go to poor, underprivileged kids who didn't choose a life of crime."

"Hey," Mica put in, "you're preaching to the choir here."

His press secretary glanced at his chief of staff. Thorn added, "I just found out she's throwing her weight behind Lawson."

"What?"

"Publicly. She told the *Sun* she'd be volunteering for the young councilman's campaign bid for the Democratic primary for senator next year so he can run against you in the November election."

"Oh, this is just great." Clay scowled. "Get the governor on the phone."

"Clay." Mica spoke gently from where she'd gone to stand by the window that overlooked Delaware Avenue. "You can't afford to antagonize him again about this. He likes Bailey O'Neil."

"The only reason that woman has his ear is because she helped his niece when the girl was being lured into that gang."

Clay saw Mica and Thorn exchange frowns this time.

"Okay, okay, I know. She's done some good. She's saved some kids. But she broke the law to do it once that we know about, and God knows how many times she's broken it since then. She should be brought up on negative misprision." Not reporting a crime when a person knows one has been committed was illegal.

"You already sent her to jail once." This from Thorn.

"I don't like your semantics. I didn't *send* her to jail. She went to prison for Accessory After the Fact. For a crime against the United States of America." He cocked his head. "If I'd needed vindication, which I don't think I did, the kid she harbored was found guilty of the murder."

"The whole thing only made her a martyr. Groups fought to get her out early. Even the former governor was torn." Thorn paused. "Look Clay, you've got to get a handle on this public feud with O'Neil. We can't let that old case endanger your chances of reelection. And of being considered for the vice presidential nomination."

"That's over a year away."

"Close enough to watch everything you do now. In any case, your feud with O'Neil was negative publicity eleven years ago, which you overcame by concentrating on what you'd done to stop youth gangs as well as other juvenile crimes as a D.A. Then we effectively buried it in the last election. You can't let the case resurface and get out of hand for the next one. You've got to make peace with Bailey O'Neil now."

"Hell, it'd be easier to sell her the Brooklyn Bridge."

"I think we should set up a meeting with her. Better, you should call her. Ask nicely for one."

He struggled to be rational. "When am I due back in New York?"

Whipping out his Palm Pilot, Thorn clicked into Clay's schedule. "Thursday. You have a late meeting with Homeland Security on Wednesday afternoon so you can fly out at dinnertime." He fiddled with some buttons. "You have a window of time that morning before you do the ribbon cutting for the women's shelter. I could have Bob set up a breakfast."

Taking in a deep breath, Clay shook his head. "No, I'll call her, like you said. And ask nicely."

His phone buzzed. Mica crossed to his desk and pressed the speaker button. "The senator's son is on line one."

Clay's steps halted. Jon rarely phoned him. And almost never at the office. He felt the familiar prick of loss shift through him. "We done? I'd like to take this in private."

Thorn nodded. "Sure."

His staff left and Clay tried to calm his escalated heartbeat. *Fine commentary on your life, Wainwright, when a simple call from your son affects you like this.* Dropping down in his chair, he caught sight of the picture that sat on his desk of him and Jon, taken last year when Jon went off to college. Same dark blond hair. Same light brown eyes. Same broad shoulders. But they were as different as night and day. At least now they were.

Clay picked up the phone. "Hello, Jon."

"Dad." The ice was still in the kid's voice, though a bit thawed. "How are you?" Pleasantries at least. Better than the accusations the last time they'd talked . . .

You know, I may not even vote for you. That bill you cosponsored shortchanged the environment across the board.

That bill provided needed funds for shelters for battered women.

Yeah, the token bone, tacked on to get guys like you to vote for it.

Pushing away the bad memories, Clay asked, "How are you, son?"

"Whipped."

"Anything new?"

"Uh-huh. I'm in charge of the fund-raiser for our Earth Environment Group." Jon attended Bard College as an environmental engineer major. He'd gone up to school in mid-July with some other students to plan the year's activities for their organization. Jon coughed as if he was about to do something unpleasant. "The dean asked if you could come to the event we're sponsoring to kick off our fund drive. He thought maybe you could give a talk to the students who'll be here for orientation and community members who would jump at the chance to hear their senator speak."

Ah, so the kid wanted something from him. "If I can. When is it?"

Jon named a date and time. "I already checked with Bob, to see if you were free. Congress will be on recess."

So you didn't have to ask a favor for nothing. "Well, then, let's set it up. Can we do something together, just you and me, while I'm there?"

A long pause, which cut to the quick. "Like what?"

"Go into the city. Have dinner. See a show."

"I guess."

At one time, Jon issued the invitations . . . *Let's catch that Knicks game . . . I want you there, Dad, at my debate . . . I need to talk about a girl . . .*

When on earth had they lost that? During the long campaigns when Clay wasn't home much? After all the school events and baseball games he'd missed? In the midst of the messy divorce from Jon's mother, who, Clay suspected, bad-mouthed him on a regular basis?

Because he wanted badly to mend their fences, he said with enthusiasm, "Okay, then, we're on. I'm looking forward to it."

"Yeah, me, too. It'll be a great fund-raiser."

Not what he meant, and his son knew it. Clay wondered if

Jon distanced him on purpose. Angered by the thought, he tapped a pencil on his desk, and let the frost creep into his own voice. "I'll talk to you before then."

He put down the phone, thinking of a time when conversations had ended with *I love you*. Because the fact that they no longer automatically said those words hurt, he tried to focus on something else. Absently, he picked up the paper and stared again at the editorial page. Now Bailey O'Neil was aligning herself with the man who was after Clay's seat in Congress.

Hell, he didn't want to lock horns with her again. Grabbing his phone again, he said to his assistant, "Joanie, get me Bailey O'Neil in New York, would you? I think we have her work phone on file." Gripping the receiver before the call was punched through, he said aloud, "Okay, sweetheart, time for another round."

SO, WHO ARE you? The words scrolled across the screen of Bailey's computer, like so many others, typed casually.

You know who I am or you wouldn't have come to my site, TazDevil2. Bailey was unfamiliar with the screen name.

No response.

So she typed, *I'm the Street Angel. And I can help you.*

Yeah, sure.

Why don't you tell me why you came to my site. It's just us two. She grinned in the empty office. *And I won't tell anybody else.* No matter what the good senator from New York does to me.

Chill out a minute.

Bailey waited. Kids needed time to take this big step. As she drummed her fingers on the table, she scanned her messy office. ESCAPE, her organization, which helped kids find a way out of gang life, needed more space. They'd grown so much they had to rent three offices on this floor, and still she shared hers with a coworker. But she'd rather direct the funds to programs instead of spending it on overhead. When they moved, as they did every few years to maintain their anonymity—much like shelters for battered women—their space probably wouldn't be much larger.

Her private phone shrilled into the silence, making her startle. She wondered if she should answer it while the newest visitor to her interactive website garnered his or her courage. Or got interrupted. Bailey winced. Once, she'd been on the phone hotline with a boy and he cut off abruptly. Bailey later suspected he'd been caught and killed. A body had turned up with earmarks of the teen she'd been talking to. *Don't think about the loss.* To avoid it, she picked up the phone. "Bailey O'Neil."

"Ms. O'Neil, this is Clayton Wainwright."

Oh, shit. "Senator, this is a surprise."

"Is it?"

Ah, he had seen the letter in the *Sun*. "Hmm."

"I was wondering if you'd make some time for me on Thursday of next week. I'll be in New York." His voice was deeper, huskier than she remembered.

"Um, I'm pretty busy."

"You have to eat. How about breakfast?"

Okay, enough dancing. Not only did they have a history together, but she despised his politics and the damage he'd done to social agencies like hers. No way was she going to see him in person. "Look, Senator, we don't have much to say to each other. You disagree with how I choose to help kids, and I think you're conservative and backward and that you've copped out on the potential you showed early in your career. We're never going to see eye to eye."

"Humor me."

"I don't think so."

"I'm afraid I have to insist."

"Are you for real?"

"What does that mean?"

"That you can insist all you want. It has no effect on me." Time to take the gloves off. "I'm furious with you for your two latest tricks."

"Tricks?"

"Blocking my funding for Guardian at the federal level. At least so far. And then for writing memos to the state officials about ESCAPE."

"They weren't—"

The instant message chimed, indicating someone had posted. "Look, I've got to go. Thanks for the invitation, but no." She hung up before he could respond, and read the message.

TazDevil2 was back on. *Maybe I'm thinkin' this is jackshit.*

You don't have to be tough with me. Tell me about your situation.

A pause. *I got me a set. The Good Girls.*

Bailey froze. The Good Girls had been the worst girl gang in New York City in the eighties. Swallowing her reaction, she typed, *That gang doesn't exist anymore.*

Yeah, dude, they do. We been calling ourselves that for a few months. Used to be the Shags. Decided to reincarnate that other gang 'cuz they was so tough.

Uncomfortable, Bailey toyed with the picture of Rory on her desk. *I know.*

How?

I was close to somebody in the GGs.

Hey, you got the tag right.

Yeah.

Who was it?

My sister. She was one of the original members.

Fucking A! You kiddin' me?

I wish I was. I saw firsthand what the GGs did to girls.

No comment.

How old are you?

Seventeen.

How old were you when you got in?

Fourteen.

The same age as Moira. Beautiful, troubled Moira, whom Bailey had loved unconditionally, despite the problems her half sister had caused in her family.

That her name?

Yeah. Did you jump or train in?

Jumped. I ain't no boy's slave. Bailey knew that "training" into a gang—fucking several guys fast and in a row like train cars—was the preferred method of gang initiation over "jumping" in, which consisted of being brutally beaten by the members. Except if you trained in, you were treated like scum afterward.

What happened to her?

Moira? She died.

No answer.

Again, Bailey glanced at the phone. Moira had died in prison, where a young D.A., much like Clayton Wainwright, had put her. Bailey herself had been partly responsible, too.

You sad about it still?

Every day of my life.

You got more family?

I do. Four brothers. Me, my mom, and dad.

How come she join a gang if she got family like you?

Because Dad slipped up, and had a kid with another woman. *Long story.* Since the girl seemed to want to talk, she asked, *What's your name?*

Tazmania. I go by Taz.

Tell me about yourself.

A pause. *Maybe later. Gotta jet now, Angel. Ciao.*

Ciao. And then Bailey added, *Stay in touch. Please. I'm on tomorrow night.*

No answer.

For a moment, Bailey just watched the blank computer screen. Sighing, she leaned back in her rickety chair, eased off her scuffed loafers, and propped her feet up on the desk. Idly, she noted that her jeans were threadbare and almost white at the knees. She plucked at the frayed cuffs of the oxford cloth blouse she wore. Geez, she needed new clothes. But hell, who had the time or inclination for shopping?

Shutting her eyes and linking her hands behind her neck, she tried to center herself. She became aware of the quiet. It had gotten late, and the day-shift workers had left the office. The hotline and website night crew would be in soon. But for now she was alone with her memories of Moira. With the pain that twisted her heart like an emotional vise whenever she thought about her half sister. The pain had dulled, but never really gone away. She was alone with her now-rabid zeal to save kids, which she knew was obsessive. That quest had taken over her life until her son, Rory, came along. And it was still too important to her. But she couldn't help it. She was going to make a difference.

She thought of Clayton Wainwright—her nemesis since his district attorney days. Though she didn't blame him for prosecuting her—she had been guilty, after all, of harboring the kid when he'd told her he'd committed a crime—she did hold Wainwright in contempt for his continual vigilance over her organization, and his attempts to keep her funding at bay. Her efforts had been stalled considerably, more than once, just because of him. Now, however, a new battle would ensue; there was money available from the government in a bill initiated by a senator from Massachusetts and passed by Congress for both social agencies and law enforcement. Bailey wanted some of the funds. Wainwright was just as determined not to give them to her.

If he only knew what was really what. But he lived in an ivory tower, with a silver spoon in his mouth, so he could never conceive of what street life was like for kids. Because of that he was dangerous. Best to keep her guard up. With a man like him, you needed your guns poised and your belt full of ammunition; she couldn't hand him any bullets to stop her with no matter how nicely he asked.

"Beware, Senator Wainwright," she said glaring at the phone. "I'm gonna win this round. The Street Angel·is not giving up."

TAZ TURNED UP the volume of the latest Marilyn Manson song, which already blasted from her computer, and crossed to the mirror above a dresser in her dingy bedroom. Carefully, she streaked three fingertips over her face. The Vaseline went on smooth and thick. It made her deep brown eyes glisten like the stars. Better yet, it'd protect her skin from knife cuts.

Tonight she was after some hard beef with her girls. Mazie Lennon's boyfriend had been spotted with a member of Anthrax, and Mazie had called out her home girls to teach the broad a lesson. It was payback time. Taz didn't think any guy was worth the trouble, but when your home girls wanted help, you went. Her opinion of the male species as lowlifes was why she hadn't trained in.

Did you jump or train in?

Smart girls knew it was better to jump in; training in made you boys' slaves. But most *chola* weren't tough enough to do it. Taz had been tough. She fingered her ribcage remembering that night. The older girls had cracked two ribs with the billy club they'd jacked from a cop and used in Taz's initiation. They'd blackened and bloodied one eye and it had stayed shut for a week. They'd given her killer shin kicks; her hair had been pulled so hard she'd felt her fucking eyes bulge. But she'd stuck it out longer than any chick on record, and even some of the guys in the neighboring gangs, who did jump in. Scared the shit out of all of them. Problem was she was so tough, she was always having to prove it. Which was why she went on-line tonight.

You don't have to be tough with me.

Done with her own special brand of a facial, Taz braided her hair so it was close to her scalp and couldn't be pulled; she tied an orange bandana, the GG's flag, around her head. Then she switched off the small lamp on her dresser. In the dim light from an outdoor streetlight, she slugged back on a forty—forty ounces of malt—and crossed to a makeshift desk. Picking up the laptop she'd stolen from the school—and slept with a computer geek to get bootleg Internet connection—she stuffed the machine in her closet in a locked box. If the old man found it, he'd sell it for booze.

He'd already tried to sell her.

How come she join a gang if she got family like you?

Christ, why the hell had she gone to the Street Angel's website? Taz guzzled some more beer, found her blade, and tested its sharpness in three shallow slits on her forearm; she smiled as she tasted the coppery blood. Every GG carried the same blade. She looked down at the tattoo ringing her belly button, visible under her crop top. It was a pitchfork. Hurt like hell the night they all got one.

When she heard the front door open, she spat out, "Fuck," grabbed her GG's jacket and hustled to the window. Jimmying it, she slipped out just as she heard the pounding. And the swearing. And the foul names he called her.

Her steel-toed boots clanged on the fire escape as she took the steps two at a time, clutching the forty and the blade close to her chest. In minutes, she was away from him, headed toward her real family.

Fingering her knife, she smiled. The dumb-ass cunt who had moved on Mazie's man was gonna regret her flirting all right. By the time Taz got to the rendezvous point, she'd chugged more malt and had convinced herself she couldn't wait for the games to begin.

~ TWO

CLAY LEANED AGAINST a storefront on MacDougal Street, under an overhang to avoid the rain which drummed on the small roof, and folded his arms over his chest. He had no idea why he was here, at midnight on a miserable Friday in July, scoping out the pub across the street. After his dinner with the governor, he'd been comfortably ensconced in his brownstone on the Upper East Side and had just talked to Jane. She'd not been happy that he was out of Washington tonight, and missing the birthday party she'd thrown for her father, the senator from Virginia. Jane had left the shindig to call Clay and whine.

God, he hated whining. His ex-wife had been a whiner. He suspected Jon bore the brunt of that now.

After Clay had hung up with Jane, he'd tried to work, but he couldn't stop thinking about Bailey O'Neil. The governor had talked about her and Clay's open feud, expressing his own chagrin at being caught between them. He explicitly said he thought she and Clay should bury the hatchet. It irked him that he'd felt defensive about their relationship. Hadn't he tried to meet with her? She'd flatly refused to see him when he'd made an overture.

During their discussion, the governor had also mentioned that her brothers owned Bailey's Irish Pub in the Village. On a whim, Clay had gone to the restaurant's website. Sure enough, the owners were listed as O'Neils: Patrick, Dylan, Liam, and Aidan. The senior Paddy O'Neil had turned over the business to his four sons and was semiretired. No mention of a daughter, though.

For privacy because of her job? No, that wouldn't be. Only the governor and a select few knew the Street Angel was Bailey O'Neil. She kept her identity hidden for her safety. Damn it, did the woman know the danger she was in? If she'd deigned to see him, he would have reminded her. But, of course, she'd refused.

So, after he'd Googled the pub, Clay had hopped in a cab and come here. What were the chances of her being at her family's place this late on a Friday night? Still, when the rain let up, he pushed away from the storefront and headed across the street, dodging cars, which seemed to honk willy nilly in this city, avoiding the spray of water from their tires. It was unseasonably cool, and he turned up the collar of his jacket.

The door to the pub was heavy as he pulled it open. He took time to appreciate the intricately carved oak before he stepped inside, where the lilting sound of Irish music filled the air. Scents from the kitchen made his mouth water; on the tables he saw steaming bowls of stew and crusty bread, which accounted for the smells. He stayed in the corner, in the shadows, and stared across the room. Five men and one woman stood in front of a piano, which was being played by an older woman. The males were all versions of one another, as if somebody had painted the same person at various ages of their lives: thick black hair, strong features, big eyes. The woman with them—the woman with the crystal-clear alto voice singing about the green hills of Ireland—also sported the same features, but this time the artist changed brushes and painted her with delicate, feminine strokes. A skein of inky hair rioted down her back.

Bailey O'Neil. Looking a little older than the last time he'd seen her, but not much. Her fresh-faced innocence amazed him once again.

All of them wore black pants and green shirts with an insignia on the left chest. They finished their song and the room erupted into applause, accompanied by raucous pounding on the tables. Clay hadn't noticed how crowded the pub was. One strapping young buck threw back his chair, stalked to the singers, and picked Bailey up. He kissed her on the mouth and swung her around. She whispered something in his ear and he laughed. Clay scanned the room, saw there were no unoccupied tables, but a stool at the bar was available.

He crossed to it and sat down, easing off his light jacket and draping it over the backrest to dry. The dark oak bar was U-shaped and hand-carved like the door. It was, literally, a work of art. The bartender, an older woman, hustled over to him, wiping her eyes. She'd been watching the singers. "Sorry, sir. I've a soft spot in me heart for that song. What'll ya have?"

"A Guinness."

"Build ya one right away, I will."

The woman busied herself at the tap. Clay, still in the shadows, watched Bailey chat with the others, and then head for the kitchen, calling over her shoulder, "I'll relieve you in a sec, Bridget. Let me just check on Rory."

"No hurry, darlin'."

As Clay waited—building a Guinness took a while—he scanned the interior. Tables scattered throughout. Thick planked floor. Subdued lighting. And posters everywhere. Of Ireland, houses, events sponsored by the establishment. There were photos, too. Right next to him on the adjacent wall was a corkboard of pictures. Little kids—a lot of them. "Them's the grandkids," Bridget said as she brought his beer and plunked it down on the bar. Some of the foam dribbled down the side of the glass.

Taking the mug, Clay lifted the drink to his lips, sipped the creamy smooth blend, and sighed. "Your grandkids?"

"No, the O'Neils'. There's Michael, Shea, Sinead, Kathleen, Cleary, and Hogan."

Clay grinned at the catalog of names, which sounded like an Irish school roster.

"And this here's little Rory. The newest. The devil's in him, for sure."

The boy was a miniature of all the O'Neils. Dark hair. Blue eyes. Maybe four or five years old.

Clay was about to ask after another photo, one of a young teenage girl who looked vaguely reminiscent of the O'Neils but wasn't the spitting image of them, when Bailey came up behind Bridget. "I'm here, so go rest. You've been on your feet all . . ." Her voice trailed off as she caught sight of who sat before her. Her eyes—he'd forgotten how blue they were—widened. Her pretty mouth scowled as she took Clay in. She had a few more freckles than he remembered. "Jesus Christ, what the hell are you doing here?"

"Bailey Ann, don't take the name of the Lord in vain."

Bailey heard her mother chide her, but her head was reeling with shock. Peripherally, she saw Bridget back away, and her father come into the bar area, on the opposite side.

"Bailey? Did you hear your ma, lass?"

Uh-oh. "Yeah, Pa. Sorry."

Sensing something, as only mothers do, Mary Kate O'Neil came to her side. "And who is this fine lookin' gentleman?"

When Bailey said nothing, Wainwright stood and held out his hand. "Clayton Wainwright."

Her mother's usually ruddy face turned as pale as cumulus clouds in the Irish sky. What the hell was wrong with Wainwright? He should have known better than to come here. Her parents blamed him completely for her sojourn in prison—and an Irish grudge could rival an Italian one any day.

"Woman, what is it?" Her father's voice penetrated the haze Bailey was in. He'd crossed to them and she nodded to Wainwright. Paddy recognized the senator right away. "Come with me, Mary, my girl." Pa escorted her mother away.

"What are you doing here?" Bailey whispered harshly.

"I'm sorry. I didn't think . . ." He cocked his head. "Look, I didn't commit any crime, Ms. O'Neil. You did. But I didn't realize your parents would be at your place tonight." He stood. "I'll be going. I'm sorry if my coming here has upset them."

"Not so fast, Wainwright," came a deep baritone from behind her. Oh, geez. Patrick. The Fighter. In her presence, especially when it dealt with any male on the planet, her brothers fell into their childhood roles. "Pa's takin' Ma home anyway."

Bailey sighed.

Patrick glared at Wainwright. "Hasslin' Bailey again, Senator?"

"I'd say we're about even on that score."

"Yeah, well, we got different views than you." This from Dylan, the Taunter. He flanked Bailey on the other side.

In minutes, Liam, the Manipulator, was behind Wainwright's stool. "Come down here slummin' for a reason, Senator?"

Wainwright looked over his shoulder and seemed startled but not afraid to see her third oldest protector.

Where the hell was Aidan the Peacemaker when she needed him? The youngest son, only a year older than Bailey, could diffuse this situation. She looked around frantically for him, and saw him flirting with a pretty redhead across the room. "Aidan!"

He glanced up grinning, took in the situation and bolted over. "What's goin' on, guys?"

"You know who this is?" Patrick asked.

Aidan cocked his head. "Ah, I see. You got no sense, man, comin' down here?"

The senator remained cool and unflappable, though she noticed his jaw tightened, deepening the cleft in his chin. "I'm sorry I upset your mother," he repeated. "I didn't realize your parents were still involved in the pub. I just wanted to talk to your sister, and she refused to see me."

Quickly Bailey untied the apron at her waist, scooted around her brothers, and slid under the opening at the end of the bar. "I'll see you now." She grabbed Wainwright by the arm. "We can go down the street for that breakfast you wanted. I'm starved."

Three brothers spoke at once . . .

"Like hell!"

"Over my dead body."

"We got business with him."

Aidan blocked them all. "Go, B., I'll take care of this." He looked at Wainwright, who stood unmoving. "Now, man, unless you want your nose broken."

Shaking his head, Wainwright slid off the stool and grabbed his jacket. Bailey dragged him to the door, and he heard behind them, "The asshole didn't even pay for his drink."

Aidan's voice was soothing. "Guys, it's not all his fault. You know that."

Once outside and across the street, Bailey let go of the senator. The rain had stopped and the early morning was cool and misty; she shivered in her thin T-shirt.

"Here, put this on." He slid his jacket around her shoulders. She bundled into it. It smelled male and musky. It also dwarfed her. He was a lot bigger than she remembered. ·

"Thanks."

He ran a hand through thick, sandy-colored hair. "That was a lynch mob in there."

She angled her chin. "They're overprotective."

"They all older?"

"Yep."

"You must have had a hell of an adolescence. Did you ever get to date?"

"Not much." Of course, after what happened to Moira, she didn't really care. She nodded down the street. "There's a diner a few doors away. Let's go."

He stayed where he was. "Anybody in there I need to watch my back on?"

She smiled, in spite of the circumstances. "No. They're Greeks. They don't even speak English."

They walked through the narrow street in dim light, the silence broken only by the occasional honks of horns and the curses of angry cab drivers. The diner was almost deserted and Bailey led him to a table near the window. She kept his jacket on to ward off the chill. He sat across from her in the too-small chair and stared at her. It was the first time she'd seen him, even in pictures, out of a suit. He wore a designer long-sleeved red crewneck shirt with a black T-shirt underneath. A gold chain peeked out. He'd always reminded her of Dennis Quaid, and like the actor, looked pretty damned good for a man in his mid-forties.

"So, Senator, what was so urgent that you had to come down here and practically start a riot in my family's pub?"

Clay stared across the table at the woman still wearing his jacket. With her hair pulled back off her face, she looked young and vulnerable. "I wanted to talk to you. See if we could iron some things out. I had dinner with the governor tonight and he's concerned about our *public feud,* I think he called it."

A slight smile crept across her lips. "Does this have anything to do with Eric Lawson?"

"No. I'm worried that our differences are going to hurt people."

"Hurt you, you mean?"

"No, mostly women and children. Whom I fight for."

"Not anymore. You vote down funding for helping teenagers all the time."

A waitress came and poured them coffee. Neither ordered breakfast.

"I voted down funding for Guardian because I think you're going about things the wrong way." He added meaningfully, "Like you always have."

"And who made you my watchdog?"

"The majority of twelve million voters in this state."

She arched a dark brow. "Well, maybe that'll change. Your margin wasn't that big last time. And you may have stiff competition next year. If the Democratic primary goes as I'm hoping."

"Did you side with Lawson simply to defeat me in the next election, Ms. O'Neil?"

"No."

"His emphasis isn't on women. Isn't on homeless teens and soup kitchens."

"Neither is yours these days. You're more concerned with giving the police and FBI money, not with financing community agencies. You used to be someone the people could believe in."

"I supported Clinton's bill, Feinstein's bill, and Stewart's new one to stop youth gangs. Hell, I helped Chuck draft that last one."

Her eyes glittered with resolve, turning a darker blue. Her complexion heightened in color. "The major support in those bills is for legal institutions. You used to fight more for social services and community programs."

"I still do, but contrary to you, I see the necessity for cops to have power."

She ran a restless hand through her hair. "Look, Stewart's bill does that by giving four hundred million dollars to legal institutions whereas social agencies get only one hundred mil. Isn't that enough for you for the cops?"

"I'm worried what the social agencies will do with their portion, which, by the way, I believe is too much."

"*Which* is exactly why *I* don't think you belong in office." She gave him a withering look. "I think you've copped out on the very reasons people elected you senator."

He slapped the table with his hand, making the dishes dance. "I haven't copped out! I went to Washington to make a difference at the national level."

"You haven't, though."

"Of course I have."

"Like hell," she said, her face flushing even more. "You tied up ESCAPE's funding, voted down clinic insurance to service these kids, and have so far blocked the special shelter for them I've been working like a dog to get in place. You don't care about us."

"I've gotten homeless shelters for *all* teens funded. Initiated a bill for more money to be spent on single mothers and children for health care. Not to mention my work on behalf of soup kitchens for the hungry. I just happen to think your way of helping kids is counterproductive to what the police are doing. And dangerous to you. Hell, you can't even let anybody know where ESCAPE is located, let alone the Street Angel's real name, for fear of being hurt."

"We've functioned safely this way for five years."

"Yeah, well it's only a matter of time before some disgruntled gang member who loses his woman seeks you out."

Suddenly she threw back her chair, stood, and fisted her hands on her hips. "This is exactly why I didn't want to meet with you." She leaned over and braced her arms on the table.

"Stay away from me and my family. We'll argue this out in the newspaper." With theatrical flourish, she stormed away.

After he dropped some money on the table, he followed her to the front of the restaurant and out the door. She got halfway down the street, then she turned and stomped her way back. He stood leaning against the outside brick wall, hands in his pockets, waiting for her. She marched up to him, her eyes blazing with blue fire, her cheeks rosy with pique. She reached to take off the jacket just as he put his hands on her shoulders.

They said simultaneously . . .

"Here's your jacket."

"Let me help."

A rapid *pop-pop* sounded loudly and a flash exploded in Clay's eyes. He grabbed Bailey to him, pivoted, and pushed her against the wall, blocking whatever it was from hurting her.

It took him a minute, as he held her close in a loverlike embrace, to realize he was shielding her from a camera.

Whose flash continued to go off.

"Hey, Senator, who's the new squeeze?"

Clay swore under his breath. He angled his shoulders so Bailey was completely blocked from view.

She gripped his shirt as if she was scared. "What's happening?"

Moving in even closer, his breath fanned her ear. "Nothing dangerous. I overreacted to a camera flash and probably a car backfiring."

"Oh." She still held on to him.

"Turn around and go into the restaurant; find the back way out. Use the kitchen if you have to. Scoot over to your family's pub."

"But why?"

"I'll call you and explain. Do it now unless you want to have your face plastered all over the papers tomorrow."

"Son of a bitch."

"I'm sorry." He didn't know why he did it, but he kissed her hair. She froze, then slipped out of his grasp. He waited till she was gone before he circled around.

A small man of about thirty, wiry, and dressed in jeans and a denim jacket held a camera up. He took another picture. Clay shielded his eyes. "*The Village Voice*, Senator. Who's the girl?"

"None of your business."

"It'd be Lady Jane's business." Clay's not-so-significant other was dubbed "Lady Jane" because she was a senator's daughter and had been involved, off and on, with Clay for a number of years.

"Don't you have something better to do . . ." He waited for a name.

"Hank Sellers."

"Mr. Sellers."

"The senator from New York's big news."

"How'd you know I was down here?"

"Just dumb luck, I guess."

Clay didn't believe that for a second. But who could have known where he was tonight? "You're wasting your time." He nodded to the restaurant where Bailey had gone. "Not only was that completely innocent and platonic, but even if it wasn't, my personal life is my own."

"Yeah, right."

"Do what you want. I'm leaving." He stepped into the street to hail a cab, forcing himself not to glance down to Bailey's pub.

"Senator, wait."

Clay turned.

"I'd like an interview."

He glanced at his watch. "At one a.m.? That's above and beyond the call of duty."

The guy nodded back to the Greek restaurant. Clay got the message. If he didn't give him something better to print, the reporter would speculate about tonight. "Tomorrow. I have a tour of the new women's shelter on Twenty-first Street at ten. Meet me there. We'll talk after."

"Sure thing."

Clay shook his head. This was all he needed. As he flagged down a cab and hopped in, he wondered what Bailey O'Neil was thinking of him now!

SOMETIMES, HAVING BIG brothers was a real pain in the ass. They circled Bailey around the table and fired questions at her like interrogators during the Spanish Inquisition. The fact she'd hurried into the pub still wearing Senator Wainwright's jacket hadn't helped. But, God, it smelled so good she didn't want to take it off. The place had emptied out, the music had stopped, and they all sat around a small table.

"He *what*?" This from Patrick, the oldest and most protective.

"He threw himself in front of me. Literally. I thought it was some kind of bomb or something. But it was a camera flash that went off, apparently just as a car backfired."

"He must have believed you were in danger." This from Aidan. "So he tried to protect you." Her closest sibling scanned the others. "I told you he wasn't a complete jerkoff."

"Don't mean nothing," Liam put in. "He was protecting his own ass from publicity." Though Liam was a scout leader for his son's and Rory's troop, and mild-mannered, problems with Bailey turned him into Mr. Hyde, too. She hated to upset Liam the most, because he was still sad all the time about his wife's death a year ago.

Bailey shook her head. "Yeah, guys, he was covering for himself. *After* he realized what happened. But before that, he was a regular Sir Galahad." She tucked back hair that had escaped from her clip. "Look, I don't like it any better than you, but he did put himself in harm's way for me. Much as I'd like to, I can't deny it."

"What'd he want, anyway?" Dylan asked. "To come down here." All of them looked alike, but her third oldest brother's eyes were darker, almost navy. Right now they were filled with thunderclouds as they bored into her with a stormy gaze.

"He wants to make peace." Bridget had brought them all beer and Bailey sipped hers. Truth be told she was still shaken. From the fear. And from proximity to the senator. He'd made her edgy, even before the incident with the camera. "I think the governor came down on him about our public feud."

"I told you not to write that letter to the editor." Aidan's tone was kind, despite the criticism.

"I'm pissed at his trying to block my shelter." Just the thought of his presumptuousness incensed her all over again. "Who the fuck does he think he is?"

Patrick straightened. "Hey, watch your mouth, young lady."

"Gimme a break, Paddy." She was thirty-six years old, a mother, and they treated her like a kid. Instead of biting Patrick's head off, though, she stood. "I'm gonna go check on Rory."

"Brie took him home," Patrick told her. "When she came to get Kathleen."

"Brie was here?" Things between her oldest brother and his spirited wife, Brie, were not good since she'd taken a job. Man, these guys, except for Aidan, were Neanderthals.

"After she got off work." He spat the words out. "She said Rory could stay overnight." Patrick's daughter Kathleen and Rory were only a year apart and as cousins, spent a lot of time together. Bailey had had her overnight twice this week.

"Oh, okay, I'll pick him up in the morning." She glanced around the bar. "I should get to work."

"It's almost two. Go home, we'll close up." Leaning forward, Dylan chucked her under the chin. "Aidan'll take you."

Her apartment was three blocks away, and she dealt with gang kids for a living, but still, they watched out for her. She only let them so they wouldn't get on her about her job.

In minutes, she and Aidan left the pub and walked leisurely to her house. The misty air was even cooler now and she snuggled into to the senator's jacket.

Aidan was quiet, thoughtful, as usual. "So, what do you make of all this with the good senator?" he finally asked.

"I don't know what to make of it. He drives me nuts with his conservative views and how he's copped out from the potential he had to be a good politician. Still, he would have risked his own life for me tonight, Aidan, had that been a gun or other kind of weapon."

"Not something to ignore."

She stuck her hands inside the pockets of the jacket. One connected with cold aluminum. "Oh, hell."

"What?"

"He left his cell phone in his pocket. I not only got his damn coat, but now I have his cell. Both of which I'll have to give back."

"And see him."

"Yeah." The thought discomfited her. "Damn it, Aidan. I don't want that guy in my life."

"Well, kiddo, then you'll have to stop this feud."

"Only when he leaves my gang activities alone."

"Be a cold day in hell when—"

The cell phone rang.

"Shit."

"Better answer it. He probably wants his phone back."

She drew it out. Its ring was no-nonsense, like hers. "What if it's somebody else?"

"Who'd be callin' him at one a.m.?"

"How the hell do I know? His girlfriend?"

As it continued to ring, Aidan took the phone from her and checked the identification. "It says *town house* on it." He pressed the Send button and handed it to her. "Gotta talk to the man, Sis."

She rolled her eyes and took the phone. Into it she said, "Hello."

"Bailey, it's Clay." The informality of his greeting startled her into silence. For a split second, it made her think of being plastered up against him in front of the diner. "Bailey?"

"Yes, it's me. I, um, have your phone."

He chuckled. It was an all male sound. "I know. Look, I'm sorry about that, earlier."

"What *was* that?"

"I'll explain when I pick up my things. Where are you?"

They'd reached her house—an older building ten minutes from the pub and twenty from ESCAPE. She had a walk-up on the second floor. "Just about at my apartment."

"Tell me where it is, and I'll come over."

"Now?"

"Ah, yes. Is there a problem with that?"

"I'm not sure I want you to know where I live."

"Honey, if I wanted to, I could find out where Susan Sarandon lives."

"Susan Sarandon?"

"She's my favorite actress."

Bailey couldn't help herself. She laughed. She and Aidan

had walked up to the front and climbed the four steps to the porch.

"What?" Aidan asked at the door.

"Susan Sarandon's his favorite actress."

Aidan's dark brows rose. "Oh, that's good to know."

She shook her head, still chuckling.

"Who's with you? No, let me guess, one of the Fearsome Foursome."

"Yep, the only one who *doesn't* wanna string you by your *cahones,* Senator."

This time he laughed. Deep and from his belly. It was a really sexy sound.

She smiled.

"I feel like I'm playing Peeping Tom," Aidan whispered. "What's goin' on?"

Bailey shook her head. "Hush."

"Me?" Clayton asked.

"No, Aidan."

"Your address . . ."

"Should I give him my address?" she asked Aidan.

"What are his intentions?"

"My brother wants to know your intentions?" Jeez, was she flirting? With uptight, staid Clayton Wainwright? She remembered what he looked like tonight in the red crewneck rimmed by the black T-shirt and readjusted her assessment.

"My intentions?" Again the husky laugh.

Bailey tossed back her head, trying to clear it. "Never mind. I live on St. Patrick's Place. Number twenty-four, apartment 3A."

"You're kidding, right?"

"Nope. It's about three blocks from the pub. Come to the front door. Ring the bell, I live upstairs."

"Is your house green?"

"How'd you know?"

"Lucky guess. Be right there."

She clicked off and shrugged. "He's coming here."

"So I gathered. Want me to wait?"

"Aidan, I meet face-to-face with gang kids sometimes."

He shuddered. "Don't remind me."

She pulled out her keys. "I'm plenty safe with the senator from New York."

"Sounded to me like you were flirting."

"God forbid." Standing on tiptoes, she kissed his cheek. "Go home, A."

"Okay, B." He kissed her back. "Be careful."

"Always."

Inside, Bailey climbed the stairs thinking about "Clay." Once she reached the top and opened the door, she resisted the urge to pick up her house—toys lay scattered around, there were a few dishes in the sink, but no dirty underwear or dried food were in evidence, so she didn't bother. Instead, she went to the stove and made coffee. For him? Of course not. She was planning to spend some time on the 'net tonight. She'd been researching shelters for the one she wanted to open for gang kids—the shelter Senator Wainwright kept trying to block. Angry all over again, she crossed to her computer, which was nestled in a nook in the corner of the kitchen, and called up her proposal. Damn it, she was going to get this off the ground, no matter what.

Engrossed, she startled when the doorbell rang. Grabbing his phone, she was out of the apartment and down the stairs in minutes. She found him on the stoop. His hair was windblown and looked . . . good. He held a brown bag in his hand.

"Hi." He smiled. "Interesting neighborhood."

She smiled back. The little section of New York was full of Irish culture—stores, churches, and immigrant families galore. People said it reminded them of Ireland, where Bailey longed, someday, to go.

"The cabbie gave me a running commentary as I came over. I could barely understand his brogue."

"Pretty different from a town house by Central Park."

She made the comment intentionally. She wanted to distance this guy. *Bailey, this is Clay.* She wasn't going to fall for his buddy business.

"I don't live on Central Park."

"Whatever." She held out the cell. "Here."

"Thanks." He looked over at her. "My coat?"

"Damn, it's upstairs." Before she could dodge away, he grasped her arm.

"Invite me up. I want to talk to you. And I don't bite."

"Only metaphorically." She glanced meaningfully at his grip on her, and he dropped his hand. "You've taken several chunks out of my hide in the papers and in Congress."

"As have you mine."

She sighed.

"I should tell you what was going on tonight. And I'd still like to bury the hatchet. It's what I wanted when I asked you to breakfast."

"If I'd gone to breakfast with you," she said with exasperation, "this whole bizarre night wouldn't have happened."

His smile was cocky. "Remember that next time."

"There won't be a next time."

He grumbled something about stubborn women as he followed her up the steps. Once inside, he scanned the area.

She turned and examined the living room, where they stood, trying to see it from his point of view. She hadn't spent much money on the decor—she hadn't had any to invest—but she'd spent time.

He said, "I guess you like Broadway."

The walls of this room, as well as all the others, were graced by posters of various plays, playbills, and some pictures of the original stars.

"Yeah, I do. I save what I can to go to the theater."

He grinned. "What's your favorite show?"

"*Phantom of the Opera*, of course. Isn't it everybody's?"

"Not mine." He said no more.

"Okay, I'll bite."

"*Barnum*."

"I never saw that one. It came out what, twenty-five years ago?"

"Hmm. I was still in college. My father and I went on one of our few excursions alone together. I can still see the elephant on stage. We were in the balcony and a tightrope walker used the ledge as his rope. It was phenomenal."

"No net?"

"Nope." He looked around. "Are there posters in the other rooms?"

"Uh-huh."

Rory's small bedroom had a huge stand-up cutout from *Seussical* in his room. Bailey was scrimping to be able to afford tickets to the play.

She grabbed the senator's jacket off the edge of the couch. "Here's your coat."

He studied her, then held up the bag. "I brought you a peace offering."

"Senator, I'm not asking you to stay. We aren't going to get chummy, here."

"It's ice cream."

Her favorite treat in the world.

"Pistachio and chocolate."

"You don't play fair."

"Don't you want to know about tonight?"

Sighing, she shook her head. "All right, for a bit." Turning, she led him into the kitchen. He scanned all the posters there: ones from *Evita, A Chorus Line,* and *Beauty and the Beast.* "Sit." She pointed to the table.

He crossed to it, pulled out a chair and stared down. He picked something up; it was Rory's New York Yankees sweatshirt. Wainwright glanced around the kitchen. His gaze was quizzical. "What are those toys doing here?"

"They're my son's."

"You have a son?"

"Uh-huh. Four years old." She got out bowls and spoons and approached the table.

"You have a son?" he repeated, as if she'd told him she'd recently walked on the moon.

"A lot of women do, Senator."

"Then what the hell are you doing risking your life every day with those gang kids?" She pivoted in time to see him run a hand through his hair and scowl deeply. "What about a husband?"

"That's none of your business."

"Man, if you were mine, I'd tie you to the bed before I'd let you do what you do."

"Which is precisely why I never married." The words were out before she could stop them.

"Hmm."

"He asked," she said defensively. "But I couldn't reconcile my job with a relationship."

"I can see why." He shook his head and took a seat, though now more than ever she wanted him to leave. "Can't be you were in love with him."

"What do you mean?"

"You wouldn't have been able to let him go if you loved him."

"It wasn't just that. I cared about him. I might have married him for Rory's sake. But I'm Catholic, and knowing it might not work out, I couldn't risk a divorce; even Dylan's legal separation almost killed my mother."

"Are you for real?"

"What do you mean?"

"Your reputation doesn't fit with who you are."

"Frankly, yours doesn't either. At least not the way I've seen you tonight." She set the bowl in front of him. "Look, I don't know how we got on this. Tell me about what happened tonight."

His light brown eyes narrowed. They were a really nice shade, like warm honey, or brandy. "All right. Sit, first."

She did, though she didn't like his peremptory attitude. He was a man used to being obeyed.

"That was a newspaper reporter. From *The Village Voice*." While he told her the story, he opened the bag and drew out Godiva ice cream. "Your choice."

She picked pistachio. "From the *Voice*? Fuck."

He cocked his head.

"Don't start on me about my language. My brothers have a fit over my potty mouth. I try to give swearing up for Lent."

His chuckle, again, was warming. "You're something else."

Charming was the word that came to mind. And Clay was astounded that he could even have that thought about a woman who'd been a thorn in his side for years.

Since you put her in jail.

"What did the reporter want? Other than to know who your new *squeeze* was?" She opened the pint of ice cream. He did the same and forgoing the bowls, they dug in.

"He was probably looking for dirt. In exchange for that, I agreed to give him an interview."

"What kind of dirt?"

"Women. Drugs. Kiddy porn. Anything that might taint my reputation."

She scowled. "Despite how much I dislike your politics, I don't remember anything like that being even hinted at about you."

"All the more reason to catch me doing something I shouldn't."

"Ah, like Rush Limbaugh's drug addiction. If he hadn't been so conservative, it wouldn't have been such a big deal."

Startled that she understood so quickly—Jane still couldn't get it—he smiled at her.

Biting into a spoonful, she licked her lips. They were full, and unpainted. "Did he, um, find out who I was?"

"What? Oh, no."

"That'd be news, wouldn't it? That we were together."

"Good news, I think. I'd like to end this feud."

"Then back off on ESCAPE."

"Bailey, I can't. It's not healthy. For kids . . ." He scanned the room. "Or for you."

"Lord save me from protective men. You sound like my brothers."

"I knew there had to be something redeeming about them."

She grinned, despite her resolve not to like him, he guessed. "They have a lot of good traits. They're truly men you can count on, believe in. But their overprotectiveness is *not* one of their better traits. That aside, I know I'm affecting the lives of kids. For the better. I have documentation."

He remembered her trial, where the stories of kids she'd helped reform, even at twenty-five, were impressive. He lazed back. This was what he wanted. A chance to talk to her. Debate with her privately. But in some ways, he was disappointed at the shift in the conversation. He liked learning about her private life. He liked seeing her face light when she talked about her family, her son, her friends. "I know you've done some good, Bailey. The governor throws it up in my face all the time. But you give the wrong message to these kids. Gangs can only be stopped by zero tolerance and increasing legal prosecution."

She licked her spoon then set it down. "Gangs can only be stopped by giving kids alternatives to joining, or helping them find ways to get out."

His own spoon clattered to the table. He said heatedly, "Your shelter would provide a haven for those who commit crimes, who are involved in a myriad of illegal activities."

"These kids need support, not punishment."

"We have to send a message that we won't tolerate crime."

"I—" The phone rang.

Frowning, he checked his watch. "Who'd be calling at this hour?"

"I'm sure it's Aidan. Though maybe Patrick. Rory's there. I hope he's all right." Motherly concern transformed her face. She seemed vulnerable and . . . and very lovely. She bounded off the chair and snatched up the phone. "Hello." Her stiff posture relaxed. "Oh, hi, A. Yeah. He came over." She waited. "Um, yeah, he's still here. What?" She giggled and shot Clay a teasing look. "Aidan wants to know if you can find out for him where Julianne Moore lives."

"Sure thing. I'll get right on it."

"What's with guys and redheads?" she asked into the phone. "Never mind, I don't want to know." A pause. A very sentimental smile. "No, I'm fine. Quit worrying. Yeah, good. Sure, about ten. See you then." She smiled at the phone after she hung up. "They have their uses."

"Who?"

"My brothers. He's picking up Rory at Patrick's and keeping him for a while so I can sleep in. I have a late shift at work tomorrow night."

Without thinking, Clay said, "Let me come. See what you do."

"What?"

"Let me come to work with you. It's Saturday. I have some things scheduled during the day, but let me spend time at ES-CAPE and see how you operate."

"Absolutely not."

"Why?"

Leaning against the counter, she studied him shrewdly, no longer seeming vulnerable. "Well for one thing, ESCAPE's headquarters are a secret."

"West Fifty-third. About twenty minutes from here by subway."

"How do you know that?"

He gave her a withering look. "Please."

She sat down again across from him, but didn't speak, just watched him. Her intense gaze, the set of her delicate features, did something to him.

Finally he said, "I could learn something from visiting you. If you're so sure you're doing the right thing, then I might come to a better understanding of what ESCAPE does. We might even make a truce." Which he doubted. But he could probably get even more ammunition to shut her down. That thought didn't sit well, though; he felt guilty dissembling. Especially since she wasn't at all what he had expected. And he kind of liked her. "Bailey?"

"All my instincts tell me no."

"Override them for once. Give it a shot."

"Well, I'll probably live to regret this." She sat back in her chair and sighed. "Okay, you can come. But be warned, Senator, if you use anything you see or hear there to seek out the kids, or to try to close me down, I *will* string you up by the balls."

She looked cute, all angry. So he said, "Watch your mouth, woman." And made her smile.

THREE

"I THINK I'VE made the worst mistake of my life." In her office, with her feet up on her battered desk, Bailey glanced at the clock and sipped strong black coffee while she spouted off to Suze Williams, her colleague and good friend.

"What'd you do now?" As she spoke, Suze typed into the computer, updating a database for shelters that would accept gang kids trying to go straight. They had a network all over the city. The clicking of the keys accompanied Bailey's dark thoughts.

"I agreed to let Clayton Wainwright visit ESCAPE tonight." She glanced at the clock. "He said he'd be here about seven."

Peering through wire-rimmed glasses at the screen, Suze absently rubbed the tattoo of a reptile she sported on her left wrist. It was a souvenir from her stint in the Lizards, a girl gang in the eighties. Suze had been its leader. Consequently she was a damn good social worker in youth anti-gang activities. She manned the interactive website on opposite shifts from Bailey, who still couldn't believe her good fortune in

snagging Suze for ESCAPE. "I must have heard you wrong."
As always her unflappability soothed Bailey.

"Nope. The illustrious senator who'd like to close us down
is coming here. I caved when he asked."

Suze swiveled around to face her. Her dark hair fell in soft
curls, and her mahogany eyes shone with surprise. Her skin
was a gorgeous coffee color. "When on earth did you see him?
Last I heard, you wouldn't give him the time of day."

"Long story."

"I got time."

When Bailey finished the bizarre tale of Friday night, Suze
shrugged. "I think it's okay for him to come here. Actually, it
could work to our benefit."

"What if it backfires?"

"What more could he do to us? He knows about all our programs, right?"

"Yeah, sure. I agreed to submit our activities for review
when I charmed Governor Friedman out of that last cool hundred K."

"Well worth it. Besides, we're proud of what we're doing.
It's all on the up and up." Suze smiled. "Nothing he can put
you in jail for again."

"He didn't put me in jail. He was just doing his job." She
shook her head.

"What?"

"You should have heard Ma and Pa when I dropped Rory
off. They went up one side of me and down the other for even
talking to the guy last night."

"Hard to forgive somebody who puts your baby behind
bars."

"Did I hear the word *forgive*?"

Bailey turned to the doorway. "Hey, Father Tim, I didn't
know you'd be in today."

The blond, blue-eyed Catholic priest, who looked more like
a movie star playing a man of the cloth, winked at her. "Gotta
see my girl."

"How sweet. Do you need something here?"

"Just to give you this." He held out a paper. "I found another counseling site."

Part of Bailey's program included meeting with gang kids who wanted out; they were called Face-to-Faces. Problem was, they had to have secure, protected sites so that ESCAPE workers weren't unduly endangered.

What the hell are you doing risking your life every day with those kids? . . . Man, if you were mine, I'd tie you to the bed before I'd let you do what you do.

"*You* are an angel, Father Tim." Bailey dropped her feet and swiveled toward the computer. "Wish you weren't a priest. I'd marry you in a second."

"Ah, don't tempt me, sweetheart." He perched on the edge of her desk. "St. Pius. In Harlem." After he gave her the rest of the information, he glanced at Suze. "So, who do we need to forgive?"

Suze told him about Clayton Wainwright.

"I could come back tonight."

"I don't need a chaperone. I'll be fine. Besides, Joe and Rob are working with me."

"Well, then I'll pray for the good senator." Both Joe Natale and Robert Anderson disliked Clayton Wainwright, but Joe particularly was rabid about the guy. For a moment, Bailey allowed herself to bask in the good friends, colleagues, and family who cared about her.

After Tim and Suze left, Bailey worked at her computer until the buzzer sounded from the entry to ESCAPE. She checked the clock. "Right on time," she said to herself, heading out to the front. Unsnicking the four locks and disarming the security system, she let him into the outer office area. "Hello, Senator."

He smiled, calling attention to the small nick on his jaw. He must have just showered and shaved because he smelled like fresh soap. "Bailey." He'd dressed casually tonight, as they all did here; he wore a Harvard sweatshirt with jeans and loafers.

"Come on back." She led him through the narrow corridor, off of which were the three offices of ESCAPE.

"We don't spend much on amenities here," she said, vaguely self-conscious of the worn, but clean, space.

"I wouldn't either."

"Yeah? I've seen pictures of the Russell Building. All that expensive wood and those Persian carpets."

"Traditional décor, I'm afraid."

She reached her office and turned to him. "I figured you to be big on fancy digs."

He angled his head. "I appreciate nice things," he said, his jaw tightening a bit. There was that cleft again. "I'm not going to apologize for that."

"Didn't ask you to. Come on in." She showed him into her space. It was about fourteen-by-twelve, housed two computers, filing cabinets, a small fridge, and books tumbling out of shelves and scattered in stacks on the floor. The scent of strong coffee emanated from a brewing pot in the corner.

He held up a sack, which she hadn't seen him carrying this time, either. "Can I put this in the refrigerator?"

A grin. "You bring me ice cream again?"

"Yes, ma'am."

"Go ahead."

She watched him cross to the fridge, bend over, and put the treat away. *Nice ass*, she thought.

"What?" he asked, turning around. "You're smiling."

Oh, Lord. "Nothing." Purposely, she glanced at the clock. "If I'm gonna show you our digs, it should be now. The website gets active around eight, and I need to be near the computer then."

He swallowed hard and turned his head away. Now this was the senator she knew and hated. Disapproving. Authoritative. She shook her head. "You sure you should be here?" she asked. "You're gonna freak about everything you see."

"No, not everything." He stuck his hands in his jeans pockets. "But truthfully, since last night, I keep thinking about your son."

"Rory?"

"Yes, and how you endanger yourself."

Because it was something she wrestled with all the time, she jammed her hands on her jean-clad hips. "It's no different if I'd chosen to be a cop or firefighter."

"In some ways."

"Would you keep women out of those professions if you could?"

"I don't honestly know. Mothers, maybe." He spotted the picture on her desk. "Is that him?"

She picked up the sterling silver frame. "Yeah, my little guy."

Taking it from her, he studied the photo. "Sometimes, I wish Jon was that age again."

"Jon?"

"*My* son."

"How old is he?"

"Twenty."

"He in school?"

"Yes. At Bard College."

She chuckled.

"You know the place?"

"Not your cup of tea, is it, Senator?"

"It was fine with me. My father had a fit he didn't choose Harvard, though. Bard's a good school."

"Yeah, but liberal as hell. I heard that they were looking to hurl the worst insult to their rival Vassar and they put up signs all over that said, 'Vassar students are Republicans.'"

"Well, that suits Jon." The sadness in his tone kept her from teasing him about his conservative views.

"Don't you get along with your son?"

"We used to." His eyes narrowed on her. "Now, he thinks like you do."

"Well, there you go. Your kid's got smarts." He grinned and she was glad. "Come on, I'll give you the grand tour." Ignoring the fact that she felt good about erasing his sadness—she sure as hell didn't want to *like* this guy—she motioned to the space surrounding them. "This is the office I share with another worker who's on the opposite shift from me. We also have a few volunteers who use this space."

He crossed to one of the computers. "State of the art."

"Yeah, we got a grant from Donald Trump to update our technology. Best thing is it's ongoing."

"Donald Trump, huh?"

"Uh-huh. You probably could find out where he lives, too."

"You want to know?"

"No, thanks." She pointed to her computer. "This one we use for the website that you hate so much, and the other is mostly record-keeping."

"For what?"

"Shelters that will take gang kids, psychologists who've volunteered to work with them, the database for the Gang Protection Program."

"Ah, the innovative GPP. Was that your idea?"

"Uh-huh." She leaned against her desk. "You have a problem with it, if I recall."

"I think it's unique to set up a form of a witness protection program for ex-gang members."

"Yeah, you called it that in your comments to the governor."

"But the cops should run it."

"And how many kids would go to the cops?"

"Enough."

"No, not enough. One loss is too many." Like Moira. For a minute she was tempted to tell Wainwright about her sister. But she shook off the stupid idea. He was the last person she should be sharing confidences with. "Come on, I'll show you the other offices."

They traveled down the hall. At the first one, Bailey stopped. It was a bit smaller than hers, and at a desk sat her buddy. "Hey, Joe. Want you to meet somebody."

Slicing gray eyes looked up from the computer screen.

Bailey strode over to Joe and put a hand on his shoulder. "This is Joe Natale. Joe, Clayton Wainwright."

"I'd say it's nice to meet you, but I make it a habit not to lie." Still, Joe stood. Bailey suspected it was to alert Wainwright to his size. Swarthy of complexion, he was six-four, about two fifty, with muscles to die for. An ex-cop, he worked out religiously; he also still had contacts at the precinct.

"What are you doing?" Clayton asked, nodding to the computer.

At Joe's questioning look, Bailey said, "He's here tonight so we can get him off our back by showing him we're careful." She crossed her arms over her chest and nailed the senator with her best tough-guy look. "And that we obey the law. Joe's an ex-cop."

Wainwright nodded.

Joe told him, "I'm handling the phone hotline and trying to contact people for the Gang Protection Program."

"Oh, good."

"Yeah, right." He looked to Bailey. "You sure you know what you're doin', doll?"

"Absolutely. We'll let you get back to work."

Squeezing Bailey's shoulder, he sat back down. He completely ignored the senator.

Nonetheless, Wainwright bade him good-bye. "Thanks, Natale. I appreciate your honesty."

With his back to them, Joe barked, "Thank the little lady. Because you threw her in jail and have been attacking her ever since, I'd have decked you as soon as I saw you if it wasn't for her."

They left, the senator shaking his head. "You seem to surround yourself with protective men."

"Do I?"

"Yes." He followed her to the next office. "That's good."

"Spare me."

Though he was as big and muscular as Natale, Rob Anderson exuded a serenity that Bailey admired. A recovered alcoholic—she credited the 12-Step Recovery Program for his calm—he was now a top-notch psychologist and one of ESCAPE's most valued workers. "Hey, beautiful." Standing, he kissed Bailey's cheek. He shot a glance at Wainwright, then back at her. "You okay?"

"Just peachy. Rob, this is Clayton Wainwright."

"I know the face." He stuck out his hand. "Jocy give you trouble?"

"Enough."

She nodded to Wainwright. "Rob's a psychologist, and when I get in trouble, he bails me out."

"As if."

"What do you do here?" Wainwright wanted to know.

"Mostly I work on the Face-to-Faces."

Bailey saw the senator's jaw tighten again. She knew he objected strongly to this program.

"They bother you?" Rob asked.

"I'm afraid so."

"Maybe you can ease his mind, Rob."

"Sit."

Clay took a chair next to the computer and Rob's hands flew across the keyboard, calling up a series of sites. "These are the places we meet with the kids. As you can see, many of them are in churches. Some in social agencies. All of them have two-way mirrors. A second person watches through it. We go by the rule of three."

"What's that?"

"Three ESCAPE workers go at a time." Rob held up his fingers to count off. "Say Bailey is the face. I watch from behind the glass. A third person checks the kid or family out for weapons, dope, anything else."

"Bet the clients don't like that."

"No, actually, it's all right with them. By the time they get to this phase, they're pretty desperate."

Wainwright shook his head. "Oh, well, that makes me feel better."

Bailey suggested, "Show him the stats on our success rate."

Rob called up numbers on the Face-to-Faces. Leaning over to get a better look, Clay studied them on the screen. Finally, he sat back. "That's impressive. Do you track the recidivism?"

Sitting forward, Bailey bristled. "Of course! We don't fake anything. Of the number that gets out, about a third go back in."

"Hmm."

"And about a third of those get out again," Rob said. "And stay out."

"Not bad." He thought a minute. "Who conducts the interviews?"

"Bailey and I share them. Some kids relate better to her, some to me."

"How do you decide?"

He cocked his head. "Good question. Sometimes the kids say who they prefer. Sometimes, girls want Bay, boys want me. Depends."

"Still, they sound dangerous."

"We take precautions," Rob told him easily.

Wainwright faced Bailey. "I know you've had some trouble with these. You've gotten hurt."

"Okay, a kid shoved me once and I got a concussion."

He shook his head as if she'd just told him she'd been mortally wounded. "Then it's crazy that you still do this."

Rob intervened. "Hold on. Me and Joe corralled the boy. He broke down, told us about his two brothers in the gang." Rob's warm brown eyes beamed and he shared a knowing smile with Bailey. "We got all three kids out. One went on to college, one works in a film studio." Here he grinned. "And one's a deacon in Father Tim's church."

Clayton's eyes narrowed. The color seemed to deepen when he was displeased. "You shouldn't be risking your own lives."

Bailey stood. "Let's go. This is a stalemate."

The men rose and Rob put his arm around Bailey. "We do a lot of good around here, Senator. Remember that the next time you attack our Street Angel."

On the way back to her office, Wainwright said, "I don't attack you. Both of them said I do, but I don't."

"Well, as *you* said, they're a protective lot." She smiled. "Rob's a big Meryl Streep fan. Maybe you could . . ."

"I know—get her address."

They were chuckling when they entered the office.

Bailey crossed to the computer and checked the website, making sure it was set. Then she thought of something and whirled around. "You can't read what comes on here, Senator."

He arched a brow. "I thought nothing was secret at ES CAPE."

"There's a difference between private and secret."

"I see."

"I want your promise that you won't be skulking around and lurking over my shoulder to see what's going on. It'll make me nervous."

"I do not skulk, or lurk."

She bit back a smile at his indignation. "Promise."

"Fine. I won't. Just tell me—"

The phone rang and the computer chimed at the same time. Bailey sat down at the desk. "Our private line. Let the answering machine get it. I've got to make this contact."

She clicked on and recognized the screen name immediately.

Hey Street Angel, how ya hangin'?
Hangin' just fine, Taz. How are you?"
Phat, as always.

Bailey was about to comment just as she heard the answering machine pick up. "Bailey, this is Eric Lawson. I wondered if we were still on for our date tomorrow night."

"What the hell?" Clay said.

Just as Taz typed, *I need some help.*

THAT'S WHAT I'M here for, Taz. Let me help you.

Taz stared hard at the screen, dissing herself big-time for contacting the broad again. But she was pumped and edgy from what had gone down. *Something happened tonight.*

Something?
We had to jet out fast.
Why?
The 5-0 came.
The police? Why?

Taz didn't answer.

Where are you?
My house.
What can I do?
Nothin'.
Talk to me . . .

Fucking shit. She shouldn't be doing this. Everything was going down the tubes. Her set had almost got caught tonight. For simple shoplifting . . . jacking beer from the corner store. The old guy who worked there had gotten royally pissed when they showed up and started messing around. . . .

"Get outta here, I don't want no trouble."

Mazie cornered him. She'd shifted so he could feel her blade in her pocket. If the law did come, he'd never be able to say he saw it. "Shut up, grandpa." Over her shoulder, she called out, "Quinny baby, Taz. Do it."

Quinn had lifted the beer and they booked. Just as they got around the corner, they heard the sirens.

Taz, you there? The Street Angel had been typing all this time. *Talk to me.*

Yeah, I'm here. Shit, she was sick of this. Sick of life.

You want to talk about getting out, Taz?

Don't court out of no gang, lady. I told you.

Yes, yes you do. ESCAPE has programs. We have people trained to help. We can protect you.

She looked around the seedy room with its dingy walls, filmy windows, and constant stench of old garbage from the alley below. *Nobody can protect me.* From herself. From the old man. From Mazie and the girls.

As if to confirm that, she heard a knock on the window. She looked over to see her homies on the fire escape.

Gotta go. Ciao.

Taz wait . . .

But she signed off.

Crossing to the window, she yanked it open. Tall and limber, Mazie climbed inside, with Quinn behind her. Mazie shook long blond locks out of her face and socked Taz's arm. "Why'd you come home, girl? We were supposed to meet at the crib."

"Felt sick," Taz said, not glancing at the computer.

Still, Mazie wandered over to it. Taz hoped like hell it didn't show the ESCAPE logo. She'd signed off fast and couldn't remember if she'd exited the site. Suddenly, the screen went dark.

Mazie crossed to the bed and plunked down. "Got just the thing for what ails ya." She yanked a joint from her pocket, lit up with a gold-plated lighter she'd stolen from her stepfather. After he'd fucked her, she said.

Taz hesitated.

Quinn took the second drag.

"Tazzie, baby? Here."

Mazie held out the blunt.

Taz waited again, then shrugged.

Street Angel versus getting stoned? No question who won.

"FUCK!"

Clayton sat on the far side of the room, watching her. He was still trying to process all he'd seen so far tonight. He glanced at the clock. And it was only nine. "What happened?"

"I lost her."

"Lost who?"

"A girl who's new. She wants out of her gang, I think. But she signed off halfway through." Bailey swiveled around and laid her head against the back of the chair; she was off somewhere, thinking about something other than her surroundings.

He waited, wondering about the girl online. "What do you do when they tell you've they've committed crimes?"

Bailey's head shot up, her eyes snapping blue fire. "They don't tell me that. Besides, it's all anonymous. What can be done?"

"When they come in for a Face-to-Face, they could be questioned for what they told you online."

"And just how many kids would take us up on our services once the first arrest was made? The street is a small world."

"You'd stop impending crimes that way."

"No, it would only be a Band-Aid. You need to go to the root."

"You can't stop gangs by getting out all their members."

"We can save kids from them. That's enough."

Clay stood, because she was impossible to argue with, and because he really did think this was a dangerous place. To quell his pique, he walked around the room, checking out the books. . . .

A Guide to Understanding Street Gangs; *Sugar Creek Gang Books*; *Gangs and Their Tattoos: Identifying Gangbangers*; *How to Save Our Children from the Street*. There were several more, all on the same theme.

Pivoting, he gestured to the shelf. "You really believe all this, don't you?"

"Of course, we all do here."

"I don't."

Sitting forward in her seat, she gripped the arms. "Senator, why can't we just agree to disagree?"

"I don't see how we can peacefully coexist. And since I'm the official representative for this state, I have to make the best decisions for it. Especially its funding for social agencies like this one."

She hit the chair arm with her palm. "You're not God.

You can't control everything. Anyway, are you so sure you're right?"

"Yes."

She rolled her eyes. "What was I thinking, letting you come here? It hasn't helped."

"No, it has. I see dedicated, smart people working hard. I just think your talents should be put to better use. Something controlled by the government."

"Oh, yeah. You guys have done a great job stopping gangs so far."

He glanced at the phone where the light blinked. "Is that why you're hooking up with Lawson?"

She actually blushed; the crimson flush rose from the scoop of her white shirt to her face. "I think Eric Lawson would make a good senator."

That angered him, though he didn't know why, because he knew she felt that way. "He's not experienced enough for my position."

"He's the age you were when you were elected. He'll learn." She raised that cute little chin and now her blue eyes sparked with challenge. "And maybe he won't cop out like you did."

Clay felt his hand fist. "We've been over this before."

"You're right." She swiveled to the computer, away from him, trying to shut him out, he guessed. "We're spinning our wheels. It's probably best you leave."

"Probably." He jammed his hands into his pockets. "Tell me one last thing."

"What?"

Though he ordered himself not to go there, he asked nastily, "Are you involved with Lawson?"

"What?"

"The date, on the phone message. Is it his politics you support or are you sleeping with him?"

She came off her chair like a shot. "You bastard. How dare you . . ." She sputtered. "Get out of here right now, Senator. This little experiment is over."

⌇ FOUR

JON WAINWRIGHT SAT in the back of the crowded, stuffy room and stared at the man who hoped to put Jon's father out of a job. This preliminary meeting was to start mobilizing workers for Eric Lawson's bid for the next Democratic primary. Lawson was just finishing his speech and things were winding down.

Thank God, because Jon felt like a shit being here. True, he and his father were eons apart on everything these last few years, but when Jon called him, his dad had agreed to speak at Bard, then asked to spend the day with him. His totally indestructible father had seemed—what was it?—*vulnerable*. So Jon had changed his mind about working on Lawson's campaign. Then his mother had called him this morning and whined about his father. It resurrected a lot of old baggage, and Jon found himself heading here despite his decision not to work against his dad. Not to do what he knew would wound Clayton Wainwright big-time.

It had been a stupid idea all around. He hoped nobody saw

him. There was no official sign-up yet so maybe he could claim that he was a spy if anybody found out he'd shown up here.

With old anger at his father fading, Jon slinked back into the shadows when the socializing began. Damn it, how did he keep getting into these positions with his family? He remembered when Clayton Wainwright had been his hero, when he'd do anything to please the man. He remembered when he'd really believed in his father. Now, sometimes his resentment at his dad was so great he wanted to howl at the moon. And sometimes, it just evaporated.

"Hey, Jon, nice to see you." Lawson had approached him; the guy was always so friendly. Of course getting the son of your opponent to work for you would be a coup. Jon's insides twisted at the thought.

"Hi, Mr. Lawson."

He had a pretty, dark-haired woman with him. "I've got somebody I want you to meet."

The woman studied Jon intently. "You look familiar."

Lawson chuckled. "Probably because he's the son of your nemesis."

Her brows arched and there were questions in her nice blue eyes. "My nemesis?"

Lawson continued, "Jon Wainwright, meet Bailey O'Neil, the Street Angel."

Jon shook his head; he knew the stories. "You sure give my old man a run for his money."

Her face blanked. She said nothing. Her lips parted slightly but she just stared at him, making him shift on his feet and jam his hands in his pockets.

Someone called out, "Eric, we need you over here."

"Oops, excuse me." He squeezed the Street Angel's shoulder. "I'm sure you two have a lot to discuss."

Lawson left and the woman still watched him.

Jon asked, "Have I grown two heads?"

"Two faces, I'd say, like Janus."

"Who?"

"The Roman god who had two faces. He's the archetype of hypocrisy." Her blue eyes had become steely. "And betrayal."

Damn, his stomach flip-flopped now. "I, um, thought you hated my father."

"No, I don't. In some ways I respect him. But obviously, *you* hate him."

"Me? Of course I don't. You don't hate your parents." Jon scowled at her. "Didn't he put you in jail?"

"Well, he was the prosecutor in my trial. But I did break the law."

This was out of focus, like a camera with a lens you couldn't quite get right. "I can't believe you're defending him."

"And I can't believe you'd turn on a member of your family like this. Won't he be devastated if he finds out you were here today?"

"Look, I haven't signed up to do anything. I'm probably not going to."

Her eyes shot daggers at him. "Your just being at this initial meeting will affect your father. It'll hurt him like nothing else could."

How could the Street Angel know that? "I don't get it. You gotta be here because you don't think he should be reelected."

"It's why I originally came. Now, I'm not sure." She glanced around at the gathering, and shook her head. "Truth be told, I'm not comfortable being here, though I can't fathom why." Her gaze focused again on him. "I do, however, understand one thing."

"What?"

"That a son does not side openly with someone else against his own father. I'll give you some unsolicited advice. Family is the most precious gift you can be given. Tossing it away out of some notion of rebellion is not only foolish, it's stupid."

Goddamn it, Jon thought as the woman stormed away— and out the door he noticed—this whole thing wasn't going quite as he had expected it to. Hell, would nothing ever be clear-cut with his father?

THE FISHER AUDITORIUM on the Bard College campus was full with a lively audience of freshmen who had arrived for an early orientation, environmental students who'd come down before the regular school year began, and many community members. On the stage, Clay sat off to the left with his son and the head of the Environmental Science Department. The president of the college walked to the podium to make a few remarks and then would introduce Clay. As he waited, Clay took in the interesting décor: the light oak woodwork was breathtaking, the acoustics were so good the president didn't need a mike; and, Clay was told, the unusual upholstery of the graded seats displayed the names of the graduating class the year this billion dollar, Frank Lloyd Wright-ish building had been constructed. It was said to be the biggest and best Performing Arts Center between New York City and upstate New York.

Jon had greeted him more warmly than usual when Clay flew in from Washington. They'd had lunch at a small restaurant in Tivoli, a nearby town, and Jon had been excited about tonight. He still maintained some of that damnable distance of the last few years, but he'd asked about Clay's well-being and even the upcoming campaign. Because they always disagreed, they usually avoided discussing their politics.

Is it his politics you support or are you sleeping with him?

Man, Clay had blown that one with Ms. Street Angel. It had been two weeks, and he still thought about her. A lot. They'd had no contact at all and had managed to avoid any public dispute in the papers, so he didn't know why she was on his mind so frequently.

Hell of a thing.

When the president announced, "And now I give you one of New York's illustrious senators, Clayton Wainwright," Clay stood and approached the podium. He'd been touted as one of the best speakers in Congress, and he really wanted to do well in this venue.

Everybody clapped. Including Jon. At center stage, Clay smiled at the audience. "It's nice to be here, to speak to such an enthusiastic crowd." He glanced to the left. "And especially since my son asked me to come. As some of you might know, a twenty-year-old son thinking his dad has something important to say is a rarity."

Jon smiled and the audience laughed.

Clayton spent ten minutes outlining Congress's latest bill

to stop fossil fuel burning. He spent ten more minutes on two other environmental initiatives. He discussed the ozone layer in upstate New York, because a study had appeared in the paper about the air in Rochester. After a half hour, he panned the audience. "I'd like to open this up to questions. I find the heart of the matter comes out then."

Several students had good queries. Several more asked pseudo-intellectual questions. All about the environment. Then a blond woman stood. "I was wondering about your campaign next year, Senator. Will you be emphasizing the environment in your platform? And what else will be on it?"

Succinctly, Clay outlined what he'd been planning for environmental programs. Then he presented some preliminary information about battered women and teens.

You've copped out on your commitment to helping kids . . .

"And I plan to continue my tough-on-crime stance with juvenile crime."

Hands shot up. He glanced to the side and did a double take. In the third row sat Eric Lawson. What the hell was that guy doing here? For a pulverizing moment, Clay feared his son might have asked his potential opponent to attend. But he forced himself to think rationally. Despite their differences, he didn't believe Jon would do that to him. Just the thought of it cut to the quick. Calling on his expertise as a speaker, he fielded other people's questions; when Lawson continued to raise his hand, Clay thought, *Fuck it, I'm not running from a fight.*

With his most ingratiating smile, he peered out at the audience. "You're in for a treat," he said. "One of the wannabe candidates for the New York senate spot next year is in the audience and has his hand up. I'm going to call on him." Again the smile. "This should be interesting."

Lawson stood. He was Clay's height but thinner. Full head of black hair. Broad shoulders. Did Bailey like those dark looks? "As a matter of fact, Senator, I have several questions."

To the audience, Clay quipped, "I imagine you do."

The excitement quotient in the room climbed noticeably. People moved forward in their seats and there was a low murmur rumbling through the crowd. Clay liked the challenge.

"What did you think of the article in *Time* magazine about the national trends in anti–youth gang activity? Specifically where it said traditional methods obviously are not effective." The man did a bit of smoozing himself. "And how the reporter cited ESCAPE and your nemesis the Street Angel as an innovative and progressive way of helping kids."

"I hope your next question isn't quite as difficult," he said. "To answer this one, I will tell you that last month I had a tour of ESCAPE." He explained to the audience what the organization was. "I found them all to be intelligent, dedicated people. I wouldn't want to close them down if they were working within the system."

"The article said that's precisely why they succeed."

"Vigilantes succeeded in stopping crime, too. That doesn't mean they were right in what they did."

"Surely, you're not comparing the Street Angel to a vigilante? No, wait, that would be the epithet she'd throw at you."

A laugh from the audience—at Clay's expense.

"The Street Angel and I had a very civil, if spirited discussion. We voiced our differences and made some headway in understanding each other, I think."

When their time was up, the president stepped forward and thanked Clay. He was proud of himself that he hadn't been blindsided by Lawson. He felt like he could scale mountains when he saw the approval on Jon's face.

They were at a reception in the president's residence before he got to talk to his son alone. "So what did you think, Jon?"

"You did good, Dad." He looked at Clay without a trace of animosity. "I'm shocked as hell the Street Angel let you visit her place."

What was I thinking, letting you come here? It hasn't helped.

"It was an interesting night."

Jon nodded across the room. Again the approval. "He didn't throw you, Dad."

"No."

"I agree with his politics more than yours, but you held your own."

"Thanks, son. That means a lot to me. So, are we on tomorrow, for dinner and a show in the city?"

"Yeah, sure."

A pretty blonde approached them and after Jon introduced her, they stepped away; right behind them, a political science professor came up to Clay. As Clay listened to the guy, his gaze strayed to Lawson, and his mind to Bailey O'Neil.

He remembered the clear blue of her eyes, how she looked in his coat, how she trembled in his arms when he tried to shield her with his body. He remembered how she ate the ice cream with relish, smiled at her son's picture, her warmth and affection for her coworkers.

When the man left, Clay heard behind him, "Hello, Senator, how's it going?"

Turning around, Clay drew in a breath. "Good, Lawson." He shook the extended hand and somebody snapped a picture.

Lawson said, "The *Sun*'s here."

"Hmm."

"So you toured ESCAPE. Bailey didn't tell me."

"No?"

"I wonder why."

"I wouldn't know."

Lawson's expression was smug. "She's working on my campaign, you know."

"So I heard." Clay set his drink down. "Give her my best when you see her. Now, if you'll excuse me, I'd like to spend some time with my son. I don't see him enough."

"I was under the impression you two didn't get along."

"How on earth would you come to that conclusion?"

"Maybe because he showed up at a meeting I held to see who was interested in volunteering to work for my election to the Senate."

BAILEY SMILED ACROSS the room at her son, her niece, and her brother. Amid little ones running around and the noisy chatter of both parents and kids, she watched Rory and Aidan try on the *Where the Wild Things Are* costumes. Kathleen studied them from the sidelines. Paddy's daughter, six, always thought before she did anything. Her older brothers said she was scoping out the situation. Bailey and Aidan had taken both kids into the city to the Strong Museum for this special exhibit on her favorite book. Maurice Sendak was her favorite children's book author.

Clayton Wainwright would probably know where he lived.

Damn, that man kept creeping into her thoughts. She could still picture him jumping in front of her when he thought she was in danger . . . eating ice cream with sumptuous delight . . . the twinkle in his eyes when he talked about Susan Sarandon.

In an attempt to get him out of her mind, she picked up the newspaper lying on the bench beside her. What the hell? There he was. Oh, my God, shaking hands with Eric Lawson?

Is it his politics you support or are you sleeping with him?

How dare he ask her that? It was rude and insulting. He was overbearing, controlling—and had years of practice at it. Powerful men were always that way. Not her taste at all in the opposite sex.

She scanned the article. He'd been giving a speech at Bard. For some reason, she hoped it went well with his son. She couldn't believe that Jon Wainwright had gone to a rally for a man who wanted to run against Jon's own father. To her, the betrayal of family was unconscionable. Her parents instilled loyalty in all of them, and were loyal to a fault themselves. Oh, sure they argued openly with each other, criticized each other. But even when her dad had fathered an illegitimate daughter, her mother had taken the girl in, and Paddy O'Neil wouldn't allow any of his other four children to bad-mouth Moira. How could Clay's son take sides against him?

"Mommy?"

She looked up to see a little imp standing in front of her. He was dressed like the boy Max from the book when he goes to the land of the wild things; right now Rory sported pointed ears, tail, and claws. Behind him stood a still-uncostumed Kathleen.

Next to them was Bailey's brother, dressed like one of the wild things. "Rumpus, rumpus," Aidan growled.

Bailey laughed. "Oh, my, you two are frightening."

"Max is mad at his mommy." Rory bared his teeth. His dark curls peeked out of the costume, and his blue eyes shone with mirth. "Better watch out."

She shivered. "Why's Max mad at his mommy?"

"She makes him go to bed early."

Ruffling his hair, Bailey quipped, "Uh-oh." Her son was a night owl and one of her biggest struggles was getting him to sleep. "I'd better watch out."

Rory hugged her, then slipped away with his cousin. "Gonna watch the show." Three feet away, they plopped down in front of one of the many TV's set up with an animated version of the book, and got engrossed immediately.

Aidan whipped off his mask and dropped down on the bench next to her. "He tires me out."

"Me, too."

Aidan watched her. "You look it. Have a hot date last night with Lawson?"

"Speaking of which . . ." She held up the paper. "He's been busy."

Aidan took the paper. Skimmed it. "I liked that guy."

"Eric? You've been making nasty comments about him every time we have a date." In truth, she liked Eric, but didn't really trust him. Was he courting her just to get ammunition against Wainwright in order to run against him in the future?

"No, not Lecherous Lawson. Clay Wainwright."

I liked him, too.

But no, that couldn't be true. Wainwright was clearly her enemy. Things had ended badly with them.

You bastard. How dare you . . . Get out of here right now, Senator. This little experiment is over.

"Sis, where'd you go?"

"Nowhere." Her cell phone rang. "I have to get that. Something might be going on at ESCAPE."

"Bailey Ann, it's your day off. Don't answer it."

She fished the phone out of her pocket. Checked the caller ID. It read *Unavailable*. Pressing Send, she held it to her ear. "Bailey O'Neil."

"Ms. O'Neil, this is Jeremiah Friedman. I hope I'm not catching you at a bad time."

"No, Governor, you're not."

"*The* governor?" Aidan asked.

Bailey nodded.

"I'll cut to the chase. At the direction of Congress, each state is setting up a task force to recommend how to spend its allotment of money from Chuck Stewart's Youth Crime Bill."

Bailey had been plotting to get some of its funds. Was this her opportunity? Her pulse speeded up. "I see."

"I want you on the task force."

Yes! "I'd be happy to be on it."

"Good. Our first meeting is in two weeks. I'll have my secretary call you with the details but I wanted to issue the invitation personally."

Something made Bailey ask, "Governor Friedman, will Clayton Wainwright be participating in this committee?"

"Yes, he'll be New York's representative. As I said, one senator from each state will be on each task force. Then that person will take the recommendation back to Washington."

"Shouldn't Alex Case"—the other New York senator—"be on this task force? Since Wainwright's on the parent committee?"

"Clay asked specifically to be part of this, and I don't see any conflict of interest. Regardless, Case is tied up with some ongoing work with Homeland Security." A long and meaningful pause. "Is there a problem with Clay being on this task force?"

He knew there was. "No, of course not. I'll look forward to sparring with him."

"Not exactly what I had in mind."

Best to take the bull by the horns. "Surely you expect some fireworks."

"What I'd like is a truce."

Let me come to work with you . . . We might even call a truce.

"I'm not sure you're going to get that. However, I'll do my best to be civil." She said her good-byes and clicked off the phone.

"What?" Aidan asked.

"Looks like round three's coming up." She explained the situation, excitement pumping through her veins like a direct shot of caffeine.

"You don't seem unhappy about working with Clay Wainwright."

"Of course I am. The senator's a pain in the ass."

"Uh-huh." He stood. "Come on, B., let's go play with the wild things. Something you're really good at," he added.

"Much to Wainwright's chagrin." She wondered what he was thinking about this turn of events.

FIVE

ALONE IN HIS den in his New York town house, Clayton stared at the computer screen; its low hum was the only thing breaking the silence. He was studying a proposal for the Appropriations Committee to be discussed in September and his eyes kept closing. It wasn't that he was tired. He was bored. *Focus on the committee,* he told himself. It was in a session of Appropriations that he'd gotten the Street Angel's funding stalled for Guardian.

You bastard. Get out of here right now, Senator. This little experiment is over.

Maybe he should try to contact her again. They were going to be working on the governor's task force together, and Jerry Friedman has asked him once again to come in peace. Clay had her email address at ESCAPE. He drummed his fingers on the mouse pad. Hell, maybe she was there. He stifled the thought that he was using the committee as an excuse to contact her.

Dear Ms. O'Neil. Nah, he knew her better than that. *Dear Bailey, I'm sorry our last meeting ended so badly. I'd hoped we could get to know each other better. I shouldn't have made that crack about Lawson.* Truthfully, Clay had been jealous.

Shit, he sounded like a teenage boy. *Are we going to be able to bury this hatchet?* He signed it simply *Clay* and pressed Send, staying online in case she was at work and responded back immediately.

She did.

Dear Senator, Apology accepted. I lost my temper with you, too, which seems to happen when we're in the same room. I think I need anger management where you're concerned.

He smiled. Her response was a peace offering. He typed, *Where are you now? Do you have Instant Messenger, so we can talk live?*

A longer wait. Clay got up and went to the teak sideboard to pour himself a scotch. He appreciated its zip as he took a swig and chided himself for contacting her. A chime indicating an answer coming in. He went back to the computer. *Not a good idea,* was the message.

He typed and sent, *Please.*

Finally, capitulation. *IrishCream.*

He chuckled, and returned *ClayFeet.*

In minutes, he added her to a buddy list under "personal" and clicked into IM. *How are you?*

Tired, came the instant reply. This was a lot better. It was like talking to her. Grinning foolishly, he settled in.

Why?

I couldn't get Rory to sleep last night.

How late was he up?

Until midnight. I read him five books and sang an easy eighteen songs.

Without thinking, he said, *I wish I had those days back with my son, Bailey. Treasure them.*

What would you do differently?

That was easy. *Be home more.*

A long pause. *I'm not home enough.*

I have some suggestions that would keep you home more. He put in a ☺.

I'm too tired to fight about that, ClayFeet.

Okay. Do you exercise?

Exercise is highly overrated.

Not if it's fun.

What do you do to keep in such good shape?

Hmm. So she thought he was in good shape. *Racquetball. I'm really good.*

And modest, too. A long pause. *I used to play.*

When?

In prison.

Clay drew in a breath. Thoughts of her behind bars made his blood run cold. *I hate to think of you in prison.* And his own role in putting her there.

Then don't. Maybe I'll challenge you to a game of racquetball. The winner could compromise on his or her philosophies.

He chuckled. *You wouldn't have a chance against me.*

Pride goeth before the fall, Senator.

I'm bigger than you are.

I'm smaller and faster. And I pack quite a punch.

No doubt about that. *Bailey, look I . . .*

Suddenly a message came on screen. *IrishCream has logged off at 12:30 A.M.*

What the hell? She cut him off? Or, oh God, had something happened to her? She was at ESCAPE. He pictured the area where the building was. The small quarters. Were those locks effective enough? Damn it, anything could have gone down. He reached for the phone, angry all over again at her carelessness about her safety.

TAZ, IS THAT you?

A long pause from the interactive network. The message had come on suddenly when she was talking with Clay. She'd clicked off her personal IM fast to answer the website visitor.

Taz, talk to me. I haven't heard from you in a while. I've been wondering how you are.

She waited, and as she did, the phone rang. She snatched it up.

"Bailey?" Clay's tone was concerned. Overly concerned.

"I'm okay. I got a hit on the website. I can't talk."

"Thank God. I thought something might have happened to

you." His relieved tone, the intimacy of his voice across the lines, warmed her.

Because it did, she said, "I gotta go."

"All right. Stay safe," he told her.

"I will."

Just as she hung up, another message came across the website.

I'm here, Angel.

What have you been up to?

Just been in the mix. Nothin' serious. A pause. *My old man and me been squabbin'.*

What are you fighting about?

He wanted me to knock boots with some jerkoff he owes money.

Oh, Taz. You don't have to live like this.

Thinkin' about livin' with my set. We got a crib . . .

Uh-oh, if Taz told her where the GGs crashed, was she legally bound to report it? Damn it, now Wainwright had her thinking like him!

Before you do that, meet with me. We have a thing called Face-to-Face. I'll come with two others. We can just talk.

Wasn't born yesterday, lady.

It's safe, and no one will try to make you do anything you don't want.

Snort, snort.

I mean it. Try to believe me. I'm trustworthy.

Word on the street has it you went to jail for not blowin' somebody in.

I did.

Maybe I'll meet with you. Alone, though, outta the way.

Should she do it?

She remembered Clay's words. *How can you risk your life when you have a son depending on you?*

Of course she shouldn't. But when had she let that stop her? *Okay, girl. Here's the plan . . .*

By the time she was done, she had a date to meet Taz. The shrill of the phone into the quiet office startled her. Bailey didn't answer it. It was probably the senator, and she didn't want to talk to him now. He'd read it in her voice that she'd just made an appointment to meet with a gang kid alone.

"AND NOW, GIVE a big hand to Senator Clayton Wainwright, who made this whole project possible."

Clayton smiled at the woman who introduced him; she was the manager of Tales for Tots, a new bookstore in town. When he took the microphone, he said, "I think that's an exaggeration, Donna. I helped get some funds for this terrific place but your committee did all the work."

The manager wouldn't be swayed. "You pushed our grant through, you persuaded a top architect in New York to do the plans without charge, and you've been a consistent moral supporter during the year it's taken to get this bookstore established."

More clapping. Clay demurred. He'd wholeheartedly worked on this project to benefit an underprivileged area of the city and had made a point to attend the ribbon-cutting ceremony of this very worthwhile venture. He wondered if Bailey knew about it. If she acknowledged at least some of the good he did.

Then he wondered why he cared. She'd disconnected a couple of nights ago when they'd been making some progress in getting to know each other, and he hadn't tried to contact her since. *Concentrate*, he told himself, as he peered out at the fairly decent crowd of kids, adults, and some of the press.

In his remarks, he cited the bookstore's layout: children's reading centers scattered throughout, indicating different topics by various primary colors. There was an adventure section that sported action figures hovering in the air over the stacks, pillows and chairs of all sizes. There were similar areas for nonfiction: trains and race cars acting as seating areas, trees, rocks, and the like. It was a child's paradise, designed to get kids interested in books. The undercurrent of children's chatter and excited squeals indicated the level of enthusiasm he'd hoped for.

As he finished his talk and a crowd began to gather around him, he had a flash of reading to Jon. When he was a district attorney, Clay was home more than after he entered politics, and remembered how his son liked the Grimm Brothers fairy tales. Karen had said they were too dark, but Clay had enjoyed reading them, then watching the videos of *Fairy Tale Theater.* A far cry from the time they spent together—or didn't spend together—now. Thinking of their last conversation, a sense of loss ambushed him like an emotional sniper, setting him off balance for a minute.

I can't believe you'd do this to me.

I didn't do *anything. I just went to Lawson's preliminary meeting.*

Going's enough. He hadn't even tried keep the hurt from his voice.

And, as he always did when they argued, Jon went on the defensive. He'd straightened to his full height and squared his shoulders. *Worried about the public's reaction?*

No, Clay remembered thinking, *you broke my heart.*

There had been no dinner and a show that trip for father and son.

He was distracted from his unpleasant memory by a tug on his suit coat. Looking down, he saw a little black-haired boy with startling blue eyes staring up at him. "Wanna read to me, mister?"

Clay grinned. "I'd love to." Something about the kid . . . "Is your mom or dad here? I wouldn't want them to think you're lost."

The boy nodded. "My uncle's over there."

Clay glanced up to see a man with looks similar to the boy watching them from about fifteen feet away. He raised his coffee cup in salute to Clay. Ah, he got it.

Squatting down, he faced the the kid eye-level. "Your name wouldn't happen to be Rory, would it?"

Owl eyes now. "How'd ya know?"

"I met your mom and uncle. And I saw your picture."

"Mommy's got lots of pictures. Uncle A. takes them." He held out a book. "Read me this," he said in the tone of a child used to being read to.

"Okay. Let me check with your uncle first."

Rory grasped on to his hand; his fingers were a little sticky, and very small. Clay was touched by the gesture.

When they reached the uncle, Clay extended his other hand. "Aidan, right?"

Bailey's brother shook his hand warmly. "Yeah, hi, Senator."

"Clay, please." He smiled down at Rory. "Your nephew asked if I'd read to him."

Eyes exactly like Bailey's were amused. "I know. He said he wanted *that important man* to read him his favorite book."

Clay glanced at Rory's choice of reading material. *Where the Wild Things Are.* "Now why doesn't this surprise me? Like mother like son."

"You got that right. It's Bailey's favorite, too. We all went to see the exhibit at the museum downtown."

His heartbeat speeded up a bit and he glanced behind Aidan. "Bailey with you?"

"Nope. She's workin' in 'that awful place'."

Clay smiled. "She know you're here?"

"She knows I was taking my man here to do something educational. I wanted to hear what you had to say. I'll tell her we saw you." He pulled out a camera. "As a matter of fact, I'm gonna document it. My sister's real big on Kodak moments."

A tug on his pants. "Mister?"

Leaning down, Clay scooped Rory up. Nostalgia washed over him once again at the heavy weight of a child in his arms. His estrangement from his own son felt suffocating. It kept growing every day, and this latest thing with Lawson had caused another huge gulf. Pushing away the more-than-unpleasant thought, he carried Rory over to a chair that fit the two of them, plopped down, and began to read.

Rory knew all the parts. Clay could imagine Bailey acting them out with him—he was sure she'd choose to be one of the wild things. Halfway through, Rory nestled close into his chest. Absently, Clay kissed his head—as Aidan did indeed take some pictures.

When they were done, Rory perked up. "I'm hungry."

Refreshments were provided at the front of the store. "Want some juice and cookies?"

"Ice cream sundae. Hot fudge," he said emphatically.

Like mother like son, Clay thought again. And again, the image of Bailey eating pistachio ice cream assaulted him.

He rose with Rory in his arms and found Aidan across the room, flirting with a redhead. "Aidan?"

"Oh, sorry. You have to leave?"

"Actually, I'd like to treat my new friend here to ice cream."

"And his uncle?"

Clay grinned. "Sure. I wouldn't mind talking to you about a certain person we both know, anyway."

"There's a diner across the street."

"You're on."

Soon they were settled in a booth in the restaurant with their treats. A small afternoon crowd had gathered in the bright, sun-drenched diner. Rory shoveled down his ice cream, then asked if he could go look at the aquarium full of colorful tropical fish that was the restaurant's main decorative touch. Since it was only a few feet away, Aidan gave his permission and Rory scampered off. Soon his face was pressed to the tank, mouth open in awe.

"So," Clay began after he and Aidan had eaten most of their dessert and had ordered coffee. "How's your sister?"

Aidan scowled. "Workin' too hard, as usual. I try to help her out, but hell, she has erratic hours at ESCAPE and fills in at the pub three times a week." He nodded to the boy. "She spends the rest of her time with this one. I don't know when she sleeps."

"Can't she forgo the pub?"

"She needs the money. ESCAPE doesn't pay much. The rest of us can't afford to help her financially." He gazed at his camera. "I'm tryin' to . . ." He shook his head. "You don't want to talk about me."

"Sure I do."

"No, you wanna know about her. I can tell." He smiled. "So, if you promise to get Julianne's address for me, I'll tell all."

"Julianne?"

"Moore."

Clay laughed. "I'll put the FBI right on it."

Aidan watched him. His gaze was intense, and again reminiscent of Bailey's.

"Aidan, why is she into the gang thing? She's bright, funny, interesting. She could be a lot of things. I know she's been offered several social work jobs with the state government, which pay more."

Aidan's dark brows knitted. "Because of our sister."

"You have another sister?"

"We did. She died." He stared out the window, obviously thinking about another time. "In prison."

Clay stilled. "Tell me."

Aidan toyed with a napkin as he talked. "Moira was three years older than Bailey. But she didn't live with us until she was fourteen. Dad . . . he, oh, hell, he cheated on Mom and got caught. To give him quarter, they were fightin' like cats and dogs then and had a temporary separation. But we didn't know about Moira until her mother died. By then, she was into a girl gang."

At fourteen. How sad.

"The Good Girls were the—"

"She was in the GGs?"

"Yeah. They got into a particularly bad street fight just past her sixteenth birthday, and were rounded up. A D.A. sent her to Greenfield Detention Center."

"I know the place. It's for hard-core teenagers."

"She found her niche there, too. She died squaring off with an in-house rival gang leader."

Clay's heart went out to Aidan and Bailey. "I'm sorry."

"Bailey took it the hardest. They were the two girls so they shared a room. She loved Moira."

Things about Bailey made more sense now. He wondered why he didn't know this about her background. It hadn't come up in her trial, or at least he couldn't remember it.

"Clay?"

He sipped his coffee. "Hmm?"

"I wish you two could bury the hatchet. You've caused her a lot of grief already."

He swallowed hard, glanced at Rory who was busy tracing patterns with his finger on the glass of the fish tank. "You mean when she went to prison."

Aidan's pleasant face tensed. "Uh-huh." His brow furrowed.

"She never talks about it. I don't think we know the whole story of what happened to her in there."

Clay said, "Andersonville is less dangerous than Greenfield. Where Bailey went was minimum security."

Her brother's jaw hardened. "I know. But in some ways, that's what I was afraid of. Other prisoners had . . . easy access to her."

Clay cleared his throat. "I checked on her."

"What?"

"After she was convicted. I visited Andersonville before she went up and then kept tabs during the year she was inside. There were a few scrapes."

"Yeah, I saw a black eye once and some bruises when I visited her."

Clay swallowed hard. He leaned over. "I'm not sure about the other—the sexual stuff. The guards said no, it didn't happen to her, that she'd gotten the protection of an inmate . . ."

Aidan shrugged. "She said she wasn't sexually assaulted. That somebody had protected her—a gang leader who'd known Moira on the outside. I just, um, didn't know what Bailey would have to do to get that protection."

Clay went cold. "Do you think she was lying?" *Please Lord, don't let her have been.*

"She could have been. I know my sister better than anybody. She's the baby but she'd feel the need to shelter us." Aidan gripped his spoon and stirred his coffee. "It's why we don't know the details of what happens at ESCAPE. It drives my brothers nuts."

Releasing a heavy breath, Clay shifted in his seat. "It drives me nuts, too."

Aidan studied him. "Am I missing something here?"

"What do you mean?"

"I don't know. Guy stuff. You seem . . . fond of her."

He started to object. Then he held Aidan's gaze. "I . . . am. I never expected to like her."

A laugh, deep and from his belly, escaped from Aidan. "Oh, wow. This is something. Particularly because I think she feels the same about you."

"She told you that?"

"Nah. But as I said, I know her better than anybody." He sobered. "You're not married, right?"

"Divorced."

"Got somebody?"

"I see a woman, but nothing formal." Jane's pale hair and slender form came to his mind. "It's been on-again, off-again for a while." He thought about it. "I don't believe it's going anywhere."

"If it is, if there's another woman, stay away from Bailey, Clay. I don't want her hurt."

"And if there isn't one?"

He snorted. "I'd watch my step if I were you."

"Why?"

"Bailey's never taken a man seriously."

"Not even Rory's father?"

"She liked him well enough. But I don't think she's ever been in love." He smiled. "She and I joke that we were both born lacking the love gene."

"No special girl for you?"

"Nope. My brothers, they're a different story. Bailey and me . . . *nada*. Truthfully, I don't think she's ever found anybody who's man enough to handle her. Or one she can believe in enough to trust her heart with."

Clay was still digesting that when Rory raced over. "I'm thirsty."

Aidan smiled. "Okay, champ." He signaled the waitress.

Sitting back, Clay watched the two of them. "Thanks for telling me all this."

"Just remember what I said. I'm more mild-mannered than my three brothers, but I'll break your legs if you hurt her."

"You gonna break his legs, Uncle Aidan?" Rory asked.

Aidan ruffled Rory's hair. "Just a figure of speech, kid."

But it wasn't. Oh, Clay didn't believe Aidan would do him bodily harm. Probably not. He didn't think so anyway. But Clay could tell this brother meant to protect his sister.

As he watched the O'Neils leave, he pondered what he'd

just heard. Bailey was an even more complicated woman than Clay had realized.

That he wanted to know all those layers, peel them off one by one, shocked him. This was *not* good.

THE GIRL WAS beautiful. She looked like Jennifer Lopez, though her hair was darker and her eyes more hazel than brown. No wonder her father tried to whore her out. Son of a bitch.

"Can't believe you're here, Angel."

Bailey smiled at Taz. "Why? I'm just having coffee at my favorite bookstore cafe." The one near Columbia University's campus, where scads of people were around, but Taz wouldn't stick out. She was dressed in fatigue pants, an army-green T-shirt, and combat boots. Around her neck were distinctive beads, which indicated her gang affiliation. She didn't fly the gang colors, though.

Bailey herself had on jeans and a T-shirt. To the casual eye, they'd look like two students having coffee. Students and teachers alike gathered in the airy space, which brought the outdoor sunshine in through a huge wall of windows. The interior was redolent with coffee and a variety of breads they were famous for.

"Nice shirt." Taz nodded to the GIRL POWER, glittered across Bailey's chest. She watched Bailey keenly, with eyes full of a wary intelligence.

Taz said, "You're pretty young to be doin' this for a living."

"So are you, Taz."

"I can take care of myself." Her eyes clouded though, and she began to rip apart a napkin in front of her. "I, um, this last thing . . . fuck, I only did it once 'cause they said they were gonna cut off his fingers, one at a time. I ain't doin' it again."

"Of course you're not. We have to get you out of that house."

"I said I can live with my homies."

"I can get you into a shelter."

"No way. Five-ohs bust those places on a regular basis."

"The shelters ESCAPE uses are havens. The police leave

us alone." She smiled. "Anyway, they don't know all the locations where we stash our kids."

Taz's smile made her even prettier. "Everybody says you don't play by no rules."

"I play by rules that are fair. So, what do you think? Are you going to let me help you?"

Bringing her coffee mug to her lips, Taz once again studied Bailey. Finally, she said, "For a place to flop, maybe. Nothin' more. Least not right now."

"All right. That's enough." At least for right now.

~~ SIX

AS CLAYTON RODE in the taxi from his office to the governor's, he drew a folder from his briefcase. Opening it, he startled at the face staring out at him. God, her eyes were blue. They sucked you in. Against his will, he reached out and traced a few freckles on her nose. Shit! Why had Josh included this picture in the file? Probably to bust his balls. Josh Lewis, his roommate from college, who ran a private investigation firm, happened to be in New York the night after Clay had toured ESCAPE's offices, and had been the unexpected recipient of Clay's venting.

"You got a thing for her, buddy?" His most trusted friend had asked as they'd kicked back with a beer in Clay's town house.

"No. Except that she gets under my skin."

"Not a lot of women been able to do that."

Thoughtful, he peeled the label from the bottle. "What if I wanted to know what she was up to for a few weeks? Could you do it? Discreetly?"

"Yeah, sure. Nothing illegal about keeping track of a foe. 'Course, if it was personal, it could be considered stalking."

"It isn't personal, it's professional."

"Yeah, I can see that," Josh said dryly. When Clay didn't respond, he said, "What the hell? Let's do it."

He knew what Josh was thinking, but he was wrong. This was purely professional. Nothing personal. Clay wanted ammunition against her, that was all.

Then why'd you change your suit today, twice, when you knew you were going to see her?

Fuck, he couldn't believe he was attracted to the Street Angel. She wasn't drop-dead gorgeous. She didn't have that sophisticated veneer he liked in women.

Disgusted with himself, he zeroed in on the contents of the folder. By the time he got to the governor's office, all thoughts of attraction had flown from his mind; he wanted to strangle her again. Hurrying from the cab, he strode into the Public Safety Building, which was buzzing with the drone of computers, phones ringing, and work chatter. He strode to the bank of elevators hidden around a corner, thinking that some man really needed to take Bailey O'Neil in hand. God help the guy who tried, though.

The doors to an elevator opened and just before Clay stepped in, he heard, "Hold it for me!" as a bundle of blue flew toward him. "Thanks, I—oh . . ."

"Bailey."

"Senator."

While they stood staring at each other, the elevator doors closed.

"Damn."

She swore, too. Averting her eyes, she pushed the call button and waited, shifting from one foot to the other.

He tried to think of something glib to say, something polite. But she looked tired and vulnerable. Why not, after what she'd been up to? Remembering the file in his briefcase, he gripped the handle tightly, and tried to rein in his pique. "I trust you've been well since we last spoke."

"Yeah, thanks. You?"

"Fine."

They stared straight ahead; she said, "I saw your picture in the paper last week. How was Bard?"

"Liberal as always." He didn't want to think about how that weekend had ended with Jon. "How's *your* son?"

"Rory? Great."

Mention of the boy got Clay riled up all over again about the danger she put herself in, when she had a child to care for. Somehow it had become mixed up with his problems with his own son, too, but he couldn't figure out how. In any case, he kept remembering Rory's little-boy haircut and joyful grin, how he cuddled into Clay's chest, how content he seemed. What if something happened to Bailey because of her insistence on meeting gang kids face-to-face? Frustrated by that, just as the elevator rolled to a stop and pinged, he reached out and dragged her around the corner into an empty hallway.

"What are you doing?" she hissed.

"I could ask you the same. Don't you ever think, woman?"

"What are you talking about? And why did you pull me away from the elevator?"

"Because what I have to say to you is private and has nothing to do with the governor's task force."

Straightening her shoulders, she faced him. She wore a plain navy suit and light blue blouse. The outfit could be nun-like if it wasn't for how she filled out the stretchy material. Today her glossy hair fell in waves around her face and down her back.

"Spit it out, Senator."

"I thought Face-to-Faces were conducted by the rule of three."

She had the good sense to blush. "They are. Everything we told you when you toured ESCAPE is true."

"You left a little something out."

She tried to sidle around him, but he stepped in front of her. They were close momentarily; she smelled like flowers. Then she stepped back. "What?"

"You met alone with a gang member."

Her blue eyes widened.

"Don't bother denying it. You were seen."

"I don't have to confirm or deny anything for you. Or anybody else. I run ESCAPE as I see fit. As long as I'm not committing a crime, you can't touch me."

"If that braided, pierced, and tattooed bombshell told you she did anything illegal, you've broken the law. Again."

"Oh, and did you, or whoever it was that *saw me,* overhear our conversation?"

"No, I'm not privy to what was said." He ran a hand through his hair. "Don't you care about your safety? You have a child to consider, for Christ's sake."

That stopped her. And made her tongue loose. "Look, I met with Taz in a very public coffee shop at ten o'clock in the morning. It was perfectly safe." She frowned. "How do you know she was in a gang?"

"She was gang material, though she wasn't flying her colors." He peered at her. "She was one of yours, right?"

"Well, I'm trying to get her out of a gang."

"Did you?"

Her smile was sun bright. It knocked him off kilter for a second, and he braced himself against the wall. "No, but I got her into a shelter."

Clay didn't say anything.

"See, Senator, I do some good."

Again she tried to move around him to get to the elevator. He blocked her way a second time. "You met a gang kid alone. That is *definitely* not a good thing."

"I wasn't at risk. For one thing, she was tiny. I could take her if I had to."

"Oh, that's just great. What if she had a knife? God help that four-year-old who depends on you."

Furious because he kept hitting that hot button, Bailey snapped at him. "What do you know about me and Rory?"

"Enough to know you shouldn't be risking your safety, for him if nothing else. He's a wonderful boy. Inquisitive. Happy . . . How would he be changed if he lost his mother at such a young age?"

"How do you know all that?"

"All what?"

"All that about Rory."

"Because I met him."

"Where?"

"Your brother and son were at the opening of Tales for Tots. I gave a speech and cut the ribbon."

"Why didn't Aidan tell me he saw you?"

"I have no idea."

"What else happened?"

"We got ice cream. Aidan and I talked for a while."

Her gaze narrowed, and she assessed him shrewdly. "About me?"

"Some. Don't worry, he didn't tell me state secrets." Uncomfortable with the direction of the conversation because of what Aidan *had* told him, Clay glanced at his watch. "We've got to get going." He circled around her and they strode to the elevator. Immediately, the doors opened and she stepped inside. He followed her.

Bailey was acutely aware of Clay's size as he stood next to her. His shoulders were linebacker material, and she'd forgotten how tall he was. He smelled like expensive cologne. And she liked his brown pinstripe suit. It did nice things to his eyes.

Damn, she was acting like a school girl noticing how a guy was dressed. She needed to annoy him and keep her own annoyance *with* him in the forefront. Luckily, it wasn't at all difficult. "So, what, you had me followed?"

"Somebody ought to have you followed, for all the common sense you have. And don't even ask. I won't tell you how I know."

"It had to be that. Who else could have seen me?"

"Any number of people. Including other gang members who wouldn't want you to get your claws into one of theirs."

"In that place? Never."

No comment.

"Look, I've worked with girls like Taz for years. They respond well to me."

He sighed heavily. "Is she in high school?"

"Yes, and she's smart. I think she's going to be one of my success stories." When he didn't respond, she added forcefully, "Damn it, Senator, give me a break."

He let out a frustrated breath, then reached out and hit a button. The elevator came to a jolting halt.

Bailey jerked forward. "What the hell are you doing?"

"Look, I'm worried about you, all right? On top of disagreeing with just about everything that pops into that pretty little head of yours, I'm *worried*."

"Why?"

"Damned if I know. Meeting you. Your family. Hearing about your life. I've been thinking about you a lot lately."

I've been thinking about you, too. "You shouldn't be thinking about me as anything but an enemy."

He looked like he'd been slapped. Then his eyes darkened to a smoky quartz. "All right, sure, fine. Forget it." Giving her his back, he went for the button to release the elevator.

Without thinking of what she was doing, Bailey reached out and grasped his arm, effectively stopping him. "Clay."

The use of his name, the way she uttered it, seemed intimate. Felt intimate. She slid her hand to his wrist and lightly grazed his bare skin. It was sprinkled with dark blond hair.

Suddenly the air felt oppressive, hot; the elevator became an emotional powder keg. She tugged her hand back.

He pivoted. There was heat in his eyes. A kind of heat she'd seen before from men. *Oh, my God,* she thought just as he grasped on to her, pressed her against the wall, and covered his mouth with hers.

From there, it got very wild, very fast.

"FIRST, I'D LIKE to thank you all for consenting to be on New York's Youth Gang Task Force." Governor Friedman's look was sincere as he scanned the ten people at the oval conference table in his stately office of cherry wood paneling and expensive furniture. "I know you're all busy. But I chose each of you carefully for your diverse views. That said, I'm hoping you can pool your expertise and come up with concrete suggestions for using our share of the hundred million dollars provided by Stewart's Youth Crime Bill, earmarked for social agencies to counter gang activity in our state."

People nodded. Smiled. Some sent surreptitious glances at

Bailey, then Clay, who were, of course, well-known adversaries on this topic. Yeah, sure, and that adversary just had his hands underneath her blouse in the elevator, for God's sake. God, she hoped she'd tucked it in right. He'd tried to help her.

Here let me.

She batted his hands away. *No!*

Right now, he could barely look at her, and she'd die before she caught his gaze. They'd both been late to this meeting, though thank the good Lord, no one else knew why.

The governor gave his committee an ingratiating smile. "Let's introduce ourselves. Tell us who you are, and why you're here."

He nodded to a plump woman of about sixty. "Marion, would you start?"

"I'm Marion Hocker. A Sister of St. Joseph. I work at the Baden Street shelter that takes in gang kids. I'm here because we need to make some progress in housing for these kids." She smiled at Bailey. The nun finished with, "I fully support ESCAPE's proposal for Guardian House."

Next up was a police captain, Ned Price, who had extensive anti-gang experience. "I'm tired of competing efforts. We need to work together." His steely gaze focused on Bailey. "And to know our places."

The senator went next. "I'm Clay Wainwright. I've made no secret of my tough-on-crime stance, especially with youth gang members. And I agree with Ned. We need to work together, and know our roles. I have some ideas where I'd like that money spent."

The others followed.

A state senator.

A single mother who used to be in a gang.

A social worker.

A teacher and a principal.

A female pastor.

When it was her turn, Bailey smiled congenially at everybody—with lips that felt slightly swollen. From *his* mouth. "I'm Bailey O'Neil, otherwise known as the Street Angel. I run ESCAPE and know some of you but not all. Since this is money earmarked for social agencies, and the federal govern-

ment already got its four hundred million"—here she took a
bead on Clay—"for prosecutors, the FBI, and other legal ea-
gles, I wonder why the local senator and the federal senator
are even participating."

Clay leaned forward to answer that. There was still a flush
on his face, and on his neck was a red mark from her mouth.
"We're here to make sure you spend this money wisely."

She gave him a blistering look. "That should not be your
decision."

"Oh, and who should decide? You?"

"These allocations should be decided by the people who
will get the social agency money."

Clay started to say more when the door opened and hit the
wall with a thud.

"Sorry I'm late." Gazes flew to the entry.

"Ah, Councilman Lawson. Glad you could make it." Friedman addressed the rest of them. "When he got wind of this
committee, Eric called and asked to be part of it. As a lawyer,
with his background in juvenile crime, it seemed appropriate."

Lawson crossed to Bailey and sat down close to her. She
inched back and shot a surreptitious glance at Clay. He scowled
at Lawson's proprietary gesture. She scowled back at him.

After the introductions were completed, the governor
clicked into his Power Point presentation. "The three objectives of this committee and the outcomes are listed here. Take
a minute to read them, then I'll tell you how we'll go about
achieving them."

Bailey read the objectives.

1. To assess current community-based programs.
2. To compile crime prevention research.
3. To explore a variety of intervention services for
   gang members and at-risk youth that might receive
   government money.

"For expediency's sake," the governor began once everyone
had time to read the objectives, "I've broken you into subcommittees according to the above. I'd like you to get together a
couple of times before our next full task force meeting, and

come back with a report on the headway you made. Let's split into groups now and take a few minutes to brainstorm some places to start, then set a time for your subcommittee to get together."

Bailey peered up at the screen. Sure enough, she was grouped with Sister Marion, Ned the cop, and the senator. The governor had obviously given his choice of participants and subcommittees a lot of thought. Their task was to assess current community-based programs.

From the corner of her eye, Bailey saw Clay peruse the screen. Then his gaze swung directly to her. The look was hot and heavy—a lot like his mouth had been. It took her a minute to realize she'd raised her hand to her lips, was touching them. His eyes narrowed possessively on the gesture. Oh, hell.

The meeting broke up, and Bailey wanted desperately to get out of the room without a confrontation with Clay. She didn't know what she was feeling. Unfortunately, Eric was at her elbow when she reached the door. "Hey, wait up."

"I'm in a hurry."

"To get away from the good senator, I'll bet."

"Eric, don't put—"

"Excuse me." Clay's deep voice raised goose flesh on her still sensitized skin. "I was wondering if I might speak to you, Ms. O'Neil." He nodded to Eric. "Lawson." Bailey noticed his address was even cooler than usual. She wondered if he knew about Jon showing up for Eric's get-together.

"I'm trying to have a word with her myself." Eric's blue eyes gleamed as he regarded Clay. "By the way, Senator, did Bailey tell you how much she enjoyed meeting your son at my campaign organizational session?"

CLAY PUNCHED IN the number of her cell. After two rings, she answered in that husky voice of hers, that tonight, ran along his nerve endings. "Bailey O'Neil."

"It's me, Clay."

A long intake of breath. "Hi." Her tone was conciliatory. She didn't bite his head off, as he half expected. "How did you get this number?" When he didn't respond, she said, "Like you get addresses? And emails?"

"The governor. I told him we'd forgotten to exchange numbers for our subcommittee. He obviously felt it was safe to give it to me."

"Goes to show how much he knows."

He chuckled.

"I'm glad you called. You left so quickly after Eric dropped that bomb."

"Yeah, well, my son and my greatest enemy working in collusion on an opponent's campaign made me speechless." And hurt, but he didn't voice that.

"It wasn't a campaign meeting. It was just a pre-session to see how much support Eric might have." Clay didn't respond. "Still, I'm sorry about what Jon did. And we weren't in collusion. I thought it was very wrong of him to be there. If it's any consolation, I told him so that night."

"You did?"

"Yeah. Did you talk to him about it?"

"Yes, and it ended in another yelling match."

"For what it's worth, he seemed really uncomfortable with what he'd done. And chagrined when I said something about it."

"Well, that helps. I'm stunned by his actions." He waited. "And I hate the fact that you were there, that you're going to work for Lawson." A pause. "Especially after today."

More silence.

"Where are you?" he finally asked.

"Home, I just put Rory to bed."

"Enjoy this part of your life with him."

"You'll work it out with Jon, Clay."

He didn't want to think about that, so he let himself wonder what she was wearing. He remembered the peek he'd gotten at some scraps of blue lace when her blouse pulled apart. By his teeth.

"Where are you?" she asked.

"At my town house here in the city. Congress is on recess a few more weeks so I spend a lot of time in New York."

"Ah."

Ohhh, ahhh, Jesus . . .

Hurt?

No. God, no.

"I'd like to see you. We need to talk." Even he could hear the intimate pitch of his voice.

"That's not a good idea. I think we should stay away from each other."

"We have a meeting next week."

"On neutral ground. With a lot of people around."

"Have dinner with me afterwards."

"No."

Silence. He saw in his mind Lawson escort her out of the governor's conference room, close, holding her elbow. "Did you go out with Lawson tonight?"

"That's none of your business."

"It was about five hours ago when you wrapped yourself around me in that elevator."

"Oh, God. I don't know what happened there. We don't even like each other."

"You don't like me just a little bit?"

Nothing.

"You're smiling."

"How can you tell?"

"I just can. Come on, the world won't tilt off its axis if you see me."

"It did today."

"What? Tilt off its axis?" He guessed she didn't mean to say that. "For me too, honey."

A huge intake of breath. "Don't call me that."

"Sorry. What was I thinking?"

"I have to hang up."

He rose and began to pace. "Are we ever going to talk about it, Bailey?"

"No. We're going to forget it happened."

"I'm not sure I can do that."

"Well, try."

"Listen, I—"

"Good night, Senator. Don't call me again."

"You can call me. You've got my cell number in your phone now. On incoming calls." He paused, smiling. "And my email and IM addresses."

"I'll erase everything as soon as we're done."

"Wait. You might need me."

"I won't need you."

He chuckled. "You seemed to in the elevator today, babe."

"Don't keep *talking* about that."

"I'll stop. For now. Sweet dreams, Street Angel."

"You too, Senator."

"Hmm." He could guess what *those* would be. "Good night."

SEVEN

WITH A POWER Point clicker in her hand, Bailey stood before fifty teachers from Carson City High School who'd signed up for a special in-service course called Teens at Risk. She'd just been introduced. "Good afternoon. Thanks for asking me here." She nodded to Nick Michaels, the School Resource Officer who'd set up this presentation. "Nick speaks very highly of all of you." She nodded to the screen, said, "Let's get started," and clicked into the computer.

"When you're a Jet . . ." The opening to one of the most famous scenes of *West Side Story* came on. The Sharks and the Jets danced down the street, pretending to punch each other and spar with knives. If only . . .

When the film clip ended, Bailey faced the teachers. "Real gang life's not like this. It's brutal." She then clicked into actual footage one of the local stations had taken. Emergency vehicles swarmed to a scene, sirens screeching, red lights blinding; gunshots rang out. People screamed. A person was filmed running—and suddenly he took a bullet in his back. The camera shifted to a young boy, on the ground, his life blood spilling into the street. The segment ended with a shot of a boy named Marcos, taken in his Face-to-Face, his own features obscured, talking about the gang. "I was ten when I joined . . . my sister trained in . . . I sold drugs to five-year-olds . . ."

A hush pervaded the room when this portion of the presentation ended. Bailey paused for effect, then said, "That's real gang life. And your school district needs to take precautions so that it doesn't happen here."

She called up her first slide. "All right, this is a test." She smiled engagingly. "Teachers like tests, don't they?"

"Except for correcting them," someone called out.

"Nick's passing out the paper version. See what you know."

The test was a series of fifteen questions, which would highlight risk factors to determine if a school or community was in danger of gang activity. Usually, there was spirited debate among educators on whether or not gang encroachment was happening in their area.

This nice little school outside of the city was no different. After giving them several minutes to take the test, she initiated a discussion. To the first question, Do you have graffiti on or near your school?, most agreed that graffiti was there, but felt that it wasn't necessarily gang related. For number two, Was the graffiti crossed out?, they agreed it was. Bailey told them this signified rival gangs. The low rumble of voices indicated the teachers were surprised at this fact.

"Are there drugs, weapons, and physical violence here?" she asked, pointing to number five of the questions.

"Yes," answered a counselor. "But all schools have those. This doesn't mean they're related to gangs."

"Right. But it could mean that. We're looking for risk factors here. If you have a lot of them, you need to know."

More murmurs.

"Here's an important point. Do students wear distinctive jewelry, clothes, and flash hand signals?" She knew they did. It was one of the reasons Nick had called her.

Louder rumblings went through the crowd. To bring the point home—teachers were a tough crowd to convince, yet her favorite to work with—she demonstrated several hand signals adult gangs used, and youth gangs often imitated. She heard some comments: "I've seen those . . . Oh, dear, I recognize that one . . . I caught a kid . . ."

The questions on beepers, pagers, and cell phones set off a whole round of discussion. Obviously, the use of that technology in their school was a hot button, and the faculty debated whether or not it could be gang related.

"The last one is very significant, and I'll confess, I know this is happening here. Nick has told me." She referred to the question asking if there was an increase in the presence of informal social groups with unusual names. "I understand there are two groups. You've reported tattoos, drawings on notebooks and clothing, graffiti in the bathrooms, and the wearing of certain colors associated with the gangs we know as the Beasts and the Cannibals." She nodded again to the resource officer. "And Nick tells me there's a preponderance of tilted caps, suggestive earrings, and belt buckles being worn." She panned the audience. "I'm sorry to tell you that your school has the earmarks of youth gang activity."

The teachers looked a little stunned. There was absolute quiet in the room until a pretty blond woman raised her hand. "Susan Smith, health teacher. Why would this happen here?" she asked. "We're small. We love our kids. Most of them come from good homes. I agree there's a problem, but I don't get why."

Bailey was prepared for this. She put up another slide. "Here are some reasons kids join gangs. You tell me which might be applicable here."

The list included: looking for a sense of respect and power; gangs become family, when kids have real or imagined problems at home; encroachment from a larger city nearby, sometimes engendered by transfer students; for self-protection from other gangs; to make money, have nice things.

"Though I'd like to debunk some myths, if I may. Gang activities, especially youth gangs, don't always make the kids a lot of money. By the time they pay off the gang, there isn't much left. However, I do understand your community has experienced some downsizing lately. Parents have lost their jobs, giving kids a need for employment, which they can't get either. That could make their homes dysfunctional so they turn elsewhere for support."

Once the issue of gang encroachment was accepted by the faculty, Bailey turned off her computer. "It's a big step to admit you have a problem. From here, we'll look at what you can do about it." She smiled. "I'll be back in the fall to do some in-service training for every member of the staff at meetings like this. Our experience at ESCAPE can help you to take steps so that your school and community are not run by gangs."

When she finished, she felt energized, as she always did after working at schools. Educational institutions were the places to start eradicating gang activity because they had so much influence over kids. Her work with them was tangible proof that she was doing some good. As she received a standing ovation, and teachers gathered around her asking more questions, she wished Senator Wainwright could have been here to see this.

CLAYTON LOUNGED BACK in a comfortable chair as Chuck Stewart called the meeting to order. The subcommittee, appointed by the Health, Education, and Welfare Committee and the Appropriations Committee, had been charged with doling out the money from the Youth Gang Bill by November first. Though Congress itself was not in session, and most senators were in their home states dealing with local business, Stewart had asked the members of this subcommittee to fly in for this special meeting to give the reports on their own states, and the others they had reporting to them.

"All right, let's see what we have going here. I want to know what's happening in each of the states so far." He smiled. "Clay, since you worked so closely with me on getting that bill passed, you go first."

Clay leaned forward. He liked the mild-mannered senator, who was rumored to be a front-runner, along with Clay himself, for the next vice presidential candidate. Stewart would make a damn good one, as would Clay. "New York's Youth Gang Task Force has met and gotten organized. We've just split into subcommittees."

"How's it going?"

He thought of being with Bailey in the elevator. "Not as expected."

"I assume your worst critic is on it," Tom Carter asked.

Clay struggled not to squirm at the irony of Jane's father inquiring about Bailey. "Yes, she is, Tom."

"Were there fireworks?"

You don't know the half of it. He recalled vividly how her skin had burned under his hands. "Yes. But I did finagle a tour of ESCAPE."

Another senator, who leaned toward social programs to stop gang violence asked, "That soften you toward her activities, Clay? You know I like that organization."

"I can see why, Carol. They're good people, hard-working. They just take too many risks and walk a fine line as far as obeying the law."

"In your opinion," Carol said.

"Mine, too," Tom put in.

Others joined in. A discussion ensued.

When it began to wind down, Stewart called the meeting back to the question and polled the other representatives for how other states were spending the money. Several were considering programs like Bailey already had in place. Her model seemed popular. It made Clay uncomfortable as hell at the prospect of ESCAPE being a national prototype.

After the meeting broke up, Tom approached him. "I understand you're coming to dinner tonight with Jane."

Holy hell, he'd forgotten. Jane had gotten back this afternoon from a cruise with her mother. Truth be told, he hadn't thought much about her since that day in the elevator with Bailey. "Yes, I am. How was the trip home?"

"Good. We'll see you at Citronelle at eight."

Feeling faintly annoyed by this commitment, Clay tied up some loose ends at his office, thought about going home to change but decided instead to call Jon. He hadn't talked to the boy since they'd clashed over Lawson. He punched in his son's cell number.

"Yeah, Jon here."

"Jon, it's Dad."

"Oh, hi."

"I just wondered how you were."

"I'm okay. I got an A on my Buddhist Thought and Practice paper."

"Good, good." A strained silence. For some reason, he remembered reading to Rory O'Neil and the sense of nostalgia that had come over him. "Saturday's your grandfather's seventieth birthday party."

The boy offered, without Clay's asking, "I'm going, Dad."

"Good." After a pause, Clay took the initiative. "Can we talk then? Things between us were left badly, and I don't like it."

His son jumped on that. "Me either. I can come up early Friday."

"Good. It's a date."

Clay felt a little more lighthearted when he left to meet the Carters at Citronelle in Georgetown's Latham Hotel. He'd always liked the unique glass-front kitchen and wall, which changed color every sixty seconds.

At a table with a good view of the goings-on, Jane stood and greeted him warmly. "Hello, darling."

He tried to participate in the hug. "Jane." They'd talked several times when she was away so he knew how the cruise had gone. He smiled at her. "You're looking tanned. A bit thinner."

"Thank you."

He hadn't necessarily meant the latter as a compliment.

After greeting her mother, whom Jane resembled, Clay sat down for dinner.

During drinks, his mind drifted from Jane's elegant Chanel suit to Bailey's stretchy knit one.

During salad, his attention went from Jane's neat chignon to Bailey's wild curls.

During dinner, superimposed over Jane's thin, elegant face, were Bailey's full lips, rosy cheeks, and mischievous eyes.

Damn it, this was not good.

Things went downhill from there when they got into a cab and he gave the driver her father's D.C. address. She put her hand on his arm and, sidling in close, she changed the directions to Clay's town house. "It's been too long, darling."

Maybe she was right. Maybe he needed to be with Jane and he'd forget all about Bailey O'Neil.

* * *

THE NIGHT OF her presentation at the school, Bailey met Eric Lawson at a small crepe place in the city. Diners crowded the small, wood-paneled interior and there was a healthy mixture of conversation, china clanking, and some soft background music.

"So, how did the talk go today?" Eric asked congenially.

Had she told him about the presentation? She didn't remember. "Good, the faculty was cooperative. And interested. I'll be going back every Wednesday in September."

"Is that common?" He asked the question but was busy scanning the restaurant. To see if he knew anybody, probably.

"Only when I take off my clothes."

"Oh, good."

She shook her head, hating it when men she was with didn't listen. Suddenly, she remembered Clay's intense gaze when she talked about ESCAPE, his focused attention when they toured the place. She saw him laugh and ask questions about Rory. Analyze her Broadway posters.

She thought about telling Eric she didn't like being ignored, but didn't have the energy—or interest—to do it. She'd just eat and go home. After devouring cheesy chicken crepes and a few glasses of wine, Bailey was feeling mellow. Outside the restaurant, Eric hailed a cab.

"Thanks," she said, as he opened the door.

"Not so fast," he told her and slipped inside. "I'll see you home."

At her door, she was reminded of Clay's visit there nearly a month ago. How he'd stood on her porch with ice cream and wheedled his way upstairs. Damn it all! This wasn't good. So she slid her arms around Eric's neck; he needed no more invitation.

His lips were warm, his hands smooth on her back, in her hair, finally on her hips, pulling her close. When she found herself shrinking from his touch, she tried harder to participate. He took it as a green light, and his hands moved to her breasts. "Invite me up, Bailey," he said as he nibbled at her lips.

In the lamps from the streetlights, she stared at his flushed face and wondered if making love with Eric Lawson would banish her thoughts of Clayton Wainwright.

"HI, IT'S BAILEY." She gripped her phone and raised embarrassed eyes to the ceiling of her bedroom. "O'Neil."

"I got it on *Bailey*." Clay's voice was sleep slurred, but amused.

"Were you asleep?"

"Um, no. What time is it?"

"Midnight. What were you doing?"

"I'm in bed." He cleared his throat. "Give me a second."

Ohmigod, he's with somebody. Quickly, she clicked off the phone. *Shit, shit, shit.* She bolted from the bed, strode to the kitchen, and opened the refrigerator. She'd been prowling around here since Eric left and had stupidly given in to the impulse to call Clay.

And he was with a woman. At least he sounded like he was. Jane Carter, she bet. The beautiful, feminine, cool senator's daughter. Bailey had seen pictures of the two of them together. They were well matched. She glanced down at the pretty peach nightgown she'd bought years ago but didn't wear much. She'd been thinking about Clay when she'd slipped into it tonight— alone. Unable to go through with anything physical with Eric, she'd given him the boot hours ago.

Her cell phone rang from the counter where she'd left it. She checked the identification of the sender. Unavailable. "Hello."

"Why did you hang up?" His husky voice rumbled over the phone. It made her shiver, though the night was warm.

"I, um . . ." She was flustered. "Fuck, I realized you were probably with somebody."

"Why would you think that?"

"Because you left the phone. And your voice sounded . . . oh, never mind."

"I'm not with anyone." His tone pitched even lower.

She blew out a breath.

"That sounds like relief, sweetheart."

"Don't call me pet names."

"All right, Bailey." He sounded frustrated. "What did you want?"

"Damned if I know."

He laughed. "How have you been?"

She found herself telling him about the school talk she gave that day. He listened without interrupting then asked several specific questions. "I'd like to see that presentation sometime."

"Why?"

"Because it's something you should be doing. And I'll bet you're good at it."

"You think I should be doing it because it's safe."

"That too. There's a lot of need for experts like you in education today."

Hoisting herself up, she sat on the counter and kicked her feet back and forth like a teenager nervous about calling the school football hero. "How have you been?" Oh, Christ, could she get any more inane?

"We had a meeting today about spending the Youth Gang Bill money."

"I thought Congress was on recess until September."

"This committee has to hit the ground running in the fall. We all flew in to meet. Stewart wants the money distributed ASAP."

"How'd it go?"

"I told him about our task force."

"Hmm."

"You remember the task force meeting we had, don't you, Bailey?"

Silence.

"And what happened before. In the elevator."

"Clay . . ." The word came out breathless. Because just his tone heated her body.

When she didn't finish, he asked, "Did you go out tonight?"

"Yes."

"With whom?"

"Eric."

"Shit."

"Did you have a date tonight?"

"With Jane."

Double shit.

"I don't like the idea of you out with other men."

Ditto. "There's no *other*, Clay. That implies you're one. Or the most important one."

"Sorry. I thought maybe because I had my hands under your blouse two weeks ago, I had a right to say that."

"Did you have your hands under Lady Jane's blouse tonight?"

"Do you care?"

No answer.

His voice rose a notch. "Did Lawson get to first base?"

"I won't talk to you about that."

An exasperated sigh. "I didn't make love with Jane."

"Oh, God. I shouldn't have asked about her."

"She wanted to. She's been away for a few weeks."

"Did you miss her?"

"Not as much as I should have." He waited. "Do you miss me?"

"No." Yes.

"Bailey, something's going on between us. I keep thinking about you. I couldn't be with Jane tonight because of you."

"Clay, don't."

"Give me some crumbs."

"I didn't sleep with Eric."

"Tonight or ever?"

"Ever."

"Good."

"What's happening here isn't good, Clay."

"You kept my cell number."

No response.

"You called me tonight."

"I know. It was a moment of weakness."

"Then you admit there's something between us."

"All right, but I don't like it."

"See me this week? I'll be in town for the task force."

"We shouldn't. Besides I'm swamped."

"Then at least go out with me after the meeting Thursday."

"I'm afraid to."

"Why?"

"Because I don't know what will happen if we're alone."

"Nothing would ever happen that you don't want to."

"How did we get here, Clay? We've been adversaries for years."

"It doesn't feel like we're adversaries now."

"But we are."

"Maybe professionally. Personally, we seem to hit it off rather well."

"Look, I gotta hang up."

"Say yes, about dinner, and I'll let you go."

"Maybe. It's the best I can do tonight."

"All right. I'll call you in a few days."

No answer.

"Bailey, before you go. Tell me what you're wearing."

She looked down at her silky nightgown. "Good night, Clay."

"That good, huh?"

⤳ EIGHT

CLAY HAD CALLED the meeting of the Youth Gang Task Force
subcommittee on community programs for six on Thursday at
his office in town. His New York headquarters were big and
imposing—a lot like him—with wooden paneling, heavy furniture, and expensive-looking drapes. The place even smelled
powerful. Bailey viewed his day-to-day surroundings as just
another thing that separated them.

He hadn't phoned or sent her emails all week—which was
good, really it was. He had called her this morning, though, and
told her he'd made a reservation at a restaurant a block away
from the office. She'd hedged, but he'd insisted and she hadn't
objected. Her mind was reeling with a thousand different
thoughts and her heart was conflicted with as many emotions.

"Thanks for coming, everybody." He smiled at Ned the
cop, Marion the nun, and Bailey, the Street Angel.

His gaze encompassed her only briefly but she was acutely
aware of herself; she'd worn a slim-fitting off-white raw silk
skirt—one of the few expensive skirts in her wardrobe—and a
bright lagoon-blue top that Aidan had brought her from the

Bahamas. She'd fussed with her hair, finally pulling it back off her face with some clips. Thank God she'd resisted the urge to put on makeup.

With brisk efficiency and the authoritative command of a man used to being in charge, Clay passed around an agenda. He was all buttoned up in a starched white shirt, gray suit, and paisley tie. How could she *like* that conservative dress? "First, let's review our assignments from last time: Ned, you're to report on which youth gangs are operative now in town so we're all up to speed. Marion, you're to give us an accounting of the shelters that take gang kids, and what medical facilities are available." He faced Bailey. "I know you have your hand in all these reform activities, but your task is to summarize what exactly ESCAPE does and the other organizations like yours in the state." He glanced at them all. "Everyone agreed?"

They did.

"I think we should alternate taking notes. I'll do it tonight." He sat down, loosened his tie, opened a thin notebook computer, and fiddled with some buttons.

Price eased back in his chair. He was about fifty, in top shape with shrewd, if world-weary eyes. "The police are aware of four youth gang elements in the city. Two are front-runners—the Barracudas and Anthrax. The other two are up and wannabees—the Conquerors and the Legends." He sighed. "They all accept girls. The first two have splinter groups which operate for females."

"That's the extent of it?"

"Far as we know."

Clay glanced up from his computer screen at Bailey. "Anything to add, Bailey?"

"Anthrax is gaining a following. They're one to watch." She looked at Clay. "And the Conquerors' girl group has a name."

"The Shags," Ned said.

"No, they've changed it to the Good Girls."

The cop frowned and sat forward. "How would you know that?"

"Really, Captain Price, you don't expect me to answer that."

"The Good Girls was one of the most brutal youth gangs

that ever hit this city." Ned glared at her. "If they're reincarnated, we're in trouble."

Bailey ignored the emotion inside her at the thought of Moira's gang legacy. "I know. They're going to be a huge problem."

"Where do these gangs operate?" Marion asked.

"The Conquerors have the West Side of the city." Ned scowled. "I imagine the GGs are over there."

"Bailey, is Ned right about all this?"

"I have no idea. I never ask those details."

"Well, you should." The captain scowled. "What's more, you should have reported to the police that the GGs are back in business."

Bailey leaned forward, feeling her temperature rise; it was easier being pissed at the police than thinking about Moira. "Listen, Captain, and listen good. I received no illegal information from that girl. She came on the interactive network and told me she was tired of gang life. I have a better than fifty percent chance of getting her out. Telling you anything about her would put an end to saving her and countless others." She straightened and peered down her nose at him. "If you're going to badger me like this, I'll have to rethink my position on this entire committee."

"Fine, quit. You won't get any money for your programs."

"All right, both of you, that's enough. The last thing I want is for anybody to quit." Clay faced her. "Is this the girl I . . . know about?"

"Yes."

He looked at Sister Marion. "Did you shelter her?"

The older woman folded her hands and stared hard at him. "Yes, but I won't divulge where, Senator. And I agree with Bailey. If this is how the committee's going to go, I'll reconsider my participation."

Clay sighed. "Well, I guess we didn't get started off on the right foot, now did we?"

After things settled down, they talked about their task more calmly. Marion had managed to give a list of shelters and an overview on medical help available, and Bailey gave a recounting of her organizations without drawing any more blood.

When the meeting ended, Sister Marion and Ned went out talking civilly. Bailey gathered her things and started for the door by the time Clay was able to grab her arm and pull her back. "Hold on a second."

She turned to face him. He'd done a good job with diffusing the situation, but she was stinging from the cop's remarks. Still the understanding in his eyes did something to her insides. "I have to go."

"Why, because somebody other than me questioned your actions?"

She shook her head. "There are other reasons." She didn't expect the ambush, and talking about the GGs had made her feel vulnerable.

Clay drew her back and closed the door. "Bailey, I know about Moira."

It was the last thing she expected. *"What?"*

"I know about the GGs and Moira."

"Did you have me investigated?"

"I didn't have to. Aidan told me."

"My brother? I'll kill him."

"Don't. I probed that day we took Rory for ice cream. We got talking about you, and I asked why you were so obsessed with getting kids out of gangs."

Exhausted, she leaned against the wall. "I guess it doesn't matter if you know."

"Come and sit." He led her to a stuffed chair in the corner then crossed to the cooler and poured her some water. He dropped down across from her and gave her the drink. "I'm sorry if tonight resurrected old feelings."

She sipped. The water choked her. "I . . . sometimes it creeps up on me. Overwhelms me. Especially when I'm least expecting a reminder."

"Want to talk about it?" His question was so sincere, his face full of understanding.

"How much do you know?"

"Not much. That she came to live with you when her mother died, and that you loved her."

Bailey closed her eyes. She could see Moira with her Mohawk hairdo, with her pierced naval and tongue. But unbeknownst to the others, she also had memories of Moira climbing into bed with Bailey and talking to her about her dreams.

"I loved having a sister. She'd braid my hair, show me how to put on makeup. She wanted to be a ballerina. But her mother never told my dad, you know, that he was her father, so there was no money for her to do things normal kids do. We used to sneak down to a studio near the house and peer in the window, stare at the girls who could afford lessons. It was like she was two different people."

"Gang kids often are."

"I couldn't believe it when she died. I missed her so much."

Clay reached in his pocket and handed her something. A handkerchief. "You can shed those tears you're holding back, you know."

She shook her head vehemently. "I stopped crying when I went to prison."

His face blanked, then looked pained. "I . . ."

"Don't, Clay."

"All right. Tell me about Moira."

She gave him a weak smile. "I used to beg her not to go out at night. When she first came to live with us, she got me to swear I'd never tell my parents about the gang stuff." She looked up at Clay. "I never did."

"Now why doesn't that surprise me?"

"Yeah, even then, huh?" She swallowed hard. "Maybe if I'd told somebody she'd still be alive."

He reached out and grasped her hand. "You knew she was out the night she got arrested, didn't you?"

The gentle soothing touch felt so good, she let him hold her hand, trace her fingers with one of his own. "Yeah. I kept vigil at the window all night." She swallowed hard. "She never came home. She'd been picked up by the cops." She sighed. "Grand larceny."

"Aidan said she was sent to Greensboro."

"She died in Greensboro."

"I know. I'm sorry."

"Dad blamed himself. Said if he'd known about her being born, maybe he could have done something." Her throat closed up. "Do you think ballet lessons might have helped?"

Sliding an arm around her, Clay tried to pull her close.

"No, I'm all right."

"You're not all right." He tugged harder.

Still she resisted. "Clay, don't. I lose it when people try to comfort me."

"So tough," he said, brushing back her hair.

She watched him. He was sincere. Empathetic. And she was tempted to rest her head on his shoulder and bawl like a baby.

But she wouldn't. She had to be strong. And clear where this man was concerned. "Don't let me do this, Clay. Please. It won't help. If I think about it too hard, guilt overwhelms me. And I can't break down. I won't."

"Maybe you should talk about it to ease some of that guilt."

"No. Just let me handle this my way."

"All right. If that's what you need." He stood. Held out his hand. "But I won't take no for an answer on dinner, now. We'll go to Pipers."

"I don't want to talk about any of this."

"Okay, you can tell me about your brothers."

"And you can tell me about your family."

"It's a deal."

Slowly, she put her hand in his.

BAILEY COULDN'T EVER remember a better conversation with anybody. And Clay had never found it this easy to talk about his feelings . . .

"My brothers are all two years apart. Patrick's the most conservative; he doesn't even want his wife to work. I'm afraid they aren't going to be able to stay together if he doesn't wise up soon. . . . When I insisted on going away to college, my parents sent me upstate to a small Catholic girls school. Aidan was at the boys' school down the road. It's how we got so close. . . . I liked regular social work enough but I wanted to help kids like Moira so I left the traditional agencies after a year. . . . Rory was a complete surprise. His dad was a singer and had a stint at the pub; he was handsome as sin. I liked him but didn't love him. We used birth control every time, but my cycle's erratic so I didn't even know I was pregnant until he was gone. By the time I confirmed it, he was busy with something else; he offered to marry me, but we'd gone our separate ways. . . . My family's close—we have each other's kids all the time so the cousins are like siblings. . . . The future? Well I don't see any more kids in the picture, but I'd like to find a soul mate. Wouldn't you, Clay?"

"MY PARENTS WOULDN'T hear about anything but Harvard and raised hell when Jon refused to even apply there. They're cold, proper people. I could never get close to them, and tried hard, at least when Jon was little, not to be that way with him. . . . I always wished I had siblings but mother was too busy with charity work and supporting my father's political career. . . . No, I wanted politics, I saw it as a way to change the world. I have in some ways, but—now don't use this against me—I feel stymied in Washington sometimes. . . . My marriage was preordained. My parents were best friends with Karen's parents. She went to Radcliff, we got married our senior year in college. Yes, the divorce was totally unacceptable. Finally, when they found out she cheated—don't look so surprised, but thanks for the compliment . . . My biggest regret in life is not being close with Jon now. We used to be like you and Rory. Somehow we drifted apart. Every time I try to get back to what we were when he was little, it goes south. Any advice, Bailey?"

HE SAW HER home in a cab. Rory was at a sleepover with his cousins so Bailey hadn't been in a hurry. Clay had been so enthralled by her, by the way talk of her son and family lit her eyes and made that pouty mouth smile, he hadn't even noticed the time. And he'd ignored four calls on his cell.

They were quiet on the trip across town, having talked for four hours. The whir of traffic and occasional static from the radio were the only sounds in the car. They sat close enough so he could smell her perfume . . . lilac scent. They pulled up to the curb on St. Patrick's Street.

"Wait here," he said to the cabbie. Then to her, "I'll see you in."

She put a hand on his arm. "No, Clay."

"Why?"

Her eyes glimmered in the light from the street lamps on the lawn. "You know why. Stay here, don't say anything, and by all means, don't get out of this cab."

Reaching over, he tipped her chin. "Afraid?"

"You're damn right. And you should be, too."

"I'm not afraid of starting something with you."

She smiled sadly. "Did you hear us tonight? Not only are we sworn public adversaries, but our whole lives, past and present, are so different. There's no way to mesh them."

"What if I don't agree?"

"It doesn't matter. I'm sure enough for both of us." It seemed in spite of herself, she lifted her hand and ran her palm down his cheek. He leaned into her touch. "You're a good man, Clayton Wainwright, and I'm glad we got to know this side of each other. But you're not for me." Leaning over, she kissed his cheek. "Good-bye."

He let her go, watched her get out of the cab and make her way to the front door. God, he wanted her. His body was as taut as a tightrope, and his heart yearned for her. But he'd respect her wishes.

From the front seat, he heard, "If I were you, buddy, I'd strike while the iron's hot, if you get my drift."

Clay watched her fish in her purse for her keys.

I'll leave if she gets inside fast. But if she looks back . . .

His body tightened even more as he continued to watch her. She found her keys. Was probably putting them in the lock. The front door opened. She stepped inside and Clay couldn't remember a time he'd been more disappointed.

Then, she turned and looked back at him.

He stuffed several bills into the taxi driver's outstretched hand and bolted out of the cab. He strode up the sidewalk and steps, never taking his eyes off Bailey. She stood in the doorway, as if frozen. He reached her, stared down at her, and waited.

After an interminable time, she stepped inside, and back,

to allow him in. He entered before she could change her mind, shut the door, and locked it. Then he faced her.

Her eyes were huge, dark, and very vulnerable.

"Bailey, I—"

She raised shaky fingers to his mouth. "Shh, don't say anything."

He wasn't sure if he liked that, but then she stepped close and he could see her lips tremble. She slid her hands up his chest, wrapped her arms around his neck and pressed her body into him.

It was all the encouragement he needed. His arms clamped her in a vise so hard it probably hurt. She only tried to get closer. He buried his mouth in her neck as she stood on tiptoes and did the same to him. He kissed her, sucked there, primitively hoping to leave marks. She bit him, soothed the nick with her tongue. Pivoting, he shoved her against the wall and hiked her up. She wrapped her legs around his waist. With his hands on her shoulders, he took her mouth. Ravaged it. He reached for her buttons, fumbling, he was so enthralled in her. Her top was open, then some scrappy lacy pink thing that passed for a bra unclasped, and she spilled into his palms. She was full, lush, and womanly. He massaged her, whispered, "You are so beautiful," and took a nipple in his mouth.

She moaned and clasped his head, anchoring him there. His groin bumped her crotch, ground against her, and for one terrifying moment, he was afraid he was going to go off.

"Clay, oh, God, yes, there."

His hands went everywhere, to her bare shoulders, naked rib cage. All the while he suckled her.

"Your skirt," he growled, "I can't get it off with your legs like that."

"You first." She was tearing at his tie, popping the buttons off his shirt. With her still anchored against the wall, he shed his jacket and shirt. Bare skin met bare skin. She jolted, he swore. She took a bite out of his shoulder, and he lowered his head to her breasts again.

They were breathing like bellows when he said, "This fucking skirt! *Get it off*, Bailey."

He stepped back, she slid her feet to the floor and went for the buckle on his pants. A moment of sanity claimed him, and he became aware they were at the bottom of her stairs, in a tiny foyer.

"Upstairs." Grabbing her hand, he started to drag her. They only got three steps up, before she clamped her arms around him from behind. He fell to his knees; she was kissing his spine. Her hands went for the buckle on his belt. She dragged the whole thing off, threw it down and its buckle clanked on the steps; still from behind managed to yank at his zipper. Her fingers dove inside, closed around him and the world dimmed. "Goddamn it."

Somehow, he managed to still her actions and turn around so he was sitting a few steps above her; she promptly dragged off his slacks, shoes, socks. Kneeling on a lower step, she buried her face in his lap. Without conscious consent, his hands grasped her head; he tunneled his fingers through her hair, kept her where she was. After moments of ecstasy, he stopped her.

"Nooo . . ."

"Shh . . ." Shakily he stood, drew her up and pushed her skirt down over her hips. "Fucking son of a bitch . . . A garter belt? Oh, God. That's it." He dragged her up into his arms.

They climbed the rest of the stairs, though she didn't make it easy. She fumbled for her keys and nearly dropped them twice before she unlocked the door.

Once inside, he stumbled to the couch. Dropped her down. Again, sanity resurfaced. "I don't have a condom. Tell me, God, you've got some."

"Top shelf of the medicine cabinet in the bathroom."

He darted away, found the bathroom, and practically pulled the cabinet door off its hinges. He was back in seconds.

Bailey couldn't think, could only react. When Clay returned holding the box of condoms, she caught a glimpse of dark, tight jockeys, of him—full, aroused, and pulsing. He struggled with the condom packet so she took advantage by yanking down his briefs and taking him in her hands, kissing him, fondling his back side. When he finished his task, she felt herself pushed—not gently—to the couch. He placed a knee on the cushion, bent her legs up high. He said only, "Look at me," as he plunged into her.

She was filled like no one had ever filled her before. He was holding on to her knees, but was still.

"Don't stop."

"Shh. I need a minute or I'll . . ."

She grasped his hips and yanked him toward her.

He tensed, swore, and thrust violently.

Only twice before she was eclipsed by explosions of colors and sounds and feelings so intense she almost lost consciousness.

The next thing Bailey became aware of was Clay, impossibly heavy on her, his breath coming in heaving gulps. He was still inside her. Her hand went to his neck, played with the soft, silky hair she found there. She kissed his shoulder. His ear. Still, he didn't move. She inhaled him. He smelled male and musky.

"Clay?" she said finally. "Are you all right?"

He mumbled into her neck, "I can't believe I'm still breathing."

She chuckled, felt an answering rumble in his chest. Finally he managed to pull back. Bracing his arms on the pillows next to her head, he stared down at her.

Never in her life had a man looked at her like that. She'd left a light on and in its dim shadow, his expression was so profound, it humbled her. He brushed his hand down her cheek.

"Wow!" he said.

"Wow, yourself."

"You pack a powerful punch there, lady."

"So do you."

"It was—"

"Incredible."

"I'm—"

"Destroyed."

"It meant—"

"A lot, Clay." She stared at him, fearing she'd just done something irrevocable. "Too much."

"Shhh, none of that," was all he said.

CLAY STROKED A hand down her naked back; a lush tingling radiated to her nerve endings as she buried her face in her pillow. Leaning over he kissed her spine. "Your skin is like cream."

"Hmm. Your hands feel so good on me."

He massaged the small of her back. She groaned. He ran fingertips over her bottom, the tops of her thighs. She shivered. Slowly he raised her foot and kneaded the instep, hard. Bailey sighed. "That's decadent."

Again, he bent over and kissed her neck. "You've got marks, sweetheart, from my mouth. My hands."

Lifting her head, she glanced over her shoulder. "Now there's a surprise."

"Was I too rough?"

"I have no idea, I was out of my mind."

He laughed, sounding like a well-satisfied male. "So was I. I've got a bruise or two."

"I'm sorry."

"God, I'm not."

He sifted his fingers through her hair, massaged her scalp. She let his ministrations continue for a while but eventually, something had to be said.

"Clay, we aren't going to do this again."

"Of course we are." She felt him rise and swell deliciously against her thigh. "And damn soon, I'd guess."

"That's not what I meant."

His hands stilled. "What did you mean?"

"After tonight. This was just, you know, a thing."

He began petting her again, making her shiver. "Do I have a say in all this?"

"What do you mean?"

"Whether we see each other again, like this, after tonight."

She rolled over. He was angled on his side, his right hand bracing his head. God, he looked good, his eyes gleaming like amber gems, his face ruddy. He was sexy and masculine as hell. But he didn't belong to her. "Surely you aren't thinking there's any future for us."

His face darkened. He grew serious. "I don't know what I'm thinking, Bailey. Truthfully I'm still reeling from having the top of my head blown off."

"I blew your head off? Cool."

He kissed her nose. Brushed back her hair. "That you did, darlin'."

Her heart thumped in her chest, but she had to keep this in perspective. "It was wonderful for me, too, Clay. I meant what I said earlier. It's never been this good."

His grin was wolfish. "You can't know how good that makes me feel. I *am* forty-five."

"It's true, but—"

His fingers came to her mouth. "No *buts* now."

He kissed her, deeply, then worked his way down her body. When he reached the juncture of her thighs, she closed her eyes and sighed and let him take her with his mouth.

Later, after she returned the favor, he held her next to his heart. In the semidark, silent bedroom, its steady beat lulled her. His lips in her hair, he whispered, "Now I have something to say."

"All right."

"You can't possibly think, after that, I'm going to let you walk out of my life."

She kissed his breast bone. "Clay, we need to be realistic, practical."

"Screw practicality."

"You won't say that if anybody in D.C. finds out about this." She added meaningfully, "Or if our respective families do. My brothers would tar and feather you, shorn me, and have me sent to a convent."

"Isn't that a bit of an exaggeration?"

She stiffened; every time she thought of that year in Andersonville, her body reacted. "They blame you for my going to prison."

His hand stopped midway down her back. "Don't you, honey?"

She ignored the endearment, and the warmth it caused to spread through her. "No. I broke the law. I wish you hadn't been such a good lawyer, but the justice system sent me to Andersonville, not you."

"Are you always this generous with people who've hurt you?"

"Speaking of being hurt . . ." She had to face him to tell

him this. Coming up on her elbows, she braced her hands on his chest. "Clay, this was wonderful. Too wonderful. I don't think we should let it go further and risk either of us getting hurt."

"What do you mean?"

"Don't you know?"

"I know, but I want to hear you say it."

"All right. Because we have a connection. We click. Not just in bed."

"It's why I don't intend to let you go just yet."

"Any relationship between us is doomed."

"Why?"

"Because we differ so much in philosophy about our work that we could never coexist in a relationship."

"You'd choose your work over me?"

A blast of icy realization hit her in the face. "Is that what this is all about? A way to get me to stop my work with gangs?"

She found herself flipped over on her back so fast she lost her breath. He manacled her wrists. "Don't *ever* say anything remotely like that to me again. How could you even think it?"

"I . . ."

His eyes were blazing fire. "Do you have any idea how insulting that is?"

"I'm sorry. Of course you wouldn't do that." She hoped not, anyway, but he was so mad, she had to recant.

He fell back into the pillows. "Damn it, Bailey, all I want is you in my life somehow."

"For better or for worse, I'm in your life professionally."

He came up on his elbow again and reached out, cupped her breast. "I want you like this."

Don't do it, she told herself. *Don't*. But as usual, she didn't listen to her sensible side. "All right, we can have a sexual relationship. That's all, though."

"You think that would work?"

"It's the only thing that has a shot in hell of working."

He seemed thoughtful.

"Without anybody knowing."

His brow furrowed. "It sounds seedy. Sordid."

"Take it or leave it, Senator. It's all I'm offering."

He waited an incredibly long time.

And then he took it. And her, again.

"BAILEY." THE VOICE penetrated her sleep-drugged mind. She willed it away and cuddled up next to the man who slept beside her.

From outside her bedroom door, she heard, louder, "B.? It's me, Aidan. You'd better come out here."

Slowly she lifted her lids. "Huh?"

Clay lay beside her. Still asleep, he gripped her tightly when she tried to move away. He smelled so male, felt so warm, she cuddled into him.

"Bailey, now! Or you'll be sorry."

She managed to ease away from Clay, took a moment to relish the sight of him—big, muscled, unshaven, and completely relaxed in her bed—grabbed a robe from the floor and headed to the living room, wondering how to keep Aidan from knowing who was inside her bedroom. He wouldn't care that she was with a man, but Clayton Wainwright was another matter. Right now, she regretted giving him a key to the doors.

"Hold your horses, I . . ." She closed the bedroom door tight and turned around. Oh, God . . .

Patrick leaned against the wall, looking murderous.

Dylan was tossing one of Rory's baseballs up and down.

Aidan was trying to hide a grin.

"Where's Liam?" she asked, stupidly.

"Taking your son and his kids for breakfast so they wouldn't see what we saw when Aidan opened the front door downstairs."

Her mind was muddled from sleep and sex. For a minute she didn't get it. Finally Aidan held up a pink bra. When she remembered hers and Clay's clothes were spread from the foyer, up the steps and into the living room, she blushed.

Dylan started for the bedroom door. Bailey blocked him. "Don't even think about it."

"We wanna know who it is."

"Why?"

"Somebody's doin' my sister, and I don't even meet him?" Dylan's eyes were as hard as shards of glass. "Far as I know, you haven't brought a guy around."

"No, I haven't." She scanned the room. "Maybe this is why."

"Think of your son, girl." Patrick had the uncanny ability to sound just like her father. "And you're supposed to have Liam's kids all day."

"I forgot that you were bringing them back, all right?" She'd forgotten her name, but they didn't need to know that.

Unable to forgo a shot, Aidan chuckled. "It was that good, huh, Sis?"

"This is not funny." Patrick again.

"I agree." Bailey tried to sound haughty. "You shouldn't be interfering like this."

Dylan stepped forward. "I can take her, Paddy, so you can get to the bedroom."

Bailey knew how to be tough. "Do that and you will no longer be a part of my life."

It was a threat they wouldn't risk. Since she'd gone to prison, they treated her opinions, her ultimatums, differently. As if they knew she'd do what she said.

Patrick and Dylan shrank back. She felt sorry for them. She crossed to Pat, encircled her arms around his neck, and kissed him. "I love you, Paddy. All of you. But I'm thirty-six. I have a life."

"So we saw, spread out from your door down the stairs." At least his tone was dry, not angry.

"I'm sorry I was careless when you were going to bring Rory and the boys back. I probably scandalized the neighbors, too."

Patrick hugged her. She repeated the gesture with Dylan.

To Aidan, she shot a look saying, *Help me out here*.

"Come on, guys, we'll meet Bailey at the diner where we sent Liam and the kids. The place a block over where we usually go B.," he said, telling her they wouldn't be able to spot whoever was leaving her apartment.

As her two oldest brothers trundled out, Aidan walked over

and handed her something. "Lucky *I* found this, kiddo, and not them."

It was a butter-soft leather wallet.

"Did you look inside?" she asked.

"Didn't have to." He nodded to the engraved initials. *C. W.* He kissed her nose. "See you in a bit. I'd hurry it along, or they'll come back."

Squeezing Aidan's arm, she followed him down the stairs, scooped up all the clothes, and as she was on the way up, she heard Dylan say, "Musta been some night. Didn't know our little sister had it in her."

She chuckled. They'd be okay. And they wouldn't ever have to know who was her partner in the orgylike scene.

For some reason, the notion made her sad as she opened the door and once again found Clay asleep. Her heart swelled when she remembered last night—the sex, yeah, but the tenderness, and the intimacy. Jeez, who would have thought?

She crawled onto the bed and woke him with kisses. His sleepy-eyed smile made her grin. "Hi, big guy."

"Hi, love."

She bit her lip at the endearment. "You missed all the action."

His hand dipped inside her robe. "No, I didn't."

She held it there. "My brothers showed up."

His thickly lashed eyes widened, and he sat up, plumping a pillow behind him. "When?"

"Just now, you slept through it."

"Good sex does that to me."

"Clay, remember what we did before we reached the apartment?"

He scowled, then awareness dawned. "Oh, God. Our clothes . . ."

"Luckily Aidan found your wallet or the guys would be in here right now." She drew back. "I have to go meet them. They gave me ten minutes."

"Now? No way in hell." He reached for her.

"No, Clay, really. They'll come back."

"Why were they here anyway?"

She slipped off the bed, and dropped the robe.

His jaw went slack. "Shit, Bailey, get back here."

"No. She went to the bathroom and did her thing, then came out, wrapped in a towel. He was still sitting there like a sultan watching his harem girl. She kind of liked the idea. Would have pursued the fantasy if her family wasn't waiting.

Dragging underwear out of a drawer, she slipped it on and answered his last question. "They have Rory and I'm watching Liam's kids today. Liam was bringing them all here. The others tagged along so we could go to breakfast together."

"Did Rory see anything?"

"No, Liam hustled him to the diner."

She pulled on jeans and a Nazareth College T-shirt and stuck her feet into slip-ons. "I gotta go." She crossed to the bed and gave him a big kiss. "Stay here and have coffee. We'll be about an hour. Be gone by then."

"No."

She threw him a quizzical look. "No?"

"Let me come with you. Talk to them about us. We don't have to hide this."

"Have you forgotten last night?"

His gaze was intense. "Not one single thing."

"Well one, apparently. This is just sex, Clay, and nobody's going to know about it."

"Did I agree to that?"

"Sort of."

"I don't want it that way."

"Look, I gotta go. It's all I've got to give."

Watching her head out, he called from the bed, "I'm not happy, Bailey."

She reached the doorway and threw an impish grin over her shoulder. "After last night, of course you are. Don't forget to lock the door on your way out."

∼ NINE

Taz rolled over in her cot; through slitted eyes she could see three chicks sitting in a circle on the floor. All had a bleached streak of hair that made them look more like skunks than bad girls. All had something pierced—nose, belly, tongue. Wannabees. They thought they were so salty. But they didn't know shit about what it was really like on the streets. Taz heard them say they'd run away and Gentle House shelter was trying to get them to reconnect with their parents. Not her problem, though.

"What you looking at?" one asked.

"Nothin'." She turned back over but she could still hear them.

"Out all night . . . did the guy . . . I'm gonna get her."

It was only about ten p.m., but Taz was tired and it was safe to crash here. No sleazebag was gonna wake her up in the middle of the night with his liquor breath and sweaty body.

Thanks to the Street Angel.

Taz dozed. She was little again, with her mother, who

smelled like lilacs. They were on her tiny bed reading. Taz
loved to read aloud. "Good night moon, good night sun, good
night stars, good night everyone."

"You are so smart." Her mother's melodic voice warmed
her. Mommies were good. Daddies were bad. "I love you,
sweetie. You're the best thing that ever happened to me, and
when you grow up, I hope you have a little girl just like you."

Taz nuzzled in closer.

A door slammed and her mother tensed. Yelling. From outside the safe cocoon. Taz plugged her ears and buried her face
in her mother's chest.

Clomping on the floor.

"Oh, no." Her mother bolted off the bed, carrying Taz near
her heart. They darted for the closet. Their sanctuary. "Shh,
now baby. Don't say nothing and he won't be able to find us."
From inside, her mother snicked the lock shut; she'd put it
there herself so they could keep her father out.

Shaking in the dark and stuffy closet, Taz hung on and
prayed he wouldn't find them. . . .

Taz startled awake. She sat up in bed, breathing fast, grop-
ing around for her mother. Where the hell was she? Then,
in the slice of light from the moon coming in the windows,
things came into focus . . . the ten cots lined up like an army
barracks, a cross on the wall, an open doorway. There were a
few sleep-slurred murmurings and some soft snoring from
the others in the room. Taz was in a shelter the Street Angel
had arranged for her. And her mother was dead, from a hit-
and-run driver that left her beloved baby to be raised by a
monster.

Shaking off the sweet memory of the dream and the
nightmarish reality her life had become, she dug out her cell
phone from under her pillow; since they'd jack you blind in
these places, you had to hide everything. The lighted face said
three a.m. Lying back down, Taz closed her eyes. But sleep
wouldn't come. It wasn't great being here. She was bored, and
didn't jive with the other girls. But it was better than being
home, plus she believed the things the Street Angel said about
starting small. Sighing, she closed her eyes.

A memory of the Street Angel surfaced. She'd smelled like lilacs, too.

IN HER ROOM where she'd been watching a video with Rory, Bailey climbed off the bed, stopped the tape and was startled when Clay appeared on the TV. He was walking into an office building, when a reporter waylaid him. Her entire body reacted at the sight of him. He looked good, rested, young. He moved with grace, athleticism.

What do you do to keep in such good shape?
Racquetball. I'm really good.

On the screen, he answered a question the reporter had asked; the deep timbre of his voice made her shiver. She hadn't seen or talked to him since the night they'd been together. *It's just sex*, she'd told him. So she hadn't expected flowers or phone calls. Still . . .

"Wanna see that guy again," Rory said from the bed.

"What guy, sweetie?"

"That guy." He pointed to the TV and smiled. "He read me *Wild Things*."

"Yes, I heard." She crossed back to where her own personal little wild thing lazed in light cotton pajamas. Soon it would be cold and he'd need the ones with the feet.

I wish I had those days back with Jon, Bailey. Treasure them.

"I like him, Mommy."

"That's nice. Okay, baby, time for sleep."

"Mom-my."

"Rory, you're such a night hawk. It's ten o'clock."

"Took a nap for grandma."

"All right, one story." Yawning, she picked up a book from the stack on his nightstand, but he circumvented her and snatched out another.

"This one," he said, mischief lighting his eyes.

"You are a bad boy." He knew that Tomie dePaola's *Nana Upstairs, Nana Downstairs* made her teary-eyed.

He snuggled in. Sure enough she sniffled all the way through it.

When she was tucking him in his own bed, he stuck two fingers in his mouth. "Night, night." Then he sighed sleepily, "Can I see him?"

"Who?"

"The guy on TV."

"Maybe sometime. Now go to sleep."

Bailey wandered out into the kitchen and made coffee. She was restless. She'd *been* restless since . . . no she wouldn't go there. She noticed a big manila envelope lying next to the pot. Aidan had given it to Rory to give to her and she'd forgotten about it. While the java brewed, she sat down and opened the flap. Slid out the contents. "Oh, for God's sake." The guy was haunting her. These were the pictures Aidan had taken at the opening of Tales for Tots. The first was of Clay alone at the podium, probably addressing the group. He looked tall and incredibly handsome, just like on TV. She traced his sculpted nose. His square jaw. The photo was black and white, but she could see in her mind the interesting amber color of his eyes and how long his thick lashes were.

The next shot was of him and Rory reading. Oh, God. He cuddled her little boy to him; Rory was wide-eyed as they both stared at the book. Both intent on the antics of the wild things. She couldn't wrest her gaze from them. Finally she looked at the last one. Shit. Shit. Shit. Rory had snuggled in close like he always did, and was nosing into Clay's expensive Italian suit. Aidan had caught Clay kissing Rory on the top of his head. The tender gesture made her heart clench.

Tossing aside the photos, she stood, poured coffee, and sat down at the computer. When she booted it up, her instant messenger connected. She was about to close it, when she heard Rory call from his room.

By the time she got back, there was a message from ClayFeet on the screen. *All right, IrishCream, I waited two whole days to contact you. I didn't send you the pretty peach roses I stared at in the flower shop for ten minutes. I didn't call so I could hear the sound of your voice. Give me some crumbs, honey.*

Honey. Tell him not to call you pet names. Remind him

that it's just sex. Don't slip into this like some naïve girl who won't admit what she's doing. *How are you?*

I suppose I'm well. Have you missed me?

We aren't supposed to miss each other.

Easier said than done, lady. He stopped typing. Started again. *I can't stop thinking about what you felt like under my hands.*

She didn't answer right away.

Should I not have said that?

No, naughty talk's okay.

Naughty talk? Oh, God, you make me feel fifteen again.

Same here, big guy.

What were you like at fifteen, Bailey?

Really ugly.

I don't believe it. Was your hair as curly? I love the way it cascades down your back.

Cascades. God, he actually used that kind of language. Of course he did. Clay was smart. He'd gone to Harvard; best remember that, Bailey O'Neil.

Yeah, it was curly. I hated it then.

It feels like watery silk.

Oh, Lord. She sipped her coffee. Sat back. Stared at the screen.

Then the chime. *Your turn.*

Fishing for compliments, Senator?

Damn right.

She laughed out loud. *You're great in bed, Clay. Really great.*

Tell me something specific.

Specific?

Uh-huh. What you liked. When we were together.

Everything. I loved the way your fingers felt on me. So strong, masculine. Powerful.

I loved the sounds you make when you come.

I make sounds?

Hmmm. Very feminine. Very sexy. He didn't type anything and neither did she. Then, *I need to see you again.*

No, it's too soon. *Okay.*

Congress is in recess. I'm in town. I can make myself free during the week.

My week is crazy.

Please.

Maybe Friday, during the day. I don't have to work until four.

All right. In the morning. We'll spend the whole day in bed.

I spend the afternoons with Rory. He has preschool in the morning.

Hell. That's not enough time.

It'll have to do.

My place then. 148 Parkland.

She didn't want to go to his home, and she thought it best to keep him out of her house after last week's fiasco with her brothers. *No. A hotel would be better.* And clearly spell out that this was just sex.

Only if I can pay. I'll reserve a room at the Suffox on Forty-fourth and Park. They have early check-in. Then he asked, *Can I call you this week?*

I don't think that's such a good idea.

Please.

She had to be strong. *No.*

A long pause. *Fine, I'll see you Friday morning about nine.* Then the notice, ClayFeet has signed off at 9:44.

Well, that was rude.

He didn't like that she refused to let him call her. But damn it, they couldn't afford to get close. She shouldn't even be sleeping with him. But she'd been unable to cut him out of her life completely so she told herself she'd settle just for sex.

Getting up, she wandered over to the table and picked up the pictures again. Looking down at him and her son, she firmed her resolve. She simply had to be strong and put clear ground rules on this *thing* between them.

"WHAT DO YOU think, Clayton?"

"Pardon me?"

Lew Jacobs, the mayor of New York City, who was in charge

of this meeting, stared down the table at him. "I asked for your opinion on the last point."

"Sorry." He looked at his notes. "I agree with it . . ." He explained his position, forcing himself to concentrate on the task at hand.

When they took a break, they mayor approached him. "Where's your mind today, Clayton?"

Thinking about a woman who won't give me the time of day. That wasn't exactly true, but he was annoyed at how his conversation with her had ended Wednesday night. She wouldn't let him call her and he wasn't used to being treated like a teenage boy whose girlfriend set the parameters. And he couldn't stop thinking about her. So much so that it was interfering with his work. "I'm distracted, I guess."

"I'm looking forward to your father's seventieth birthday."

"So am I."

"Clayton Sr. and I are playing golf at noon on Friday."

"Ah."

"Tom Carter's joining us. Are you making up the foursome?"

"Foursome? Um, no." He had a special kind of twosome scheduled, and wouldn't change his plans if God asked him to. His father hadn't been pleased.

The mayor can be an influence on your career, son. You need to put that ahead of everything else. Having done exactly that for years, Clay balked, leaving his father angry and dismayed.

The mayor laughed. "I must say, Clayton, you're out of it today."

Tom Carter had told him the same thing when he'd called about Clay being on a new Homeland Security subcommittee in the fall. *Is something wrong, Clay? Jane says you're acting strangely. You seem distracted, as if you're always thinking about something else.*

Clay knew Jane's comments stemmed from the fact that he wouldn't sleep with her that night in D.C. Then, last week she'd phoned him and wanted to come up early before his father's party to spend a few days at his town house. But he'd said no. She hadn't bought his lame excuses, and had been whiny about his lack of attention to her.

Finally the mayor reconvened the committee. Grateful for the reprieve, Clay listened to the superintendent of the city schools give his pitch. "These are the preliminary numbers for the outlay of money to provide after-school tutoring for inner-city kids."

Something Clay supported. He wondered if Bailey would be in favor of it. She'd probably want a special program for her gang kids to be tutored. He wondered what she was doing right now? He checked his watch. Only twenty-four hours till he'd see her.

It's just sex.

Okay, so it was. He'd get his brain to wrap around that and forget about anything else with her. He would.

"Clay?" The mayor again. "I asked you another question!"

TAZ POPPED AN upper and sank onto the mildewy chair; she was kicking it with her homies at the GG's crib. The hard rock pulsing from the boom box grated on a headache beginning to bud in her brain.

She closed her eyes, thinking about the day. At the Street Angel's nagging, she'd gone to school and registered to go back this fall. The guidance counselor had ragged on her about how far behind she was already, and the principal wanted to make himself clear that they wouldn't put up with her absences again.

She'd thought, *Why bother?*

The Street Angel had had an answer for that one.

Because you're smart, Taz.

How can you tell?

Good instincts. You have potential.

"How's it hangin', Tazzie girl?"

"Hey, Maze." Her friend had long blond hair, baby blue eyes, a sweet mouth. Real Barbielike. And she could be as ruthless as any Crip or Blood. Rumor had it Mazie had taken somebody out; lots of the GGs claimed they'd put in some work, but who knew how many really had?

Taz hadn't. Yet. But she knew the longer she stayed in the gang, the closer that day got when they insisted she kill somebody. That was why she'd been having crazy thoughts about getting out, like the Street Angel said she could. She sprang to her feet. "Gotta go."

"Where? Home to your old man?" Mazie's smirk was knowing.

"Not stayin' there."

"Then how come you ain't crashin' here?"

"I dunno. Look, I'm bookin' ."

She left before Mazie could ask any more questions.

The street was quiet for eleven p.m. Residents had to be back at the shelter by midnight. Little Cinderellas. She headed over there; along the way she passed on two hits of coke, three offers from johns. Jesus. What a world.

She reached Gentle House just before curfew. Sister Marion, the head nun, waited for her in the entryway. "Hello, Taz-mania. It's a little late to be out, isn't it?"

"I made curfew."

"I know that, dear. I was worried about you."

Geez, lady, don't do that. "Are you for real?"

"Gen-u-ine article." The nun smiled.

Taz hid one of her own. It didn't pay to get friendly with people. Who knew what lurked behind that habit? There'd been all the scandals with Catholic priests . . .

"I'm tired. I gonna hit the sack."

"All right, dear. But, you know, if you ever want to talk, I'm here. We give more than shelter."

"Yeah?"

"We give guidance."

"Oh, sure."

Taz found her way to the communal sleeping area. Lights were still on; most of the girls were in bed already, but the skunky threesome gathered on one cot.

"Here's Her Highness," she heard one of them say as she found her bed.

Taz ignored it. Like the kids at school, these chicks got their rocks off by dissing her.

"Think she got a boyfriend?"

"Nah. Seems pretty cozy with the sister, though. You a fag, girly?"

Taz whirled around. "None of your fucking business,

assholes. Listen and listen good. You don't want to mess with me." Out of her backpack she pulled her gang bandana. "Or my set. You got what I'm sayin'?"

They apparently did. They didn't have a smart-ass comeback, and looked away. It wasn't enough. Taz strode over to the leader and pulled her up by the shirt. "Answer me, cunt."

"Yeah, sure, I got it."

"Fine. Now leave me the fuck alone." Taz crossed to the cot.

The Street Angel's words came back to her. *You don't always have to be so tough.* She was sure wrong about that.

BAILEY FELT OUT of place as she walked into the posh lobby of the Suffox Hotel at nine the next morning. *You're out of place in Clayton Wainwright's life, that's why.* He was already here, in room 2234. He'd left a message on her voice mail saying he'd arrived and telling her where to go. Tucking her hands into the pockets of her long denim skirt, she rode the elevator. She hadn't fussed today—she'd worn a plain pink T-shirt with the calf-length skirt; no, she hadn't fussed—except for her underwear. A lacy white thong and bra to match. She'd been saving last year's birthday present from Suze for a special occasion. How pathetic. It took her almost a year to use it. That must be why she wanted sex with the man whom she'd fought bitterly with for over a decade and thought she hated.

But she didn't hate him. She couldn't wait to be with him again.

She knocked on the double wooden door, hoping he'd answer it, drag her inside, and ravish her so her head would stay on straight. The door whipped open right away. He stood in a little foyer-type space, in jeans and a navy blue T-shirt, barefoot. His hair was tousled and a bit damp. He had a little nick on the corner of his jaw from shaving. "Morning," he said flashing her a toothpaste-commercial smile. God she wanted that mouth on her.

"Morning."

He stepped aside so she could come in. Wow! He'd gotten a suite. The place resembled Richard Gere's penthouse in *Pretty Woman*. It consisted of a huge living room with modern mahogany leather furnishings. A dining room. And she guessed a bedroom off to the left. Drawing in a breath, she pivoted to face him. His hands were in his back pockets and his pose was . . . cocky.

She said, "Ready?"

"Oh, yeah." He closed the distance between them and once again she was surprised at how much bigger he was than she. His size, and his scent when she got a whiff of him—soap and aftershave—made her heart stutter. He took her face in his hands. Lowered his head. She waited for desire to slam into her, and him, to combust them both. Instead, his lips met hers and tasted, tested. His tongue coaxed apart the seam of her mouth. She went up on tiptoes and tried to wrap her arms around him, but his position didn't allow it. All she could do was let him kiss her, explore her, with a tenderness that was unnerving. She felt herself sinking into it by degrees.

Desire came, not bursting, but as a tiny bud beginning to unfold. After forever, he left her mouth and kissed his way to her neck. His arms banded around her in an encompassing but so gentle embrace she sighed with it. His fingers slid down and explored the hollow of her back. His actions were accompanied by murmurs of appreciation and contented sighs.

Finally he let her hold him, run her hands over those linebacker shoulders, flirt with his nape, sift her fingers through his coarse hair. She felt a ripple go through him. Nudging the pink cotton aside, he tasted her skin, plucked at her bra strap with his teeth. Then his mouth was at her ear, his breath whispering into her hair. She felt as if she were melting into him, like a candle left out in the sun. His words, too, were a gentle caress. "I missed this. A lot."

She drew back. His eyes shone with deep and dark desire. Yet there was a lazy expression on his face, an unhurried set to his body. This was not good. Not safe.

"Let's go to the bedroom."

"All right."

Instead of scooping her up in a fit of passion like the last time, he leaned over, slid muscled arms under her and lifted her. Then he cradled her against his chest and kissed her head. His tenderness was killing her. And it was so romantic only a stone wouldn't react. He carried her into the bedroom. She had an impression of slatted blinds allowing half the morning light in, a lake of a bed, and dark wood furnishings. He set her on her feet and she immediately went for her belt. He batted her hands away. "No way, lady. I get to do all of this."

"Clay, don't—"

He put his fingers to her mouth. "Shh. You said just sex right? Just the physical."

"Yeah. But this—"

His big hands deftly released her belt. Slowly drew it off. "—is within the rules."

Oh, no, it wasn't, she thought as he let his fingers brush her bare rib cage on their way to taking her top off. He wasn't playing fair; surely he had to know that. Unzipping her skirt, he eased it down so it fell to the floor. Then he stepped back. "Oh, sweetheart. Could you be any sexier?"

She shook back her hair. Straightened her shoulders. He wasn't going to get the upper hand here. She could take this. He circled around her. Studied her. Sniffed her. There was a hint of arrogance in his perusal, a smugness about his smile, like a man appreciating the sight of a feast he was about to enjoy. It sent delicate threads of desire dancing through her. To defuse the sensual web, she said, "I'm ten pounds over the weight the insurance company recommends for my height. I should probably go on a diet."

"What do they know?" he said from behind. His jeans scraped her bare legs and made her quiver.

"You're probably exactly where you should be." She was babbling but couldn't help it. "I'll look it up for you. How tall are you?"

"Six-three."

When he came back around front, his smile was knowing; he reached out, released the clasp of her bra and let it fall to the floor. His eyes sparked with interest, with appreciation; he lowered his head, let his tongue tease first one nipple, then the other. His fingers skimmed her hips, and he brushed the lacy scraps down, knelt to take them off. Like a worshipper, he kissed her shin, her knees, her thighs, her tummy. The brush of his lips sent involuntary tremors over her skin. When he stood, he picked her up again and placed her on the mattress; its cover was already pulled back; the sheets were baby soft. Again, an intense gaze. "All mine," he said as he went for the hem of his T-shirt. "For now, all mine."

CLAY COULD BARELY move. He lay on his side, still nestled in Bailey's body. She was flushed, sweaty, but her skin glowed and her eyes shone like polished sapphires. Her velvet warmth encompassed him, as aftershocks rippled through him, and her. He thrust forward to maximize them.

She whispered, "Please, stop. I can't take any more."

He hoped his smile wasn't too smug. He'd practically killed her with gentleness, arousing her slowly, searching and exploring every inch of her delicious body. When she'd become impatient, urgent, he'd gone even slower.

It had tortured him too—he'd wanted to explode about ten times; yet he'd bathed her in tenderness. Because he had to find a way to use this *just physical* mandate to bring them closer. He wouldn't examine why, didn't want to, really. He was just going with his feelings.

"Why are you frowning?" she asked.

He brushed knuckles down her cheek. "Was I?" He gathered her against him.

"Yeah, Senator, you were. Though I'm not sure why," she mumbled into his chest, kissing him there. "You won."

"How did I win? It was just sex." He tried to keep the triumph out of his voice.

"Like hell."

"I don't know what you're complaining about, Ms. O'Neil." He leaned over and breathed in her ear, "You came three times."

She sighed and stayed where she was. "I know."

He just held her. Cupped the back of her neck. She let him. Finally, he said, "How much time do we have?"

"Um, a little longer than I thought."

"Really?" He half expected her to bolt out of here after what had just happened.

"Rory was invited to a friend's house for lunch after pre-school. I don't have to pick him up until two."

"Well, that makes my day," he said. "Four more hours."

"Mmm. Whatever will we do?"

"Oh, we'll think of something."

He ordered food first. When it came, they were still cuddling in bed. He threw on his jeans, got the cart and wheeled it into the room. She was sitting up in bed looking like a present that had just been unwrapped. He had to close his eyes not to dive right back in. He managed to control himself.

"What did you get? I'm starved."

"I'm not surprised. We worked up quite an appetite."

"Are you bragging, Senator?"

A loud pop. He poured the champagne and turned to hand her a glass. "A bit, I guess."

She looked at the flute. "It's ten o'clock in the morning, Clay."

He clinked their glasses. "I know. To . . ." He arched a brow. "Just sex."

Her eyes narrowed, she raised the glass to her lips.

Then he reached over and plucked a strawberry out of the bowl. "Open up," he said, and she bit into it. He felt the gesture in the pit of his stomach. She nibbled on the rest of it, and tantalized him more in the process.

"What's that?" She nodded to a basket as she sipped more champagne. He drew out a flaky croissant. "Oh, God, I love those." She reached for it.

"Nope." He held the roll to her mouth and fed her.

"Mmm, it's still warm."

He saved the best for last. Triple chocolate almond ice cream, which he fed alternately to her and to himself, stopping occasionally to lick the chocolate from the corner of her mouth. The ice cold creamy confection tasted almost as sinful as she did.

By the time the impromptu meal ended, her nipples were beading against the sheet. He brushed them with his knuckles. "See, that was just sex, too."

Lazing back into the pillows, she sighed. "If you say so, Senator."

*   *   *

SHE'D ASKED, "WHAT have you always wanted to do with a woman and never done?"

That's how they'd ended up here, in front of the mirror, surrounded by the scent of vanilla candles that he'd brought with him and lit all around the room. It was nearly noon, and she faced the beveled oval glass, while he stood behind her. "I want you to watch me fondle you." His voice was gravelly, even to his own ears.

"Hmm."

His hand seemed huge, kneading her breasts. When he took the nipple between two fingers, she closed her eyes. "No, no, watch."

Her arm went up and around his neck, plumping her breasts even more. "Clay . . ."

He worked the other breast.

He nibbled on her ear.

He kneaded her waist then let his hand drift lower. His eyes held hers in the glass. The blue of hers deepened to the color of midnight as he grazed her curls with his knuckles. "Clay, please . . ."

"All right, but watch yourself come. For me, Bailey. Come for me."

"I HAD NO idea you could be so kinky."

"It's not kinky."

"My wrists are tied to the headboard of the bed. Call me old-fashioned, but to me that's kinky."

"You could pull them free. I knotted our belts loose." She looked down from where she straddled him. Suddenly she was embarrassed. "You don't like this, do you?"

"Are you kidding? I love it." He grinned. "Besides, turnabout's fair play. I got my fantasy, you get yours."

"All I wanted was free access to your body."

"It's a tough job, Bailey, but somebody's got to do it."

"At least I didn't ask to beat your butt."

"Oh my God. You're not into *that* are you?"

She shivered. "Not in the least. I just like you powerless."

"A Park Avenue shrink could do wonders with that."

She felt a blush rise up from her neck to her face. "I never, you know, did this with anyone."

His gaze was hot and intense, accented by the burned-low, but still-flickering candles. "Good. I want everything between us to be new."

That worried her, but it was too much of a temptation not to enact her secret fantasies when he asked to return the favor. After all, this was just sex. Good sex, though.

In fifteen minutes, his body was swollen from her hands and mouth. Still, he didn't release the bonds. He pleaded though, "Bailey, enough . . ." then he demanded "Now, Bailey, I mean it or I'm stopping this game . . ." and finally, he broke his hands free, impaled her on him and came instantly with volcanic force.

Of course, she did too, so it was okay with her.

"THIS ISN'T JUST sex."

His eyebrows rose innocently. "It's physical; we're sharing a bathtub together." He sipped his champagne. "Come on, tell me what you'll do with Rory today."

She scooped up some bubbles and blew them into the air. He'd brought the bath things along with the candles this morning. "I'm taking him and Dylan's son Hogan to the movies to see *Shrek 3*." She sighed.

"What?"

"Rory wants to see the musical *Seussical,* but I can't swing the tickets. I'm going to work some extra shifts at the pub on weekends so maybe we can go for his birthday."

"When's that?"

"September twenty-first." She watched him. "Are things going all right with Jon? You said you were having dinner with him."

"We haven't seen each other since the fiasco with Lawson. I'm hoping to mend some fences."

"He's only twenty, Clay. He's still trying to find his way separate from you."

"I know." His look turned playful and he set his glass on the rim of the huge tub and grasped her foot. "Here, lift up." He drew her leg out of the water and reached for the soap and a loofah that was on the edge of the tub. He began to wash her leg, scrubbing the rough sponge over it.

"Hmm." After a moment, she asked, "Will the party for your father be fun?"

"More like a command performance. It's at the Pierre Hotel. Legions of friends and political acquaintances will be there."

"How long was he a senator?"

"Twenty years."

"Tell me about your childhood."

"I already did that, the night we first made love. Lift the other leg."

She did and sank back against the bath pillow. Closing her eyes to relish the steamy water and his decadent ministrations, she said, "Tell me specifics about it."

"It's such a cliché. Typical rich-kid stuff. A series of nannies. My mother's charity and political-wife career. My father not home. "

"I'm sorry."

"Yours was fun, I'll bet."

She opened her eyes. "With four brothers? What do you think?"

"I think they treated you like a princess."

Bailey laughed. Hard. From the gut. By the time she was done telling him about how they wouldn't let her cross the street alone until she was ten, how they hung up on boyfriends when she was a teenager, and checked her drawers for birth control, drugs, or even guys' phone numbers when she was home from college, he was laughing, too.

This time warmth spread through her, but not the sexual kind. The *I-want-to-get-to-know-you* kind. The *wow-it's-great-to-be-together* kind. The *I-can-believe-in-you* kind.

No, no, no, this wasn't going to happen. As nonchalantly as she could, she sat up. "Look, it's getting late. I have to leave."

His gaze was piercing. "What's the matter, Bailey? Enjoying my company too much?" It was hard to conceive that he could look and sound so superior while he was lounging naked in a tub. But he did.

"Maybe I am. If that's the case, it should stop now."

She went to stand but he grabbed her around the waist and pulled her down so she was straddling him. The water rose and sloshed over the side. "Maybe it shouldn't stop."

"I can't have a relationship with you, Clay."

This time he was rough. He dragged her head down and gave her a bruising kiss. Afterwards, he said, "The hell you can't."

Quickly, she drew back and managed to get out of the tub without slipping and breaking her neck. As she dressed in the bedroom, she heard the water drain in the bathtub, and caught a glimpse of him in the mirror dropping towels to the wet floor.

When he came out, dressed in a white robe, flushed from the heat of the bath, she was fully clothed.

He watched her slip into shoes and grab her purse. She headed for the door but when she reached it, she couldn't leave without saying anything, so she turned around. He was leaning against the archway of the bathroom, his shoulder jutted up against it, his arms crossed over his chest. And her breath caught at the sight of him. Not just because of how incredibly sexy he looked, but because of what they'd done together in this room. Unwittingly, it had forged a bond between them, and she knew *he* knew she recognized that. "I'm sorry, Clay. This just can't happen."

"It already has."

"No, no, up until the bath, it was just sex."

"Whatever you say, darlin'."

She lifted her chin. "I say that it was."

"Fine," he said smugly. "Then we can do it again."

ON FRIDAY NIGHT, Taz startled awake. She'd heard something. Shit, she was in a house full of people, of course she heard something. Still, she listened. Whispers. Jesus, the skunk girls were at it again. She rolled over. Then a voice at her ear. "Help, please." It sounded like a little girl. "Sister Marion's in trouble."

Taz flipped over. Nobody was there.

For a minute, she lay in bed, then got up and stumbled into her shoes. She wore pj bottoms and a T-shirt. She stuck her cell and watch in her pocket, then, for some reason, she reached in her backpack for her blade. You weren't supposed to be carrying in a shelter, but any home girl worth her salt was always equipped.

She crossed the room. Seemed like everybody else was asleep. As she crept out to the hall, she heard something again. This time it was a moan. She followed the sound.

The living area was big. She could see it in the moonlight. TV. Couches. Two chairs. A lump on the floor. Fuck! She crossed to a lamp and switched it on. "Goddamn!" She rushed to the body. Sister Marion. A big statue lay on the floor. She recognized it as the Virgin Mary. She reached for it, when the overhead lights went on.

"Oh my God, what'd you do?" The skunk sisters were lined up looking as innocent as Jesus.

Taz stared at them, realizing she'd been had.

TEN

"YOU'RE DIFFERENT TONIGHT, Dad." Jon sat across from him at a rib place in the city and sipped a Coke while his father nursed a beer. "You look . . . relaxed."

His dad glanced away. "Do I? I took it easy today."

"No, it's more than that." He smiled; going with safe subjects was a good idea. "Things cool with Jane?"

"Not exactly." He stared over Jon's shoulder. "That relationship is lacking something."

"She's a little stiff. But I thought you liked your women sewn up tight."

"I thought I did, too." Again a faraway look in his eye. "Not anymore, I guess."

Holy shit! Was Clayton Wainwright mooning over a woman? It couldn't be. "Is there somebody else?"

His father hesitated. "Not really. I don't know. Maybe. It's complicated." He grinned at Jon. "How about you? That little blonde I saw you with at Bard seemed pretty interested."

"Yeah, I like Alice. She's terrific."

Their orders came and they dug into the barbeque ribs and spicy fries. Usually his father didn't eat high cholesterol food.

When they were done, Jon decided to take the bull by the horns. "When you were at Bard? What we fought over?"

"Yes?" His father hadn't brought it up, probably to keep peace, but things had to be said.

"I'm sorry for what I did, going to Lawson's meeting. It could be really bad publicity for you."

"Fuck the publicity. It hurt, Jon."

Hurt? His father? "Jeez, Dad, I never heard you talk like that."

"The swearing? Sorry."

"No, that family was more important than politics."

Now his dad looked like Jon had kicked him in the nuts. "I've really messed things up with you then. You are much more important to me than politics. My relationship with you is."

"Thanks, Dad." He rolled his eyes. "Alice had a fit when I told her what I did. So did that woman I met there."

His father's eyes sparked. "What woman?"

"The Street Angel. Lawson thought she'd get a kick out of seeing me at his meeting, but she reamed me out good."

"I think Bailey knows the importance of family."

"Bailey? How well do you know her, Dad?"

"We have a history together. You know about my role in her going to jail?"

"Yeah, sure. And she takes you on in the press whenever she gets a chance."

His father picked up a leftover French fry and nibbled it. "We're on a committee together now, so recently I've had some contact with her."

"She's a looker."

"Is she?"

"Yeah, and young."

"She's thirty-six."

"She married?"

"No, but she has a son." He shifted in his seat.

"She's working for Lawson."

His dad's jaw tightened. "So I heard."

Jon leaned forward. He wanted to touch his father, but they didn't do mushy things in his family anymore, though he remembered a lot of affection when he was little. "I won't work for him, Dad. I'm not saying I agree with your politics, but I won't undercut you like that."

"My views might be different from what you think." He reached out and covered Jon's hand with his own. "I'd like a chance to talk to you about those things without fighting."

Jon was shocked. Something was definitely different about his dad tonight. "All right, let's do it."

"COME ON, COME on." Taz had was at a computer in one of those all-night cyber cafes, signing on to the Internet. Shit, what were the chances of the Street Angel being on tonight, anyway?

The screen pinged and buzzed into a connection and she went right to the ESCAPE website. *Hey, anybody there?*

I am. Hi, Taz. I recognize your screen name.

Hi. It was important to be tough. *How you doin'?*

Good. Great actually. How's the shelter working out? I'm so glad you're there.

It was important to be casual. *Oh, that? It didn't.*

Didn't?

Work out. I bounced . . . Shit, her throat clogged. The Street Angel was turning her into a regular sissy.

Tell me, sweetie. It's okay, whatever happened.

Sweetie. What her mother called her. What she imagined calling her own daughter some day. *Somebody blamed me for somethin' I didn't do.*

Was it serious?

Yeah. Sorry I let you down.

You didn't let me down. We'll find you someplace else.

Any place just gonna be a repeat. I need to get my own pad to crash.

Where are you now?

Nowhere. It doesn't matter. I gotta go.

Taz, please, don't go. Talk this out with me.

Later, lady. Ciao.

Taz clicked off. She sat back in the hard chair and stared at the screen. Damn it, this woman stirred up all kinds of things inside her. Made her hope. Not good, not good at all.

THE BAND WAS in full swing, right now playing some cool jazz. Waiters floated around the ballroom, serving champagne and caviar to tuxedoed men and women glittering in diamonds. Clay leaned against a post and watched Jane dance with her father.

"She looks lovely tonight, doesn't she?"

"I think she looks a little too thin," he told his mother, who had come up to him.

"Darling, a woman can never be too thin."

I'm ten pounds over the weight the insurance company recommends for my height. Well, Clay for one liked those curves.

A waiter passed by and offered him champagne. He couldn't take a glass. It reminded him too much of being with Bailey yesterday. "I'll have a scotch, if you wouldn't mind getting it."

"Certainly, sir."

"What's the matter, Clayton? You're brooding like Heathcliff."

"I'm restless, Mother." He turned to look at the woman who gave him birth. She was also too thin; at sixty-five, her meticulously cut, styled, and tinted-just-right hair framed a rather unlined face for her age. She wore a dress like everybody else's—long, black and expensive.

"Over what, dear?"

"My life I guess."

"Maybe it's time to talk to your father about the next step, then. The party's been whispering about you for the VP spot in the next presidential election."

At one time, her encouragement, her confirmation of what he himself had heard, would have elated him. "That's a bit premature isn't it?"

"Not necessarily." Her gray eyes narrowed. "I understand that little creature you sent to jail is giving you trouble these days."

He stiffened. "She's not a little creature. She's a nice woman who made a mistake. Is still making them, but her heart's in the right place."

"Your father says she can do you damage. Especially after those editorials in the *Sun*."

"The Street Angel wrote something else?" He couldn't believe she'd do that to him, not now. Not after . . .

His mother's frown was as old as he was. He remembered hating the thought of displeasing her. "No, nothing recent. Clayton, you sound, I don't know, sympathetic to her."

"I'm not. We're on a committee together and I've gotten to know her some. She believes everything she says."

"Well, know thy enemy. Perhaps you can sway her if you get more friendly with her."

Is that what this is all about? A way to get me to stop my work with gangs?

The song ended and Jane stood talking to her father and someone else who'd come up to them on the dance floor. His mother nodded toward her. "I think perhaps it's time you made this official, too, Clayton."

"Official?"

"Yes, you and Jane. It would look good for a prospective vice president to be married. Especially after that scandal with Karen."

"Which she created, Mother."

"I know." Jane left her father and approached them. His mother said to her, "I was just telling Clayton how lovely you look, dear."

"Thank you, Marsha. As do you." She fluttered heavily made-up eyes at Clay. "I'm afraid your son has hardly noticed, though."

He was thinking about Bailey's eyes, unadorned with makeup, the freckles on her nose, her long hair, casual and sexy as hell. "I noticed, Jane. I told you how wonderful you look."

"No, darling, you didn't. But Father says you're distracted these days, just as I thought."

"I wish people wouldn't keep saying that about me." His tone was harsher than he intended.

His mother and Jane exchanged surprised looks.

Clay pushed away from the post. "I'm going to find that drink I ordered. Excuse me."

"Just a moment, Senator." He turned to a familiar looking man with a camera. "Hank Sellers. *The Voice*."

Ah, now he remembered. The reporter on the street that first night with Bailey. "Mr. Sellers."

"May I have a shot of you and Lady Jane?"

Jane blushed becomingly at the epithet. Moved in close so her breasts grazed him. He was forced to slide his arm around her waist.

"Smile," Sellers said.

Clay smiled, feeling trapped, unhappy and . . . fuck it . . . lonely for his Street Angel.

BAILEY STUDIED THE pub. Her mother and father were singing a duet, and it brought tears to her eyes to hear their melodic voices joined. She was so lucky to have them as parents. The whole place felt warm and comfortable tonight, with the aroma of home-cooked food and drifting sounds of people having a good time.

Tell me about your childhood.

I'll bet yours was happy.

It had been. Except for the jail thing and Moira's death, she'd had a good life. So why was she feeling miserable?

"Here you go, darlin'. And watch out for that handsome one's hands. They'd be likin' to wander all over you."

"How would you know that, Bridget?" she asked, picking up the tray of Guinness.

"He's lookin' at you as though you're tonight's dessert."

Bailey hustled over to the table. The guys gathered around it were cute. And the blonde was definitely interested. "Ah, there she is, me girl." He tried really hard to mimic an Irish accent, but wasn't succeeding. He was handsome in a young sort of way. He had brown eyes, but they were dark, and not as penetrating as Clay's.

As soon as she had the thought, she chided herself, *Don't do this!* But she couldn't help it. She'd been *doing this* since yesterday morning—thinking about Clay. And not just the sex.

The talk about their families. The way he cradled her to his heart. The romantic, silly things he'd done, like sweeping her off her feet, the champagne, feeding her strawberries and ice cream, his ministrations in the bath.

". . . go out with me darlin'?"

"Excuse me?"

"I asked what I had to do to get you to go out with me."

She gave him a saucy smile. "See those four guys over there?"

"Tell me they're not boyfriends."

"No, worse. They're my brothers. You'd have to get through them to date me."

"I'd slay dragons to date you, honey."

"That would be easier."

She left the group and went to serve more tables. After a while, she glanced at her watch and realized she'd been on her feet for three hours. "I need a break," she told Bridget as she set her cocktail tray on the bar.

"About time. Go in the back and take a load off. Margie can cover for you."

Bailey headed to the rear of the pub. She found her mother in the big sitting area, off a small bedroom, watching an old episode of *JAG*.

"Hello, dear."

"Ma."

She moved over on the stuffed and worn couch. "Sit."

Bailey sat.

"No, scoot down there. Stretch out and put your feet up. I'll rub them."

Thinking about Clay in the bathtub, she lay back, closed her eyes and let her mother tend to her. From the TV, the familiar music and dialogue continued for a bit, then went silent as her mother turned off the set. She said, "Want to be tellin' your ma about it?"

Bailey would love to pour out the whole story, but Mary Kate O'Neil would freak if she knew the reason for her daughter's funk was the man who her parents blamed for putting her in jail. "Nah. It's nothing important." She raised her arm and rested it on her forehead. "Rory okay?"

"Sleepin' like a baby, after I read him a good number of books. That boy, now he's smart."

He's as smart as a whip, Bailey, Clay had said.

"Why'd you moan, darlin'?"

"How do you keep yourself from thinking about a guy, Mama?"

Her mother's laugh was youthful. "Never found the answer to that myself, love. I tried everything I could to get your pa out of my head. It never worked."

Bailey sat up a bit. "He loves you, Mama."

"I know." Her mother's face shadowed. "That business with the other woman was my fault, in part. I wasn't showin' him enough attention, then."

"He shouldn't have done it."

"No, he shouldn't have. Poor Moira paid the price."

"I got a girl I'm working with now; she reminds me of Moira."

Her mother watched her. "You were never the same after that, child."

"Don't you think so?"

"No. You got so serious." She drew in a deep breath. "Then, after that man sent you to jail, it only got worse."

"Ma." She grasped Mary Kate's hand. "I broke the law, and got the punishment I deserved."

"The good Lord wouldn't have held you accountable for helpin' a young lad." Her face hardened. "It was *his* fault."

Shit, Bailey didn't need this. She started to get up.

"No, stay here. I'll go do your tables for fifteen more minutes. You're dead on your feet, girl." Her mother got up and leaned over her, brushing Bailey's hair back. "You sure you don't want to talk to your Ma about this man?"

Bailey shook her head.

"All right then."

After her mother left, Bailey nestled back into the cushions and sighed. Damn, nothing was going right. Taz hadn't come back on the website again. And Bailey hadn't heard from Clay.

Can I call you this week?

No.

Hell, if she really didn't want him to call, why did she carry her cell phone around in her pocket all night?

Because she did want to hear from him. Desperately.

No sooner did she have the thought than her phone rang.

It probably wouldn't be him, anyway. He was at that fancy party with his family, and his *girlfriend*, for God's sake. Maybe the call was something about work. Something about Taz. Bailey had asked Suze to notify her if the girl came back to the website.

Still lying on the couch, she fished out her cell. "Hello."

"Don't hang up, please." The husky timbre of his voice curled through her like a kiss.

"I won't hang up." A pause. "I'm surprised to hear from you."

"Why is that?"

"Aren't you at your party?"

"Yes, where are you?"

"At the pub, taking a break. It's been a zoo."

"You work too hard, honey."

"Clay, don't—"

"Call you pet names, I'm sorry. It slipped out."

"Are you having a good time?"

"Yes. No."

"Well, that's definite." Her dry tone made him chuckle.

"I . . . I'm having a hard time . . . I keep thinking about yesterday."

"With Jon?" she asked to divert the direction of his conversation. "How did that it go, anyway?"

"No, I didn't mean with Jon. But it went well. We talked for hours, some of the time about politics. I think he saw we have more in common than he realized. And he made me think I *have* copped out some."

"Clay, that's a huge step." *I'm so proud of you*, she wanted to say, but didn't have the right.

"He talked about you. How you 'reamed him out,' I think he said. Thanks for coming to my defense."

"You're welcome."

A long, uncomfortable pause.

"What I said earlier? I meant I couldn't stop thinking about yesterday morning."

No answer.

"You remember yesterday morning, don't you?"

She drew in a breath, sucked into a sensual whirlpool of his making. "I remember." She wanted to say, "The sex was great," but she couldn't, just yet, minimize what had happened. So she told the truth. "Clay, too much happened yesterday."

"Which time?" Now his tone was teasing. "On the bed? In the bath? In front of the mirror?"

"Oh, God."

"I'm miserable being here without you."

She didn't respond.

"Don't you miss me just a little bit?"

Damn, damn, damn. "Maybe a little."

He let out a long breath.

"It doesn't matter."

"It matters to me."

"I was just talking to my mother. She brought your name up."

"Not in a good way, right?"

"They blame you, Clay. Even if there wasn't anything else between us, which there is, my going to prison will always be your fault to my parents."

He waited a few heartbeats, then asked, "What happened to you in prison, Bailey?"

"I . . . I never talk about it."

"Will you tell me, someday?"

"I . . . shit, Clay . . ." Why did he make her feel like she could tell him things she'd never told a living soul?

The door to the back room swung open. "Hey, Sis." Aidan stood there. "You got a visitor."

"Just a second," she said into the phone and put it on mute. She was shaken by what Clay made her feel, even over the phone. "Who?"

"Councilman Lawson's out here looking for you."

"Okay."

"Ma's coming back to be with Rory."

"Fine." After Aidan left, she clicked into the phone. "I gotta go."

"I heard Aidan say someone's there to see you. Who is it?"

"Clay . . ."

"It's Lawson, isn't it?"

"Yes."

"Did you make plans to see him tonight?"

"No! He came here on his own."

"Tell him to go home."

"I can't do that."

"Fuck it, Bailey. Didn't yesterday morning mean anything to you?"

"Of course it did."

"Promise me you won't let him touch you. Not even a kiss."

"Hello, dear, I'm back." Her mother stood in the doorway, a quizzical look on her face.

Into the phone she said, "I've got to go. My mother's here."

"Promise me!"

"All right, I promise."

"I'll call you tomorrow."

"Good-bye."

Her mother came closer. "Sweetheart, what's wrong, you look like you're going to cry."

Bailey stuffed her cell into her pocket and raised shaky palms to her cheeks. "Do I?"

"Who was that on the phone?"

"Nobody you need to concern yourself with." Rising, she kissed her mother and headed out to the pub fast. Because Mary Kate O'Neil was right. Her daughter was perilously close to tears.

ELEVEN

ON THE STOOP of Bailey's building, grasping a bakery bag in one hand, Clay rang the buzzer. Shifting from one foot to the other, he chided himself for being here. But something had happened on the phone last night and he was damned if he wasn't going to find out what it meant.

It had cost him to come here . . .

His parents' disapproval . . . *What do you mean you can't make brunch?*

Jane's disappointment . . . *Clay, darling, I thought we'd spend the day together.*

Only Jon hadn't pressured him. His son had given him a knowing smile, said he was off to Bard anyway so he didn't care what Clay did today. He wondered if Jon was thinking about the woman they spoke of Friday, though Jon didn't know she was Bailey.

As he waited—and rang again—Clay glanced around her street. Late August was hot in the city, but trees were still green. Soon summer recess would be over and he'd be back in D.C. Not around to visit her like this. He punched the buzzer again. Where the hell was she? Church maybe? He would have called but he was afraid she'd tell him to stay away.

Finally, she answered the buzzer. "Hello?"

"It's Clay."

A pause, and then she buzzed open the front door. He bounded up the stairs to her apartment, and the door opened as he reached it. Clay just stared at her. She'd obviously been in the shower. Wearing a short pink terry robe and a turbanlike towel around her head, she looked young and fresh and very desirable. Her face wreathed with a genuine smile, before she quelled it. "Clay, what are you doing here?"

He held up a bag. "I brought you breakfast."

"It's only nine."

"I know. I hope I didn't wake you."

"Are you kidding? Rory got me up two hours ago."

Reaching out, he traced a smudge under her eye. "You must be exhausted. What time did you get in?"

"Two. But it took me a while to wind down. Coffee helped this morning," she said when he gave her a doubtful look.

"Got any more? There are croissants and donuts in here."

She glanced behind her. "Rory's here."

"I know, silly. You just said he got you up."

"He'll—"

"See me." He tucked together the lapels of her robe and got a whiff of lotion. "I know, honey. It's okay."

"He's a blabbermouth."

"We'll talk to him about that. Aidan told me the day at the bookstore that he and Rory play a game of keeping secrets. We can work something out with the boy." He gave her his best ingratiating look. "Truthfully, I was looking forward to seeing him again, too. Let me come in."

She hesitated. Leaning over he took her mouth. It was a possessive, consuming kiss. "Bailey, please," he whispered against her lips.

Cuddling into him for a too-brief moment, she whispered, "All right."

She stepped back and opened the door for him to enter. He crossed the entry hall into the living room and found her little boy in New York Yankees pajamas, playing with his toys. From beneath shaggy dark bangs, his eyes rounded when he saw Clay. "Hey, mister. You read to me." He gave Clay a grin that stole his heart. "We got pictures."

"Do you now?" Clay bent down and scooped up Rory. "Nice pj's, champ."

"Like those Yanks," he said.

Bailey rolled her eyes. "My family, the consummate Yankees fans."

"Hey, you have good taste. I love the Yanks, too."

"You read to me again?" Rory asked.

"Sure."

Bailey frowned as if she didn't understand all this, then nodded. "I'll get dressed."

His eyebrows arched. "Not on my account, I hope," he called to her retreating back.

When she returned wearing worn jeans and a Yankee shirt herself, Clay was seated with Rory on the couch reading *The Teddy Bear's Picnic.*

When he took a breath, Rory said, "Fun picnic."

Clay chuckled. "They're having a teddy bear's picnic in D.C. in the fall. It was one of Jon's favorite books, so I noticed the ad in the *Post.*"

"Can I go?" Rory asked innocently.

Bailey frowned. "Senator Wainwright is a busy man, Ror."

"Not that busy. I'll check my schedule to see if I'm in town then. I'll get back to you." He cuddled Rory closer. "Now let's finish our story."

"I'll make fresh coffee."

When Bailey returned, she handed him coffee and cuddled up on the other end of the couch watching them, sipping from her own mug. Clay finished reading the story then glanced over at Bailey. She was asleep with the half-filled mug snuggled in her lap, her drawn knees securing it.

"Mo-mm . . ."

Clay clapped a hand over Rory's mouth. "Shh, champ. Let Mommy sleep."

The boy's eyes narrowed in a what's-in-it-for-me look.

Food was always good with kids. "Let's go have some donuts."

"'Kay. I ate my cereal."

When they finished donuts and small talk—Rory had a king-size hero worship of Derek Jeter—they crept back into the living room. Bailey was out cold. "Wake 'er up," Rory said, bounding for his mother.

Clay held him back by the shirt. The kid must have something against Bailey getting enough sleep. Clay spied a mitt, ball, and bat in the corner of the room. "Hey, want to go hit some balls?"

Rory's eyes widened, then glanced at Clay's big frame. "Yeah. Mommy hits like a girl."

"Go change and we'll find some place to play."

"Park," Rory called over his shoulder and disappeared.

Clay crossed to the couch. Bailey was cuddled into a ball at one end, but there was a pillow behind her. Gently, he drew her legs down. She stretched out easily and stayed comatose. He covered her with a blanket and kissed the top of her head.

Rory came back wearing a Number 2 Jeter T-shirt, jeans, and two different color sneakers. "Lookin' good, champ," Clay said and held out his hand.

Rory grabbed the mitt, gave Clay the bat and ball and put his free hand in Clay's.

It felt good.

"I GUESS IT'S all right now. Gentle though, okay?"

The words came as if in a dream, far off. Bailey turned her head into the pillow to block out the sounds. She was in bed, with Clay, nestled against his shoulder.

"Gentle don't work, Clay."

"All right. Let me do it." Something nudged her hip. She could smell Clay's aftershave now. "Hey, Sleeping Beauty, wake up before your son dive bombs on you."

Clay's voice.

Her son.

Bailey bolted awake. "Oh, my God. Rory."

"Shh." He grasped her by the arms. "It's all right, sweetheart. Rory's fine."

"I fell asleep." Her tone was disbelieving, horrified.

He scowled. "You didn't commit a crime."

"He could have gotten hurt. But he never lets me sleep . . . I don't understand."

"Bailey, he was with me. I was reading to him when you dozed off."

"Oh."

"Then I wouldn't let him wake you. We had a nice morning."

"Morning? What time is it?"

"One."

"In the *afternoon*? You came at nine."

"I know." He brushed back her hair. "You shouldn't work so hard."

She glanced over at Rory. "Hey, buddy, you okay?"

He approached Bailey, holding something.

"What's that?"

"A kite."

"Where'd you get it?"

"Store. Got Jeter on it."

"You went to a store?"

"Uh-huh. After lunch." He yawned.

"You ate lunch?" She sounded like a fool but she was disoriented.

"At McDonald's. Got a happy meal."

Clay said, "We left you a note in case you woke up and were worried."

Her gaze swung to him. "I . . . I don't know what to say."

"He hit me balls. Better than you, Mommy."

She noticed the smudge of dirt on the knee of Clay's perfectly pressed khakis, and his beautiful wine-colored polo shirt was a bit damp. He smiled. "From what I gather, that's not much of a compliment."

"I liked it."

Clay tousled his hair. "I did, too. We'll have to do it again."

Rory yawned a second time.

"Honey, want to go watch a video on Mom's bed?"

"'Kay." He crossed to Clay, who stood so Bailey could get up. "Thanks." Spontaneously, like he did everything, he threw his arms around Clay's legs.

Clay bent down and hugged him. "You're welcome."

Bailey's throat seized up at the sight. "I'll be right back."

After she had Rory settled—this was the only way he'd fall asleep for a nap—she took a minute to brush her hair; it was so wild from washing it and not drying it, she gave up and twirled it into a scrunchie, letting it hang in a ponytail down her back. Checking her image in the mirror, she left the room.

Clay was leafing through a photo album that had been on the coffee table.

Bailey approached him and eased onto the arm of the couch, so she was looking down at the pictures. "Aidan's handiwork."

He smiled, the dimple appearing in his chin. She wanted to kiss it. "They're wonderful. He's got talent."

"That he should do more with. Check out the ones at the end."

He turned to the back. "Ah, me and the champ. Wow, Aidan can certainly capture a mood."

She stared at the pictures of Rory and Clay. "That one shows how much you enjoy him."

"I do. We had a great time today."

"I'm sorry about that. You didn't come over here to babysit."

"I said I had a great time. Can't remember my last double cheeseburger and sundae."

"Your tastes run more to caviar."

Setting down the album, he turned so fast he unbalanced her. She toppled onto his lap. "My taste runs to you."

His mouth closed over hers. The kiss was deep and drugging; he tasted like Coke and peppermint. He undid a button on her shirt and nosed into the opening. "Hmm. You smell so good."

She sighed.

A second button opened, then she heard the buzzer ring. "Don't answer it," he mumbled into her bare skin.

She ran her hands over his shoulders. "It'll wake Rory up."

"Damn."

Pulling away, she grinned at him. He was a man clearly aroused.

"Get rid of whoever it is."

"Maybe." She stood up.

He whacked her gently on the butt. "No maybes, woman."

Bailey was giggling like a school girl as she walked to the intercom. "B., it's Aidan." After the time her brothers caught her with Clay, she made them promise to ring before they entered her home. She buzzed him in and opened the door before he reached the top of the steps.

"Aidan . . ." She got a look at his face. It was murderous. "What's wrong?"

"I need to talk to you, B."

"Is everybody all right? Safe?"

"As far as I know." He held out a newspaper. "It's something in here."

He pushed past her into the apartment. She was so worried she forgot to warn him that Clay was here.

Which was too bad. Because when Aidan reached the living room, the first person he saw was Clay.

"Aidan, hi." Clay had stood and faced her brother.

Who, without warning, shot across the room, saying "You bastard," and took the senator from New York down.

CLAY FELT HIMSELF stumble backward, hit the wall, and crack his head on something hard. Glass shattered. Bailey screamed, and a fist pummeled into his jaw. He was on the ground, Aidan straddling him, raising his arm for another punch when Bailey jumped on her brother's back, knocking him off Clay. "Aidan, don't . . ."

"Mommy? I'm scared."

Bailey looked up, still holding on to Aidan; they both froze. Clay rolled to his feet and went to Rory. "It's okay, son, just a little misunderstanding."

"Like hell," Aidan said.

Picking up the boy, Clay cuddled Rory to his chest. "Mommy and Uncle Aidan were wrestling."

"How come you got blood on your mouth?"

He wiped his lip. "I, um, got in the way." He turned. "Come on, let's go back to the video."

By the time he came out of the bedroom, Bailey was sitting on the couch with her brother, staring down at a newspaper.

She had her hands over her mouth. Aidan's palm made circles on her back. "I'm sorry, kiddo."

"What's going on?"

Bailey looked up. Eyes that had been dancing with mirth just minutes ago now were . . . bruised.

"What's wrong?" he asked.

She rose from the couch. He'd never seen her move so stiffly as she crossed the room, handed him the paper, and turned her back on him.

Befuddled, he looked down. There was a big, color photo of last night's party. Of him and Jane. They were smiling, but Clay remembered feeling phony in the pose. He looked up, frowning. "I don't get it. You knew I was there with Jane."

Aidan practically spat out, "Read the caption, you fucking bastard."

He gaze fell back to the paper. The words underneath his and Jane's picture stood out boldly. *Senator Clayton Wainwright celebrates former Senator Wainwright's seventieth birthday party with fiancée Jane Carter.*

Fiancée? Who the hell? His gaze swung to Bailey. "Listen, I—"

She spun around. "Get out of here. Now. I know I said we'd just have sex, without any commitments. But I had no idea you were engaged."

"I'm not."

Aidan crossed to her; she turned to him and buried her face in his chest. "Get him out of here, please." Her voice cracked on the last word.

Her brother smoothed her hair down and whispered something to her; then she fled to the bedroom. Clay heard the loud snick of a lock.

He stared over at Aidan. "I'm not going anywhere until this is cleared up. It's a misunderstanding."

"You cocksucker. I knew you were sleeping with my sister. I thought it was good for her. But I didn't know—"

"I'm not engaged."

"Get out of here!"

"No."

Aidan watched him, then yanked his cell phone out of his

pocket, punched in his speed dial, and after a moment said, "Paddy. Get Dylan and Liam. I need your help to dispose of something. I'm at Bailey's house."

Holy hell, this was like a grade B movie.

Aidan clicked off. "They're on their way over."

"Then the four of you will have to drag me out of here. I'm not engaged. And I'm staying until I make Bailey believe that."

Aidan glowered at him.

"I care about her, man. I want this relationship to go further; I have all along and she's put on the brakes."

"We'll beat the shit out of you."

"So be it. I'm not leaving. I won't let her think what she's thinking."

Aidan stared at him. For a long time. Then he picked up his phone again.

"I'M STILL HERE, Bailey. Aidan left. I'm not going anywhere until we talk."

From the other side of the door, he heard, "My brother wouldn't leave me alone with you."

"Come out and see."

"No."

"I'm not engaged. I don't know for sure who told *The Voice* that I was, but I'd hazard a guess it's my mother. She was pushing for the engagement last night. And Hank Sellers was scrounging for a tidbit."

"I don't believe you."

"Then I'm staying right here, in your living room, until you do."

After a long time, he heard the lock turn. Thank God. He figured when Aidan left, he had a chance here. But he knew firsthand how stubborn Bailey could be.

The door opened. She stood straight, her shoulders back, her head held high. Man, he admired her grit. He knew she was hurt, but right now she looked like an angry goddess. She said haughtily, "I can't see how you're going to convince me."

"I'll tell you the truth. Come sit down."

She crossed the room and sank down into a chair. He was forced to take the couch adjacent to her. "So go ahead."

"I've been seeing Jane Carter for a few years, off and on. It's suited us well. But she's been pushing for more, and I've backed off."

"Why? She's everything you need in a political wife. Beautiful, polished, well-connected. She probably doesn't even have a job."

"She works on her father's campaign from time to time, but you're right, she doesn't have a career."

Her curiosity surfaced, he guessed, despite her resolve to remain aloof. "How do people live if they don't work?"

"Family money. Jane has trust funds."

"Do you? I mean, do you have to work?"

"Ah, no. I don't."

She shook her head; to her that only underscored their differences. "Where's this going, Clay?"

"I'm not in love with Jane. I've been backing off from the relationship, like I said, but you're right, she's perfect for me and I was lonely, so I've kept company with her. Now, however, things have changed."

"Are you sleeping with her?"

"I was. I haven't been with her, or anyone else, since you and I made love."

He could tell she wanted to believe that, and it gave him courage to go on. "Bailey, you're upset, right?"

"Yes, of course. I don't take men away from women who they've made a commitment to."

"So it's just philosophical? There's nothing personal about your reaction?"

She drew in a breath. He wondered if she'd tell him the truth. Holding his gaze, she whispered, "It's personal. It hurt to think you belong to someone else after we were together like we were."

Rising he crossed to her and knelt down in front of her. He took her cold hands in his. He kissed them warm. "What does that tell you, honey?"

She held his gaze and he knew she wouldn't dissemble

now. "I know what you're saying, Clay, but we'd have to be crazy to let this go any further than sex."

"It already has."

She bit her lip, a gesture that put every protective gene he had on red alert.

"You know it has. That's why you're upset."

As if looking for answers, she stared at the ceiling. "This is so stupid. I don't know how it happened."

"Stupid or not, it's a fait accompli. I feel the same way, of course. The thought of Lawson's hands on you kills me." He kissed her fingers again. "You haven't slept with him, or anyone else either, since we've been together, have you?"

"No. But Clay, forget about Eric and Jane for a second. Look at this logically. We're sworn enemies about gang intervention and youth crime legislation. We've become public about it. And we're going to clash big-time on this committee."

"That's professional."

"I know, but if we let something more than sex develop between us, and I'm beginning to think that in itself was a huge mistake, we'd fight over what goes on in the committee, over my safety, over how I run my life, and how you operate politically."

"We can separate our work and our personal relationship. Or at least we can try." He brushed her cheek. "Don't you want to try?"

She turned her face into his palm. "That's not all of it. Say we were able to separate our professional conflicts from our private lives, what about our . . . unsuitability? I spent time in jail. I have a child and never married his father. I work in a pub, for God's sake."

"I don't care."

"The press, and your constituents, might."

"I'm not going to live my life according to someone else's standards."

"You agreed to do that when you became a senator."

"The hell I did. Look, if that's the only thing holding you back, think about this. Hillary stayed married to Bill after he cheated on her and perjured himself about it. And she was still elected to the senate. It's not like you think in the public arena."

He could see that made some inroads. Standing, he drew her up, cradled her face in his hands, and peered down at her. She looked like a little girl trying to resist temptation. "For some reason, Bailey, we've connected, and not just in bed, though that's been spectacular. I like you. I like your energy, your refusal to give up on what's important to you, your loyalty to your family, the kind of mother you are. I'm not going to let you out of my life until I see if we have something here."

She shook her head. "I like you, too. A lot. You're not what I thought."

He kissed her nose. "Can't we just see if we have something good together? And if we do, we'll take it one step at a time."

"Maybe." She stepped back. "I have to think about this and I *can't* think when you're touching me."

Well, that was good news. He jammed his hands in his pockets and forced himself to keep quiet. He'd given his best defense. If she said no, he'd probably appeal, but he'd see where she took this first.

"Give me some time to figure this out?"

"I can do that." He moved closer though and tipped her chin. "But I'm done with the seesaw, Bailey. I'm tired of going back and forth. Take your time, make a decision about us and stick to it." He kissed her nose, smoothed down her hair, and turned to leave.

"Clay?"

He glanced over his shoulder. "I'm sick of the seesaw, too."

"Good."

IT WAS SO lame. Bailey hurried from her office, glancing down at the outfit she wore. She'd fussed today. For Clay. She'd ransacked her closet for something special that she could wear to this committee meeting and found the pants and tunic in the back of her closet. She'd bought it on a whim and had only worn it to important meetings and once or twice to dinner when she needed something sophisticated. Slate blue, its knit material hung well on her frame; her brothers had made a fuss about it looking *too good*, so she guessed it did the trick.

Also, Joe and Rob, who were working her shift today, whistled when she'd come in. And when Suze relieved her at four, she said, "Who are you, and what have you done with my friend Bailey?"

She'd laughed it all off, but refrained from putting on mascara and blush until now, when she boarded the subway. Clay had called and asked her to go out for a drink after the meeting. He told her he expected good news, and he was going to get it. After a long night of soul searching, she'd finally decided to give her relationship with him a real shot.

As she rode to his office, she thought about her decision. It scared her to think of what she was going to commit to, but he was right: this back and forth wasn't working. And she'd meant what she said about liking him—a lot. She arrived at his building in fifteen minutes. Her heart started to beat faster as she rode the elevator.

When she reached the doorway to his office, she found him standing by the sideboard, sipping coffee and talking to a woman Bailey had met when she was here once before. He wore a beautiful heather brown suit today with a beige shirt and paisley tie. He looked wonderful. When he caught sight of her, his amber eyes lit. "Hello, Street Angel." He turned to the woman. "Thanks, Mary. That's all. You can leave at your usual time."

"Thanks, Clay." The woman nodded politely to Bailey, but gave her a cold glare before she left. No surprise there. His staff all probably hated her.

Bailey came farther into the room. "Hello, Senator."

"Ms. O'Neil." His gaze cruised down her body. "Did you do this on purpose?"

"What?"

"Wear that thing?"

"On purpose?"

"To drive me to distraction."

She chuckled. "Now there's a thought. But no, I just wore it."

He angled his head.

"For you."

"Does that mean you have good news for me?"

"Maybe."

"You'd better sit at the end of the table, then."

She batted her eyelashes. "Why?"

"You know damn well why."

"All right." She smiled and sat. "You can serve me coffee."

He brought her a mug and took a chair a few seats down from her. "How are you?"

"Fine. What will we do in the committee today?"

"Go over your lists and Sister Marion's. Then I think Ned's gathered some information on the GGs." He glanced at his watch. "We should be done by four."

"Hmm."

"Where's Rory?"

"Aidan has him."

He rubbed his jaw; up close, she could see a bit of bruising by his mouth. "How is Aidan?"

"He's sorry he hit you. But he's still wary about our relationship."

"I can win him over."

"Maybe. Of everybody, Aidan's the least protective."

Clay touched his jaw again. "God forbid I have a run-in with the others."

"Does it still hurt?"

His eyes twinkled like he was going to tease. "Yes, but you can kiss it and make it better."

"I—"

Ned appeared in the doorway. His face was grim and his posture stiff. "Hi. Sorry I'm late."

Clay glanced at his watch. "No problem. Sister Marion isn't here anyway."

He frowned. "Don't you know?"

"Know what?"

"Sister Marion's in the hospital."

Bailey set down her mug. *"What?"*

"She was attacked in her shelter Friday night by one of yours, Ms. O'Neil."

Bailey glared at him. "What are you talking about?"

"Tazmania Gomez is wanted for questioning in the assault

of Sister Marion Hockman Friday night. She's gone underground and we can't find her."

"Is Marion all right?" Bailey asked.

"She's being released tomorrow. She had a bad concussion."

Clay leaned forward. "How do you know it was the girl?"

"Several residents testified to her guilt."

"Did the others see her attack Marion?" Bailey asked.

"One did. The rest came in after it happened and found Gomez holding the statue that gave Marion the concussion."

Bailey straightened. "So it's the first girl's word against Taz's."

"We don't know Taz's story, as she bolted."

Bailey sat up straight. "Well, I do."

"What do you mean?"

"Taz came on the network Friday night. She told me she wasn't living at the shelter anymore because she'd been unfairly blamed for something."

"That girl admitted to you Friday night that she committed a crime?"

"That's not what I said, Captain."

Ned raised a brow. "Oh, sure, like that's never happened before." His gaze swung to Clay. "This came up the last time we met, Senator. I made my point then and I'll say it again. The Street Angel's up to her old tricks. *What* are you going to do about it?"

Bailey rose so she was more eye level with Price. "Senator Wainwright has nothing to do with this. A girl I'm trying to get out of a youth gang told me she was unfairly blamed for something that happened in a shelter where I placed her. That's all. I didn't break any laws here."

"This is fucking nuts, Clay. She's coddling criminals."

Bailey looked at Clay for the first time. His face was strained and a muscle leapt in his jaw. "I have to say, Bailey, I'm not happy about this. Did you think to contact the police?"

"We've been through this before. Several times. I refuse to explain myself again."

Ned shook his head. "You're a piece of work, lady."

"Watch what you say, Ned. We might disagree but no need to insult her."

Ned stared at Clay. "I got better things to do with my time. This subcommittee, this whole committee's a joke. I'm resigning."

"Ned, wait."

But the cop stalked out.

Bailey looked after him, then turned to Clay.

The muscle in his jaw pulsed. "Tell me this isn't the girl you met near Columbia."

"Clay, listen . . ."

"Answer me. Is it?"

Her gaze narrowed at his peremptory tone. "Yes."

"And she attacked a nun."

"So one girl in a shelter says. That's not the whole story."

He stared hard at her. "You won't be meeting with her again."

"Excuse me?"

"You heard me. I want your word you won't meet with Taz Gomez again."

"Absolutely not."

"I won't have it, Bailey."

"You have nothing to say in this."

"Your safety's in jeopardy."

"We've covered this ground before, Clay. Back off."

"Things are different now."

"I hope you're not saying what I think you're saying."

"Which is?"

"That our relationship changes things."

"Bailey . . ."

"Well, so much for keeping our personal and professional relationships separate."

Briefly he closed his eyes, visibly struggling for control. "Honey, I care about you and I'm concerned about your safety. I cannot tolerate you meeting with a gang member suspected of assaulting a nun, for God's sake."

She sighed heavily. "I was right, wasn't I?"

"Right?"

"You're trying to use our personal relationship to sway what I do in my job."

His face flushed. She remembered how he flipped her

down on the bed after the last time she accused him of this. "I thought we already rang that bell."

"We did. Apparently, you forgot what it sounded like." She stood. "I'll be leaving now."

"You're kidding, right?"

"No." She started for the door. He grabbed her arm.

"What was your decision about us before you came here?"

"It doesn't matter now."

"It matters to *me*."

"Let go of my arm."

"After you tell me what conclusion about us you came to."

"The only conclusion there *is* about us is that we were both foolish to think there was a shot in hell of our relationship working." She shook off his arm. "Good-bye, Clay. Don't contact me again."

Bailey hurried out of his office. He didn't call her back. Which was good. Maybe he'd finally come to his senses, too.

~ TWELVE

TAZ RAISED THE billy club and faked a smile. She hated initiations, and would've boned out on this one but Mazie had caught on that she was always sick or busy during the induction of a new member—shit, they sounded like a goddamned sorority—and had made a point of Taz being here tonight.

Tazzie baby, what's goin' on with you lately?

What do you mean?

I dunno. You always on the computer of yours. Again Taz had worried that Mazie had seen the screen for ESCAPE that day they came over.

I'd hate to think you coppin' out on your homies.

Shit no.

Then be at the jumpin' in.

As the new recruit ran through the gauntlet, Taz halfheartedly swung the club on the chick's butt. The other GGs weren't so kind. The girl was bleeding everywhere, and limping already. Feeling her stomach churn, Taz concentrated on why she was here.

Everybody but the gang had japped out on her. She'd had

to deep-six the shelter. The skunk girls set her up, and got her in trouble with the 5-0. So she'd gone home; in the past, she'd left her house before for a few days; sometimes the old man didn't even notice. Sometimes he just beat her up.

This time he'd raped her. He'd never done that. He'd tried twice before but he'd been so drunk she could fend him off. He wouldn't have succeed last night if he hadn't knocked her senseless first.

She surveyed the scene. The stoned and vicious posse. The battered wannabee. Hell, this was her only family? What did that say about her? Was her life even worth living?

Finally the initiation was over. She let down in the aftermath—booze and lots of it, a little pot, but left when the GGs all started fucking the boys in the Conquerors who'd come to watch. At her father's apartment, she climbed the fire escape and went in through the window. Maybe he wouldn't know she was here. Maybe he wouldn't be home. She fingered the blade. She was done letting him do anything to her.

The place was quiet. She dumped her stuff and went to the locked closet. Beneath piles of junk, she found her computer. She plugged it in and went on to the 'net, and right to ESCAPE's website.

There was a notice box where they published things sometimes. When they had a new program. When they wanted to get in touch with somebody. Sometimes just an inspirational saying. Tonight there was a note from the Street Angel. "TD2, please come on to the network. I need to talk to you. SA."

Taz stared at the screen. It was dated last week. She'd avoided the site since the incident with the nun. But after tonight, damnit, she wanted big-time to be out of the GGs.

What the hell. She clicked on to the network.

That you, Street Angel?

No, it's the Street Angel's coworker and buddy.

Never mind then.

If this is Taz, please, stay, I'll talk to you.

No.

I used to be in a gang. I can help, too.

When she gonna be on?

Tomorrow morning. Please come back then. She's so worried about you.

Maybe. Ciao.

So the Street Angel was worried. Smart broad, Taz thought kicking off her boots and lying down on the bed. She had blood on her pants and smelled like weed and booze but she was too tired to change. Without even taking off her clothes— she might need to make a quick escape—she slid the knife from her pocket, grasped it in her hand, and turned her face into the pillow. Like a child's teddy bear, the weapon made her feel secure and she held it through the night.

CLAY RAISED HIS racquet and slammed the ball into the front wall so hard it echoed like a gunshot, bounced back and caught Thorn in the shin. "Son of a bitch," his press secretary said.

"Sorry." Clay wiped his face with the sleeve of his shirt. He was dripping with sweat and smelled to high heaven. "My point." He went back to the serving line, tossed up the ball, and whacked it. "Ace."

Thorn mumbled something, but Clay didn't ask what. He was playing like a maniac, as he'd done everything else this past ten days; he'd lost five pounds between the games of racquetball, running, and lifting. It was the only way he could stop thinking about her. He was so pissed he wanted to rip something apart, and the exercise helped.

"That's it," Thorn said after a while.

Clay pivoted. "Huh?"

"You won, Senator. Again."

"Oh."

Thorn closed the distance between them. "Besides, you have a meeting in two hours."

"With Stewart, right?"

"Yep. He wants an update on New York's Task Force. How's that going?"

"Don't ask. What's after that?"

"An ad hoc committee of taxpayers on the new energy bill. Followed by the Senate hearing on the new Seahawk, and a bipartisan brainstorming session with the president on some new antiterrorist measures."

Clay nodded. He'd been packing his schedule since Congress reconvened in September in order to stay busy. In order not to *think*. "Good."

Thorn gathered up his bag and towels as Clay did, and accompanied him out of the court, down to the locker room. Once they'd showered and dressed, Thorn checked his watch. "You have time. Get some coffee with me?"

"I don't think so. I want to—"

"It's important, Clay."

Since Thorn rarely called him anything but *Senator*, Clay paused. He wondered if something was wrong with his press secretary. He'd hardly noticed what was going on around him all week, and now was ashamed of that. "Sure."

They stopped in at the coffee bar on the ground floor of the Russell Building. When they were seated, Thorn faced him. His shrewd eyes held a hint of what? Exasperation? "I drew the short straw."

"Excuse me?"

"Mica, Joanie, Bob, me—we're all wondering what happened."

"Happened, when?"

"Oh about a week ago when you turned into a slave driver."

"A slave driver? Have I?"

"Clay, you work from dawn till dark, come back here after the party's evening events, never take a break, and have stopped eating lunch. We're all exhausted trying to keep up with you."

"I'm sorry if I've worked everybody too hard."

"It's not just that. We're worried about you."

With good reason. But he hadn't realized he'd turned into an inconsiderate boss. Hell. He stared over at Thorn, wondering, not for the first time, why he didn't have anybody he could talk to about these things.

You could talk to Bailey.

Not without ringing her neck.

"Clay?"

"I've got a personal problem."

"With Jon?"

"No, actually things are going fairly well with Jon."

"He's not still intent on supporting Lawson, is he?"

"No."

"Thank God, what a political nightmare that could be."

"It was more than that, Thorn. It hurt like hell to hear what he'd done."

"Sure, I know that. I just look at the professional side of things all the time."

"Because I've wanted that, haven't I?"

Thorn gave him a quizzical look. "You going to get all touchy-feely on me now?"

"Go to hell," he said good-naturedly.

"Seriously, we've been working together for ten years. If you want to bat something personal around, I'm here."

"Thanks." He sipped the café au lait, enjoying its sweet taste.

"Is it a woman?"

"Why would you ask that?"

"You have all the signs of a troubled love life."

"It's not love."

"Lady Jane seems in love to me."

Over the rim of his mug, he stared at Thorn. "It's not Jane."

Thorn's brow furrowed. It was his formal Chief of Staff scowl. "Is there somebody else?"

"I thought there might be, but it didn't work out."

"Clay, everybody's expecting an announcement about your engagement after the picture of you and Jane in the paper last week. I've tried several times to discuss this with you since your father's party but you blew me off."

He'd gone ahead and broken off with Jane, despite the fact that Bailey had nixed their relationship. Or at least he'd told Jane how he felt. She hadn't listened, suggested they take a hiatus from each other, and not do anything rash. He'd reiterated that they were through, though. At least he was sure about that aspect of his life.

"No, there isn't going to be an engagement."

"I see. We'll have to put some spin on that."

"Christ, Thorn, I'm breaking up with a woman, not making

decisions about strategic arms. Who the hell's business is that?"

Thorn sipped his coffee and his cool gray eyes regarded Clay thoughtfully.

Clay ducked his head. "I guess I can see what you mean about getting the short straw." He sighed. "All right. I'm breaking it off. What do I have to do so it doesn't bite me in the ass?"

"Are you sure there's no one else?"

He pictured Bailey, cuddling into him and telling him she was hurt by his relationship with Jane. Then he pictured her saying that final good-bye. "No, there's no one else."

"HOLD ON, KIDDO, I can't keep up." Aidan bent at the knees and gulped the fresh September air. "Hell, I had no idea you were in such good shape."

Good shape, oh, yeah, that'll be the day. Bailey stopped jogging. "You used to be able to outrun me."

Finally her brother straightened. "Methinks you're outrunnin' something else, Sis."

Bailey stretched her calf muscles beneath a tree; the leaves were on it and September was still sunny, so she appreciated the shade. Aidan had worn gray sweats today, but Bailey only had on spandex biking shorts and a white T-shirt. "I have no idea what you mean."

Aidan stretched too. "Okay, lie to your favorite brother."

"You'll just get mad."

"I knew it was about him. What did the good senator do now?"

"The senator is history."

"I thought you said you believed him about Lady Jane."

"I do. Something else happened."

"What?"

"Promise you won't rail on me, too?"

"I promise."

"A kid I'm working with is suspected of a crime. She came on the network and talked about it in vague terms. Said she was being framed."

"That's not so bad."

"When Clay found out I knew about it, he told me not to meet with her again."

"He can't . . . you met with her?"

"Uh-huh." She pushed off from the tree. "Come on, let's run." They picked up a leisurely pace. "A while back. He found out about it."

"You told me Face-to-Faces were safe."

"They are. It wasn't a Face-to-Face. I met her alone."

Aidan halted on a dime and plopped his hands on his hips. "You're kidding, right?"

Bailey kept going for a few paces but then stopped, too. "At a public place with a lot of people around."

"I don't care if it was Grand Central Station. What's the matter with you? You got a kid who depends on you. A family who loves you. If something happens to you, we'd be devastated."

"I know."

"We all almost lost our minds when you went to prison. B., you're overstepping now. Even I can see that."

"That's what Clay said."

"I knew he had some sense. Maybe he *is* good for you."

"Doesn't matter." She felt tears prick her eyes. Damn it. "It's over. We had a huge fight and he went back to Washington when summer recess ended. I haven't heard from him."

"And you haven't called him."

"No."

"Hmm."

"You think I should?"

"I think you should join a convent."

She rolled her eyes. They started running again.

After a while, Aidan spoke. "For what it's worth, I think he's a good man, Bailey."

She threw her brother a sideways glance. "You punched him in the face just a little over a week ago."

"I know, but I thought he was using you."

"He wasn't."

"I figured that out. When he refused to leave and was gonna face the wrath of all your brothers, I decided he was the real deal. Then he did that with Rory."

"Did what?"

"When you were on my back tryin' to keep me from Clay, Ror came out. Clay jumped up and comforted him. It was like when he tried to protect you on the street that day. Basically, he's a good guy."

Bailey stopped. She closed her eyes. "I like him a lot. But the whole thing seems impossible: our families, our public animosity."

Aidan touched her shoulder. "When did little things like that ever stop you?"

Bailey was still thinking about Aidan's words when she entered ESCAPE an hour later. Suze was coming off the night shift. "Your girl was on the network," she said without preamble.

"Taz? Really?"

"Yep. She wouldn't talk to me. I said you'd be here this morning."

"Oh, thank God."

"She's still wanted for questioning."

"No, she's not." Joe Natale, the ex-cop with current connections at police stations, stood in the doorway.

"What happened?" Suze asked.

"The witness in the shelter ran away. The other girls confessed that she attacked Marion and they lied about Taz—they were out to get her."

"Damn." Bailey sighed. "If she comes on today, I'm going to set up a Face-to-Face."

"Good. Let Rob and me know."

Suze said, "Bailey, don't meet with her alone."

Joe scowled. "Of course she won't do that. She's not stupid." Silence. He shifted. "You haven't, have you?"

"Just once."

"Son of a bitch, Bailey. That's against the rules. What's wrong with you?"

Because she was beginning to think there was a conspiracy, she said, "I got it, okay. You're the third man to rail on me about it."

"I'd kill you if you were my girl."

If you were mine, I'd tie you to the bed.

Hell, nothing was going right.

The computer chimed. Bailey bolted to it.

Hey, Angel, you on?

Bailey dropped down at the computer. *Yes, Taz, I'm here. Are you all right?*

What do you think?

I'm sorry about the accusation at the shelter.

It don't matter.

Yes, it does. She typed in what she'd just found out. *You don't have to hide now.*

From the 5-0 maybe.

Who else would you be hiding from?

No answer. *Taz, did something happen with your father?*

Still no answer.

Taz? Please answer me.

I gotta book.

No, please, don't. Meet with me and some of my staff. We'll show you your options.

Maybe I'd meet. Just with you again, though.

No, Taz. With all of us. I can't meet alone with you anymore.

Thought you didn't play by no rules.

This one I have to.

Oh, I get it. You got in trouble for that.

Not trouble exactly. Meet with us, please.

No can do.

And then she clicked off.

Bailey sat back in her chair.

Joe put his hands on her shoulders. He and Suze had been reading the exchange over her shoulder. "You did the right thing, girl. Now stick to it. Promise me."

"I promise." He was right of course. But she wanted to help this girl. What if she couldn't do it within the system?

WHEN CLAY GOT back to his office, there was a delivery waiting for him. He opened the envelope. Inside was something he'd asked his assistant to arrange weeks ago. He stared at the glossy program and tickets. He should just dump them in the garbage. But he recalled the face of a little boy he'd come to care about and he quelled his temper. Quickly he wrote a note, addressed the envelope, sealed it, and left it with Joanie on his way out of the officer to meet with Stewart.

"How's it going, Clay?" Chuck asked when they were settled. A tall slim man, he was mild-mannered; Clay liked him.

"It's been better."

The other senator's face showed surprise. People in Washington usually played things close to the vest. "Personal or professional?"

Clay laughed. "Both, but I was referring to the trouble on this task force." He filled Chuck in on the difference of opinions, the attack on the nun, Ned's quitting.

"Did you contact Price about coming back?"

"Yeah, I'm having lunch with him when I go to New York next week."

"How about the Street Angel? Hell, she sounds like a real ball buster."

That made him bristle. "She's headstrong and stubborn and totally unconcerned about her safety. But she's good-hearted, too."

"So you're making headway with her."

"I was. This last thing with the nun was a pitfall."

"She staying on the committee?"

Clay glanced away. "I don't know."

Stewart waited a bit, then said, "Check it out. We need her cooperation."

After they batted around some other ideas, Clay rose.

Chuck did, too. "Before you go, I want to tell you something."

"What?"

"I'm not throwing my hat in the ring for the VP slot next time around."

"No? You're a favorite."

"My wife just found out she has breast cancer. It's in the early stages, so there's a good prognosis. But it put things in perspective. I'd rather be with her and the kids than go on a campaign trail."

"I'm sorry about your wife." He asked after her and they talked briefly about treatments and her state of mind. Then, after a time, Clay said, "This is big news about the VP."

"I'll make it known soon but I wanted to tell you. There's been talk of you for that job. For what it's worth, I think you'd represent the party well."

"Thanks, Chuck. I appreciate it."

"You're not married, are you?"

"No, divorced."

"Maybe the campaign would be easier on you then."

For some reason, that made Clay feel bad. He left Stewart's office thinking about the emptiness of his life.

THE PUB WAS decorated in Yankee motif. Big NYs were suspended from the ceiling. Blue and gray streamers floated in the air. Posters of the team adorned the wall. The O'Neils celebrated their birthdays in style.

Her son sat in the middle of his cousins, friends, aunts, uncles, and grandparents, ripping paper off a stockpile of presents. Some adult chatter, soft Irish music, and squeals of delight filled the room. Bailey stood back, sipping beer from a bottle, watching him.

"Hey, girl." Paddy came up behind her and slid his arm around her shoulders. "You look like you lost your best friend."

Immediately, she thought of Clay. She leaned into her oldest brother. "Nah, got all my best friends here."

"Not all." He squeezed her tight.

She examined Pat's face. "Brie isn't coming?"

"No. She had a business appointment."

"Wanting a career and pursuing it isn't *wrong*, Paddy."

"Shea and Sinead are grown up enough. But she should be home with Kathleen."

"Your daughter is fine," Bailey said pointing across the room to where Kathleen sat with Rory. "She doesn't need her mother twenty-four seven. And she has you and the rest of us to fill in any gaps, just like we do for Liam since they lost Kitty. Give Brie some space."

"Spoken like a true feminist."

"Spoken like a sister who loves you."

He sipped his own beer. "Relationships are tough."

Bailey didn't answer. God knew that was true about her and Clay.

"Still seein' that guy?"

"What guy?"

He snorted. "The guy whose clothes were all over the stairs."

"No. Like you said, relationships are tough."

"Mommy, look." Rory held up something in his hands.

Glad for an excuse to end the conversation with Pat, she crossed to her son. He held a manila envelope that had come in the mail with other birthday cards. Out of it slid something colorful and another envelope. "What is it, honey?"

"Seussical."

"The musical?" She got a good look at the thing. It wasn't a Playbill, but one of the larger, glossier programs sold at Broadway theaters.

"Yeah."

Aidan, who was standing over him, said, "See what's in the other envelope."

Rory tore it open. "What are these, Mommy?"

She took them. "They're tickets to the show. They're for this weekend." She glanced around at her family. "Who did this?"

Everybody's expression was blank.

"Come on, guys, it's so nice. But too expensive."

Aidan came closer. "We didn't do it, B."

"What?"

"Is there a card?"

Rory held one up. "Read it to me, Mommy."

Her hands shaking—she had a feeling about this—she opened the Yankee motif card. "Dear Rory, Happy fifth birthday. I know you wanted to see this show. Enjoy it. Clay Wainwright."

A gasp went through the room.

"What the hell . . ." Paddy said.

"Holy Mother of Christ." This from her mom.

"That had to cost a couple a bucks," Dylan put in.

Her father glared at her.

She said, "Don't look at me. I couldn't be any more surprised."

Later, after the party was over, and she was tucking Rory into bed, Bailey tried to keep her mind off Clay. "We need to write thank-yous for the presents."

"'Kay. We gonna see *Seussical*, Mommy."

"I know, sweetheart."

"Uncle Dylan says that costs lots of money."

"It was very generous of Clay."

"Wanna call him. Say thank you."

"What?"

"On the phone." He sat up. "Now."

"No, honey, you're just trying to find an excuse to stay up."

"Wanna call him."

"Baby, go to sleep."

"No."

"Rory, I'm not kidding. It's time for bed."

He pointed to the phone. "After."

Ten minutes later, when he was still demanding, and getting crankier and crankier, Bailey gave in. In truth, had it been anyone else but Clay, she would have thought Rory's was a great idea. "He may not answer. If he doesn't you've got to go to sleep."

"'Kay."

The phone rang twice. Bailey held her breath. Then a deep baritone came on. "Wainwright."

"Clay, it's Bailey."

A long silence. Before he got the wrong idea, she said, "Rory insisted on calling you. He got your present today."

"Ah."

"Gimme, Mommy!"

When Clay said no more to her, she handed Rory the phone. "Thanks, Clay! I'm gonna see *Seussical*." He must have answered. "Yeah, a Jeter backpack." Her son listed off the rest of his presents. Laughed. Smiled. It just about broke Bailey's heart. "'Kay." He gave the phone back to her and cuddled down into the blanket.

She said into the phone, "Clay? Are you still there?"

"Yes."

"Hold on a second, will you? Let me tuck Rory in."

When she'd done that, she hurried out of the room and spoke into the phone. "Thank you so much for the tickets. It was his favorite present."

"You're welcome."

"It was too much."

"Little boys should get their wishes on their birthday."

"Well, I appreciate it."

No response.

"How are you?"

A pause. "I'm fine."

"Are you? I'm not."

"No?"

"Clay, I—" She didn't know what to say. He was so cold and distant. "Are you coming in for the meeting tomorrow?"

"I'm already here, at my town house."

"Oh."

"Are you going to the meeting? I half expected you to quit the committee."

"I'm going. Maybe we can talk after."

"Do you want to?"

"I don't know what I want."

"Well, you were pretty specific about what you wanted— correction, what you didn't want—last time I saw you."

"You sound mad."

"Are you kidding? I'm pissed as hell at you. How could you give up on us? Oh, wait, I forgot, there is no us."

"You were out of line asking me not to see Taz."

"Look, this is old ground. I'm not going over it again. You made it very clear how important I am—or am not—to you. I'll see you at the meeting." He disconnected.

"Damn it." Bailey stared at the phone. Then she punched in a number.

"Hello."

"Aidan, it's me. Could you come over for a while?"

"Yeah, I guess."

"Oh dear, are you with somebody?"

"Don't I wish. You need to talk?"

"Yeah, I need to talk. Not to you, though. Can you come

and watch Rory for a while? There's something I have to do."

"Sure, be right there."

CLAY WAS LIKE a caged tiger. "Son of bitch," he said aloud to his empty town house. He stalked around the bedroom, where he'd been futilely trying to read, but once she'd called, it had been useless. Rain began to patter against the windows, which were partly open, so he shut them and swore. "Damn her." He threw on pajama bottoms and trundled down the stairs; he crossed to the wet bar in the living room, poured himself a double scotch, leaned against the furniture and replayed everything she'd said.

He should have hung up when she asked him to hold on while she tucked Rory in.

He couldn't.

How are you?

Fine.

Are you? I'm not.

What had she meant by that?

Oh, hell, he knew damn well what she meant. He wasn't fine and apparently she wasn't either. He should have taken the opening, but then she'd been so surprised he was angry at her, it pissed him off all over again.

Maybe we can talk after . . . I don't know what I want . . .

He should have been more understanding. He glanced at the phone, stared at it a good few minutes. Sipped his drink. Fuck it, she'd made a move. He could be conciliatory. He'd just punched in her number when the doorbell rang. Still holding his cell, he walked to the foyer and peered out the window.

And there she was.

He clicked off just as she pulled out her own phone. He opened the door. "Hi."

"Hi." She held up her phone. "Someone called me. I have to see if this was Aidan. He's watching—"

"It wasn't Aidan. It was me." He noticed the rain had made her hair curl, and her cheeks were dewy with the moisture outside.

"You called me?"

"I'm afraid so. I should have waited a few more minutes. Saved face."

She smiled weakly. "Can I come in?"

He stepped aside and tossed his phone on a table, closed the door, and leaned against it, watching her. "I don't know whether to kiss you senseless or take you over my knee and paddle you."

An eyebrow arched. "You said you weren't into kinky."

"You bring out the worst in me." He nodded to her raincoat. "Here, let me have that."

After he'd hung up her coat and set her purse down, he faced her; she surprised him by stepping closer and resting both hands on his chest. "I vote for kissing me senseless."

He turned her fast and, bracing her against the wall, ravaged her mouth. She ravaged back. When he drew away, he pulled her head to his bare chest. She nosed into him. "Damn it, Bailey. You make me hard in seconds."

"We can make love first, if you want." She kissed his pecs, ran her hands over them, inhaled him.

"First?"

"Before we talk."

He stilled. "What are the chances of us talking, and your storming out of here without hitting the sheets?"

She laughed. "I hope none." She drew back. Sobered. "I've missed you so much, and I'm sorry about what happened."

"Aw, honey, I missed you, too. And I'm sorry."

"You were right, I was ready to agree to giving our relationship a try. I shouldn't have bolted at the first sign of trouble."

"And I shouldn't have been so autocratic." He sighed and rubbed her shoulders, leaned in closer so he could smell her hair, the scent of her lotion. "These are real, divisive issues, though."

"Insurmountable, do you think?"

"I hope not." He took her hand and led her to the couch. "Come on, let's talk."

"Okay." She followed behind him. "But I gotta tell you, Senator, you look really cute in jammies."

"I'll let you borrow the tops, if you want."

She sat down. "I want."

"Look," he said earnestly. "I was wrong to yell at you about Taz. We should have talked it out."

"But?"

"But you can't meet with her or any gang kids alone."

"I know."

"It's too— You know?"

"Yeah. Aidan got on me about it. Took your side. And then Joe had a fit. I guess you're all right. I need to consider my safety first."

"Wow, I never expected this."

"But Clay, I'm going to have a Face-to-Face with her. And I'm going to continue doing that with other kids."

He sighed. He didn't like it, but he knew he wasn't going to change this woman, not really, though she'd given a big concession just now. "All right, I'll try to deal with that." He brushed his hand down her cheek. "I'll compromise about your job."

"Thank you."

"But no more seesaw, Bailey. We're done fence sitting about this relationship. Promise me you won't go back on trying to make this work between us." He leaned his forehead against hers. "I've fallen for you, honey. Hard."

"Me, too. I've fallen for you. And I won't change my mind, won't bolt. I promise. I believe in us, Clay."

"Good. Now," he said pulling her onto his lap. "Kiss me."

"Yes, sir."

They didn't even make it off the couch. He consumed her, breathed her into his body and soul. She let him, took, and gave. At one point they tumbled to the floor.

"Bailey, love . . ." he said leaning over her.

"Clay, come inside me. I want to feel you there."

Their lovemaking was sweet, and tenderly cataclysmic. Afterward, he grabbed some pillows and a blanket from the couch and lay on the rug with her, cuddled her to his chest, kissed her forehead. "How long can you stay?"

"A while. Aidan's bunking at my house."

"How'd you explain going out?"

"I told him the truth."

"I wish I had a brother I could talk to like that."

"I'm lucky." She sighed and looked up at him. "You can talk to me, Clay, about anything."

They'd come a long way.

"Tell me about your week? What happened?"

"It was miserable." He filled her in on Thorn's "short straw" comment. She laughed. He told her about his meeting with Stewart and the senator's comments about her.

But he didn't bring up the VP thing. It would only muddy the waters, divide them more. And as he hugged her to his chest, he didn't want to be separate from her. He wanted to be closer.

Eventually, to that end, he began kissing his way down her body.

THIRTEEN

BAILEY O'NEIL THREW herself into her relationship with Clay just like she did everything else—completely and without reservation. As he watched her across the room putting the finishing touches on dinner—with Rory's help—he knew he'd already become utterly enthralled with her. For him, there was no turning back. For her, psychologically, the jury was still out, though her actions did not indicate her reservations.

"Be ready in ten minutes," she said glancing over Rory's head to where Clay sat ostensibly reading the *Washington Post*. Dressed in jeans and a simple cotton sweater set of ruby red, she gave him a private smile that made him hard in seconds. The sex had been even better since they'd admitted their feelings for each other went beyond the physical. He'd never been so satisfied in his life.

"No hurry." He nodded to her son. "I'm enjoying the show."

She swiped at her nose. "Do I still have potatoes on my face?" Rory had gotten carried away with his task of whipping the potatoes and had smushed some on his mother's nose.

"Nope. Now it's in your hair."

A look of sham outrage came over her. "Rory O'Neil, did you . . ."

"Nu-uh. He's teasin', Mommy."

Clay laughed.

"Not funny, Senator."

"Sorry."

He couldn't imagine Jane or Karen allowing this kind of play to go on while cooking a meal—if they cooked at all. Nor had he, as a child, been privy to this kind of interaction with his mother. Which was how this whole dinner came about. Earlier in the week when they had talked on the phone—as they did every single night—the subject of his nannies had come up. His favorite had made him pot roast. He'd been shocked as hell to walk into Bailey's apartment today and smell that meal cooking.

"Rory, go set the table while I sit a minute."

"Clay, too."

"No, Clay's on cleanup. You do it."

Rory climbed off the stool, passed by Clay at the table, gave him a hug, and dragged a high step stool to the other side of the kitchen. Bailey encouraged all kinds of independence, as well as the affection the boy routinely showed. Rory's demonstrativeness toward Clay still stunned him, and pleased the hell out of him.

The only dark spot, he thought, glancing down at the paper in front of him, was that Bailey insisted on keeping their relationship a secret. Their ruse with Rory had worked—they all pretended it was a game of keeping secrets, as Rory did with Aidan, and so he hadn't talked to anyone about Clay. But Clay had wanted to go to *Seussical* with them yesterday and Bailey had objected. . . .

Somebody could see us together. You're a public figure and would be recognized.

I'm not ashamed of how I feel about you.

No, I'm not ashamed of my feelings either; but why give people ammunition? After all, this might not work out between us.

She'd been washing her face in the master bath of his town

house and he'd been lying on the bed; he'd gotten up when she made the remark, stalked over to the bathroom and grasped her by the arms. *I hate hearing you talk like that.*

Clay, you've got to be realistic. Let's just see where this goes. Anyway, we can't publicize our relationship. People would want to know about me. Then it would come out that I'm the Street Angel, and I couldn't do my job.

Because public exposure would put you in more *danger.*

Clay . . . stop, please. This kind of conversation is just pulling us apart.

He'd stopped, mostly because he had no choice. And he *had* agreed to be reasonable.

She set a scotch-on-the-rocks in front of him and sat down at the table with a glass of wine while Rory worked happily in the dining area off the living room. He was singing a song from *Seussical.*

Bailey lifted her glass.

"Faol sadl chroi!" Her face was flushed from the stove heat, with little tendrils of dark hair curling around her face. It reminded him of how she looked after sex. At his questioning look she said, "Long life and happiness." He shook his head. "What?" she asked, her blue eyes darkening.

Reaching over, he swiped her lips with his thumb. "Do you know how *happy* you make me?"

She kissed his hand. "I want to make you happy."

"It's why you cooked this dinner."

"Yes. I hope you like it."

He had to clear his throat. Stupid to get choked up about a silly meal. But Bailey really listened to him, and she went out of her way to please him with little things like this. It meant a lot. "I'll savor every mouthful. Thank you." He grazed her lips with his. "You look tired."

"I am. I was on nights Thursday and Friday at ESCAPE and Rory woke me at the crack of dawn today."

"I'll put you to sleep tonight."

"Sounds good to me." Though they'd agreed he wouldn't stay overnight when Rory was home, Clay knew they'd make love when—finally—the boy went to bed. The kid was an owl, but Clay had the best luck in settling him down.

Bailey rose to go back to the stove. He watched her, wondering what had gone on at ESCAPE this week. They rarely talked about work, or the task force or their public disagreements. Monday they'd had a subcommittee meeting—the first since their commitment. It was surprisingly low-key as everybody just reported their findings. Marion was back and recovered, thank God. Tomorrow they were meeting as a whole group again, which was why he was officially in town; they'd really get to the nitty gritty then. He expected fireworks from the little chef across from him.

The meal was sumptuous. The roast beef was so tender it seemed to melt in his mouth, the gravy was dark and rich, and the vegetables tasty. Rory helped Clay clean up in exchange for tossing a ball with him outside. While Bailey was getting the boy down for the night, Clay went to her bedroom to wait for her and was watching a news show from Washington. The chair of the Health, Education, and Welfare Committee was being interviewed.

After other topics had been covered, the host asked, "Senator Smith, how is the anti–youth crime movement going? Congress said it was a priority."

"It's going well. As you know, Stewart's new bill will provide millions of dollars to fight against juvenile crime."

"Especially against youth gangs, correct?"

"That's right."

"When will the money provided for by his bill be allocated?"

"We're gathering information this month in each state; home senators will report their recommendations in a few weeks; we expect to have funds earmarked by Thanksgiving."

From the doorway, Bailey said, "It's coming up soon."

Clay looked up. "Yes." He gripped the remote.

She came fully into the room and dropped down onto the bed. "This is hard, isn't it?"

He nodded.

"Think we can handle it?"

Tossing aside the remote, he reached for her. She fell onto his chest. He kissed her soundly. "Yes, we can handle this. Especially if we're honest with each other."

"I think that's important, Clay. Even if we disagree. Or if it causes problems."

"I know." Grasping her neck, he kissed her again. "But no more negative talk tonight."

She didn't say anything, just studied him in that way she had that made him want to squirm like a grade-school kid. "All right." Her eyes glittered, and he felt her hand drift down his abs, below his belt to cup him boldly. "I can think of one way to assure that."

"Can you now?" he said closing his eyes.

AT FOUR ON Monday afternoon, Clay surveyed the Task Force Committee and watched Bailey across the room talking to Eric Lawson. Dressed in the denim skirt she'd worn that morning she'd come to the Suffox and a long-sleeved navy T-shirt, with her hair pulled off her face, she listened intently to something his rival was telling her. Clay thought back to leaving her twelve hours ago.

He'd climbed out of bed trying not to wake her. Still, she turned over and faced him. "Clay?"

"It's late. We both fell asleep. I've got to get out of here now, or I'll be zonked for good." He was naked, standing in the dim moonlight. While she watched, he drew on the jeans · he'd worn. A breeze drifted in from the window and she shivered; he bent over and drew up the covers.

She grasped his hand. "I don't want you to go." God he loved how she reacted so spontaneously, didn't hold back.

"It's either that or explain to the little guy why I slept with Mommy."

She sighed and closed her eyes. After the discussion of the task force, their lovemaking had been unbelievably tender and poignant. He truly didn't want to leave her.

She said, "Damn it."

He sat on the side of her bed and brushed back her hair. "Just so long as you like it as little as I do."

"That's an understatement. You know, I thought getting to see you more would stop this . . . need to be with you." She took his hand and brought it to her breast. "It's just the opposite."

"Aw, sweetheart, for me, too." Leaning over he kissed her other breast. "I'm becoming addicted to IrishCream."

She laughed at the pun, and he'd been tempted to crawl right back in the bed with her.

"I'll see you at the meeting . . ."

Ned Price approached him just before they got started. "O'Neil's here," he stated gruffly.

Pretending to check the time, Clay nodded. "Yes."

"I wish she hadn't come back to the committee."

"She deserves her say, Ned."

"Yeah, but she just doesn't get it. These kids are violent criminals. I heard rumblings about the girl gangs at the precinct last night."

"What kind of rumblings?"

"Action's stepping up. Apparently Anthrax has some beef against the GGs." He dropped his voice. "The cops are working overtime on a strategy to get those kids and cripple both gangs."

Briefly, Clay thought of Taz, the girl Bailey was trying to get out. Would she be caught in the police's net? He knew it would hurt Bailey, a lot, if she was.

"I think we can get started." Jerry Friedman had approached the table and spoke up.

Clay glanced up to see Bailey lean over to listen to something Lawson had to say. She smiled weakly, her gaze panning the table. When it fell on him, her expression was full of feeling, then she turned away.

A spurt of anger shot through him. He hated this dissembling. He hated her sitting with Lawson. For a brief moment, he wondered what would happen if he declared how he felt about her to the whole committee.

The governor checked his agenda. "Today, we'll give our reports from the subcommittee meetings. Once everybody has all the information, I'll let you have some time to study it, then we'll call a final session to vote on a recommendation." He set another meeting date and the reports began.

"The first committee's task was to assess current community-based programs already in existence." He nodded to Clay. "You ready to go?"

"Sure." He passed around the document they'd assembled. "We started with the city. As you might expect, we have the most programs because we have the most problems. If you look on page twelve, you'll see a list of our operations." At the top of it was ESCAPE.

"I see several cities are modeling ESCAPE's prototype," Eric Lawson commented after scanning the document.

"Yes." Bailey smiled at the younger man. "I've gone to Albany, Rochester, and Buffalo to talk to the staff of the groups about what we do. They're well underway to implementing at least some of ESCAPE's programs."

Clay rapped his knuckles on the report. "We don't want to lose sight of the shelters, clinics, and food kitchens available to all youth, and that assist kids in gangs. ESCAPE isn't the only game in town."

Again Lawson. "None, specifically for kids trying to get out of gangs, though, are there?"

"You know there's not, Lawson."

"Yet."

Bailey caught Clay's gaze. She said, "It's no secret we're trying to get money for Guardian, but Senator Wainwright's blocked it. And we need clinics which will take these kids if they're hurt. Those are particularly necessary."

"Because your kids are so violent," Clay said.

"Because my kids are in danger, Senator."

Sister Marion intervened. "Could we look at the research from subcommittee number three, which explored a variety of current intervention services for gang members and at-risk kids in the rest of the country? Let's see if these kinds of special places exist or are effective?"

The state senator held up his document. "We did the research on that. There are a few organizations in California that we might want to look at."

After they'd reported their findings, the third subcommittee on crime prevention research presented.

Clay listened to the recap of the two sides: social intervention versus legal intervention: Bailey's views versus his.

"So," he said when they finished. "There are no cut-and-dried answers."

"Nothing's black and white," Lawson said in a dry tone bordering on sarcastic. "No matter how much you try to make it so."

"I don't do that," Clay snapped.

The governor checked the time. "We need to wind this up. Here's what I propose. Everybody takes the documents home. Come back next meeting knowing how you want to spend the money. We'll argue it out then. I think we can solidify our recommendation at that point, too."

Lawson spoke up. "What will happen to this recommendation?"

Friedman studied the young lawyer. "Is that a loaded question?"

"Sort of. I hate when a committee puts time and effort into something, then the people running it don't pay attention to the official recommendation."

Friedman stiffened. "Each senator on his or her state's task force will meet with Stewart's committee. Obviously, Clay will represent us. Then the rest of Stewart's committee will make the determination of use of funds from the new bill."

Like a dog with a bone, Lawson zeroed in on Clay. "You're on the D.C. committee, too, aren't you Wainwright?"

Price spoke up. "What's this all about? We're not in a political arena here, Lawson. Save your attacks for the newspapers."

Lawson raised his eyebrows. With a shock of dark hair falling over his forehead, he looked rakish. "Isn't anyone else concerned about this? Wainwright's views are well-known. If we come up with something other than what *he* believes in, what difference will our recommendation make? He'll veto it on the parent committee. He's double dipping. He gets to present our findings with whatever spin he wants to put on it, then act as a decision maker with Stewart."

Marion leaned forward. "I'm concerned about that. There are obvious sides here. We can't do anything about his membership on Stewart's committee, but that the conservative senator is our sole representative worries me."

Bailey shot Friedman a look; something telegraphed between them. She said, "I mentioned this point to you when you asked me to be on this task force, Governor." Her gaze transferred to Clay. "I have concerns about that, too."

"Are you questioning my integrity?" Clay asked.

"No," Bailey said. "We're worried about your biases, Senator."

"Perhaps Ms. O'Neil can be there when you present our report," Friedman said. "We can send two people to give New York's input."

Clay sat back. Bailey sat back. Lawson said, "I think that's a great idea. She'd make sure our side got fair representation."

The others agreed. Friedman nodded to Bailey. "Ready for a trip to D.C., Ms. O'Neil?"

She looked directly at Clay. "I'm more than ready to go to Washington, Governor Friedman."

Of course, no one else knew Clay wasn't totally unhappy about this turn of events.

BAILEY WAS LATE for dinner at her parents' apartment. The pub was closed Mondays so they tried to make family time together then. Having sold their home in Queens, her mother and father now lived above the restaurant in a spacious second floor apartment. Now that they were retired, they spent the winter months in Florida and the rest of the time here.

She entered their home with Rory in tow and found everybody already seated. The adults were in the big dining room and the kids were happily settled in the kitchen.

Her father said, "There's my girl."

Bailey kissed his cheek. "Sorry I'm late, Pa. I had a meeting for work." She hugged her mother, who was just putting lamb stew on the table. "Hmm, smells wonderful. I'm starved."

She scanned the members of her family. Dylan, Liam, and Aidan sat on one side, with Patrick adjacent to them—alone. Uh-oh. If Brie had to work tonight and miss a family dinner, sparks would fly.

She sat down, and amid the chatter, her mind wandered to just an hour ago . . .

"Where are you going now?" Clay had asked, pulling her to a dim corner in Penn Station. As prearranged, after the meeting, she'd taken a cab there with him to spend a bit more time together.

She glanced up at the huge overhead clock. "Dinner at Ma's. I'm late."

He brushed his lips over her forehead. "Will you miss me?"

"Uh-huh." She stood up on tiptoes and kissed him hard.

He held her to him. "I hated clashing with you on the committee."

"Yeah, me too. You okay with it?"

"For the time being. Call me tonight. I have a party fundraiser thing, but I'll be done by eleven."

She'd hung on, not wanting him to leave . . .

"Hey, B., you're in never-never land." This from Aidan.

"Sorry." She paid attention to eating the stew and joined in with the conversation by tossing her brothers a few barbs.

When they were having coffee, Patrick leaned back in his chair, and cleared his throat. "I got something to say."

Bailey stiffened. His tone indicated it wasn't good.

His face was lined with fatigue and his blue eyes were dull. "Brie and I are separatin' for a while."

"Separating?" Her mother acted like the word was foreign.

"I know this'll be hard for you, Ma. And you, Pa. But it's best for me right now."

"And what about your three children?" Mary Kate asked. "What about vows you made?"

He looked to Pa. Her father had made vows, broken them. "Katie, don't. We were apart for a while. It worked out."

Except he'd had an affair and a kid.

Her mother's face indicated she was struggling with that. Aidan reverted to his peacemaker role. "I'm sorry, bro. What can we do?"

Paddy faced him. "For one thing, you can let me move in with you for a while."

"You could live with me," Liam put in. Bailey knew that since his wife died, Liam was lonely.

"Or me." Dylan offered. "I got Hogan's room when he isn't there."

"A separation didn't work out for Dylan," her mother added.

Dylan shook his head. "The verdict's still out there, Ma. Let Paddy make his own way."

"The church frowns on that."

This time, they avoided each other's gaze. The church frowned on a lot of things the O'Neils did.

They talked more. Discussed arrangements. It wasn't until Bailey had left and gotten Rory tucked in that she let herself think hard about what had happened. Her mother was so upset about Pat. What chance did she have with them accepting Clay? He was a public figure. Who'd been instrumental in her going to jail. And he was a divorced man.

At eleven she phoned him. "Clay Wainwright."

"Hi, it's Bailey."

His tone softened. "As if I wouldn't recognize your voice."

"Hmm."

"It has some worry in it, lady. What happened?"

Already he knew her so well. She told him about Patrick.

"I'm sorry, I know you're close to them."

"I feel bad. Paddy and Brie were so in love when they married. Now, because they disagree on her work, they're splitting."

"The work thing's a tough nut to crack."

"Too tough?"

"I hope not." He waited. "I handled today, honey."

She said nothing.

"We don't need to dredge this up now, though. Let's talk about Patrick some more. Where's he going to live?"

"All right." This was safer ground.

The conversation went well. Still, when they hung up, Bailey felt sad. Really sad. Tonight with her family, today at the meeting, highlighted so many of their differences.

When she climbed into bed, she drew the covers up and pulled the pillow where Clay had slept to her face. It smelled like his aftershave. That calmed her some.

KAREN COLLINGTON WAINWRIGHT fit her name. She was tall, blond, and cool. She even smelled sophisticated; her signature scent was French perfume and cost three hundred dollars an ounce. Jon used to think his father was a perfect fit for her, but these days his dad seemed different. Jon guessed he had a girl stashed somewhere that he wasn't telling anybody about. More power to him.

Home for a long weekend, Jon sat in his mother's house in New York keeping company with her parents. She'd asked them for dinner specifically to see Jon since he hadn't spent time with them when he was in New York for his other grandfather's party. His mother demanded equal time for her family. It took Jon all of a half hour to realize they were working him.

"So, Jon," Zachary Collington said easily, "how are your courses this year? Remember your grades have to be good enough for law school."

His gaze swung to his mother, hoping for some support. She said weakly, "Now Dad, you know nothing's been decided."

"Never too early to prepare, just in case. Besides, your father told me the last time I saw him he'd be devastated if you didn't follow in our footsteps." Both grandparents were lawyers.

That didn't compute. At dinner his dad had said, *You have to follow your own way, son. Politics was for me. I knew that, even though my family pushed for it. But you can still do good for the world in other arenas*. They'd talked then about those options.

"That's not what Dad said the last time I had dinner with him. I told him I might want to be an environmental lobbyist."

"Need law school for that."

"Not necessarily."

"Darling," his grandmother added, "it isn't as easy as it looks in the movies."

"Speaking of which," his grandfather said to his mother, "I hear talk of Clay and the vice presidential candidacy next year in the same sentence."

"My father's going for vice president?" Jon asked. Geez, his Dad had said nothing to him about that. He felt a little betrayed.

His mother straightened. "Yes, of course, it's always been in the plans. I won't, however, be second lady." Clearly ticked off at the notion, she got that pinched look on her face that meant trouble.

His grandmother looked at Jon. "So, when is the wedding?"

"What wedding?" Jon asked.

"Your father's and Jane's, of course."

"Dad's engaged?"

His grandfather frowned. "*The Voice* reported it the day after Clay Sr.'s party."

His mother stood. "Mother, would you come to the study with me? I want to show you some new books I got for our charity bazaar. They're signed by the authors."

The women left, and Jon and his grandfather discussed innocuous things. When his grandfather tired of talking to him, he turned on the evening news. Jon got up and went to the sideboard. Normally he didn't drink in front of his parents, but the whole night was getting heavy. Not that anybody else noticed. He went outside on the patio to think.

He stood looking at the lawns. It was fall, his favorite time of year. He remembered his dad taking him to a pumpkin farm, then trick-or-treating. It had been so easy in those days. He'd believed everything his dad said; he'd believed his dad could do no wrong. When had all that changed? When his father started campaigning for the Senate? When he started spending less time at home and more in Washington after he was elected? When he started missing significant events in Jon's life? He had reason to resent his father, but he thought they were starting off on a different foot, now.

On his second stolen scotch, Jon wandered into the kitchen to see when dinner would be ready. He stopped in the hallway just before he reached the room. "Do you think he's going to marry her?" his grandmother asked.

"Jane?"

"Yes."

"Probably. He was, after all, seeing her on the side before things came to a head between us. Clayton likes his women, more than one at a time."

"Typical presidential material, I'd say."

"Hmm, like Clinton and Kennedy." He heard his mother

sigh. "Let's change the subject, Mother. I have conflicting feelings about Clayton Wainwright."

Right now, Jon knew exactly how she felt.

CLAY SAT STARING at the computer, thinking *three steps forward, two back*. Damn it, how could Jon believe these lies about him? Clay thought they'd made such progress that night before his father's party.

He reread parts of the email . . .

When were you going to tell me about running for VP? . . . Damn it, Dad, you know how I feel about law school . . . how could you cheat on Mom? . . . I won't be coming down to D.C. this weekend . . .

It didn't take Einstein to figure out what had happened—Jon had had dinner with Karen and the elder Collingtons. This was so typical of them—the innuendos, the half-truths, but did they honestly tell Jon that Clay had cheated on Karen?

He checked the time on the computer. Midnight. He'd already talked to Bailey before he got this email, but he needed her now.

The phone rang three times before he heard a sleep-slurred, "Hello."

"Hell, I woke you." And he knew she needed rest. "Sorry. Go back to sleep, babe."

"Clay? What's wrong?"

"Nothing. I'm sorry . . ."

"Clay." Her voice was intimate. Sexy. "I was dreaming about you."

He chuckled. "Was it good?"

"You were great."

Another laugh.

"What happened?"

"I got a disturbing email from Jon." He told her about it, and out poured his frustration with his family, his anger, his shock. The only thing he didn't discuss with her was Jon bringing up the possibility of Clay being considered for the vice presidency. He hated concealing that, but it was necessary for now.

He talked for a half hour; she asked pointed questions. By the time he finished, he was clearer on what he was feeling.

"So, what are you going to do about it?" she asked.

"I don't know. I have a dilemma. I've gone to great pains to keep Jon's relationship with the Collingtons and his mother on an even keel. He never knew about Karen's cheating."

"Why?"

"He was fifteen at the time. A vulnerable age. Just wait until Rory hits adolescence. Anyway, we also kept it quiet here in the city. Bad politics. All anybody knew was there were irreconcilable differences."

"It sounds so phony. How can you live in that fishbowl?"

"It's necessary to do what I do." His tone was clipped.

"I wasn't being critical, Clay."

"I'm sorry, I'm raw right now."

"Why don't you call Jon?"

"The email asked me not to. He said he didn't want to discuss anything right now. He just wanted me to know what he's feeling."

"Then you should respect his wishes. You could email him back."

"And say what?"

"Do you want my honest opinion?"

"God help me, but I do."

"Tell the truth. He's twenty years old, Clay."

"I know." He thought for a moment. "What if it hurts his relationship with his mother?"

"Maybe you have to make this decision based on what's best for his relationship with you. No other adult is going to look out for that bond."

"You're right." He sighed. "How'd you get so smart?"

"It's common sense. When you're emotionally involved, you can't see the forest for the trees." She waited a beat. "And something else I do know for sure?"

"What's that?"

"Your ex-wife must have been a complete idiot to have cheated on you."

He laughed heartily. "I like having you in my life, Bailey O'Neil. You're good for me."

"Quite a change from three months ago, isn't it?"

"Yeah, it sure is." A hesitation. "We're gonna do this, honey."

"I hope so, Clay. But we're getting side-tracked. Go write your email to your son."

"All right. Thanks for helping me with this. Good night, sweetheart."

"Good night, love."

He hung up before it hit him what she'd called him. Love. Hot damn! Invigorated by that, he turned to his keyboard.

⟿ FOURTEEN

"HERE ARE THE tickets you ordered, Senator." His administrative assistant, Joanie, stood before his desk. "I'm still working on the other thing."

"Thanks, Joanie."

She smiled. Young and freckle-faced, she was nonetheless a good asset to his staff. "That'll be a great game. Hope they make it to the series."

"Are you a Yankees fan?"

"Not born and bred there but I love those Yanks." Her comment reminded him of Rory.

They chatted about baseball for a few minutes then Joanie left; Clay lazed back in the chair and stared at the tickets. He'd ordered them and with any luck could convince Bailey to come along with him and Aidan. The latter had been his partner in arranging it. . . .

"So you're back in her life!" Aidan had said on the phone when Clay called him.

"Yes."

"We tellin' anybody yet?"

"If I had my way we would."

"Well, that sounds better. Now maybe my brothers won't beat the crap out of you."

"I hope not."

"Of course if you could find out where Angie Everhart lives, that'll help."

"You like your redheads, don't you?"

Aidan chuckled, then sobered. "It's only a matter of time before people find out about you and my sister."

"We'll deal with it then, I guess," he told him. "For now, help me get her to go with us . . ."

Clay put the tickets in his pocket just as Mica and Thorn appeared at the doorway.

"Ready for that strategy session?"

Mica went to sit by the window and Thorn approached his desk. "Better read this first."

"What is it?"

"The Street Angel's at it again."

"Excuse me?"

"She took another cheap shot at you, Senator. Publicly."

Clay couldn't believe it. He opened *The Voice* to where Thorn had folded it. And read:

In our continuing series on youth violence in the city, we have an exclusive interview with the Street Angel, who runs a hotline/web network for kids in gangs. Hank Sellers has spoken with her . . .

The article was set up in interview format:

TV: *Tell us about your organization.*

Briefly Bailey explained ESCAPE.

TV: *What kind of success rate do you have?*

Bailey gave Sellers the same statistics as she'd given Clay.

TV: *It's no secret that there's animosity between you and Capitol Hill. Is it true you're working for Eric Lawson's campaign and against Clayton Wainwright.*

SA: *I've been to a couple of campaign meetings for*

Councilman Lawson. I think he'd make a worthy opponent to the senator from New York.

TV: *What specifically do you object to in the senator's views on youth crime?*

SA: (offering a hint of a smile) *It would be easier to tell you what I agree with.*

From there she succinctly described their differences. Seeing it in black and white was startling. Finally the interviewer asked the last question.

TV: *Do you think Lawson has a chance against Wainwright?*
SA: *Yes. I think he does.*

Clay threw the paper down on the desk and forced his breathing to stay even. He couldn't reconcile this with the woman he felt closer to than any other person in his life, the woman who talked to him late at night about *everything,* the woman who made love to him like there was no tomorrow.

"You all right?" Thorn asked.

"Yes, of course."

"Damn that woman. She'd been quiet awhile. I thought she was calming down about us since you've been on that committee together."

Clay stared at his picture in the paper; hers was not there, for privacy, but Lawson's was. Clay looked a lot older than his challenger. "This was probably done before the task force started."

Mica and Thorn exchanged concerned looks.

"What?"

"The interview was given a few weeks ago. It says so in the credits."

After they'd slept together. "You're kidding."

"No, check it out."

Clay checked. He'd missed the date in the opening lines. "I can't believe she'd do this to me."

Thorn's frown was deep. "What does that mean?"

"She . . . we . . ." He glanced up at his staff. "Nothing, I just thought we'd come to some kind of understanding is all."

"Are you sure, Clay? Your demeanor suggests there's more to it." Mica had moved in closer. "If there is more, we need to know what it is."

"No, no." He fingered the tickets in his pocket. "There's no more to it."

BAILEY TOOK A break from working at the computer and picked up a copy of *The Voice*. She was tired, but happy. Clay was coming to town tomorrow for some state legislature stuff and she'd see him afterward. Absently, she scanned the contents page of the paper and stopped short. Oh no. Opening to page six, she found the interview she'd had with Sellers three weeks ago.

"Good press," Rob Anderson commented over her shoulder.

"Huh?"

"Good press for ESCAPE. Not for the senator, though. I'd say you scored on this one."

I didn't want to score against Clay.

Joe came into the office. "What are we looking at?"

"Our fearless leader got the senator again in the press. Not that I'm crazy about Lawson."

Bailey just stared down at her public criticism of Clay.

"Why?" Joe asked.

"He's slimy. At least Wainwright's aboveboard about everything."

Not everything, Bailey thought.

"Honest but a jerk."

"No he's not!" Her head whipped up; she had spoken more harshly than she intended.

Joe scowled. Rob folded his arms over her chest. "What's this all about?" Joe asked.

"Nothing. I've just gotten to know him on the task force and he's a decent guy."

"He's been trying to close us down for years," Joe retorted. "What's gotten into you? First you let him come here, then you defend him."

"Nothing's gotten into me."

"If you say so." Joe turned and walked out.

Rob said, "This is all we need."

"What?" she asked.

"Some male-female stuff between you two."

"There's nothing . . ." Suddenly she couldn't utter the lie.

"Don't bother denying it, Bay. I'm a psychologist. I get vibes. When he was here for that visit, you two gravitated to each other physically. And you watched each other. Then . . . I heard you talking to him on the phone one night. I wasn't eavesdropping but I caught the tone of your conversation."

"I never meant for this to happen." She shook her head. "It's . . . complicated."

Rob nodded to the paper. "More than you know, probably. If it hasn't gone too far, I'd end it now if I were you."

And for the first time, Bailey admitted to herself, as well as to anther person, "It's gone too far."

"I see." He pushed off from the desk. "Then you'd better call him. He's probably pissed as hell about this."

"No, he'll be hurt."

Rob squeezed her shoulder. "I'll man the hotline and the computer in here while you do it. Use my office."

Bailey went into Rob's office and called Clay's cell. No answer. She called his home. Still none. She tried the town house, hoping maybe he came in tonight. Nothing.

Then things got busy on the hotline and on the network. She had a dialogue going with a new kid from Anthrax. The girl mentioned the GGs and some territory that was in dispute. Bailey was so startled when ESCAPE's front door buzzer rang she jumped in her seat.

Natale and Anderson rushed into her office. The alarms were all on, but no one visited here unless expected, especially at this hour of the morning. So this wasn't good.

"Stay here," Joe said, drawing his gun. "If anything happens, call nine-one-one."

"Oh, Lord." Bailey went to the phone, picked it up, and punched in nine-one. She held on to the receiver, waiting to hit the last number in case of an emergency. "I'm ready."

"I'm coming with you." Rob followed him out.

With the phone poised, Bailey waited. What a night. First Clay, then this.

Finally the guys returned. With Clay in tow!

"Clay, what are you doing here?"

His face was stony. "I saw *The Voice*."

"Fuck!" Natale said, holstering his gun. "What's going on, Bailey?"

"Come on, cowboy, let's leave these two alone."

"Why the hell would I do that?"

"I'll explain it to you." Rob all but dragged Joe out.

Bailey closed the door and turned to Clay. He was dressed in jeans and a dark long-sleeved thermal shirt. His hair was windblown and his face taut. "The ex-cop needs a gun here, Bailey."

"I know."

"Shit."

She waited. "You saw the article."

"Yes."

"And you're angry?"

He jammed his hands in his pockets. "When'd you give the interview?"

"Three weeks ago."

His jaw hardened, accenting the clef that she loved. "You said those things about me after we'd made love?"

"Clay, I said those things about your politics. Not about you as a man."

He shook his head. "Same thing."

"No, no it's not."

He scrubbed his hands over his face, looking exhausted.

She glanced at the clock. It was two a.m. "What made you come down tonight?"

"I had to see you." He nodded to the paper. "About this. How long is your shift?"

"Till six."

"Would you stop by the town house on your way home?"

"Yes, of course."

Just then the computer network chimed and the phone rang. He sighed. "Get that. I'll see you in a bit."

Though they were busy as hell, the rest of the night dragged. At six, Bailey hurried to Clay's town house. They made love, but it hadn't seemed to take the sting out of her public criticism of him. Bailey desperately wanted their closeness back. He was preoccupied and somber as she made coffee for them in his kitchen. To avoid talking, she guessed, he switched on a small TV in the corner for the morning news from Washington.

"Prison reform is necessary," she heard a member of the House of Representatives remark from the set. "Even our minimum security ones pose risks."

Clay's hand clenched into a fist on the table. She studied him as he listened to the broadcast. His big shoulders were encased in a dark T-shirt he'd thrown on with pj bottoms. She wore the top. Right now, his face was set in stern, uncompromising lines. How long had she been able to read those lines, read his expression so well?

Finishing with the coffee, she crossed to the set and switched it off. He arched a brow at her gesture. She folded her arms around her waist. "You want to know, don't you?"

He waited a minute to answer. "I've always wanted to know. More so, I want you to trust me with it." He cleared his throat. "Today, I need that trust even more."

Nervously, she glanced at the set. "I've never talked about it. Not even to Aidan."

"You can tell me anything."

She took in a deep breath. "I was never raped. I told my brothers that but I don't think they believed me."

He watched her.

"But I would have been, if somebody hadn't intervened. I worked in the laundry." She closed her eyes momentarily. She could smell the soap and detergent. Feel the stuffy confines of the dank room that had made her skin clammy. To banish the sensations she opened her eyes and met his gaze, drew strength from it. "I was jumped one night not long after I got there. Four women took me down to the floor, behind the dryers." She bit her lip, feeling the helplessness again that washed over her as she hit the hard concrete. "They stripped my clothes off." She rubbed her arms, chilled as she'd been then. "They . . . touched me. Everywhere. They were rough."

"Oh, Bailey."

"They had some things, you know, sexual things to use to do the rape. I started to cry, begged them to let me go." She bit her lip, tasting the coppery blood, just as she had that night. "They laughed." For a second she heard the ugly sound, couldn't speak over it.

He cleared his throat. "Finish telling me, honey."

"They were just about to do it when the door swung open."

"A guard?"

"No, three members of the other gang in prison. I didn't know it then, but somebody ran and got them when the first gang jumped me. The leader of the second had been a friend of Moira's almost ten years before. They were close. Actually, I met her once when I was with my sister, but didn't remember her."

"She did, though? Remember you?" His voice was gravelly.

"Uh-huh. She knew I was inside, but didn't want to let on about her connection with me so I wouldn't make any unnecessary enemies."

"And she stopped them."

"Yeah, there was a huge brawl; she told me to run, just as it started. I grabbed my clothes and got out of there. All of them were punished. The rival gang members were transferred. The woman who saved me got solitary and six months added on before she came up for parole."

"So she became *your* guardian angel."

"Yeah, and asked nothing in return." Bailey reached up and rubbed her eyes. "It was a nightmare, still, being in jail. But the word got out and nobody tried to make me her bride again, so to speak."

The humor fell flat. Clay just watched her. He didn't swear, didn't fly off the handle. He didn't even say how bad he felt, or that it was his fault, none of which she wanted to hear. He simply looked sad. After a few moments, he got up and crossed to her. Reaching out, he cupped her cheek. "You are a remarkable woman. I'm humbled to be your friend, your lover. You've done so much, survived so much. And I'm so, so sorry that happened to you."

She shook her head. "You could hold me now."

He did. He drew her close to his heart, kissed her hair, and just felt the grief, bitterness, and disgust along with her.

It was at that moment that Bailey realized she was in love with Clayton Wainwright.

"MOMMY, LOOK! THERE he is." Rory's voice was pitched high with excitement. "See Mommy, number two."

"I see, sweetie." Through sunglasses and beneath a baseball cap, Bailey watched the New York Yankees, who were two games away from the World Series, take the field. "He looks big."

"As big as Clay. Six-three, 195 lbs, right, Clay?"

Wearing a matching cap and glasses, jeans and Jeter T-shirt, Clay nodded from the other side of Rory. Like her, he was unrecognizable.

"Read me more," Rory said, cuddling up to Clay.

As Clay enumerated the stats on Derek Jeter from a special program, Bailey pretended to watch the team warm up and thought about how she'd gotten here.

Rory had been so excited when Clay had produced the tickets yesterday, Bailey was afraid he'd never sleep. Only an admonishment from Clay and threats from her made him settle down. She came out into the living room where he was watching the recap of that day's game and sat down next to him.

He took her hand immediately. "I want you to go with us. I know you'll object, but I want you to see the playoffs with Rory, Aidan, and me."

"So do I."

"Then come."

"We'll be right out in the open."

"Not really. I know how to blend in so I'm not noticed. I'll wear sunglasses, a baseball cap, and jeans. Nobody will recognize me, therefore they won't be interested in who you are."

She hesitated.

"I want you with me, sweetheart. All the time, I might add. I won't apologize for wishing you'd come along with your son and me to a game he'll love."

With no more fuss, Bailey had decided maybe a disguise could work. . . .

"And his best friend's name is Alex Rodriguez."

"He plays for New York now," Aidan commented.

"Yep."

"A-Rod. Holy cow." Rory's eyes rounded like an owl's. "My best friend's name is Alex."

Clay ruffled Rory's hair. "You got a lot in common, champ."

They all enjoyed the game. Partway through, Rory climbed on Clay's lap. Aidan leaned around him and gave her a *You're dead meat* look. Sighing, she realized she was in way over her head.

But it was when the game was over, she realized she was about to drown. "Ready, champ?" Clay asked standing.

"For what?"

"To go to the locker room. I got special permission to bring one friend to meet DJ."

Rory threw his arms around Clay's leg. "Golly, Clay, I can't believe it."

Clay turned to her and Aidan. "Sorry, guys. Only two people can go."

"How did you arrange this?"

"Need you ask?" He winked at her. "Meet you two in the car."

CLAY WAS AT work late the following Tuesday and went on-line. He saw on his buddy list that she was up and running. *Hey, IrishCream, how are you?*

Hanging in there. Rory's still flying about the game.

Me, too, he teased. *I'm glad they won.*

That's not what I mean. He's sleeping with the ball Jeter gave him. He's in seventh heaven.

When he's old enough, I'll have to set the boy straight on what's really seventh heaven in bed.

A long pause. She'd ignore this, he knew. She always did when he brought up the future. And it was wearing on him. Every day he wanted more of her.

You can't ignore the future, honey.

We're not sure there is a future.

I'm sure! I wish you were.

Are we going to fight now?

Maybe.

I don't want to fight with you online. Only in person, where we can make up in bed.

Which happened all the time and was beginning to worry Clay. Sex was great, but he wanted all of her, not just her body. Turning away from the computer, he caught sight of a memo from Chuck Stewart to the party chair. He'd copied Clay in on the missive declaring he did not want to be considered as a candidate for VP. In it, he also suggested Clay be the front-runner.

Clay, are you still on?

Yes. He searched for a neutral ground. *How's Patrick?*

Sad. He misses Brie and the kids. Separation is hard. He has them for my birthday party, but Brie won't be with them.

Hell, he didn't even know when her birthday was. *Your birthday party?*

Yeah.

And I'm not invited, right?

Clay, you can't come to that. The party's at the pub and everybody who's important in my life will be there.

Well, that puts me in my place.

I didn't mean it that way.

I know. I'm sorry, this is hard for me.

I'm sorry, too. Can't we just avoid conversations like this for now?

I suppose we should. He fingered the memo from Stewart. If they did talk about the future, he'd have to tell her about *this* and she sure as hell wasn't ready to handle that.

I wish I could see you now.

I'll be in town for the task force meeting in a few days.

Where he'd vote against her on allocation of funds. *I know. Can you come in a day early?*

Why?

We could celebrate my birthday privately. And because I miss you. She paused. *I think it would be a good idea to be together, be close, the night before the vote.*

All right, see you then.

After he disconnected, he stared into space, thinking about the vote—where he'd block her funds for Guardian. And about the memo regarding the vice presidency. Clay stood and crossed to the window. The odds seemed impossible tonight as he stared out at the street, quiet at midnight. How could they ever mesh their lives?

But what was the alternative? Never see her again? A montage of pictures flashed through his mind: her with her baseball cap and glasses on; her face distraught as she told him things she never told anyone else; her asleep, next to him.

No way in hell was he going to accept that they didn't have a future together. He'd find a way to keep her in his life—and pursue his career.

FIFTEEN

"YOU THINK YOU so tough," the Anthrax gang chick spat out to Taz. "Let's see what you can do with the rag." She whipped out a purple bandana.

The alley was dark, and Taz, Mazie, and Quinn had been strolling down it, minding their own business, when three members of Anthrax had leapt out of a doorway. They were all flying their colors, so they weren't peace-n, but they weren't looking for trouble, either. After dissing each other, there'd been the challenge.

Mazie reached into her pants and drew out the *fila* she always carried at her waist, like a cell phone. "Here you go, Tazzie." She tossed the knife to Taz. "You go, girl."

No way out of this one, Taz thought as she caught the knife. The cold steel felt foreign in her hand. She dropped the gin she'd been drinking straight out of the bottle and unzipped her jacket. Her heart thudded in her chest, but if she ignored Mazie's command, she was in deep shit. This time, she had to get down.

She fingered the blade, while the other *chola* got herself

ready. In minutes they were bent at the waist, each with one hand behind her back, the opposite tips of the rectangular bandana in their mouths. Taz was so close, she could see the red eyes and smell the sweat of the other banger.

The cunt took the first pass, missing Taz. Taz struck back before the girl could snatch her hand away and drew blood.

"Son of a fucking bitch."

Taz's homics cheered.

Circling to the left, Taz planned her next move; the girl, whose name was Annie-O, went to the right. Taz stopped quick and got a nick in her leg. The rule was three hits and you won. Nobody was supposed to buy it. This was a just a ritual they played out when they happened upon each other.

The third time Taz lunged for the girl's arm, a siren in the background distracted her, and Annie-O bent low and sliced her leg through her cargo pants.

Taz went down, the sirens got closer, and everybody else boned out.

CLAY LAY NEXT to her, breathing hard. He'd gotten in late and had missed seeing Rory; he and Bailey had headed for the bedroom practically as soon as he got his suit coat off. Both knew that tomorrow, when the Task Force would make its decision, was going to be tough. But she fully believed they could weather it. They'd gotten too close, shared too much, to let this old argument separate them.

Her cell phone rang from the bedside table. In the early morning stillness, it was shrill and startling.

"What the hell?" Clay frowned. "Who'd be calling now?"

Bailey bolted up. "It's either ESCAPE or something's happened in my family." She grabbed the phone. "Bailey O'Neil."

"Bay, it's Suze. We just got a call on the hotline. Taz has been hurt."

"Hurt? How?"

"A knife fight."

"Where is she?"

"It happened on Houston and Allen. The paramedics are taking her to a clinic. She called us on her cell."

"Okay." She caught sight of Clay's worried face. "It's the hotline," she told him. The concern only deepened.

"Joe and Rob are on their way to the Baden Street clinic."

"I'm going, too."

"I wouldn't have called but she's asked specifically for you. I had to promise I'd get in touch with you before she'd tell me what happened." Those kinds of promises had to be kept or ESCAPE would lose its reputation.

"It's fine. I want to know."

"Keep me posted."

Bailey clicked off. "I've got to go."

Clay scowled. "Go? Where?"

"There's been an incident." She threw off the covers and slid out of bed. Crossing to the dresser, she dragged out some clothes. As she stuffed her legs in underwear and jeans, she said, "It's Taz. She's been hurt. She called the hotline on her cell."

Clay sank onto the bed, scowling now. "You're kidding, right? You're not really going out in the middle of the night to rescue a gang kid."

"Of course I am." She slipped into a bra and sweatshirt.

"You told me you wouldn't see any gang kids alone, Bailey." His tone was curt.

"I won't be alone. Rob and Joe are on their way."

"That makes it all right?"

"Yes, it's almost like a Face-to-Face, which I said I'd be doing."

"Those are under strict security conditions—or so you told me."

"Clay, she's hurt. I don't know how badly." She found loafers and slipped into them.

"Hurt?"

"A knife fight."

"Oh, this is just great."

"Don't start—"

After a moment, he said, "Let the paramedics handle this!"

Raising her chin, she leveled an angry glare on him. His shift back into a righteous autocrat was difficult to handle right now. "No, I have to be there."

He rose, strode to her, and spun her around. "This is un-safe! you shouldn't go."

"Look, I don't have time to walk you through this."

He stiffened. "Oh, well, sorry for my concern." His amber eyes flared with hot temper. "Do you have time to make arrangements for your son? Or do you usually leave him alone when you go play Charlie's Angels in the middle of the night?"

"I never leave him alone!" She felt her own temper spike. "I'll call Aidan if you won't stay."

He stared at her. She could tell he was visibly reining him-self in. Finally he said. "I'll stay with Rory."

Standing on tiptoes, she gave him a hug, hating this dis-tance after they'd been so close earlier. "Thanks. I'll call you. And don't worry, I'll be safe."

"Yeah, sure, I won't worry."

CLAY SAT IN the last Youth Gang Task Force meeting waiting for Bailey to arrive. He had no idea what was going to hap-pen—either here or with his *life*, and he was edgy.

What he *did* know was that she'd not made it back to the apartment before Rory went to preschool. She'd called and said she was still tied up at the clinic; she was waiting with Taz to talk to the police, then she was going to find a shelter for the girl to stay in for the time being. She'd arranged for Aidan to come over to get Rory off to school. It had been awk-ward at first when her brother arrived. . . .

"Aidan."

"Hey, Clay." Bailey's brother glanced at Rory. "Go brush your teeth and hair, kid. I'm takin' you to school."

"Where's Mommy?" Rory had been cranky since he awak-ened and found his mother gone.

Clay had only told him she needed to go out.

Aidan squeezed his nephew's shoulder. His warm expres-sion reminded Clay of Bailey. "You know she gets called out at night sometimes, honey."

"Don't like it," Rory had declared before he marched off to the bathroom.

"Neither do I," Aidan had mumbled, looking after the boy.

"Then why the hell do you allow this?"

Pivoting around, he'd faced Clay. "Because she's my sister and she makes her own choices."

Clay paced the kitchen, ready to take a bite out of someone's ass. Aidan was the closest target. "I don't believe you condone her endangering herself like this."

Her brother raked a hand through his hair. "It doesn't matter what I think. When you love somebody, you let her make her own decisions and then you're there for her when she does."

That had sobered him some. After Aidan poured coffee, he turned and leaned against the counter. "Where's all this going with you two, Clay? You're here again. You obviously care about her."

"I do."

Aidan studied him. "You in for the long haul?"

Clay waited before he answered. "I thought I was. But this . . ." He gestured to the whole apartment "I'm not sure I could live like this—calls in the middle of the night, the jeopardy she puts herself in . . ."

Aidan's gaze was shrewd. "Then again, if Bailey hooks up with you, she wouldn't be living like this either. If she was in the political eye, her whole life would have to change."

Which would be a good thing, he remembered thinking, but Rory returned ready for school so he didn't say it aloud; the O'Neils left him alone with his angry thoughts.

Bailey appeared in the doorway to his office. She'd changed into a plain pair of black slacks and pink blouse and her hair was pulled off her face, which was lined with exhaustion. Of course, she'd been up all night, and probably spent all day—her day off—dealing with the gang girl. Just how she wore herself down for these kids was enough to set Clay off, let alone the danger she knowingly courted.

She searched the room; when her gaze landed on him, she gave him a weak smile. He nodded, and she took the empty seat at the end of the table.

Governor Friedman began the meeting. Soon, they hit the crux of it. "Our committee needs to make a recommendation for the money allocated to New York from the Youth Crime

Bill. I'd like everybody to put in their two cents, then we'll vote on the propositions." He turned to Bailey. "You go first, Ms. O'Neil."

She picked up her notepad. "I'd like the money to be divided according to size and the number of kids they service among the existing social agencies in New York that deal with gang prevention." She hesitated. "With the exception of three hundred thousand to go to setting up Guardian House. This would be a prototype for other shelters, therefore, in the long run, it would benefit all the agencies."

Clay stepped up to the plate. "You'll need more than that to open a shelter."

"I've got other money."

"From where?"

"All right, you two," Governor Friedman said. "Discussion comes after brainstorming."

Several people had recommendations. Lawson suggested a clinic just for gang kids, which never would fly. Finally, it was Clay's turn. "It's no secret I object to the singling out of shelters or clinics for youths involved in juvenile crime. I do however, concur with Ms. O'Neil's initial proposal. The agencies we have are good, solid ones. The money from Stewart's bill should go to them." He looked pointedly at Bailey. "All of it. I'll even concede to letting ESCAPE have some of our funds. But I'll never agree to let her build Guardian."

The debate took an hour.

Then came the vote.

Wisely, the governor had put eleven people on the committee. However, one of the member's child had taken ill and she'd been unable to finish out her stint. And so the vote ended up in a tie.

"Stewart's committee will have to decide about the money for Guardian," Jerry said. "The rest we seem to agree on."

"Fine." Bailey stood. "I'm still going to Washington, right? When the senator presents our findings?"

"Absolutely." Jerry Friedman smiled. "You've got one more chance for your baby."

The meeting broke up. Clay didn't try to catch her; instead he talked with Friedman about what a good job he'd done leading a difficult group, then headed out of the Public Safety Building. Though he felt good about most of what happened in the committee, he was still mad as hell about last night.

"Clay?"

He turned and found Bailey out front, standing in the shadows.

"What's your schedule now?" she asked.

Checking his watch, he said, "I'm going back to my town house for a while. Then I'm catching the train to D.C. tomorrow."

"Can I come home with you?"

"I don't know if that's a good idea, Bailey. I'm really angry with you about last night."

She nodded to the building. "You're not exactly on my top ten list either right now."

He shook his head, walked to the curb and hailed a cab. When it pulled up, he opened the door.

And turned to her. He nodded to the taxi. Wordlessly, she crossed to the vehicle and got inside.

HE SLAMMED HER against the wall once they were in the foyer of the town house. Which was fine with her. She needed some outlet for what she was feeling. Squelching the inner voice that said she needed *him,* she gripped his shoulders, matching his passion. What was between them now was desire mixed with anger, and they both knew it.

He ravaged her mouth. She bit his lip, his jaw, his shoulder once she got his jacket and shirt off.

He ripped at her clothes, and vaguely she wondered what she was going to wear home.

Grunts. Groans. An "Oh, shit, help me with this." Another, "Fuck, I can't get it off."

Naked, needy, and almost desperate, he hiked her up. She wrapped her legs around him and he plunged inside her.

"Bailey, oh, God, I . . ."

"Clay . . . Clay . . ."

They came in seconds. Together. Mindlessly.

Afterward, Clay held on to her. When he could finally move,

he stumbled to the couch, sat down with her still wrapped around him, and sighed. Once reality dawned, she could feel the separation coming. His body spoke it like a second language.

And so she moved in closer and anchored her arms around his neck. "Please don't pull away."

"This didn't solve anything."

"I know." Still she held on to him.

After a moment, he set her back. He didn't look as tense now, but his face was grim. "I'm mad as hell about what you did last night."

"And I'm mad about how you're handling last night. It's old ground." She shook her head. "Not to mention that you voted against me just now. I want that money, Clay."

"I didn't vote against you. I voted against your idea. If you recall, that's exactly what you told me about the interview you gave to *The Voice*." He sucked in a deep breath. "We knew this would happen."

"We can handle it, Clay."

He waited a minute, then said, "I want to."

She hugged him tight then. "Thank God."

He hugged her back and snorted. "I think you got that wrong, babe. I'm beginning to think the devil's got his hand in this whole thing."

She chuckled. "Then let's give the devil a run for his money."

BAILEY WAS DRESSING to go pick up Rory, and Clay had slid into his trousers but was bare-chested; he lounged on the couch watching the six o'clock news. She felt better now that they'd talked; she believed in him, in herself, in their relationship and vowed they were going to make a go of it somehow.

The drone of the TV became louder; as she slipped into her shoes, she saw Chuck Stewart was being interviewed on the show out of Washington that Clay liked to watch. "No, I don't regret my decision not to be considered for the vice presidency next summer."

Bailey stilled. "Stewart's not going for VP next time around?"

"Ah, no."

She turned back to the set.

"So, this paves the way for others," the announcer said. "Who's the front-runner?"

Stewart smiled. "I think that's obvious. Clay Wainwright's the party's best choice."

Her world shifted. For a moment, she couldn't speak. Then she whirled around to face him. "Well, so much for honesty. When were you going to tell me about this?"

There was an assertiveness about his expression, almost an arrogance. "You really want honesty?"

"I said I did."

"I was waiting to tell you about this potentiality—and that's all it is—until you'd fallen in love with me and wouldn't leave me over it."

Tears clouded her eyes. She couldn't believe this. "Well, Senator, that's exactly what you've done."

He looked startled. Pivoting fast, she headed for the foyer; he caught up with her just as she opened the door. Slamming it shut with a flat hand, he barked, "Hold on."

"No, I've got to get out of here."

"Like hell. If you think you can say something like that and leave, you're crazy."

She leaned her head on the wood. "I am crazy."

"Bailey?" His tone turned tender. He tried to pull her around, but she resisted. He tugged hard until she finally faced him. "Oh, God. I've never seen you cry."

Her throat clogged, she shook her head.

"Bailey." Gently he grasped her cheeks in his hands. "Sweetheart, did you say what I think you said?"

She cried harder. He drew her to his chest. "Do you love me, Bailey?"

Only able to nod, she held on to his shirt.

"Oh, baby. That's wonderful."

"It's awful."

He drew back. "No, no it's not. I've been in love with you for weeks and have been afraid to tell you."

"You have?"

"Yes."

She swiped at her tears and glanced at the TV. "But if you're going to be the vice presidential candidate, there's no way I can fit into your life now."

BAILEY SAT ACROSS from him in his dining room, playing with the shrimp takeout he'd ordered for her. He'd devoured his chicken teriyaki. She was conflicted; he could tell by the shadows that chased through those gorgeous blue eyes. Clay, however, couldn't be more elated. She loved him and that changed everything.

"You're not going to avoid talking about this by pushing your food around your plate, you know."

"I know." She shook her head. "It would help if you were a little less chipper."

Lazing back in his chair, he grinned. He felt better than he could ever remember feeling, except maybe when Jon was born. "Why shouldn't I be? The woman I love tells me she returns my feelings for her, and I'm supposed to be depressed about it?"

She just stared at him.

"I'm sorry you're sad, sweetheart. But don't ask me to regret that this has happened." He leaned over and grasped her hand. "I love you, Bailey. More than I've let myself admit until you said the words."

"I love you, too," she whispered achingly. Biting her lip, she rubbed her eyes. "I'm sorry. I'm all messed up about this."

"Would it help to talk about the obstacles?"

"No. We've run that train into the ground."

"Except for this new wrinkle—the vice presidency." He watched her. "You're angry I kept this from you."

"Yes, of course. But we've got bigger fish to fry."

He straightened. "Bailey, it's not a fait accompli. Even if the party wants me, I don't have to say yes."

She stared hard at him. "But you want it, don't you?"

"I've always wanted it. And more, maybe. But first off, the appointment is several months away. And second, I don't even know if the presidential candidate—whoever that's going to be—will choose me."

"What are you saying, Clay? That we go along, keep falling more and more in love, then you *do* go for the VP slot. Where does that leave me?"

"At my side, maybe."

"Publicly."

"Yes." He watched her. "I know what that means."

"That I'd have to give up my work at ESCAPE, or anything else like it."

"There are a lot of things you could do for at-risk kids, especially as the VP's wife."

"Oh, my God, don't make that jump, Clay."

He didn't like her shock, or the revulsion underneath it. "People in love have been known to consider marriage."

"People like us don't fall in love." She looked so afraid and vulnerable it softened him.

"Talk to me, Bailey. Tell me why the idea of marriage frightens you so much."

"For one thing, it's too soon. I haven't accepted my feelings for you and you're talking about making this permanent." She sighed. "Second, you're logic's off; I couldn't do better things for kids as the vice president's wife if the vice president himself disagrees with everything I believe in."

He was silent. She was wrong; there were a zillion things she could do in Washington.

She got up then, and crossed to the window.

"What are you thinking?"

She shook her head.

"Tell me, honey. It's time to put all the cards on the table."

"It's selfish."

"I don't care."

"Why would I be making all the sacrifices, Clay?"

He stretched out his legs and crossed his arms over his chest. "You shouldn't. I said I don't have to go for the vice presidency unless it works for us."

"You'd give it up for me?"

"I want this relationship, Bailey. I think I've known that since I showed up at your family's pub that night. I'll do almost anything for it to work."

She just watched him.

"Look, I—" His cell phone rang. He checked the caller ID. "It's Karen's number."

"Your ex-wife?"

"Uh-huh." He answered it. "Hello."

"Clay, it's Karen."

"What's up?"

"Jon's been hurt in some kind of an accident. You have to get to Kingston right away." Kingston was the closet hospital to Bard College.

"Is he all right?"

"I think so. He has a broken arm. No internal injuries. But he's got some scrapes and bruises, maybe a concussion and he's in a lot of pain. The school called me as his emergency contact. One of his parents should be there."

"Where are you?"

"In the Bahamas. On a ship. Where are you?"

"At my town house in New York."

"Do you want me to come back?"

"No. I'm on my way. I can handle this." He clicked off and stood. "Jon's been in an accident at college. I have to get up there."

"Oh, Clay. Is he all right?"

"Karen says so. A broken arm. But . . ." He shook off the thought. "Look, I have to leave. I think I can get a train to Kingston now."

She looked at her watch. "Then let's go. I'll call on the way to Penn Station and see if Liam can keep Rory for a while."

"You're coming with me?"

"Of course."

"What about keeping our relationship private?"

"You're not making the trip alone when your son's hurt. We'll deal with anything that happens about me coming along with you later."

"THERE'S NO REAL damage to my face, right Dad?" Though he was confused and angry—somebody was lying to him—Jon was more afraid now that he'd maimed and scarred himself in his rebellious outburst, than concerned about his parents' being up-front with him.

His father's scowl lightened. He'd never seen the man so worried. "The doc said you're going to be as handsome as ever."

Jon hadn't looked in a mirror, but he could feel his face swelling. "You sure?" Hell, he sounded like a little boy, but he needed his dad's reassurance.

"I think it looks worse than it is." His dad studied him as they waited for the resident who casted his arm to come in. "What happened, son?"

Glancing away, Jon swallowed hard. "I had too much to drink. We were at a party on campus, one of those blow-out things in the old gym, and I had a few too many beers. I fell off a human pyramid we were building."

"Hell." The scowl deepened again, the lines in his dad's face were groovelike. "I didn't know you drank, Jon."

"I don't normally. Not much, anyway. I was upset."

"Why?"

"I had a huge fight with Mom. Then she flew off to the Bahamas without a care in the world while we were still pissed off at each other."

"What did you fight about?"

"You."

His dad folded his arms across his chest. "Does this have anything to do with our email exchange?"

"Yeah."

"I knew we should have talked this out."

"I confronted Mom."

"And?"

"She said you were having an affair, no matter what your story was. She said *she* found somebody after that."

"Oh, Jon, I don't know what to say. That's just not true."

"I figured she might be lying 'cause she got so pissed at me for asking about it." He shook his head. "That's what she always does when she's wrong."

"She used to do the same thing to me. It drove me nuts." His father stretched out his legs. He was dressed in suit pants and a shirt. At least he was beginning to relax. "Does it even matter, now, what your mother did? People make mistakes. Karen and I were having a lot of problems for a year before we divorced."

Jon closed his eyes. He didn't know what to think. And he was tired. "I guess it doesn't really matter."

"Look, let's table this. You don't need all that on your mind now. I think you should come to the town house and stay with me for a few days. I'll arrange for a car to take us there."

He liked having his dad make this decision. "Shouldn't I go back to school?"

From the doorway, a doctor said, "In a few days. Now, you should be with somebody because of that concussion. Go home with your father."

"Okay, sure."

After the doctor gave instructions to Jon, his dad stood. "I'll be right back. I'm going to talk to somebody out there about a car."

As his father headed out, Jon called after him. "Thanks, Dad."

Clay turned at the doorway. "For what?"

"For coming here, helping, not being pissed."

"I'm pissed about your underage drinking. But for the other, you can count on me, Jon. I wish you'd believe that."

"I hear ya, Dad."

BAILEY SAW HIM come toward her from where she sat in the waiting room of Kingston Hospital. His clothes were wrinkled, his hair a mess; he looked tired and unhappy but not worried. She stood and gave him a hug. He hung on. "Jon's all right," he said when he pulled back.

"Thank God. Do you know what happened?"

"He was drinking. They made a human pyramid when they were hammered. What the hell's the matter with him?"

"College kids aren't known for their common sense."

"He had a fight with Karen." Clay told her the details. "Then she casually flew to the Bahamas without thinking what the lack of resolution might do to Jon."

"Well, like I said before, she has to be an idiot for cheating on you."

He reached out and swiped his fingers over her lips. "Thanks. Listen, I'm taking Jon back to my town house. He needs rest. I'm going to call for a car." He watched her. "You'll have to catch the train back by yourself."

Bailey knew he didn't want that.

Tucking a strand of hair behind her ear, he shook his head. "I hate sending you off alone."

"I've taken thousands of trains alone, Clay."

He nodded to the hospital rooms. "We have to think about telling him."

"We'll do it. But tonight wouldn't be good. He's already upset."

Leaning over, Clay kissed her nose, then reached out his hand and took hers. "Come on, I'll get you in a cab to the station."

They turned then, and found Jon standing before them. "Well, so much for honesty, Dad. Geez, you and Mom are a pair."

➤ SIXTEEN

"WHAT ARE WE doing, Mommy?"

"We're soothing troubled waters." Standing on the stoop of Clay's town house, Bailey held Rory's hand and clasped the dessert she'd made in the other. Clay said Jon liked sweets so she'd made him a chocolate ice cream roll. As far as peace offerings went, it sufficed.

Rory jumped from one foot to the other. Dressed in jeans and sneakers, he insisted on wearing his Jeter shirt under his jacket. "We're gonna meet Clay's son, right?

"Right."

"How come we never met him before?"

The sixty-four thousand dollar question. "Well, you will now."

Thankfully the door opened. Clay stood there in a forest green sweat suit, his color high. He must have gone running. "Hey, hi, guys." Bending down he picked up Rory. "Ready to meet Jon?"

Quietly, she asked, "Is Jon ready to meet him?"

"I think so. He's been surly, and out of sorts, but part of that is because he's in pain."

They entered the living room.

"He hasn't said much since the ride home."

Bailey nodded. "He didn't say much then, either."

"He won't talk about it. Just vegges in front of the TV. So I thought we'd take the bull by the horns." He ruffled Rory's hair. "I figure this little guy can charm anybody out of their funk."

"Oooo, that's a bad word. Mommy uses it sometimes."

"Not funk, buddy. Something else is a bad word." He smiled at Bailey over Rory's head. "Being in a funk means you're sad."

They took the stairs up and found Jon, fully dressed, on his bed, watching the pregame show for the first leg of the World Series. "Hey, Jon, I have someone for you to meet."

Jon looked up, his expression souring even more when he saw Bailey. "I already met the Street Angel."

"This is Bailey's son, Rory."

Jon inspected Rory as if he were a bug that had just crawled into his bedroom. "Yeah, hi."

Rory hugged Clay's leg. "Hi."

Jon's eyes narrowed on the movement. "He knows about you two?"

"Yes."

"How long?"

"What?"

"How long has the kid known?"

"Awhile."

"Can I watch the game with you?" Rory asked, glancing at the TV.

Ignoring the boy, Jon asked Clay, "Why're they here?"

Clay said, "Jon, don't be—"

Bailey stepped forward. "We wanted you to meet my son. And I wanted to talk to you. Clay, would you take Rory downstairs for a bit? Jon and I need to get acquainted. Alone."

Protectively, he put his hand on her shoulder. "You think that's a good idea?"

Jon jutted out his chin. "I do." The challenge was evident.

When the guys left, Bailey sat down on a chair near the bed. She knew she needed to be direct. "The secrecy about my relationship with your father was my doing, Jon. I should have cleared that up right away."

"The night of my grandfather's party, Dad lied to me outright when I asked if there was another woman besides Jane. If he lied about that, how do I know he's not lying about everything else?"

"You mean what your mother told you?"

"Crap, he shared that with you about why they broke up?"

"Uh-huh. He's not lying, Jon."

"Sure."

She scowled. "Did you hear what I said? Your father wanted to go public with our relationship right away. I insisted on keeping it quiet."

"Why?"

"For obvious reasons." None of which she'd worked out in her mind, so it was hard talking to his kid about it. "I don't fit in your dad's world."

Shaking his head, Jon leaned back against the pillow. "I get it. This is just some sleazy affair between you two."

"I'll let that pass because you're upset. And because all this is new to you. I'll even address it. This isn't some sleazy affair. But it's more complicated than you know. So I'd appreciate if you didn't make things more difficult for your father than they are."

"Why the hell are you together anyway?"

Bailey laughed. "I wish I knew. It just happened."

"You still gonna keep it a secret?"

"I don't know what we're going to do. We weren't planning to tell you yet."

"Oh, that makes me feel better."

"A lot's at stake here, Jon."

"I'm his son! I should have known. He said he'd be honest with me and he wasn't."

"At my insistence. Cut him some slack; this is an unusual situation. We both have a lot to lose."

"What?"

She explained her side, about the publicity, then tackled her background, and what that would mean to Clay's reputation.

Her honesty seemed to soften him. "I get it, for you, anyway. Still . . ."

"You're his son and you feel left out. That's okay—you have a right to those feelings. As a matter of fact, if I were you I'd be royally pissed. You've told him all that, now put it behind you and go from here."

She could tell from the look on Jon's face that was exactly what he wanted to do.

Jon cocked his head. "You're good with kids, your know that."

"I hope so. It's my job."

"That's why you run that place."

"Yeah."

"What are you and my dad gonna do about your job, your differences?"

"I have no idea. For now, we're coasting. We'd like you to keep this quiet, not tell anybody, either."

"Your kid can do that? He's little."

"We told him it was a game. One of my brothers knows."

Wearily, he laid back into the pillows. "I wish I had a brother."

She stood. "I think this is enough for now."

"You can go get Rory. He can watch TV with me."

"Why don't you come downstairs and we'll watch the game all together."

"You like baseball?"

She gave him a withering look. "You're kidding, right?"

Jon smiled. It was so reminiscent of Clay's it made her reach out and squeeze his arm. "I made you an ice cream cake."

"You did? Why?"

"As a peace offering. Since I was responsible for this latest rift with you and your dad."

"Okay. I guess I can come downstairs." He slid off the bed. She stretched out her hand and they shook.

She held on to him. "He loves you so much, Jon. He wants your relationship to flourish. Work with him, would you?"

"You're crazy about him, aren't you?"

"Yes," she said simply. "I am."

CHUCK STEWART SAT at the round table and smiled at his committee. He seemed rested, less care-worn, since his announcement not to be considered for VP. "Are the states all ready to give their reports?"

His administrative assistant nodded. "Yes. We need to set up a schedule, then let the states know their time slots ASAP, if we're going to have a decision by Thanksgiving."

"It's the agenda for today." They talked some about time frames when the committee members could meet.

When it was his turn, Clay cleared his throat. "I have a problem." Which was a huge understatement. Mostly, Bailey was a *crisis* in his life, though she'd worked miracles with Jon.

"Go ahead."

"My committee wants dual representation."

Jane's father, Tom, spoke up. "Why the hell is that? We're all on those task forces. Each senator is reporting."

"Well, our committee was divided. Half of them want the Street Angel to come to our meeting." He rolled his eyes. "Apparently they don't believe I'll give an unbiased report."

"What?" Carol Jenkins quipped dryly. "People don't trust politicians?"

Everybody laughed. Clay opened his Palm Pilot. "Here's some dates she can come to town. I'd like to accommodate her on this, rather than antagonize her off at the outset, if any of these times are available. The first one is the best for her. It's next week, though."

Bailey's choice of a time was a go. Clay had meant what he said about setting the tone, but there was another reason why he wanted the first date—because Bailey could get free and spend the weekend before with him in D.C. Apparently Rory was doing a camping thing with Liam's scout troop. It felt like stolen time.

Dates were set for the other states. When the meeting broke up, Tom Carter approached him. "Clayton, would you have a drink with me?"

He hedged. "I'm not sure I'm free."

"You are. I checked with Bob. I'd like to talk to you."

Irked at the older man's presumptuousness, Clay remembered Bailey's comment, *How do you live like that?* Some aspects of his life in Washington he really did resent.

Nevertheless Clay accompanied Tom to Barlow's, a small club on C Street where senators often socialized. It was quiet and catered mostly to people on the Hill.

When they reached Barlow's, Clay was shocked to find his father sitting at a table waiting for them. Tall, fit and as imposing as ever, Clayton Sr. was unsmiling.

"What's going on?" he asked Tom when they reached the elder Clayton.

"Sit down, Clay," his dad said.

They did. The buzz of low conversation filled the silence until they ordered drinks. Then Tom dove right in. "I asked your father to come for a drink when I found out he was in town. We both want to talk about your erratic behavior of late."

"What behavior is that?"

Clayton Sr. sat back and steepled his hands. It was a gesture Clay knew well. "For one thing, this temporary separation from Jane."

He arched his brows. "I didn't break it off temporarily."

"Did she?" Clayton Sr. asked Tom.

"Of course not. She was expecting a ring after your party."

Clay sipped his scotch, wishing he'd ordered a double, "I meant that I broke it off permanently."

"Jane doesn't know that." This from a clearly disgruntled Tom Carter.

He faced Jane's father squarely. "Jane doesn't want to know that. I told her point-blank our relationship was over. I'm sorry, Tom, but that's the way it is."

Clayton Sr. spoke up. "Jane's a perfect wife for the vice president of the United States."

He studied the staid man before him. "Aren't we jumping the gun here?"

"No. Before a choice is made, you should be married."

Clay shook his head. "I *should* marry someone I love."

Obviously uncomfortable with the situation, Tom stood. "I'm going over there to speak to Jackson Jones for a minute." He nodded to another table. "Talk some sense into him, Clay."

When Tom walked away, his father shook his head. The stern, disapproving look on his face was all too familiar. "What's this about?"

"I'm not in love with Jane, Dad."

"I'm sorry to hear that." He sipped his drink. "But it's not uncommon to marry somebody you don't love."

"I know, I already did it once. To please you and Mother, I think."

"Really? I had no idea."

Of course you wouldn't. Clay was hit with a blast of resentment so hard it made him speechless. But it also made him strengthen his resolve to keep working on his relationship with Jon.

"Clayton, what is it?"

"I was thinking about my relationship with Jon."

"Now that's another thing. We can't have the son of a VP carousing so hard he has a hospital stay."

How do you stand it?

"I talked with Jon about that. Actually, I'm more concerned with improving my relationship with him."

"What's wrong with your relationship?"

"It's started to become like ours, Dad."

Pure surprise showed on his father's face. "What does that mean?"

"It means that you and I don't communicate. It means you have no idea how I feel."

"I know your politics inside out."

"I meant my personal feelings."

Clayton Sr. drew in a breath. "I'm not good at those things."

"At knowing me personally?"

"Social things like that."

Oh, God, this is where Clay came from. He thought of Rory and Bailey, her parents, her brothers. Though they fought boisterously, they loved and supported each other. "A relationship among family is not a social thing, Dad."

"I don't understand."

"No, you don't."

"Look, could we leave my *shortcomings* for another time and talk about getting your relationship with Jane back on track?"

Clay stared at his father, then stood. He threw some money on the table, which he knew would irk Clayton Sr. "No, we can't talk about that. Because anything with Jane and me just isn't going to happen."

As he started away, his father called him back in his trademark peremptory command. "Clayton, what the hell's gotten in to you?"

He pivoted to face the man he'd, in some ways, always feared. Again, he made resolutions about his own son. "Some clear-headedness, I think. Finally." With that he walked away.

HEY, SISTER. HOW ya hangin'?

Bailey did a double take at the computer where somebody had just signed on the network. The screen name was TazDevil2. How could Taz be online? She was at a shelter.

Taz, sweetie, is that you?

You got that right.

But something didn't *feel* right. *How do you have access to a computer? Yours is home at your father's. You didn't go back there, did you?*

No way, lady. I ain't never goin' back. Me usin' one of my sisters' machines.

Are you at the crib? Why aren't you at . . .

Suddenly all Bailey's street instincts went on alert.

Who is this?

The Tasmanian devil.

You aren't Taz. How did you get her computer? Oh, God, was it her father, trying to find out where she was? *Are you her father?*

That piece of shit? No way.

Ah, she got it. *Are you in her set?*

Give the lady a cigar.

Can I help you?

We wanna know where our girl is. We wanna see her.
What makes you think I know?
You stashed her, lady.

Hmm. What if they were just worried about Taz? What if she could help these kids, too? Unsure, and pressed to decide, her stomach clenched. Without signing off, she got up and poured coffee.

True, Taz was tight with her home girls. Gang kids *cared* about each other. On the other hand, they left her alone, bleeding in the alley, probably when they heard sirens, which weren't even headed their way. Maybe they went to her house to find her and got ahold of Taz's computer. They could know she was in contact with ESCAPE, whose mission was to get kids out of gangs. Were these girls trying to find her because she betrayed them? Why hadn't Bailey thought of that earlier, when the screen name came on? She could kick herself. How much information had she given away?

She went back to the computer. Tried hard to think of something to say that would imply Taz wasn't one of hers. Before she could, another message came on. *You know what's good for you, bitch, you stay away from our girl!* Then the screen blinked, TazDevil2 has signed off.

Her heart pounding, Bailey pushed back her chair and made her way down the hall to Joe's office. "We got a problem, Joe."

"What else is new?" He turned from his computer; though his tone was gruff, his look was always tender when directed at her. "What?"

"I've got to go to the shelter and see Taz. I want you to come with me. Rob can hold down the fort."

He stood immediately. "Least you asked me to go with you," he grumbled. "Let's book."

TAZ CHILLED OUT on her bed at the shelter. Her wounds from bumping titties with Anthrax were healing and soon she'd bone out of here. At least these digs were safer than the last one. Nobody dissed her; nobody even paid much attention to her. She slouched down on the pillows and picked up a stuffed animal. Somebody had given the cute giraffe to her when she'd come here. She hated to admit she kinda liked it. Rubbing its soft fur against her cheek, she thought of her mother, and the stuffed animals she'd bought Taz. She treated kids as they should be treated, until she died. The thought made Taz sad.

So did everything else. Street life sucked. She'd been sliced in a little get-down that should have been nothing. Her home girls had bounced without blinking, ditching her to bleed alone in the alley. Taz had been mega scared. But the Street Angel had come to the rescue.

"What does that tell you, girl?" she asked herself aloud.

There was noise outside. Taz saw somebody enter the sleeping quarters. They had partitions here, but her bunk had a decent view of the door. A man and a woman stood in the doorway: the woman approached. Hmm, speak of the devil . . .

"Hey, Street Angel, how you doin'?"

"I've been better, Taz."

"What's happenin'?"

The woman was really pretty. Black as night hair. Peaches and cream complexion. Even a few freckles. She wore a pink cotton sweater and a denim skirt. A little preppy, but it was good on her. Taz glanced down at her hands to see if she had on a ring. "You married?"

She hesitated. "No."

"Got a guy?"

A bright smile. "Yep."

"Why you come here?"

"Have you heard from your posse?"

"They been callin' on my cell, but I turned it off. Don't want to talk to them yet." She frowned. "Why?"

"I think they used your computer."

"It's locked in the closet in the apartment. They find it?"

"That's my guess."

"Well, that ain't so bad."

"It is Taz. They came on to the website."

It took her a minute. "Holy fuck, they know I been talkin' to you?"

"I believe so. It's my bad. I didn't think fast enough on my

feet when your screen name came on. I indicated I knew you."
The Street Angel sat down in a chair, reached out and took
hold of Taz's hand, like her mother used to. Again Taz smelled
lilacs. "Do you know what this means, sweetie?"

"Yeah, they find me, they gonna dust me." Suddenly, she
felt young and vulnerable. She gripped the woman's hand.
"What am I gonna do?" Now she had, literally, nobody.

"We're going to put you in a Gang Protection Program."

"What's that?"

"It's like the Witness Protection Program that the government operates."

"I heard about that. You take a new identity. You never
come back to your turf. You leave everybody you love forever."

The Street Angel's blue eyes saddened. "Taz, do you really
have anybody you love? Or that loves you? Would it be so bad
to leave this town and start a new life?"

Weary, Taz sank back onto the pillows. Her leg hurt and
her head began to pound like the bass on a CD when it was
turned up too loud. Was the Street Angel right?

SEVENTEEN

CLAY SIPPED HIS scotch and stared out the front window of his town house. The mid-October air was warmer in D.C. than New York, but the days were growing shorter. As planned, Bailey would arrive here at dusk. He'd wanted to meet her at the train station, but of course, he couldn't do that. God forbid they might be seen!

"Damn it," he said aloud, then told himself to calm down. So what if they were being circumspect? He had an entire weekend with her, all alone, and hadn't been able to think about much else during the long week since he'd seen her.

Finally, headlights shone in front of his house as a taxi pulled up. He resisted the urge to run out to her. Instead, he drew back the sheer curtains on the living room window and watched her climb out of the cab; hell, she wore some slinky black skirt with big white polka-dots on it and a slim, short jacket. She even had on heels, though not too high. He smiled. His girl would never put fashion over comfort, he thought. For a minute, a vision of his mother and Jane in too-tight-to-be-comfortable dresses and so-high-they-must-hurt heels popped into his mind. Bailey could never fit into that image. He wouldn't want her to even try.

He whipped open the door before she had a chance to ring the bell. Her smile was wide; she wore makeup tonight, and he wanted to kiss the raisin-colored lipstick off her luscious mouth. "Hi, Senator."

Bracing his arm on the door, he smiled back. "Street Angel, welcome to Washington." He took the small bag she carried and stepped aside. She entered the foyer. "This is gorgeous, Clay."

"You're gorgeous." He came up behind her and circled his arms around her waist. She wore some unfamiliar perfume; it was sexy and sinful and made him hurt. "Do you have any idea how excited I am about your being here for the whole weekend?"

She pressed back into him so her cute butt bumped his groin. "Yep, I do."

"Witch." Nosing aside her hair, which was long and curling down her back, he kissed her neck. She sighed and laid her head onto his shoulder. His hands cupped her breasts. Through the silk shirt she wore beneath her jacket, he felt her nipples bead. "I'm not the only one, baby."

"Hmm. No, you're not."

"Do you want a tour of the house before or after." His hand drifted to her waist. And below.

"After," she whispered.

Turning her around, he saw the desire etched on her delicate features. He cradled her cheeks in his palms. "I'm going to make love to you, Bailey. For hours. All weekend long. The way I've always wanted to and never had enough time."

"I want that, too, Clay." She wrapped her arms around his neck. "Starting now." Up on her tiptoes, kissed him, a carnal, open-mouthed mating that went on for a long time. He could take her now, standing in the foyer. But he didn't want that. Instead he grasped her hand and led her up the steps. On the way, she ran her fingers over the oak banister. "Nice," she said, smiling. She took in the skylights, the huge windows. "This is lovely."

He didn't say anything until they reached the bedroom.

"You realize," he growled as he closed the door, cocooning them in. "There's going to be no interruptions, no worries about your brothers barging in or Rory waking up."

She grinned. Sliding her hand in her pocket, she said, "Just one concession." She pulled out her phone. "In case Liam needs to call me. Though they're out in the wilderness somewhere in upstate New York so I doubt he will."

"Well, thank God for the wilderness."

Slowly, he crossed to her. Gently, he eased the jacket off her shoulders. "This is pretty." He skimmed his hands over the white silk T-shirt and brushed his hands over her hips.

"Thanks, but I'd rather not be wearing any of it right now."

"I think I can accommodate that." He slipped the shirt over her head. "Oh, I like that." The bra was half-cupped and all lace."

"Good, I bought it just for you."

Unbutton, unzip. The skirt hit the floor. Scraps of lace to match the bra barely covered her. "Why bother?" he asked, chuckling at the skimpy panties.

"For you, Senator."

Leaning over, he drew in the scent of her. "Perfume, too. What is it?"

"A new Calvin Klein." She nosed his chest. "Aidan bought it for me. My brothers always buy me these girly things."

"Knew they had redeeming qualities."

Her skin was like cream; he ran his hands over it, exploring the hollow of her back, the curve of her butt, the oh-so-tender inside of her thigh. During his perusal, he removed her underwear. Lifting one of her breasts to his mouth, he took the nipple between his teeth. She jolted. "Hurt?" he asked.

"No, no." She reached for his shirt. "Off," she mumbled as he suckled her.

"In a minute."

At the juncture of her thighs, her curls were soft as down; he slid his fingers through them, and managed to slip one inside. "Wet, already," he murmured.

She squirmed. "Clay."

He touched her, explored her, for moments. He let his body heat at her warmth, her readiness, the way her breasts swelled.

She was so soft and pliable he almost wanted to do this forever. Almost. Stepping back, he had to hold her because she
swayed into him. "Easy, love." He led her to the bed before he
undressed. She lay there, her dark locks rioting gloriously
across his pillow, and watched him slowly unbutton his casual
dress blue-striped shirt, undo the button of his khakis and let
them fall to the floor revealing navy blue boxers.

Dropping them, he crossed to the bed, drew out a condom
from the nightstand and sheathed himself while she watched.
Her breathing speeded up and he knelt on the bed. He touched
her again, everywhere, then covered her body with his. "I
can't wait any longer, sweetheart."

"Don't wait."

"I love you," he said as he slipped into. "Love you, love
you, love you."

"I love you, too, Clay."

"OH, CLAY." STANDING on the cobblestone floor, Bailey noted
the light oak booths, caught the tune of an Irish band and took
in the aroma of traditional Irish food; she felt a sense of security and familiarity in the downtown Irish pub that she'd
feared she'd never feel in Washington. When the singers began "No Never, No More," she smiled. "I can sing that song."

Clay came up behind her and squeezed her shoulder. "Don't
tell them that. They'll have you up there joining them in a second."

"Oh, dear, that would be public." She pivoted to face him.
"Clay, what are we doing here? I was so enamored of the
place, I forgot . . . should we be here?"

"I think this is worth the risk." He winked at her. "I doubt
people on the Hill are going to frequent Fado's Irish Pub at
eleven on Friday night."

She stared at him.

"Come on, I hate seeing that scowl. Just to be safe, we won't
touch each other once."

She was distracted from their conversation by a host who
approached them.

"*Tráthnona maith agat.*" He welcomed them in Gaelic then,

and when Bailey answered him in kind, his eyes widened. "*Bean mo chroi*. We'll have to give you a prime seat, lass."

Bailey flashed Irish blue eyes at him and threw Clay a sideways—and sexy—look. "How about a private one?"

"Aye. As private as we've got."

As he led them back, Clay asked, "What did he say?"

"Woman of my heart."

"Ah, I know the feeling."

They were seated in one of the beautifully crafted booths, in the back, behind a pillar. Her gaze spanned the interior. "This is lovely."

"Designed by Irish craftsmen with authentic Irish materials in order to bring the best of Ireland to Washington." The host smiled at her. "Be sure to look at the other rooms. The Library over there is stacked with books by our boy James Joyce; the Cottage is the Shankee's home."

"Oh, I love Irish storytellers."

The host beamed. "And then there's The Victorian Room where you can see some theater about Irish politics."

After he left to bring them Guinness beer, Bailey gave Clay a private smile. "Politics, now that would interest you, wouldn't it?"

"Do I detect a lilt to your voice?" he asked. His brandy-colored eyes shone with humor and intense satisfaction. His whole body was relaxed and he looked young in a gauzy light-brown shirt rolled up at the sleeves and tan designer jeans. She wore black jeans and green light cotton sweater.

"A lilt? Maybe I . . . oh, Clay, listen." He smiled. "Oh Danny Boy," the classic Irish hit song, began to play. Immediately her eyes misted.

"What, honey?"

"I love this song. It reminds me of my family, my background."

"Well, let's listen to it, then."

Afterward, there was raucous clapping. Bailey stuck her fingers in her mouth and whistled. Clay threw back his head and laughed at her enthusiastic response.

"Galway Bay" began with the opening, "If I ever go across the sea to Ireland."

Clay smiled at her, his eyes brightening even more. "Maybe we'll go to Ireland on our honeymoon."

She sucked in a breath. "Clay."

"What? We already talked about marriage."

Bailey watched him watch her. Just a little while ago, his mouth had been all over her. It heated her blood just to think of it. Their lovemaking had been tender and breathtaking at the same time.

Finally, Clay spoke. "You can't just ignore what I said."

"I don't know how to respond."

Cocking his head, he shrugged. "All right. Let's table it. I don't want anything to ruin this weekend."

A waiter approached them with their Guinness. "*Slainté!*" he said.

Bailey and Clay both raised their glasses to toast. After they sipped, the man asked, "Will you be orderin' now?"

"We haven't looked at the menu," she said picking it up. "But I'm starved."

"Boxy is their signature dish, Bailey," Clay told her.

"Oh, I love potato pancakes. My mother makes them."

The waiter beamed. "Bailey, is it? A nice Irish girl."

She wished she could tell the waiter about her parents' pub. Damn this secrecy. Though she didn't voice it to Clay—he'd jump on her frustration and use it to move her along faster— she was tired of hiding her feelings, too. "Aye, and I'll have boxy, of course."

"What would you like it stuffed with, darlin'?" the waiter asked. "Chicken, shrimp, sausage, seafood, or portobello?"

"Oh, I love them all."

"Can we get a sampling?" Clay asked. "My friend here is in town from New York."

"For an Irish lass, I'd say Hogan will do it." He took the menus and left.

"So, you like this surprise?" he asked, starting to reach for her hands across the table, then remembering their deal and drawing it back.

"I love it, Clay. Thanks so much."

He grinned.

"For this and earlier," she added arching a brow.

"I missed you, lass."

"I could tell."

He clasped his hands together tightly on the table. "It's different now, isn't it?"

"Hmm." She sipped her beer. "More meaningful." She scanned the fieldstone fireplace and absorbed the familiar atmosphere. "More intense."

He picked up his beer. "For me too, darlin'."

"This place is even getting to you."

"*You* are getting to me."

Despite their caveat about touching, she reached over and squeezed his hand. "Right back at ya."

He laughed, she smiled, then she lifted her glass to him. She said, "Dance as if no one were watching, Sing as if no one were listening, And live every day as if it were your last."

Clay arched a brow. "Heed your own words, Bailey me girl."

She knew exactly what he meant.

BAILEY WAS LIKE a little kid on the bicycle tour of the Mall the next day. Wearing sunglasses and ball caps, they pedaled next to each other as she exclaimed over the Washington sights. A warm October breeze and bright sunshine followed them everywhere. They stopped in front of the Lincoln Memorial for a break and dismounted their bikes.

Bailey looked up at the famous American monument and grinned. "Wow, is that big. Rory would love seeing this." She swept her hand in the air to indicate the entire scope of the Mall. Although Bailey had been to Washington several times, she hadn't done the tour since she was young. And Rory had never been here.

"Then we'll have to bring him down."

She sipped her water. "Maybe."

Forcing himself not to react, Clay looked away. He wasn't going to spoil this weekend by arguing about what he didn't have. "Hungry?" he asked glancing at his watch.

"Are you kidding? Between what I ate last night and at Kramer's this morning, I'm stuffed." They'd had breakfast at the famous bookstore on Dupont Circle in the same disguise they wore now so she could get to see one of his favorite D.C. spots.

He nodded to the bikes. "This will work it off."

She moved a bit closer on the steps. "I can think of other ways, too." She brushed the side of his thigh with hers.

Since he was incognito, he leaned over and kissed her nose. "You're on, sweetheart, as soon as we get back to the town house."

They were called to return to the group and resumed the tour of sights Clay had taken for granted as long as he could remember. She was good for him, letting him view these grand monuments through her eyes. Though he had to force-fully quell his worry over what was coming Monday, he was enjoying himself.

He felt the same way when he toured the Smithsonian with her that afternoon. He saw the Women's Museum and the children's exhibits with new appreciation.

And once back home, he made tender love to her. She promptly fell asleep and was still out when the phone rang. Clay answered it quickly so she wouldn't wake up.

Thorn's voice came across the line. "Oh, great, Clay, you're in town."

Damn it, he shouldn't have answered. "I am."

"I hope you're not tied up tonight."

He glanced over at Bailey, naked in his bed, the sheet pulled up to her chin. Her chest rose and fell rhythmically as she slept deeply. "As a matter of fact I am."

"Can you get out of it? For a while at least."

"Why?"

"The head of Health, Education, and Welfare is having a tête-à-tête at the Kennedy Center tonight. You're invited."

He sat up straighter in bed. "What? I didn't know anything about this."

"The invitation got lost. His assistant called me yesterday, to ask why you weren't coming. You'd left the office early and didn't return my calls."

Clay glanced at the answering machine, which blinked an accusing bright red. "I wasn't here."

"What about your cell?"

"I turned it off."

A pause. "Why?" Thorn waited. "Does this have anything to do with the talk we had that day after racquetball?"

"Yes, in a way."

"Clay, if you're with somebody, you can bring her."

"Don't I wish."

"Oh, hell, she isn't married, is she?"

"No! Nor does she work for me. Nor is she a hardened criminal." Though she had gone to jail.

"Sorry. Role reaction. Look, you need to go to this thing, even if you just put in an appearance. It's black tie."

"Thorn, I can't."

"Just for an hour."

He sighed.

"Damn it, Clay, can't you get away from her for a little while? You have responsibilities. And if you decide to throw your hat in for VP, you shouldn't ignore events like this."

He pivoted when he heard a rustle on the bed. Bailey turned over and opened sleepy eyes to him.

"All right, I'll be there. What time?"

He hung up mad.

"You'll be where?" she asked.

"The Kennedy Center." He explained the situation to her.

She brushed his cheek with her palm. "I can amuse myself here for a couple of hours, Clay."

"It's not that."

"We were cooking in tonight anyway."

"I know." He tried to bite his tongue but he was a man used to speaking his mind. "It's the secrecy that's getting to me. I want you with me tonight. I want to show you off to the world."

"Clay."

"I know. I promised myself I wouldn't bring it up all weekend. But I didn't expect this." He nodded to the phone. "I'm sorry. But I have to go for just an hour or so."

"Of course you do." Her eyes sparkled. "Do you have to wear a tux?"

"Yes. Why?"

"I've never seen you in one."

"Well, you will I guess." He nodded to the phone. "Damn it."

She brought his hand to her breast. The sheet slipped and he felt her skin against his palm. "We've got all weekend, Clay."

And then what? he thought but didn't ask. At times like this he felt the dilemma of their situation acutely and was tempted to return to control mode, which would only irritate the lovely woman lounging in his bed like Jezebel waiting for the king.

To give her credit, she tried to lighten the moment. After he showered and began to dress, she made bawdy comments about the cut of his trousers over his butt, got out of bed to help button his studs, and teased him. "You know, while you're gone, I'm going to snoop. In your desk. Your underwear drawer, everywhere."

"Just don't reveal any state secrets," he said kissing her nose.

A half hour later, with the vision of her soft and sexy in his bed firmly planted in his mind, Clay shot the sleeves of his tux jacket as he climbed the stairs to the famous performing arts center on F Street. Built in 1971 as a memorial to JFK, the still-modern building housed several theaters and was responsible for bringing culture to Washington. It also had a rooftop restaurant, where he was headed. Finding the elevator, riding it up, he thought, of course, of what he'd left behind.

Reaching the top floor, he exited the elevator and found the private room in the back, just off the outdoor porch where events were held in the nice weather. Jim Smith, the senator from Michigan, and head of the Health, Education, and Welfare Committee and their host, crossed to where he stood in the doorway and stretched out his hand. "Clayton, we were wondering where you were."

"Apparently, the invitation got lost." He shook hands. "Glad I could make it."

As they moved to the bar, Thorn joined them, said hello, and got a drink for Clay. Jim asked, "Didn't you question why you weren't invited to this shindig?"

No, because I wasn't paying attention to the events in D.C.

"Actually, he's spent a great deal of time in New York." Thorn smiled graciously. "The Big Apple keeps him busy."

"Those Yanks are doing great, aren't they?" Smith said. "Have you managed to take in any of the games?"

"Well, he took in at least one." The other New York senator, Alex Case, had come up behind them when Jim asked about the baseball team, and clapped Clay on the back. "Tell me, did your young friend enjoy his visit with Jeter?"

"What visit with Jeter?" Thorn asked.

Case sipped his drink. "Joanie called my assistant and asked if I could arrange for Clay to take a little pal of his into the locker room." He shrugged. "I knew Jeter before he was the number one man for the Yankees."

"Yes," Clay said, uncomfortable. "My friend enjoyed that."

Thorn eyed him silently. When the others moved away, Thorn drew in a breath that indicated lack of patience. "What's going on, Clay?"

"What do you mean?"

"Don't fuck with me. Something's going on. It seems to me you have a double life. If you aren't going to tell your Chief of Staff about it, we might as well call it quits now."

Clay shook his head. "You're right. I'm not thinking clearly these days. You should know what's going on." He scanned the area. "Not now, though."

"So long as it doesn't blow up in our faces before I get to hear about it."

"It won't."

"Monday morning."

"Monday, I have the meeting with Stewart about the allocation of the crime bill funds."

"Ah, yes. Bailey O'Neil's going to be there, isn't she?"

Clay recognized this as, ironically, a change of topic, and appreciated it. "Yes."

"There'll be fireworks, won't there?"

"Probably."

Again, Thorn frowned. "She'll take you by the balls if you let her, Clay."

She already has. "I know. I have it under control."

"When she coming into town?"

Clay waved to a friend of his from Virginia. "Uh, this

weekend. Oh, look, there's Commander Ransom from the navy. I'd like to talk to him."

Thorn grabbed his arm as he started away. "How long are you staying tonight?" Clay caught his shrewd gaze.

Checking his watch, Clay said, "An hour or so."

"And then you're going back to . . . holy shit, Clay. I just put the pieces . . ."

Clay turned. "What are you talking about?"

"Bailey O'Neil. Jesus Christ, Clay, what the hell do you think you're doing?"

"HEY, STREET ANGEL, how ya hangin', lady?"

Still in Clay's bed, but wearing one of his pajama tops, Bailey smiled into the phone. "Good, Taz."

"What's cookin'?"

"I just had some time so I decided to call. Not too long until I won't be able to chat with you, girl."

"Yeah. We're jettin' soon, right?"

"Are you all right with this, Taz?"

"Yeah, I'm cool. Ready to bounce." She heard a hesitation in Taz's voice. "The new place, it'll be safe, right?"

"Yes." Since Taz wouldn't be eighteen until the end of the year, she was going to be in foster care, in upstate New York with people who'd volunteered for the Gang Protection Program. "I think you'll like the family."

"They got kids?"

"No, none of their own. Why?"

"I'd just like to be around some kids. You got any?"

"A little boy."

"Lucky."

Bailey liked chit-chatting with the girl and not solving life-and-death problems. "Do you want to have children, Taz?"

"Big-time. But not before I can take care of them."

"This move will help put you on that path." Clay appeared in the doorway, his tie undone, his hair disheveled. "Hold on a sec."

"Who are you talking to?" He looked weary and unnerved.

"Taz."

His face tightened. "Taz, as in gang girl Taz?" Now, he sounded impatient.

"Uh-huh." She went back to the phone while Clay sipped a drink he must have made downstairs. "I'll talk to you again soon with the details about leaving, sweetie," Bailey told the girl.

"Gotcha. Ciao, lady."

They disconnected and for a minute Bailey let herself be optimistic. Taz sounded hopeful. Ready to take this step. It was times like these that Bailey felt so good about her work.

From across the room, Clay yanked off his tie. "Couldn't you leave that alone for one night? And why would you use your cell? Now she has your number."

"I don't think that's a problem anymore. And since you were out, there didn't seem to be any reason to 'leave it alone.'" She studied the stern set of his jaw. The rigidity of his shoulders. "Tell me why you're upset."

Taking a hefty swig of his drink, he leaned against the dresser. "My chief of staff has guessed about our relationship. He reamed me out tonight at the Kennedy Center for keeping him in the dark."

"Guessed? How could he guess?"

"Who knows? He put clues together. I was hesitant about going tonight. I broke it off with Jane. I've been vague and secretive about things."

"But how would he know it was me? Did somebody see us last night?"

"No. Alex Case got the go-ahead for Rory to get in to see Jeter. He mentioned 'my young friend' in front of Thorn tonight. Then Thorn asked about Monday and your coming to town, and I don't know, hell, the inflection in my voice, something, must have tipped him off. He asked me directly."

"And you didn't lie."

"No."

"I see."

He set his drink down, and walking to the closet, he took off his suit coat and hung it up. "There's more I haven't told you.

My father and Tom Carter think something's going on with me, too. They don't know about you, but they do suspect I stopped seeing Jane for another woman." She opened her mouth to say something, but he cut her off. "They're right, of course."

"Clay, is *nothing* private with you?"

"I guess not."

Rolling up the sleeves of his shirt, he crossed to her and sat on the bed. He toyed with the top button of his pajamas that she'd borrowed. "I was going to tell you about all this tomorrow. Now the stakes are higher." She watched him. "I wish I could say I was sorry that people are finding out, Bailey, but truthfully I'm not. I hate this." He swept the room with his arm. "The hiding. I want you in my life openly."

She sank back into the pillows. "I know you do. I want that too. It's so hard and confusing. I wish there was some way we could change the necessity for me to stay out of the public eye."

"Would you consider some other kind of job, working with kids?"

She raked back her hair. "I don't want to leave ESCAPE, Clay. Despite the danger."

"Danger? Are you referring to something specific?"

She picked at the thread of the quilt on his bed. "I have something I've been waiting to tell you, too. Promise you won't fly off the handle."

"I never fly off the handle."

"About these things, you do."

"I promise."

"Taz is going into the Gang Protection Program."

"Really? That's good, isn't it?"

"Yes." She smiled. "I think I'm really going to get her out."

"I hope so, honey." He watched her. "How did it come about?"

"Her gang girls grabbed her computer. They came on the website, looking for the Street Angel."

"How on earth did they know about your connection with her?"

"Apparently, they had some suspicions. I've been trying to figure out the chain of events. My best guess is they found

ESCAPE bookmarked on her Internet program and put two and two together."

He stiffened. "And got minus one."

"Yes. They pretended they were her. I didn't catch on at first, and almost gave away her location at the shelter."

"You didn't though?"

"No. I caught myself when I realized who they were."

He took a bead on her. "Oh, I get it. They threatened you, didn't they?"

"Well, it was clear they weren't happy with Street Angel." She grabbed his arm. "Please, don't get mad. If it's going to work between us, you can't go off every time my job takes a turn you don't like."

He ran a hand through his hair. "It makes me sick inside to think you're in danger. I can barely tolerate it. Now, more than ever."

Bailey watched him. "I understand, Clay. Really I do. And I hate that this hurts you so much. But short of giving up my job, I just don't know what to do about it."

"Well, we have some choices to make in any case, I guess. Thorn knows. My father suspects. Jon, Rory, Aidan . . . we didn't do a very good job of keeping this secret did we?"

"No." Bailey watched him.

And, finally, she admitted to herself for the first time that she was going to be forced to choose between Clay and her career.

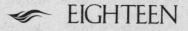 EIGHTEEN

THE CONFERENCE ROOM at the Russell Building was old—it sported antique cherry furniture, Persian rugs, an ornate chandelier, and other fancy light fixtures. It was meant to intimidate. As Clay watched Bailey face down the committee, he felt a spurt of pride that she was not, in the least, put off by her surroundings. Of course, she'd been in prison and had endured unspeakable intimidation there.

"Welcome, Ms. O'Neil," Chuck Stewart said as he began the meeting. "By the way, I know you keep a low profile, but the committee knows your identity." He gave her a dry smile. "We've talked quite a bit about you."

She returned his smile. "I imagine you have." She was all prim and proper, sitting with her hands clasped on the table, wearing the blue suit she'd worn the first time Clay had kissed her.

Stewart continued. "You're here at the request of your task force. Protocol is to let the spokesperson, i.e., the senator in charge, present the group's findings. We'll do that, then break form so you can have your say."

"Thank you for letting me be here, Senator."

"Make it Chuck." It was nice of him to not give an unfair advantage to the others who, of course, were on a first-name basis. "Clay?"

Across from her, Clay straightened and passed around a thin folder. "Our recommendation is fairly simple. Here's a listing of all the agencies in New York we think should get money from the new bill. At the top are agencies like ESCAPE, then the shelters and clinics. We'd like to see the money divided among them."

"You agreed to this, Clay? Even though it goes against most of your beliefs about social agency intervention in dealing with youth gangs."

"Well, the Youth Crime Bill's money is earmarked for those agencies, but yes, I conceded to giving ESCAPE and a few other programs I disagree with the money." He took a quick peek at Bailey. Her face was full of soft approval.

"The distribution would be according to size, location, and need, right?" Chuck asked.

"Yes. All except for three hundred thousand. There's a disagreement over the shelter, Guardian."

"Which is why you're here, Ms. O'Neil, correct?"

"Call me Bailey. And yes, that's why I'm here. I understand you'll cast the deciding vote."

"My committee will." He faced Clay. "Go ahead, present your case."

"I can see where we need to shelter kids trying to get out of gangs, so I voted for some of the money to go to places like Gentle House. In addition, they'll service other kids. However, to build one solely for gang members—criminals— would take money away from teens who need shelter and haven't done anything wrong."

From the corner of his eye, he saw Bailey stiffen. It was hard to believe he'd been inside her just hours ago. *Make me forget about all our differences, Clay.* He had, with mind-blowing sex.

Clay presented the rest of his defense with lawyerlike clarity, then Stewart turned to Bailey. "Perhaps you can enlighten us on why you want a separate shelter."

"Because we could do so much more for gang kids. In

shelters like Guardian, we'd have specially trained counselors to expedite the process of getting out. Doctors could set up ancillary clinics at the sites. Schools could be represented in an effort to keep these kids in the classroom. Eventually, we hope to have job training so they could get the skills they need to stay out of gangs. The possibilities are endless."

"Why can't that be done in other shelters?" Tom Carter asked.

"Because they don't have the money, manpower, or skills to provide for the specific needs of gang kids." She faced Chuck. "Your bill, and grants we would write for stopping juvenile crime, would give us the needed funds."

Clay felt his temper rise. "We can't cater to criminals."

"They aren't criminals. These would be kids trying to get *out*." She slapped her hand on the table. "To *avoid* becoming hardened criminals."

"How do you know the ones you're trying to get out haven't broken laws already?" Clay asked. "You won't help the police prove anything."

Stewart smiled. "Well, I can see what fuels these fireworks between you." He said to Bailey, "Would ESCAPE run Guardian?"

"We could. If we get the money, those things would have to be decided."

"Do you have the manpower?"

"We'd manage."

This time, Clay slapped his hand on the table. "By running yourself into the ground doing it."

The room stilled. Bailey's eyes widened at his personal remark. Then she recovered. "Which is no concern of yours, Senator."

He backpedaled. "It is if we give you money and you stretch yourselves so thin we lose it."

The spirited discussion was joined by all the members. After a half hour, Stewart said, "I guess that's enough. We have information to make our decision." He nodded to Bailey. "Thanks for making this an interesting morning." And at Clay. "Could you both stay a minute?"

After everyone filed out, Stewart faced them. "I can tell

this was hard for both of you. I appreciate your coming here and sharing your views despite how uncomfortable this must be for you."

The senator from Massachuttes had no idea how true his statement was.

"I want to ask you something, Bailey. Jim Smith is working on creating a post in HEW that deals with youth crime. Its parameters haven't been set, but its focus would be the schools. He'd need somebody to head it. With your background, and from what Clay tells me about your work in education, would you be interested in applying for the job?"

"DID YOU SET me up in there?" They were walking toward his office at a brisk pace. He'd practically had to drag her here, as she wanted to get away from him and think. Her typical MO.

"No, I knew nothing about Chuck's suggestion."

She was silent.

"You don't believe me."

"I don't know what to believe."

They passed Joanie's desk, and Mica's office. His press secretary looked up and her brows rose in surprise. Once inside, Clay closed the door, went to his desk, and leaned against it, trying to control his temper. He hated how this woman pushed his buttons. "I thought you believed in *me*."

"Clay, he offered me a job doing exactly what you want me to do: take an administrative position—in Washington, I might add—as opposed to working directly with gang kids."

"You like working with schools. Every time you go to one, you talk about how much you feel you've accomplished."

"That's not the point."

Ignoring her, he went on. "I told you there was a lot you could do for gang kids in Washington."

"So you did set me up."

"No. I swear I didn't. But what's the big deal even if I had? Holy hell, Bailey, don't you see this is a way we could be together?"

"Once again, by my giving up everything I love."

He arched a brow. "Everything?"

"I didn't mean it that way."

His gaze was hard.

"Don't blur the personal and professional lines, Clay."

"Those lines were blurred the minute you slept with me."

She glanced at her watch. "I have to go. My train is in an hour."

He sighed. "All right. I hate to see you leave like this." His tone was coaxingly intimate.

"I know. Me, too. I'm sorry we clash so badly."

"Don't use it as an excuse to separate us."

"We don't need an excuse."

"Bailey." He started to approach her.

"Don't. Not here," she nodded to the office. "It wouldn't be right."

"Fine. Will you call me?"

"Yes." She crossed to the door, reached for the handle, but looked over her shoulder. "Clay?"

"Yes?"

"Before this, it was a nice weekend. I enjoyed it. Thank you."

Arms folded over his chest, he sat on the edge of his desk. "You're welcome. I enjoyed it too."

She walked out of the office, leaving him with a heart full of conflicting emotions. He was angry that she'd believe he set her up with Stewart, and hurt that she still talked in terms of them not making it. There was no way in hell *he'd* let *her* go. On the other hand, he admired her spunk and commitment to what she believed in. It was, after all, what drew him to her. Was he going to lose her now, because of that?

No! He wouldn't let that happen. She was his now, in every way except legally. And once he got her to agree to that, she'd have to work things out.

"YOU'RE *WHAT*?"

"I'm in love with her."

Thorn dropped down into a chair openmouthed. Clay had never seen his staid chief of staff so rattled. "With the Street Angel?"

"Yes." From behind his desk, Clay fiddled with the picture of him and Jon on the surface. He wanted to be able to put one of Bailey out here. One of Rory.

"I'm shocked. You said she was with you Saturday night, but you're in *love* with her?" His eyes narrowed. "How long has this been going on?"

"Since July, really."

Thorn's brows rose as if he'd thought of something. "You're not using your relationship with her to get her off our back, are you?"

"No!"

"It's been done, Senator."

"Not by me. And I really resent your asking if it was."

"I'm sorry for the implication."

"You should be. Hell, Thorn, is that what you think of me?"

"No, Clay. I believe in your integrity. This is just such a surprise."

"To me, too."

"Can I ask you something?"

"Sure." He sat back and put his feet up on the desk. "Though I warn you I don't have a lot of answers."

"How did this happen?"

Clay laughed, a confused, male, stupid laugh. "I wish I knew. None of it was planned. I just *liked* her right away, that day I went up to New York. The time you suggested I mend fences. For some reason, the feeling was mutual. Then it got out of hand physically, and before I knew it, I was crazy about her."

"She feel the same way?"

"Yes, except that she fought it like a pit bull. Still, here we are."

Thorn frowned. "And where is that?"

"What do you mean?"

"Where do you see this going?"

"I want to marry her."

Thorn's jaw tightened. "Career-wise that wouldn't be a good move."

"Be careful what you say here, Thorn."

"I have to be candid. She's a single mother. Never married. She's spent time in jail. The press would have a field day with all that. Then there's your public animosity. Reporters would go wild."

"We could handle that, I think. But that's not my main concern."

His chief of staff did not look pleased.

"I'd risk all that. She's a hard-working, unselfish woman. Her successes are phenomenal. Eventually the press and voters—would see that."

"Maybe. We could put a kind of Cinderella spin on it."

Clay shook his head. "But if we go public, then Bailey's job at ESCAPE is over."

"Well, that would be good. We've wanted to close them down. You'd get the girl and your way with anti–youth gang policies."

"Chuck Stewart asked her if she'd be interested in a government post in Washington working with HEW."

"That could be tricky."

"It's all tricky."

Thorn said, "She going to take it?"

"Hell no. She's furious about the situation. She asked me if I set her up."

"Did you?"

"No." Running a hand through his hair, he stared up at the ceiling. "The worst part is, I worry about her safety all the time."

"You always said the safety of the workers at ESCAPE concerned you. Must be hard to be in love with one of them."

"It is." He sighed and took a bead on Thorn. "Tell me what you think of all this."

"It's politically dangerous. Your reelection to the Senate might withstand it, but your chance of being selected for the vice presidential candidate could be hurt by it. Somehow, I can't see Bailey O'Neil as second lady."

"She's not a Republican."

"Icing on the cake, Senator. As your chief of staff, I recommend you stop seeing her."

"How about as my friend for ten years?"

Thorn watched Clay, his cool gray eyes shrewd and assessing. "Off the record, if I were forty-five and single, and I fell in love, I'd fight for her. But Clay, this doesn't sound like your decision. It sounds like she won't change her life for you."

Why does my whole life have to change?

"Will she?"

"I don't think so."

"So, is there any choice to be made?"

"Maybe not."

The thought depressed the hell out of him.

BAILEY WALKED INTO the pub at four that day feeling bereft. Instead of the weekend making things clearer, her time with Clay only clouded the issue. She could still hear Stewart throw the newest monkey wrench into their relationship.

Jim Smith is working on creating a post in HEW that deals with youth crime . . . its focus would be the schools . . . would you be interested in applying for the job?

Rory, who was sitting at a table coloring with Kathleen, leaped up when he saw his mother, made a run for her, and practically tackled her to the ground. "Hi, buddy." She kissed him soundly and held on tight. "I missed you."

"Me, too. Camping was awesome. We saw a snake, a 'coon, and lots of beavers."

She smiled at him. "Tell me more." They both sat on stools. As he chatted, her mind kept drifting to Clay and what was going to happen with them. "Mommy, how's Clay?"

"Oh, um, good. But keep it down, pal. We still want this to be a secret."

He handed her a picture. "It's for Jon."

"Oh, honey, this is great." She stared at the stick figure who bore faint resemblance to Jeter only because of his number two Yankee jersey. "He likes Jeter, too."

She felt a presence behind the bar and turned to find a scowling Patrick there. "Welcome back." He leaned over and kissed her cheek. Rory slid off the stool and Bailey flipped the drawing over.

"Have a good time?" Patrick asked as he began to wash some glasses.

"Um, yeah. It was mostly work, though."

"Hmm."

"What?"

"You went down Friday. Never called to check in or anything. Sounds like you were busy."

"You got something to say, Paddy?"

"Yeah, I do." He braced his hands on the bar. "It's obvious you were with a guy. We saw evidence of somebody you're seein' all over your steps that morning." She just stared at him. "What's happened to you, girl? You used to talk to us. Tell us stuff. All of a sudden this guy is in the picture and you don't say nothin'?"

She watched her brother with a lump in his throat. He was right.

"Me, Liam, and Dylan decided he's married. Is that it?"

"No! I wouldn't fool around with a married man after what Dad did."

Patrick's gaze narrowed. Of all the O'Neil siblings, he had the most trouble with their father's infidelity. "Then who on earth would you have to hide?"

Bailey swallowed hard, so sick of all this. To hell with it. "I'm in love with Clayton Wainwright. And so help me God, Paddy, if you throw a fit about this, I'm gonna scream."

Patrick just stared at her, his blue eyes disbelieving; she squirmed on the stool.

"Well," he finally said, "I can see why you'd keep it a secret."

She deflated like a balloon losing air. Tears clouded her eyes.

"Aw, baby, he doesn't feel the same about you?"

"It's not that." She shook her head and forced back the tears. "He wants to get married."

"Holy shit."

"I know. Can you imagine it? Me, a political wife."

Patrick laughed deep and from the belly. "You'd set Washington on its ear, honey."

"I'd never fit in with my background."

"What's wrong with your background?"

"Pat, I spent time in jail."

"Where this guy put you!"

"I have a child and no marriage."

"Fuck it, Bailey. You raised a good kid."

"We own a pub, for Christ's sake. I don't fit into his social strata."

Now her brother's temper spiked. She could see it in the flash of fire in his eyes. "You ashamed of us, lass? Of your background?"

"Of course not. I love our family, who we are."

"So the problem is you and him."

"Uh-huh. We just don't mesh."

He picked up a towel and folded it meticulously. "I know how that goes."

Reaching over she touched his arm. "You and Brie not doin' any better?"

"She had a date last night. Kathleen let the cat out of the bag."

"Oh, Paddy."

"She told me last week since it was my decision to move out, and since I was being so pigheaded, she might as well look for somebody else."

"That doesn't sound like Brie."

His face flushed. "I was . . . out of control at the time. We'd just . . ." He glanced to the side. "Hell, you know. We fooled around, and then she got mad because I thought that changed everything."

"Oh, Paddy."

"I did, Bay. I thought it meant things were settled, that we were gonna get back together. Instead, she's *dating*."

"I'm sorry."

"It's hard when somebody's so different from you."

"Believe me I know. And it's not just that for us."

"Take my mind off my troubles and tell me."

She talked about having to give up ESCAPE.

"Well, if he'd get you out of that place, it'd be enough for me to give my blessing on this relationship."

"What relationship?" Liam asked.

Bailey glanced over to see he and Dylan had arrived for the family dinner.

Paddy looked to her. There was a question in his eyes. He was right. She shouldn't be keeping this from her family. "Okay, guys. I got something to tell you. But I swear, if you get mad, I'll never tell you another thing."

As Bailey told her family about Clay—with minimal fire-works—she realized how much deeper her whole relationship with him had gone. They accepted it like Paddy, with grim resignation, for her sake. But they were anything but optimistic about things working out.

Then again, neither was she.

"YOU HAVE EIGHTEEN messages." Taz stared at her cell phone, ready to ditch it along with her colors and her blade and everything else associated with her posse.

You don't have them anymore, Taz. They've turned against you.

Slowly she stuffed her GG's jacket, do-rags, and bandana into a paper sack. She'd be flying no more colors. She'd do no more 8-ball. She wouldn't be in the mix.

But at least she hadn't put in any work. She couldn't live with herself if she'd killed somebody.

You can start a new life, Taz. Be who and what you want to be. There are people in Rochester to help you do it.

She was just about to drop the phone in the bag when it rang. She checked caller ID. What they hell? Couldn't she at least say good-bye to her sisters? "Taz here."

"Tazzie, baby, where are you?"

"I'm gone, Maze."

"Whatdaya mean?"

"I'm leavin' town."

"Aw, come on, we need you."

"You booked, Maze. When I was bleedin' in that stinkin' alley, you jetted out."

"We came back. You were gone." Silence. "Who got ya?"

"Nobody."

"It was her, wasn't it?"

"Who?"

"The Street Angel."

They came on the website, Taz.

"Don't know nothin' about no Street Angel."

"We were on your computer."

"So?"

"We know. Come back, Taz and we won't do nothin' about it."

You safe? she'd asked the Street Angel.

Yeah, my identity and the whereabouts of ESCAPE are secret.

Still she should be careful. "What're you talkin' about?"

"How you goin' away if she ain't helpin'?" This time, Mazie's tone was cut-glass hard.

"Got a cuzz in Florida. He sent me money to come down."

"Where are you now?"

"Nowhere. Look, I gotta go. I won't be usin' this number anymore." Suddenly the enormity of what she was doing overwhelmed her. "Take care of yourself, Maze. Tell Qunnie I said that, too."

"Fuck you, hater. You drop a dime, we'll get you." The line went dead.

Hater—the term for snitch. Droppin' a dime—to blow somebody in. Jesus Christ. Taz shook her head and removed the battery from the phone. Then she threw it in the bag and made her way out to the trash. As she stuffed the contents of her gang life into the big steel receptacle, she whispered, "God I hope I know what the fuck I'm doin'."

CHUCK STEWART NODDED to the clock. "I think we can finish up today. I know everybody's anxious to get back home for the holidays." It was three weeks before Thanksgiving, and Clay would spend the majority of the next month and a half in his home state, as most congressmen would.

The Youth Crime Committee had heard all the reports each state task force had assembled. For the areas where there was no disagreement, they pretty much rubber stamped the task force's recommendation. Where there were some concerns about spending, the committee debated. Most instances they compromised. No task force except New York's had sent someone other than their senator to report to Stewart's committee; Bailey had been the only one to come to D.C. Now it was time to decide the money for the Empire State.

"Next up is Clay's state." Stewart shrugged. "I have to tell you, Clay, Bailey O'Neil made a good case. I'm nearly convinced that she should have this shelter."

Clay kept silent, in order to let everyone else speak. His views had been given loud and clear. Except that now . . .

Carol Jenkins spoke up. "I feel the same as Chuck. First, it's not that much money we'd be risking. Second, Ms. O'Neil's shelter could be a prototype where we test out this kind of housing. If it works, we're on to something."

Yeah, with Bailey as the guinea pig.

The willing *guinea pig.*

Others gave their opinions—mostly supportive. Tom Carter, who was still angry at Clay about Jane, didn't comment. Stewart turned to Clay. "Since you're the most vocal on this, any last-minute points before we vote?"

Clay took in a deep breath. He'd given this a lot of thought since Bailey had left last Monday. He scanned the committee members, then focused on Chuck. "Yes, I guess I do. Give her the money."

Startled, Chuck did a double take. "Care to tell us why you changed your mind?"

Because I love her and want to make her happy.

But it was more than that. "Well, for one thing, she wore me down on the task force. She kept battering me with good ideas. And they are good." He sighed. "They just don't align with what I think. However, the money in our bill is for social agencies, and it's going to go to gang kids, anyway. She's the expert. I guess we should let her spend it."

"I don't know what to say," Chuck put in. "Except that maybe you can convince her to take the education post if it comes to fruition."

"I doubt it."

The meeting broke up and as Clay hurried back to his office, he thought of his conversations all week with Bailey. They'd been tender, and not fractious at all, which was surprising since she'd left in a huff.

When he reached his office, most of his staff was gone. Closing the door, he went to his desk and punched out her number.

She answered on the first ring. "O'Neil." She sounded harried.

"Bailey, did I catch you at a bad time?"

"Clay, hi. Um, yeah, I'm running out of here any minute. But I'm glad you called. I probably won't be able to talk to you tonight."

"Why?"

"We're relocating Taz. I've been running around like a chicken with my head cut off with details, but I've got it all arranged."

He struggled with his temper. "*You're* taking her?"

"Me and Joe and Rob." When he didn't say anything, she added, "Clay, Joe's an ex-cop. We've done this before. We're safe."

You'll never be safe working with those kids. Instead, though, he said, "Okay, go."

"Was there a reason you called?"

"Um . . . yes. I have some good news."

"Tell me. I could use it."

"You got your money for Guardian."

A scrambling of noise. "Bailey? Sweetheart, are you all right?"

Rustling. "I . . . um, I dropped the phone. Clay, I'm shocked." She hesitated. "Didn't they listen to you? I'm sorry if they didn't. Well, I'm not really, but if it hurts your reputation, I feel bad."

Hell, he was only human. "Bailey, they listened to me."

A long pause. "What are you saying?"

"I voted to give you the money."

A longer pause. Then in a throaty voice, "Oh, Clay, that means so much to me."

"I know, it's why I did it." He told her about the other voters.

"Just a sec . . ." She talked to someone off the phone. Back on. "I have to go. The van's ready to take off. I'm sorry, I want to hear all about what happened. I'll call you if I don't get back from Rochester too late."

"All right. Good luck."

"I love you, Clay," she whispered. "You won't regret this."

"I hope not. Now go. I love you, too."

* * *

HER HEAD SPINNING, Bailey watched the Interstate 90 green signs tick down their way from New York. Soft soul drifted from the front CD and Rob hummed along as Joe drove. Taz dozed next to her.

Albany . . .

What on earth had possessed Clay to vote for her shelter?
Because he loves you.

Had he really put her beliefs first because of his feelings for her? Could he have really compromised like that?

Utica . . .

What was going to happen to them?

. . . creating a post in HEW that deals with youth crime . . . would you be interested?

To be able to be with Clay every day was a dream she hadn't thought possible. But could she give this up? She glanced over. Taz was sound asleep next to her. Today the girl wore plain Levi jeans, a red sweater and nondescript boots. Her hair was in soft curls, and she'd put on no makeup. She turned and the sweater pulled up. In the light from the lamps on the road, Bailey saw something on her stomach. She leaned over. It was a tattoo. A pitchfork. She gasped.

"What's wrong, doll?" Rob asked from the front seat.

"Her tattoo. It's the same as Moira's."

"Ah."

Memories flooded her. Of her sister coming to live with them. Sharing a room. Confidences, and secrets. And finally, Moira's demise because of gang girls.

Syracuse . . .

She looked around her. She loved this work, loved helping kids. But something was missing. Something Clay had filled.

"You guys ever get tired of doing this?" she asked after a while to the men in the front seat.

"'Bout every day," Joe grunted.

"It's a tough life." They exchanged glances. "You?" Rob asked, turning around.

"Sometimes."

Joe said, "You're young. You got a great kid. Nobody'd

blame you if you left this all behind." He checked the rearview mirror and caught her look. "Not with him, though."

Leaning back, Bailey closed her eyes. God she was tired.

I hate to see you wear yourself out like this. If you were mine, I'd tie you to the bed.

"Bay? Wake up."

Bailey startled awake. "Clay?"

"Shit," Joe said.

"Who's Clay?" Taz asked.

"We're here," Rob announced.

"I must have fallen asleep." She got out of the car with the others. Under a canopy of crystal-clear stars in a cool night, Taz studied the area. "Looks like suburbia."

"It is." Bailey took in the surroundings, too.

The house was a sprawling split-level, white with red shutters. The lawn was closely cut. The neighborhood was a little older, but was well kept. In the small suburb of Gates, Taz would go to a one-thousand-student school, with average, blue collar kids.

"How come I ain't in no city?"

Bailey slid her arm around Taz, surprised she accepted the affection. "Because this is where you belong. Away from temptation. Rochester has gangs, too, but the suburbs usually don't. Or at least they aren't open about it. The Gates School District is one of the best out here. Plus, there are two counselors I know that have experience working with kids out of gangs."

"Thought you said this was anonymous."

"It is. From now on, we'll have no contact with you. Only those two counselors will know your background, but just generally and they'll only know your new name. Tamara Golindo."

The front door opened. Out came a woman and man, both about fifty. He was tall and bald, and she was smaller in stature.

As they approached, Bailey whispered, "They're both school teachers, Taz. You'll like them."

Taz grasped on to her hand. "You know what you're doin', Street Angel, right?"

"Yes, Taz, I do. Nobody up here's going to hurt you here. Now let's go meet with the Conklins."

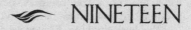 NINETEEN

"I LOVE YOU. Thank you so much for this."

At the moment, Clay was having trouble remembering what *this* was. "Hmm."

She'd stopped kissing his abs and peered up at him. Her sky blue eyes sparkled and her hair was a riotous mass of curls around bare shoulders. The rest of her was beautifully naked, too. "I'm stunned you did that for me, Clay, got the money for Guardian. I . . ."

Playfully he pressed her head back down. "Hell, not now woman!"

She chuckled—and got back to business, thank God. Afterward, he brought her to climax three times before he let her rest.

She cuddled into him, inhaling him, rubbing her hand across his still sweaty chest. "Tell me why you did it."

They hadn't had time to talk between her trip to settle Taz in Rochester and his arrival in New York. They'd rushed into bed, anxious for the connection. The confirmation.

"It's essentially what I told the committee; you wore me

down. But most of all, I decided you've got a point; and you've made me realize that one way—mine—isn't the only way. I think you deserve a chance with Guardian."

"Oh, Clay, that means so much to me."

"It's just that . . ."

"What?"

He grazed her arm, running his fingers up and down her biceps, loving the feel of her. "A lot of people know about us. I had to tell Thorn. Your brothers know. Both the kids. It's going to come out, now, honey, all around."

"I've been thinking. Maybe we could withstand the publicity, despite my background. . . . Senators get elected all the time without the 'proper' kind of woman in their lives."

"You're *my* kind of woman." Sighing he kissed her head. "Thorn called it a Cinderella story."

"Maybe."

"We still have the other problems, though. I'm concerned about your safety if, because of your association with me, people find out who you are. You've gotten a lot of kids out of gangs. Their cronies can't be happy."

"Mostly we'd have to worry about Taz's homies. Many of the kids I've worked with have grown up and so has their set. And a few gangs have been dispersed by the police."

Silence. "Have you heard from her?"

"No. We don't expect to. The host family will communicate only if there's a problem." She stirred and came up on her elbows. "Clay, I have an idea."

"What?"

"If we build Guardian, no one will know of its whereabouts like shelters for battered women."

"Right."

"Maybe I could work there. The Street Angel, so to speak, can retire. She'll just disappear and won't be working directly with kids. Then, after a time, if you and I go public, it won't be a big deal."

"You'd do that?"

"Uh-huh. It would satisfy my desire to get kids out of gangs, but I'd be safer."

"Hell, it could work. Especially since the cops are closing in on the GGs, as well as Anthrax."

"Even if the cops don't get them, maybe Mazie and the gang will fade from our radar now that Taz is out of their clutches. We'll just have to wait and see."

"All right. Until we can figure something else out, we'll keep this between us as quiet as we can."

She nestled back into him. "I love you, Senator."

"I love you, too, Street Angel. No way am I letting you go."

"Good."

THE COMPROMISE FELT terrific. For the first time, Bailey believed she and Clay really had a chance. She floated through the first week of November, feeling optimistic. And she had extra energy. Of course she was sleeping like a rock at night, mostly because she got to see Clay every day. Their lovemaking was amazing.

Dressed in her favorite light blue cotton sweater, a new pair of tan jeans, and a heavy fall jacket, she was whistling when she came into ESCAPE the next morning.

Suze, Joe and Rob were waiting for her. She stopped abruptly in the doorway to her office. "What's up? Somebody win the lottery?"

"You, maybe."

"What do you mean, Suze?"

Joe said, "There was a big bust last night. Apparently, that little altercation Taz had with the girl from Anthrax spiraled into an outright turf war. The police got wind of it, and were in place just as a big brawl broke out. They rounded key members up of both Anthrax and the GGs. Mazie Lennon was among them."

"Oh my God. Then we got Taz out just in time."

"We did." Rob shook his head. Usually unflappable, he seemed enervated. His brown eyes shone with delight. "She would have gone down with them, Bay. We saved her."

"I'm speechless." And she couldn't wait to tell Clay. "So, do the cops think this will disable both gangs?"

"Pretty much." Even Joe's perpetually dark gaze had lightened. "Of course, others'll pop up, but they think these two are diluted enough to scatter like leaves in the wind."

"Whew!" Bailey sank into a chair and removed her jacket.

"So," Rob asked nonchalantly. "What does this mean for you and your senator?"

She stared at her three friends. "A lot. If that gang is gone, and the press finds out about me, I'll be safer now." She studied them. "Particularly if I just run Guardian and you guys take over here."

Rob folded his arms over his chest. "You'd have to retire the Street Angel."

"I know."

Joe shook his head, turned, and left.

She looked at the other two. "What was that all about?"

"He doesn't like the shit Wainwright pulled on you all those years ago, especially sending you to jail. Now, you're hooking up with him." Rob sighed. "We were worried he was just using you, to . . . get you to do exactly what you've done. Leave ESCAPE."

She could feel her face flush. "He wouldn't do that. Besides, ESCAPE will continue without me."

At Rob's skeptical look, she added, "I'm in love with him, Rob."

As always, Rob thought before he spoke. "And he feels the same way?"

"Yes."

"You're sure?"

"I believe in Clay. I know in my heart we have a future together. This was not some big ploy to get me out of ESCAPE."

"Okay, okay, I just had to say it out loud. I'll go talk to Joey."

After he left, she turned to Suze, who was rummaging in her desk. "Do you suspect Clay's motives, Suze?"

She didn't look up. "I suspect everybody." She yanked out another drawer.

Bailey just watched her.

Suze glanced over her shoulder. "Listen girl, you're the best judge of how he feels. I'm more upset that you'd be leaving us." She closed the drawer. "And that I can't find a damn tampon."

"I have some." Bailey stood, crossed to her desk, and pulled out a bag. "Here."

Suze took the bag. "You're a lifesaver." She drew out the pack. "It isn't open."

Bailey frowned. "I guess I didn't need them when I bought them."

Suze went to the john and Bailey frowned. She hadn't used the tampons because her period never came. Which wasn't unusual. Bailey's cycle was about as predictable as February weather. Because of that, she kept track on her calendar when she'd last menstruated.

Her heart beating a bit faster, she sat down at her desk. She flipped the calendar from November to October. Looked for the little checks in the bottom of each box. None, as she suspected. She paged back to September and found the checks in the first four days of the month.

She hadn't had her period since early September? And she'd been sleeping with Clay since just after that. Hmm. It probably didn't mean anything. She'd gone two months before without her period. Hadn't she? Well, worrying wouldn't help.

Turning to her computer, she called up the tracking system they kept on youth gang activity and she entered the new information about Anthrax and the GGs. She thought about what it meant that Mazie and her set had been picked up. Only good things, for Taz. For her and Clay. For the city.

Her gaze strayed back to the calendar. It was hard to believe she and Clay had been sleeping together only two months. She remembered vividly that first time that had begun in her foyer. Had they used precautions every time? She thought so. Hadn't they? No, this was dumb. She was the most irregular woman she knew. Her girlfriends used to tease her about it.

Turning back to her computer, she called up the Internet

sites she'd bookmarked for shelters since Clay had told her he'd okayed her Guardian money. She smiled about it. As she was waiting for one site to download, her hand drifted to her stomach. Pressed. Would she be happy or sad if she was pregnant with Clay's child? "Dumb, dumb, dumb." She had no symptoms. None. Nada.

She'd worked for fifteen minutes before she remembered she'd had no symptoms with Rory either. Not one single sign. Wow, could this possibly be a reality? She couldn't believe it,

CLAY STIRRED THE pasta sauce in his kitchen, humming along to an oldie goldie. "I got you babe . . ." he sang, a bit off-key. He'd just heard the news about the capture of the GGs. He'd phoned Bailey right away to tell her, but her cell was off, and when he called ESCAPE, Rob had said she'd left early.

Maybe she went home to change into something comfortable. And sexy. Not that he gave a damn. He didn't care what she wore, though he himself had put on a red long-sleeved Polo shirt that she said did great things for his eyes.

He went into the dining room to put the finishing touches on the table. He'd found good china and crystal he'd forgotten he had and used it, scrounged up some candles, and had just set the CD for some easy listening when the doorbell rang.

Hurrying to the foyer, he whipped open the door. "Hello, love." He drew her inside, shrugged her out of her jacket and kissed her soundly. She held on tight. Tighter than usual. Maybe she already knew how their future had changed irrevocably today. He drew back, noting the way her blue sweater accented her eyes. "Do you know?"

Her face was flushed and her eyes rounded. "Know?"

"About the GGs?"

"Oh, yeah. It's wonderful news. We got Taz out in time."

A little stung, he said, "That's the only reason it's wonderful?"

"What?"

He peered down at her, wishing ESCAPE didn't always come first. "I thought maybe you'd be happy about the significance of this arrest for us."

She looked up at him. "I'm sorry, I'm distracted."

He didn't know why that pissed him off. He guessed he expected more enthusiasm for *them* as a couple, for their future. Since the GGs had been caught, secrecy was no longer so vital. He turned away from her and crossed to the bar, trying not to go off half-cocked about what could be an imagined slight—something he was prone to do with this woman! "Want some wine?"

"I don't think so. Not just yet."

He wished she didn't muddle his brain so much; he busied himself trying to clear his head, quell his pique. It leaked out anyway. "So you don't see this GG's thing as any more significant than its effect on Taz?" he said with more edge to his voice than he intended.

"Um, yeah, of course I do."

Ice clinked into his glass. "Don't be so enthusiastic about it."

He felt her come up behind him, lean slightly into his back. "You're angry about my reaction?" Hell, she sounded amused.

He shrugged, feeling like a little boy sulking.

"I'm sorry. Something more important came up."

He opened a new bottle of scotch. "As usual." He was pouring his drink when she reached around him and dropped something on the sideboard. "What's that?"

"Look at the box."

He picked it up. EPT. He scowled. "EPT—what's that stand—" His heart stopped in his chest. "An early pregnancy test?"

"Uh-huh."

Whirling around, he clutched the box. Blindly he stared down at it. Then he peered up at her. "It's not open."

"No." She had a smile on her face.

"I take it this is for you."

"Never let it be said the voters elected somebody slow on the uptake."

He didn't smile. "What . . . what's going on?"

Her gaze was direct. "I haven't had a period since the beginning of September."

"It's November." He frowned. "You never had your period when we were together, but I just assumed you'd menstruated the times we were apart." His frown turned to a scowl. "You've suspected something and didn't tell me?"

She shook her head, long black locks going everywhere. "No, actually until about an hour ago, I suspected nothing."

He arched a brow. "Talk about slow on the uptake."

Chuckling, she reached out as if she had to touch him. She laid her palm near his heart. "My period's erratic. It always has been. I never know when it's going to come."

He just stared at her. "That means you never know when you . . ."

"Ovulate. That's right." She drew in a deep breath. "Suze wanted to borrow tampons. I went to get mine, realized I'd never opened that particular box, checked my calendar, and saw how late I was."

His heart began to catapult in his chest. "Do you, um, think you're pregnant?"

Biting her lip, she moved in close. "I think it's a possibility."

"Have you had any symptoms?"

"No." His heart slowed. "But I didn't have any with Rory either."

"So . . ." Heart rate was double timing now. "Why didn't you do the test?"

"I wanted to wait until we were together." She swallowed hard. "Besides, I wanted to ask you something first." She watched him with those fathomless blue eyes. "Before we do it, I need to know if you'd be happy or sad if the test is positive."

He waited until he could form a coherent sentence. "I see. And do I get to ask you the same thing?"

"After you answer. I know how I feel. You have to go first, then I'll see if we match."

Huge emotion battered at his chest. Cradling her cheek in his palm, he smiled. "I would leap for joy if you were carrying my baby, Bailey O'Neil."

A grin split her face. "Me, too, Clayton Wainwright."

He dragged her to him, burying his face in her hair. "Oh, honey." He gripped her tightly, relishing the feel of her, and the significance of this whole development. Then he forced himself to think clearly. "We're getting ahead of ourselves here, though, aren't we?"

"Uh-huh. I just had to know that first."

Drawing back, he stared down at her. "What did you think I'd say?"

"Clay, this whole relationship—everything that's happened between us—has been so unorthodox, and so unexpected . . . I didn't know what to think about this latest thing."

"I'd be really happy, love."

"Well," she said taking the box from him, "let's see if there's anything to celebrate."

She briefed him on the procedure as they climbed the stairs to his bedroom. He couldn't seem to stop touching her; she could be having his child. His mind whirled with a hundred thoughts all jumbling up together. She went directly to the bathroom off his master suite, closed the door, then opened it a short time later. She had a paper cup in her hand and a wand. "It only takes a few minutes." He stood in the doorway as she set the cup on the vanity, inserted the wand. Then she faced him. "It'll say *pregnant* or *not pregnant*."

"No wands turning pink or blue?"

She shook her head.

He stared at her and smiled. She smiled. He checked his watch. She checked hers. Finally she said, "Time to look."

"All right." He grabbed her arm as she turned to the cup, and laced the fingers of both hands with hers. "I love you, Bailey."

Swallowing hard, she withdrew a hand; it shook as she reached for the wand. Peered down. She closed her eyes and passed it to him. It said simply, *pregnant.*

"Ah, love." He pulled her to him. She held on tight, then small tremors shook her. He felt his own eyes mist. Finally she drew back.

"Clay." She reached up and swiped her hands over his face. Trying to swallow the lump in his throat, he whispered,

"I'm happy." After a moment, he took her hand and led her to the bedroom. "I want to see."

She giggled. "See what?"

"Your stomach. Is it bigger?"

"No, though I have no idea whether I'm two weeks or two months along."

Slowly he unzipped her jeans. Sliding them over her hips, he found a pair of red bikini panties, cut below her stomach. Reverently, he knelt down in front of her and placed his cheek against her belly. Then he kissed her there, bringing a new bout of moisture to Bailey's eyes.

Finally he zipped and buttoned her pants and stood. "So, what do we do now, Ms. O'Neil?"

"That's easy. You're going to marry me."

"Excuse me?"

"You're going marry me, Senator."

"Well," he said dryly, "I guess that's all settled."

Then he remembered something.

You didn't marry Rory's father?

No, he asked, but I wasn't in love like I should be.

Yet she wanted to marry *him*.

Reaching down, she grabbed the purse she'd thrown on the bed. From it she drew out a little pouch and gave it to him.

He asked, "What's this?"

"Open it."

He shook the contents into his hand. Out fell two beautiful, gold wedding bands. Filagreed with some kind of design. He looked up at her.

"The rings belonged to my grandparents. They willed them to the only girl in the family. I know they're not fancy, though they are real gold; those are Celtic knots, symbolizing Ireland, and the union of two entities. And they probably won't fit. But I'd like to use them."

He watched her. She stared back at him. When he didn't say anything, she frowned, and then fidgeted. "Don't you . . . I mean, well, if this isn't what you want . . . I'm just surprised. You brought up marriage before . . ."

Gently he put his fingers to her mouth. "Shh, love, be

quiet. I'd like to say something, but you haven't given me a chance."

"All right."

"Though the old-fashioned, conservative guy in me would like to have done the asking, these rings are lovely; I'm touched. And yes, of course, I want to marry you. When?"

THE SURROUNDINGS WERE less than ideal—a small Justice of the Peace's chambers about an hour outside of New York City. In the cherry paneled room, with the smell of eucalyptus surrounding them, Clay and Bailey were married. The bride wore a simple beige dress with a lacy hem. The groom wore a heather brown suit that looked wonderful with his eyes. The witnesses were strangers to Bailey. But the couple couldn't have been happier.

George Gregory had been an old friend of Clay's from Harvard and one he trusted implicitly to keep their marriage quiet—for now. The man beamed a smile at them. "I now pronounce you husband and wife."

Since Bailey had never heard those words or said her own vows, she battled back tears. Clay gripped her hand, and she could see he was overcome with emotion, too. Once again, she marveled at fate. A year ago she was writing scathing letters about him to the newspapers. Four months ago, she refused to see him in person.

Now they were married.

"You may kiss the bride, Clayton."

"Oh, I will, George." Clay took her mouth possessively; his action said, *I'm your husband*.

Since they'd already socialized with his old friend, they were able to leave the chambers shortly after the ceremony and head toward the inn where they were staying.

"Well, Mrs. Wainwright, how does it feel to be married?" Clay asked once they got inside the car he'd rented.

Uh-oh. She shot him a sideways glance.

He caught on. "Oh, I get it. You're not going to be Mrs. Wainwright, are you?"

"Um, no. I'm sorry. We didn't talk about changing my name, but I just assumed . . ."

Placing his hand on her knee, he said, "Shh. We'll discuss it later. Nothing's going to spoil today for me."

"Not even that no one you know and love was here?"

"Well, there is that."

"Do you mind waiting to tell everybody?"

They'd decided, until she could leave ESCAPE, they wouldn't reveal they were married, then they'd have a ceremony in her church. It was an old tune for them both, one neither of them was happy about still singing.

"Hell, yes, I mind. But becoming a daddy again takes the edge off it." He gave her a lecherous grin. "Besides, you can make it up to me when we get to the room."

"Okay."

As he drove through the upscale area, he smiled. "Did I tell you Goldie Hawn has a place not far from the inn where we're staying?"

She laughed heartily at the return to their old joke. "That's right, you can find anybody."

"And don't you forget it. If you ever run away from me . . ."

She sobered. "I'd never run from you, Clay."

"I was teasing, sweetheart."

"I know. I just wanted to say that out loud." She yawned.

"Sleepy?"

She nodded. "Yeah, it's like, now that I've known about the baby for two days, I gave myself permission to feel pregnant. I'm exhausted. And last night, I couldn't eat Mama's stew."

"I hope I get to have Mama's stew sometime."

"You will, I promise. I just know this is going to work out."

For the rest of the trip, they shared silly little hopes and dreams they'd never shared before. A cottage on Keuka Lake that Clay always coveted. Bailey, of course, wanted to go to Ireland. By tacit agreement, they'd tabled all discussion of what still stood between them—like the vice presidency. She wanted to ask about the gang kids who had been rounded up, especially Mazie, but she let that go, too.

"Why the scowl, love?" he asked.

"No reason." Clay was right. This was their wedding day, and even if she did have lingering concerns, she kept them to herself.

On the drive to the inn.

Through dinner.

And later, where she did indeed make up for all the secrecy.

~ TWENTY

THE NEXT MORNING, when they got within the city limits, Bailey turned on her cell phone to call Rory, who was staying with Aidan. She sent for her voice mail while Clay told her bawdy jokes about married couples. So she was laughing when she listened to the first message. "Bay, it's Suze. Call me as soon as you get this."

There were three others from Suze, two from Joe. All said they needed to talk to her.

"What is it?" he asked when she scowled.

"Some emergency at ESCAPE. Since we're so close, I'd like to go there instead of home."

He frowned. "I'm coming in with you."

"What could have gone wrong in two days?" She asked the rhetorical question as Clay dropped her off to find a space to park; she hurried inside.

No one was in Joe's office. Or Rob's. She strode down to hers and was astounded to see Ned Price sitting at a table in the corner with them. They looked up as she entered.

"Thank God," Natale said, worry in his voice.

She hadn't told them about the wedding, only that she needed a few days off. "What happened? And why's the captain here?"

"Sit down, hon." This from Suze.

She took a seat and Price handed her a paper. It was a copy of a transmission on the website. It read, *Where's Taz, cunt? Tell me or you're dead!*

Bailey had been threatened on occasion before, but still, her heart leaped to her throat and her skin grew clammy.

"Who sent this?"

"Mazie Lennon."

Bailey shook her head. "Mazie Lennon's in jail."

"She was," Price told her. "But she gave the cops the slip when they were transferring her to a new facility."

Bailey gripped the paper. "The slip?"

"Yeah, she's out."

Ned had just finished explaining how Mazie got away when ESCAPE's buzzer rang. "It's Clay," Bailey said to Suze. "Would you let him in?"

The cop asked, "Clay Wainwright? How do you know it's him?"

Thinking fast, Bailey said, "I was meeting him here."

"Again?" Natale's scowl. "Why?"

Just then Clay came through the door. "What's going on?" he asked when he saw Price.

"Mazie Lennon escaped," the cop said. "Then these guys called me."

Clay looked down at Bailey and saw the paper in her hand. Wordlessly she handed it to him. "Jesus, Mary, and Joseph," he said after he read it. He looked to Price. "Did you question the other girls?"

"Yeah. They won't tell where the crib is, or how to find her."

"Gang kids don't narc," Bailey told them. "A hater—a snitch—is dead meat if she gets caught."

The cop's gaze hardened. "And these do-gooders won't reveal the whereabouts of the other one, so we can question her."

"The other one?" Bailey asked.

"The one you *saved*, Street Angel."

Bailey frowned. "Of course they won't reveal her whereabouts. We'd lose all credibility with her and any other kid we try to get out if we did divulge her location."

The three ESCAPE workers nodded.

Clay shook his head. Bailey could feel the tension emanating from him.

Price's jaw tightened. "She threatened you, Ms. O'Neil. Your life is in real danger now. I think you can compromise your ethics some in light of that."

"Never." She shot a quick glance at Clay. His face was stony.

Ned followed her gaze. "Look, I don't know what's goin' on between you two, but if you have any sway over this one, Senator, use it." He stood and threw back his chair. "I'm outta here." He left grumbling about social agencies.

Still, Clay was silent.

"Clay, listen, this will be okay." He just stared at her. She glanced to Suze. "We've been threatened before."

Rob said, "Maybe the police will find Mazie."

Joe Natale scowled. "If we tell where Taz is, we're done here."

Clay straightened and put his hand on the back of Bailey's chair. "I can't believe all of you. You're going to keep quiet when that gang is coming after Bailey?"

"She can handle herself," Suze said.

Natale's chin raised. "We have before."

Rob Anderson leaned back against the table and said nothing.

Clay grasped her shoulders possessively. "Yeah, well she wasn't pregnant with my child before. She wasn't my *wife* then."

All three spoke at once.

"Your wife?"

"Your child?"

"Holy hell."

"Well," Bailey said. "So much for secrecy."

A GUST OF November wind blew closed the door to Clay's town house, just after he entered. Like the weather, he was raging; he was more frustrated and angry than he could ever remember being in his life. "That woman is so fucking stubborn . . ." He saw a wastebasket and kicked it, sending the contents sprawling. Crossing to the sideboard, he poured himself a scotch and swore again, all the colorful words he could think of. Bailey just wouldn't budge. She'd asked her colleagues to leave them alone, then faced him . . .

"Our marriage and my pregnancy have absolutely no bearing on how ESCAPE operates. We never have disclosed placements and we won't now."

"Then you call Taz and ask her where the crib is."

"Clay, I can't do that. If she knew I told you her whereabouts, or even if I just asked for her help, she'd see it as a betrayal. She might run if she thinks we're using her."

"So what? You'd be safe."

"Not if she goes back to the GGs. I wouldn't know anything, and she'd be lost, and Mazie could still come after me. It would be a waste."

"How do you know she won't tell you their location?"

"Gang kids, even when they relocate, don't give up the whereabouts of their posse."

"She likes you. You have a relationship. Tell her you're in danger."

He saw it then—the confirmation that flitted through her eyes.

"I'm right, aren't I? She'd be swayed by knowing you're in jeopardy."

"No."

He grabbed her wrist. "Don't lie to me."

"Let me go."

He dropped her arm. "Doesn't it matter to you that you're pregnant? If something happens to you, it happens to our baby."

"Nothing's going to happen to me."

"You don't know that."

"Clay—"

"No!" His voice rose. "I won't listen to this. I'm your husband now. I have some say over what you do."

She bristled. "I wasn't aware that was in the vows."

"Bailey please . . ."

She'd stormed out then. He followed her but before he could retrieve the car to take her home, she'd ducked into a cab.

I'll never run from you Clay. What had that been—twenty-four hours ago?

He'd come back to his town house because he was so angry. And because he had a plan. There was no way he was going to allow this to happen. Thinking of her carrying his baby gave him the courage to whip out his cell phone.

His buddy answered on the first wring. "Lewis here."

"Josh, it's me, Clay."

"Hey, Senator, how's it going?"

"Not so well. I have an emergency. I need you to do something asap."

"Sure. What?"

"I want you to find somebody. Her name is Tazmania Gomez. But she's in a protection program for kids getting out of gangs."

"This the one we saw your friend Bailey with?"

"Yes."

"She'd be buried pretty deep. It'd take a while."

"It needs to be done yesterday."

"If I had something to go on more than the pictures . . ."

He remembered Bailey's excitement on the phone when he told her about the funding for Guardian. Ironic that giving her what she wanted had given *him* the information he needed. "She was relocated ten days ago. To Rochester, New York."

DRESSED IN CASUAL slacks, a light sweater, and a not-heavy-enough jacket for upstate New York in November, Clay leaned against a brick wall outside of Gates High School at seven o'clock the next morning. In his hand, he held a new picture of Tamara Golindo, aka Taz Gomez, and her location—school, home, even the kind of car her host family, the Conklins, drove. Goddamn, Josh was good. Clay had the information by last night; since he'd missed the last plane out of New York, and already had a rented car, he'd driven the six hours up here, arriving in time for school.

Watching the teenagers trundle off the bus with their leather jackets, headphones, and cocky attitudes reminded him of when Jon was an adolescent. God, he wondered how these teachers did it. Right now, several stood out in cold November wind on bus duty, for Christ's sake!

He turned and scanned the parking lot. If he didn't catch Taz when she arrived in the car Josh had described, he'd go into the school and use his own identity as a senator to get her out of class. He hoped he didn't have to do that. He preferred this contact to be kept a secret.

Because when he was finished here, he didn't plan to tell Bailey what he'd done. Not until Mazie was caught. She hadn't called him after their argument yesterday, and he hadn't called her. He wondered what she was doing now. If she was safe. He had Ned Price standing by waiting for a call with the location of the GG's crib and other hangouts. Clay was going to protect his wife and child even if she never spoke to him again.

Which she very well might not. He knew what the ramifications of his actions would be. Bailey would be furious, but she'd be safe.

A gray Honda civic pulled into the lot. Bingo! Immediately he headed down the grassy slope to the blacktop. Taz Gomez got out of the car; Bailey had said she was beautiful, and she was, especially now, when she looked so normal. Dressed in a battered brown leather jacket and jeans, her dark hair soft around her shoulders, she could be just any teenager at school. She was retrieving her books out of the trunk when he reached her.

"Taz, I need to talk to you."

The girl froze.

Clay moved in closer. "Taz? I know who you are."

She slammed the trunk. "Don't know who you talkin' to, mister. My name is Tamara."

Since she looked ready to bolt, he said, "I'm a friend of the Street Angel's."

Her head snapped around. "She send you here?"

"No."

A frown. "I don't get it."

"My name is Clay Wainwright. I'm a U.S. Senator and her husband."

"She ain't married."

"She is now." Stupidly he held out his hand to show her his ring. "We got married yesterday. I've come to see you because she's in danger."

"Danger, how?"

"From Mazie Lennon. Your friend's threatening my wife."

Taz slammed the trunk. "The Street Angel can take care of herself."

Clay knew he was going to have to play his trump card. "Maybe so. But she's pregnant, Taz. With my child. And I need you to help me protect her."

TAZ TROMPED INTO school just as the bell rang for first period. She was upset about what she'd done—tellin' the feds where Mazie was—but fuck it, she couldn't risk nobody's kid. So she'd dropped a dime on her homies. She was a hater after all.

"They're not your homies anymore, Tazzie baby," she told herself.

Still, as soon as the senator had taken off, she wondered if she'd done the right thing. Should she have checked out this guy? She wouldn't tell him anything until she saw his ID, a Senate badge, even his marriage certificate to Bailey O'Neil, who he contended was the Street Angel. Taz remembered the night they drove to Rochester, they called her *Bay*. But she needed to confirm it all, so she got a pass to the computer lab during study hall and Googled him.

Okay, the line items showed he was a senator, like he said. She scrolled down the entries. Jesus, there was enough on him. She got to one that caught her eye. "Washington Eagle clashes with the Street Angel."

Taz called up that article. It was an interview by a guy names Hank Sellers given by the Street Angel about Senator Clayton Wainwright. She criticized him big-time. Taz's heart beat faster in her chest. She went back to the entries. Some of these were old. But she read them anyway. They said the

Street Angel hated Wainwright. He wanted to close her down. They were open enemies. Oh my God, had she just given that guy the ammunition to destroy the Street Angel?

And to take out her home girls?

No, wait. Taz remembered something else about that night they drove up here. The Street Angel woke up disoriented and called out for *Clay*. Fuck it! Had the Street Angel set her up? Could she have fallen for this guy and betrayed Taz? Her mind screamed, *no, no, no*. But she was confused.

Immediately she went on the ESCAPE website. Clicked in. And waited until the site came up.

Street Angel, is that you?

No, it's me again, her coworker. Taz, are you all right? You're never supposed to contact us.

I need to talk to the Street Angel. When will she be on?

I'm not sure. She's off for a few days.

Shit! Now she wouldn't find nothing out. She couldn't shake the notion that she'd been tricked, that maybe the Street Angel was in on this. Fuck it, Taz knew what she had to do. She stood and headed for the door.

"Tamara, are you going somewhere?" The aide checked the clock. "You have a bit more time."

Taz shook her head. "I don't have no time at all, lady," she said, and she left the room.

"NED, IT'S CLAY."

"We're standing by. Where is she?"

"I got three locations from the girl. You'll have to check them all out."

"I'll put more men on it. Damn it, I wish there weren't so many; we could miss her going from one to the other."

"Don't."

"You all right?"

"Yeah, feeling a little like Judas, but I'm all right." And he was. He *had* to do this.

"I'll keep you posted."

"I'm driving back now. I have my cell on me so stay in contact. I want to know the minute Lennon's apprehended."

"I'll be in touch."

Clay clicked off and tried to concentrate on the road. He tried hard *not* to think about Bailey. Her face when she told him she'd never run from him. Her affirmation that she believed in him. Damn it, he thought, pounding the steering wheel with his fist. He didn't have any choice. If she wouldn't take care of herself, he had to keep her safe. Her and their baby.

Impatient to get back to New York, he stepped on the gas. He needed to see her. He was on the outskirts of Rochester when he saw a car slam on the brakes in front of him. Shit. This was all he needed, he thought, as he hit his own brakes.

Then, he felt an impact from behind.

TAZ MANEUVERED THE Conklins' car through the streets of New York. It would have been on hit having wheels in this city, but today, Taz was scared. She'd already checked out the three places she'd told the senator to look for Mazie—nobody was there—and now she didn't know what to do. So she decided to go home. Her father wasn't at the apartment. She called and he didn't answer.

Her plan had two ways to go. She'd grab her computer and try to get to the Street Angel online; if she'd been straight with Taz and wasn't in cahoots with the Senator, Taz was gonna tell Mazie what had happened and go back to the gang. If Taz returned to them, Mazie would be cool—after she knocked the shit out of her. But so long as Taz was back, Mazie wouldn't do nothing more.

If, however, Taz found out the senator *was* lying, and the Street Angel had sold her out, Mazie could go after the woman with all she had; hell, Taz would even help. After all, she even knew the Angel's real identity now. English teachers would call that ironic. In hoping to save his wife, the senator had gave them ammunition to gun her down.

But as she parked the car in an alley below her apartment, then made her way up the fire escape, Taz admitted she didn't want to do that. She felt close to the Street Angel. She hoped they didn't have to do nothing to her.

The window was ajar. The stupid bastard. Didn't even lock

up. She slid it open and crawled inside. She didn't turn on the light. God she hated how this place smelled. For a minute, her heart hurt remembering the pretty wallpapered bedroom the Conklins had set up for her. It didn't matter. She'd stay here just until she got her computer, her stash of money, and some clothes. Tamara's clothes were all gone. She let a wave of sadness about leaving Rochester rush through her. She'd only been there a couple of weeks, but the Conklins rocked, and she'd been making friends at school. "Stupid, stupid, stupid," she said as she opened the closet door.

From the dark corner of the room, she heard, "You got that right, Tazzie baby. You are one stupid cunt."

Taz whirled around. Mazie stepped out of the shadows. She was wild-eyed; she reeked of blow. And she was pointing a double deuce handgun at Taz's chest.

BAILEY HADN'T HEARD a word from Clay, which shocked and hurt her; she was sitting at her computer at ESCAPE, wondering where her life was going, when Joe Natale burst into the office. "Bailey, oh, fuck. I got bad news."

She threw back her chair and stood. Rob was right behind him. "What?"

He shrugged his shoulder. "Taz Gomez is dead."

"What?" It didn't compute. "That's . . . that's impossible. She's in Rochester, with the Conklins."

"The Conklins called here before you came in. All they knew was that Taz left school today. Apparently she drove back to New York. The police just found her in her father's apartment."

Bailey's head began to buzz; her stomach heaved; she stared at Joe, unable to internalize what she was being told.

Before she could respond, the office phone rang. Suze picked it up. Everything seemed surreal; Suze's voice even sounded far away and unnatural. "Oh, yeah, that's great. Yeah, I'll tell her. Thanks, Captain." She clicked off.

Rob had moved in close to Bailey and slid his arm around her. "What now?"

"Mazie Lennon was picked up by the police at her crib.

She had a gun on her." Suze's face was somber. "It matched the twenty-two that killed Taz."

"Oh, God." Bailey wobbled, then sank into a chair. After a moment, she asked, "At their crib? How did the police find it?"

"Price wouldn't say."

"The cops have a network of snitches," Natale put in. "One probably called in."

Bailey shook her head, as if that would help make sense of all this. "I can't believe it."

Rob, the psychologist, squatted before her and grasped her hands. His big blue eyes held a wealth of sympathy. "Bay, I'm so sorry. I know how you cared about this girl."

She gripped his hands and battled back the emotion in her throat. "I did. I . . ." She stood abruptly. "Look, I have to go."

"Go where?" Suze asked, alarmed. "Stay here with us."

"No, I have to think this out. I want to be alone." She grabbed her coat and rushed toward the door to the protests of her friends. Whom she'd lied to. She didn't need to be alone. She had to find Clay.

"YOU'RE LUCKY TO be alive, Senator."

His vision blurry, Clay peered up at the ER doctor, who didn't seem much older than Jon. A pungent antiseptic smell stung his nostrils. "I, um, yes, I know. How's the driver of the other car?"

"Drunk."

"What?" Clay had been sure his excessive speed had caused the accident on Route 90. All he remembered was slamming on his brakes when somebody stopped abruptly in front of him on the thruway. Then there was some kind of impact. Then Clay had blacked out.

"The guy who hit you from behind was drunk."

He ran his hand over his jaw. "I thought I ran into somebody."

"You did, after you were rear-ended. That driver's about as bad as you. The drunk doesn't have a scratch."

"How bad am I?" He knew his head hurt like hell; he raised his hand and felt a bandage at his temple. The movement told him he was sore all over.

"Slight concussion," the doctor said. "We'd like to keep you the rest of the night."

"Night? What time is it?"

"About midnight."

"You're kidding."

"You've been in and out of consciousness since the accident this morning."

"Shit." He reached for his cell phone in his pocket, but encountered a hospital gown. "I need my cell."

"There's no cell phone use in the hospital."

"Can I check the messages on my phone?"

The doctor nodded as he made a notation at his chart.

"I'll need to use another phone, too."

"Sure. Your clothes are over there in the bag." He nodded to the nurse. "Ms. Jackson can help you out with both." He started to walk out.

"I can't stay here all night," he called after the doctor.

The man glanced over his shoulder. "We'll talk about it when I get back."

His head still fuzzy, Clay watched the nurse, at his request, sift through his clothes. "I'm sorry, Senator, there's no cell phone in your pocket."

"Damn." He lay back on the pillows. "That's right, it's in the car."

"Oh, dear. I was told the car was totaled."

"Jesus." He drew in a breath, started to sit up, but a wave of dizziness caught him. He dropped back down on the pillow. "I need a phone. It's imperative."

"I'll see what I can do." The nurse left.

Clay lay back, his head pounding like a jackhammer. How the hell had he been so unlucky? He needed to get to New York to talk to Ned Price. He had to know if they got Mazie.

He struggled to keep his eyes open. Then he had to tell Bailey he'd betrayed her. He'd used information she'd let slip to the man she loved, to get what the senator, whom she didn't like much at all, thought she needed. What she *did* need, damn it! He wouldn't apologize for saving her from Mazie Lennon.

Though his mind was hazing over, he thought about Taz. She'd seemed all right with his explanation for why he'd violated the protection order. When they picked up Mazie, could Clay convince Bailey that Taz was still safe and they'd caught the bad guy, so his actions had been acceptable? Certainly Clay knowing Taz's whereabouts wouldn't jeopardize her safety. Maybe everything would fall into place. His eyes grew heavy. Bailey would be mad. Probably for a long time. But she was carrying his baby and she'd have to forgive him eventually.

The next thing he knew, his blood pressure was being taken. Blips and beeps surrounded him, as well as a low rumble of voices. His eyes flew open to see a different nurse doing the task. "What time is it?"

"Six a.m. I just came on."

"Hell." He glanced around. "Where's the phone?"

"What phone?"

He shook his head. The other nurse hadn't done anything about getting him a phone in here. By the time he managed to crawl out of bed and dress, he was exhausted. But he found his way to a hallway phone. At least his wallet and phone card were in his pocket. He dialed Bailey's cell first, then something made him hang up. A feeling. He redialed Ned Price. Clay should know what he was dealing with, first. If Mazie was caught, he'd be in a better place with his wife.

"Price." The guy sounded sleepy.

"Ned, it's me Clay. I'm sorry to wake you."

"Shit, Senator, where have you been? I've called your cell a thousand times."

"I was in a car accident on the way home from finding Taz. I've been in the hospital, apparently overnight."

"You all right?"

"Yeah. What's gone down? Did you get Mazie Lennon?"

Absolute silence.

"Ned?"

"Yeah, Senator, we caught Mazie Lennon. She's behind bars."

Relief surged through him. This was going to be all right. Bailey was safe. "Don't let her get the slip on you this time."

"She won't. She's in maximum security."

He thought a minute. "Isn't that unusual for a kid under eighteen?"

"Clay, look, there's something else."

"Oh, God, is Bailey all right?"

"Far as I know. Though I heard she was shaken when she found out."

"About Mazie?"

A long pause. "No, about Taz Gomez."

"Shit, Bailey knows I came up here?"

"Not that I'm aware." The tough cop's voice was hoarse. "Clay, I don't know how to soften this; Mazie Lennon shot Taz Gomez before we could get to her. When we finally did catch up, Mazie still had the gun."

His heart in his throat, he asked, "How . . . how is Taz?"

The cop said, "She's dead."

LOOPING HER SCARF tighter around her neck against the bold November wind, Bailey walked toward her family's pub; she was exhausted, and feeling hollow. It had been twenty-four hours since she'd found out Taz was dead. The young, beautiful girl was no more. Bailey could still remember her words online . . .

How come she in a gang if she got family like you?

She could still hear Taz's voice the few times they talked . . .

You married . . . you got a guy?

Any kids? I love them.

She could still see Taz's gorgeous Hershey-kiss eyes. Now the light was out in them forever.

Biting back a groan, Bailey pushed open the door to the pub. Taz was dead. Killed by her home girls because, at Bailey's dogged insistence, she'd tried to get out of the gang. . . .

Don't get out of no gang, lady.

Yes, yes you do. ESCAPE has programs. We have people trained to help. We can protect you. The words stung, the poison of guilt shooting through her veins.

As the comforting smells and feel of the pub surrounded her, Bailey pushed the memory away. If she thought about how responsible she was for Taz's death, she'd go crazy. Instead, she'd think about the baby. After she removed her coat, her hand went to her stomach. But thoughts of the baby only led to thoughts of the baby's father. Whom she hadn't been able to get in touch with nor had she heard from in twenty-four hours.

Sinking down onto the barstool, she buried her face in her hands. Would anything ever be right again?

"Hey, lass, what are you doin' here?" She looked up to see Patrick had come out of the bar. He was followed by Aidan. Paddy ambled down behind the counter and Aidan outside it.

"I had to do *something*. Once Rory went to school, I couldn't stand being alone."

Resting his hand on her shoulder, Aidan kissed her head. "How are you feeling?"

"I don't want to talk about Taz." Only to Clay; he'd make sense of this; he'd make everything better. "But I'm really worried about Clay."

"You still haven't heard from him?" Aidan asked.

Patrick took out a cloth and began to wipe down the bar.

"No. It's so unlike him. I know he's mad at me, but this . . ."

Paddy's head shot up. "Why's he mad?"

She hadn't told anybody, not even Aidan, about the baby, the wedding, or their fight about her safety; she was waiting for the right time. Then all this happened. "Long story."

Her phone rang. She checked the readout but didn't recognize the ID. "Hello."

"Bailey, it's Father Tim. I just heard about Taz. Where are you? I'd like to see you."

"Oh, Father Tim, thanks, but I . . ." She looked around the bar. Bit her lip, to keep her feelings inside. "I can't see anybody now. I can't talk about this."

"Then I'll just come and sit with you."

"No, please. I'm at the pub with my brothers. I'm going to stay here." Until Clay calls. Or comes to find me. Then things would be all right.

It took some convincing, but the priest agreed to go to ESCAPE instead, to see if he could help the others deal with what had happened. Bailey held on to the phone when he clicked off, wishing it would ring again and be Clay.

"You should go home and sleep." This from Aidan.

She ran a hand through her hair. Had she even combed it this morning? Glancing down, she saw she wore jeans and a fuzzy pink sweater that she didn't even remember putting on. "I can't sleep."

Paddy honed in on her. "Then take a pill."

Her hand went to her stomach, beneath the bar. "I can't. Look, I'll just stay here and help out with lunch."

Her brothers exchanged a concerned look. "You wanna work here?" Paddy asked.

"What about ESCAPE?" Aidan asked.

She felt her face blanch. "I'm not going back there."

"Why?"

Abruptly she stood. "Look, if you're going to rag on me like this, I'll go somewhere else." Her heart clenched. "But I wanted to be with you here today. You always make me feel better."

"We'll lay off, honey." Aidan handed her a towel, which she wrapped at her waist.

She circled around to the back of the bar. "I'll wash the glasses, Paddy. Go do something else."

Paddy kissed her head and went to check on things in the kitchen. The familiar smells were beginning to waft out and made Bailey's stomach queasy.

Aidan stayed where he was, watching her. She stole a glance at him. "I said don't start."

"What's going on with Clay? Why was he mad at you?"

She bit her lip. "Got an hour?"

"I got all day, B."

The emotion started to come again, and she couldn't let that happen. "I know you mean well, but I've got to keep this all under control. I'm not up to answering questions." She turned pleading eyes on him. "Please, A., do as I ask this time."

"Okay." He reached over the bar and squeezed her arm. "I'm here if you need somebody to talk to."

She swallowed hard. "Thanks." But, she wouldn't talk to her brother this time. She'd talk to Clay. Only Clay. He'd make her feel better. He'd make her see . . . she didn't know what, and she didn't care. She just knew she needed him now.

After she finished with the glasses, she checked her phone for messages. None. She couldn't believe it. Where *was* he? Who could she call to find him? Jon? His offices in D.C? She tried his cell again. No answer. She closed her eyes. If something had happened to him, too . . .

For a moment, the possibility made her woozy and she grasped on to the bar. No, no, she wouldn't think that way. She wouldn't buy trouble. She had enough of the real stuff.

She held on through the lunch crowd, which kept them all busy, even though she had trouble looking at the food. She even kept it together when she saw on the TV over the bar the report about Mazie. She had to turn away, though, when Taz's picture came on. Through it all, she waited for Clay.

The lunch crowd dribbled out and she was wiping the last of the tables in the corner when the door to the pub swung open. She turned.

And there he stood.

"Oh, my God, Clay." She flew to him.

He caught her and held on to her tight.

Once in his embrace, Bailey came apart.

CLOSING HIS EYES, Clay held on to Bailey as she dissolved in his arms. He bit the inside of his jaw, forcing back the guilt and self-loathing he'd been experiencing ever since his phone conversation with Ned Price this morning.

As she plastered herself to him, and wept wrenchingly, Clay was overcome with what he'd done—he'd reduced her to this. Because, as always, he thought he knew better than she what was best. How could he have been such an idiot? He was responsible for a young girl's death—he, Clayton Wainwright, who'd spent his career trying to save kids.

Her brothers, all four of them, strode to the front of the bar and stood before them. Their faces were washed with a myriad of emotions—shock, sadness, and a little bit of fear. He kissed Bailey's head and anchored his hand at her neck. "That's it, baby, cry it out."

He heard Aidan say, "She hasn't cried at all since we found out."

All the more reason to let her get rid of the emotion. She did, eventually. Her brothers stood guard until she finished the catharsis. Liam handed Clay a handkerchief, which he gave to Bailey; she mopped her face and turned in his arms. He left one hand on her neck, the other at her waist. "Don't start," she said when Paddy opened his mouth to speak.

"I wasn't going to. I'm glad you cried. You needed it. If this guy was what did it for you, fine."

Her eyes narrowed on her brother. "He's what I need, Paddy." She scanned the others. "He's my husband now." Her hand went to her stomach. "And I'm expecting his baby."

"What the hell—" This from Dylan.

But Patrick stepped forward. "Stop, Dylan. Bailey can't handle our shit now. She's too raw." He leaned over and kissed her cheek. "When you're ready, honey, you can tell us all about this." He straightened and shook his head at his brothers. Then he turned to Clay. "There's a back room. You can go there."

Clay nodded, holding on to Bailey. When they took a step and she wobbled, he scooped her up in his arms. Cuddling her to his chest, he panicked at the thought of telling her his part in Taz's death. But he wouldn't let himself think about the repercussions. He strode to the back room and tried to lay her on the couch. She clung to him, whispered, "Nooo, please," so he sat down with her on his lap, biting back a groan at the movement. He was running on empty, and he still hurt everywhere.

"I'm so sorry," he said.

"I know. Me, too." She buried her nose in his chest. "It's my fault."

Oh, God. "No, baby, no. It's not."

"Yes, if I hadn't been so sure I was right. Always so right. If I'd listened to you and let the cops do their job, instead of interfering, she might still be alive."

She'd be alive if I hadn't intervened. "Bailey, honey, you can't blame yourself."

"I do." She drew back. "If I—oh, God, Clay, what happened to you? I didn't even . . ." She touched the bandage on his temple and studied the bruises on his face.

"Car accident." *When I was coming back from betraying your trust.*

"Are you all right?"

I may never be all right again. "Yes, but I was knocked out, spent the night in the hospital."

"That's why you didn't call me. I thought for sure you'd call as soon as you heard. I . . . tried to call you." Tears again. "I need you to help me through this, Clay. I can't do it alone."

"You're not alone, sweetheart." *Even after I tell you what I did.* "You've got me and your family."

Tightly she gripped the lapels of his suit. "No, no, I need *you*. Please, Clay, promise me, you won't leave me for the next few days. I need you—just you—to get through this."

A bit shocked at her response, he swallowed hard. Had he just been given a reprieve, or sentenced to purgatory? Could he *help her through* what he himself had caused without telling her what he'd done, which he'd planned to do as soon as he saw her?

"Clay, please. I know we fought that day we came back from getting married. I know you're upset . . ."

"Shh. It's not that." He pulled her to his chest. "And of course, I'll be here. For as long as you want me."

"Forever," she mumbled and cuddled into him.

Probably not, he told himself. But for now, at least she'd take his comfort.

He was wallowing in the depths of guilt when Bailey fell asleep; he stretched her out on the couch, covered her with a blanket, then walked back to the bar proper. Her brothers deserved an update on how she was. And they probably had something to say about the bombshell Bailey had dropped.

Aidan was behind the bar. The others weren't in sight. Sinking onto a stool, he saw a beer set down in front of him.

"You look like you could use this."

Clay took a sip. "You have no idea."

Aidan angled his head to the back. "She asleep?"

"Yes. I think she needed the outlet to rest."

"I'm sure she did."

Clay blew out a heavy breath. "Listen, about the other stuff?"

"What, that you're married and have a kid on the way?"

"She would have told you. But it all happened so fast—finding out about the baby, getting married right away. Then as soon as we got back, the rest of it started to go down."

He told Aidan of Mazie's threat, of the fight they had over it, of Bailey's stubbornness about her safety.

Aidan listened, alternately swearing and thanking God. When Clay finished—omitting his part in all this—Aidan stared hard at him. "If I were you, Wainwright, and it were my wife and baby at stake, I'd have done more than yell at her."

Clay looked up. "Yeah? What would you have done?"

"I'd have gone to look for Taz. Gotten the whereabouts of Mazie and her gang from the girl to protect Bailey."

"You would have?"

"Yep."

Frowning, Clay shook his head. "Then you'd be responsible for what just destroyed the strongest woman I've ever met in my life." His voice was hoarse, just thinking about how Bailey broke down.

"Yeah, but she'd be safe. Worth it, I think."

"She'd never forgive me . . . you . . . your wife wouldn't forgive you, I mean, if you went against her like that."

"Maybe she would, maybe she wouldn't. Who knows?"

Suddenly it hit Clay. Aidan knew. Had guessed somehow. Before he could say more, her brother started talking again. "Of course, finding the right time to tell her would be the trick."

"The right time?"

"Yeah, you couldn't tell her now. When she's so bereft. You'd have to wait. I imagine that'd kill me in the interim, deceiving her like that."

"You got that right."

"But I'd do it. I'd put off confessing my guilt, dumping it on her, until she was stronger." He swallowed hard. "Especially if she was pregnant," he said. "The baby's welfare might be at stake."

"You really think that would be the right thing to do, Aidan?"

He zeroed in on Clay. "I know my sister, Senator. I've

never seen her so distraught. So dependent. She wouldn't talk to anybody about this, and only let go with you. You gotta help her through it, man."

"Of course I will."

"Without dumping the other stuff?"

"The *hypothetical* other stuff?"

"Yeah, sure, that."

Clay sighed. He'd listen to Aidan. Clay was too close to this and her brother knew her so well. Maybe it was best to get her through these few days, then to tell her what he'd done.

Not to mention you'd get time with her, before she found out you betrayed her.

No, he wasn't thinking about himself. Aidan was right. This would be best for Bailey.

Clay just hoped he could do it.

TWENTY-ONE

"HOLY FATHER, OUR God, I commend now, the body of your child Tazmania, into the ground."

The November wind picked up, blowing open Bailey's coat and stinging her cheeks. At Father Tim's words, she sucked in a breath and leaned on Clay, as she had since he came to find her at the pub two days ago. Clutching his arm, she drew strength from him to endure this ordeal.

Father Tim looked over at her and gave her a sad smile. She nodded, picked up one of the roses off to the side, and placed it on the pretty white casket. Rob, Joe, and Suze followed suit. Taz's father hadn't attended. He'd been contacted, but the man asked Rob why should he come, saying that Taz was no good to him now. She'd never had a chance.

Well, she'd had one chance, and gave it up. No one knew why Taz had left the Conklins and come back to her home girls. But the reason didn't matter. She returned to the city and now she was dead.

After Suze, Joe, and Rob all stepped forward to place a flower on the casket, Clay did the same. He looked haggard with deep grooves around his mouth. The bump on his temple had gone down and the bruises were fading, but his color wasn't good. Though he'd been her rock for two days, he seemed so breakable right now and incredibly sad. He loved Bailey so he probably just hated seeing her suffer; and she knew he truly felt bad about Taz.

When the service ended, Bailey crossed to the casket one last time. She felt Clay come up behind her. Leaning over, she kissed the simple box, and whispered, "I'm so sorry, Taz."

She drew back, pivoted, and looked at Clay; there was moisture in his eyes. God, she loved this man. As she moved in close, she glanced over his shoulder. Behind him stood her brothers, all dressed in suits. Oh, God, she hadn't seen them before. She burst into tears, then went to each one and hugged him. "Thanks for coming."

They murmured their regrets and held her tight.

"Come back to the pub," Aidan said when things broke up. "We already asked your colleagues from ESCAPE. Have a little lunch, a beer. Be with the people you love."

Her gaze swung to Clay. "Shouldn't I get Rory?"

Pat answered before Clay could. "Brie's bringing him over to the pub after school."

Again she looked to Clay. He said, "It's a good idea, honey."

"All right."

They'd rented a car again, and she and Clay found the gray sedan and climbed in. The warmth of the interior felt good after being outside. "Thanks for that," she said, her hand on the knee of his dark navy suit. Her suit was navy, too, but she'd needed Clay's help picking out her clothes this morning.

His smile was warm and loving. "I told you I'd be here for you."

"I know. It's the only thing holding me together."

"I love you. I hope you'll remember that."

What an odd thing to say. But she was too tired to figure it out. She laid her head back on the seat. "That's not what I meant, though."

"What did you mean?"

"Thanks for paying for the funeral."

"How . . ."

"How did I know? I went to take care of the bill after the arrangements were made. The director said an anonymous donor had already covered it."

"How do you know it was me?"

"Because I know you. You're a generous, honest, wonderful man." Her throat closed up and she fingered the wedding band on her finger. "I was so wrong about you."

"Oh, honey."

She shut her eyes and sank farther into the seat. After a moment, Clay reached over and pressed his hand into her stomach. "How's our girl?"

"Girl, huh?"

"Yep. And she's going to look just like you."

"You're a sap about this kid."

"Hey, I owe her. It's the only thing that saved me from your mother's wrath."

They'd told her parents and Rory, of course, since Clay was staying at her house, that they were now husband and wife. Her mother had started to cry until Bailey said she was not only married, but pregnant. Then in typical grandma mode, she'd hugged Bailey and was a little warmer to Clay. Her father, given his own past, had been more accepting, and beamed about the baby. The verdict was still out for the guys, though Aidan and Clay seemed on good terms.

By the time she and Clay reached the pub, Bailey was spent, but she felt better being encompassed in the warmth of her friends and family. Around noon, Brie arrived with Rory, and Patrick asked her to stay. She looked hesitant, then agreed. The lunch was pleasant and homey and lulled Bailey into a calm state. By two, the ESCAPE people were ready to leave.

Hugging her tight, Suze said, "Chin up, girl. We'll get through this."

Rob and Father Tim both offered their counseling expertise.

Joe Natale enveloped her in a big bear hug. "We'll take care of you kid," he said gruffly. He still wouldn't speak to Clay.

When they were left, Bailey yawned.

"I think you've had enough," Clay told her. "We should go home."

Linking her arm with his, she laid her head on his shoulder. "I need a nap."

Rory slid off the bar stool where he'd been drawing, and tugged on Clay's pants. "No nap, I'm too big."

"A nap for Mommy," Clay said and ruffled Rory's hair.

"You take me to the movies."

Bailey stiffened. Clay hadn't left her side in two days. She'd even accompanied him to his town house to pick up some clothes. She touched her son's arm. "Um, not today Ror."

"Wanna see *Spider-Man Three*." His words were spoken with typical five-year-old whininess.

Panic welled inside her. Her heart rate speeded up and she felt clammy all of a sudden. Clay sensed it. "Maybe when Mommy gets up we all can go."

"I'll take him and Kathleen to the movies," Patrick offered, having overheard the conversation from behind the bar.

Seeing Rory balk, and sensing what Bailey needed, Brie stepped forward. "I'll go too." She knew Rory loved her like a second mother. "Come on, buddy, it'll be just like when the four of us saw *Spider-Man Two*."

"'Kay." He stared at Bailey. "I like having Clay with us."

"I know, sweetheart."

"You're my mommy," he said, hugging her.

"Yes, love, I am. I'm just sad now. I need Clay to take care of me."

"Me, too."

When Bailey and Clay arrived back at her house, he took her coat and hung it up. Grasping her shoulders, he said softly, "I'm going to tuck you in, then I have some calls to make."

She grabbed his hand and kissed it. "All right." In her room, he unzipped her dress from behind. Then, in a totally possessive gesture, he leaned over and kissed her spine.

"Hmm, feels good."

He pushed the dress off her shoulders; it fell to the floor. She turned around, wearing only a slip. "Can you sleep in that?"

"Yes." She nodded to the bed. "Lie down with me."

"All right. After my calls."

Bailey lay in bed and waited for him. She cuddled in the soft cotton sheets and blanket, and thought about her life. No decisions had been made, but one thing had become crystal clear since shed found out Taz had died: Bailey was through at ESCAPE, and by extension, Guardian. Her family knew about her and Clay, and soon they would tell Jon and Clay's parents they were married. Then it would become public. She could no longer work incognito. In any case, her drive to do that kind of intervention was gone, buried in a grave in the cemetery they just left. She refused to think about what she was going to do with her life from now on. All she wanted was her family around her and Clay by her side.

She waited for him for fifteen minutes. Where was he? For the past two days, she hadn't been able to sleep without him next to her. Rising, she left the bedroom and found him at the kitchen table, with his back toward her. He'd removed his suit coat and his broad shoulders stretched tight the light blue shirt he wore. "I know, Ned. I feel bad. I just don't have any more information."

Ned? As in Price? Why would Clay be talking to him?

"Damn it, Ned. I'm dealing with my own feelings about all this now. Let it—" He moved slightly in the chair and saw her. "Listen, I have to go. I'll call you." He clicked off.

"Was that Ned Price?"

"Yes, he, um, wanted some information . . ."

She shook her head sharply. "I don't want to know if it's about Taz."

He looked surprised. "What *do* you want?"

"I want you to come and hold me while I sleep."

"I said I would."

She held out her hand. "Let's go." She glanced at his cell phone on the table. "Leave that there. I don't want anything to intrude."

He seemed pained, then his face blanked; he stood and took her hand. "All right. Let's go to sleep, love."

CLAY HAD WORRIED over several things about Bailey's behavior in the past week, not the least of which was her completely-out-of-character clinginess. He loved being with her 24/7, and had told Thorn he needed a few days off. Since Congress was on Thanksgiving recess, things were slow anyway. So it wasn't that he didn't have the time or inclination. But this dependence, this need of Bailey's to be with him was so unlike her. She didn't want to let him out of her sight.

The second concern he had was her refusal to talk about ESCAPE, about Guardian, or Taz. So he was shocked one night at about seven, when they were watching TV on her bed, that she said out of the blue, "Why do you think she came back here, after she was settled in Rochester?"

He gripped the remote, unprepared for the question. "I . . . um . . . Does it matter?"

"No, I guess not. It all boils down to the same thing."

Since she seemed inclined, and he thought it would be good for her, he shut off the television, stretched out his legs, crooked his arm, and braced his head on his hand. He had on comfortable pj pants and a green long-sleeved polo and she wore a baby pink sweat suit. Her hand rested over her belly, as if she was protecting their child. "What does it boil down to, love?"

Her face paled. "I was wrong about my approach to youth gangs. My stubbornness caused her death." Bailey turned her head to him. "Maybe if I'd let you contact her, when you wanted to . . ." Tears moistened her eyes and she bit her lip. "Maybe she'd be alive."

"That's crazy thinking, honey. I don't know as though anything was going to keep Taz alive."

She shrugged.

"But since you brought it up, Suze and Rob and Joe have called me several times. So has Father Tim. They're concerned about you."

"I'm sorry. I'll get in touch with them soon." She started to get up.

He grasped her arm and pulled her back. "What are you going to do about ESCAPE?"

Big blue eyes rounded, as if she expected he knew the answer. "Nothing. It's theirs now. I want no part of ESCAPE or Guardian." Her mouth set in grim lines. "That's a given, Clay. I can't work with gang kids ever again."

"Bailey. Taz's death was not your fault." He knew he sounded desperate, but he couldn't let her take the blame for this.

"Of course it was. You were right all along about my methods."

He swallowed hard. He had to tell her, he knew it, if for no other reason than to get rid of her unwarranted guilt. But of course, there were other reasons. There was no way they could build a life together based on a lie. He just wasn't sure if she was strong enough to hear what he'd done.

Noise sounded on the steps, eliminating the opportunity for Clay to come clean. Aidan had taken Rory and several of his nieces and nephews to a pre-holiday event at Rockefeller Center. The kid appeared first in the doorway; fully clothed in his jacket and jeans, he dove for them. Clay reacted fast and caught him. "Hey, slugger, watch out for Mommy's tummy. There's precious cargo in there."

Rory eyed Bailey. "A baby."

She squeezed his shoulder. "A brother or sister for you."

He scowled—it was an O'Neil expression. "You gonna like him better?"

"No, no, honey. Why would you think that?"

He stuck his fingers in his mouth, crawled over Clay to cuddle in to her side. She glanced at Aidan, who stood in the doorway.

Aidan shrugged. "He said you never do anything with him anymore. I tried to reassure him . . ,"

Bailey kissed Rory's head. "I'm sorry, buddy. I told you what happened. Somebody I cared about died."

"Not me!" he said belligerently.

Out of the mouths of babes . . . Clay thought.

Bailey must have been on the same wavelength, "You know what? You're right. You're alive and well and we need to do some things together." She glanced at the clock. "How about if Mommy gives you a bath and reads you a story to-night instead of Clay?"

"Want my Mommy."

She slid out of bed, and tugged him with her. "Let's go." She nodded to Aidan. "Stay and have dinner with us?"

He looked to Clay who nodded. Everybody took their cues from him. He was becoming totally entrenched with these people.

"Sure then," Aidan said. "The kids all had a Happy Meal but I refrained."

Since Clay had made spaghetti sauce, they went to the kitchen and Aidan helped Clay finish the meal. The drone of the little set in the corner and squeals coming from the bathroom were punctuated with small talk between the two of them. As Clay stirred the sauce and put on a pot to boil water, Aidan tore lettuce and chopped vegetables for a salad.

When they were finished and settled with drinks at the kitchen table, Aidan said, "So, how is she?"

"She seems a bit better." He nodded to the bedroom. "That's a good thing."

"Uh-huh."

Aidan fussed with a napkin on the table. "How long you gonna be able to do this?"

Clay glanced at the calendar date on his watch. "I have things to do Monday. I can't stay with her all day anymore."

"Maybe it's not good for her anyway. She's got to detach from you some."

"I know. Especially since I have to . . ." He cut off. Though they both knew what Clay had done, they never talked about it openly.

Aidan picked up his drink and took a long swallow. Then he stared purposefully across the table. Clay had forgotten how his eyes were the same color as Bailey's and his gaze just as direct. "You don't have to do anything."

"Excuse me?"

"Who else knows besides me?"

Clay sat back in his chair and stared down at the amber colored liquid in his glass. "Ned Price, a cop who was on the other end."

"Will he keep quiet?"

Clay looked up at Bailey's brother. "He would if I asked him to." He sipped his scotch. "Which I'm not about to do."

"Why? It would be best for Bailey."

"To begin our life together on a lie?"

•

"If that's best for her."

"No. She could find out anytime down the road. I won't do it."

"You won't do what?" Bailey stood in the doorway. "What are you two talking about?"

"Nothing."

Crossing to the cabinet, she pulled out dishes. "If it's about me, I don't want to know what you're discussing."

That was so unlike her, it broke Clay's heart. Her brother's brow furrowed with worry.

Clay got the meal on the table. As they ate, he watched the woman across from him nibble at her macaroni and push meatballs around the plate. He remembered how she devoured food before Taz died. Now she ate enough for the baby, but didn't enjoy it. Just one more piece of evidence of what he'd done to her. She was a bit pale tonight, and her eyes were always sad. Damn it, *should* he keep this to himself for her benefit? *Was* it best for her and for the baby?

BAILEY LAUGHED OUT loud for the first time in a week at a TV program she was watching while Clay showered upstairs at his town house. It was a stupid sitcom, on in the middle of the day, but it was funny.

At the commercial, she glanced around his living room. This was a nice place. In a good location. Maybe it was time for her and Rory to move in here; she and Clay needed to talk, so she was glad for the uninterrupted time today. Rory was off again, this time with Dylan, who'd taken his son Hogan and Rory for a pre-Thanksgiving weekend to the Catskills. She and Clay had the whole time to themselves.

Smiling, she thought about the bag she'd packed. In it was a sexy nightgown. Bailey had decided it was time to go on living, and despite her sadness, she was ready to make love with Clay again. She wanted to. Her hormones were kicking in and demanded attention.

She heard the shower go off, then a bump at the front door. His mail. Rising, she walked to the foyer and slipped outside in the crisp November day. Grateful for the warm gray fleece sweat suit, she got the letters and magazines out of his box and went back inside. The mail would all be personal. Everything else went to his offices. Which he had to return to Monday. She pushed the thought away and took the bundle to the sideboard. Accidentally, she dropped a few pieces on the floor. Bending over to pick them up, she saw a phone bill, a letter, and two things from Rochester, New York. Hmm. What personal correspondence would he get from up there? She examined it more closely. Strong Memorial Hospital. State Sheriff's Department. Could they be donations, or requests to speak? Senators were in huge demand to talk to their constituents. But why would the requests come to his residence and not the offices?

She heard him on the stairs, then smelled his aftershave as he came up behind her. "What are you doing?" He slid his arms around her and rested his chin on her shoulder.

"I got your mail."

"Ah, I see." He nuzzled her neck. "Looking for letters from other women?"

She turned in his arms. His face was ruddy from the shower, his hair damp. He wore jeans and a long sleeved T-shirt. He smelled like heaven. "Are there any after you, Senator?"

"Hordes."

She grinned. "Well, then, I think it's time to tell them, and your family, that you're off the market."

His face blanked. "Oh, honey. I'd love to do that. But it's too soon."

"I don't understand, Clay. You've wanted to go public for months. Now I'm offering to do it. As far as I'm concerned, we can tell the world."

He looked torn. For the life of her, she couldn't figure out why. "I—" He drew back. "All right, let's tell my family. I'll set up a time."

"Great."

He hugged her, then picked up the letters and scanned them. Stopping abruptly, he gripped one. She caught sight of the Rochester address. "I got a glance at some of the addresses. What did you get from Rochester?"

"I . . . um . . . I don't know."

"Open it and see."

He drew in a breath. Through the material of the T-shirt, she saw his muscles contract. He turned around and the look on his face frightened her. "Bailey, we have to talk."

A premonition hit her with the force of a tidal wave. Something was wrong. Something she didn't want to hear. She could see it in his dark gaze, hear it in his raw voice. "Okay, we'll talk. After."

"After what?"

Slipping her arms around his neck, she smiled. "I want to make love, Clay. It's been too long."

"Oh, sweetheart, you sure you're ready?"

"Don't you want to?" She edged in closer and felt him respond, eloquently. "Seems you do."

He gripped her waist. "I do, of course, I've missed us together. But . . ." He glanced to the letters.

Again, fear skittered through her. "You can read your mail later." She tugged his head down and kissed him thoroughly.

"All right," he said with what sounded like resignation. "Let's make love. Then we'll talk."

FORCEFULLY CLAY PUSHED away all the things running around his brain—Aidan's comments about keeping his actions a secret, the letters from Rochester, Ned Price's need for answers—and led Bailey up the stairs. Once in his bedroom, she went into the bathroom; he slatted the blinds, turned on the stereo in the corner, then drew down the sheets. When she came out, his heart began to beat fast. She wore a peach silky slip of a thing that outlined every beautiful curve. His throat clogged at the thought that this might be the last time he'd see her in something like that.

Fiddling with the spaghetti strap, she raised flirty brows to him. "You don't like this outfit?"

"I love the outfit. I love *you*."

"You look so sad," she said, crossing to him and soothing the lines round his mouth. "Why?"

"You mistake desire for sadness." He drew her to him, playfully rough, and ground his groin against her. "Intense, primitive desire. I ache for you, love."

She mirrored his actions. "I ache for you, too," she whispered. "I want to make love to my husband again."

"Ah . . ." He choked back emotion. "I like the sound of my wife saying that."

"Good, because I'll be saying it for decades."

No, you won't. Again he banished the thought. Slowly, he eased down the straps, and the oh-so-feminine garment fell to the floor. He brushed his lips over her shoulder, traced the delicateness of her rib cage with shaky fingertips, then his palm curled into the curve of her body. "You are so lovely."

"Soon, I'll be fat." The words came out breathless, and she clung to his arms.

His hand found its way to her belly. "Beautiful. You'll be so beautiful, I'll want to look at you all the time." *If I'm around.*

He tunneled his fingers through her hair—thick glorious locks that he might never feel again. Gently, he slid his hands down, threaded through the curls at the juncture of her legs.

He eased a finger inside her and she startled, gasped, moaned; they were sounds he wondered if he could live without. Emotion welled in his throat as he coaxed the moisture from her, then withdrew his finger, cupped her, and rocked her against him.

She came, not like the brisk wind outside, but with the gentleness of summer rain, flooding him with her warmth. Her words were petal soft and as sweet. "Clay, God, yes, Clay."

He held her while she calmed, then he knelt before her. Oh, Lord, would he never taste her again? He devoured her, but still with utmost tenderness, with a reverence he didn't know a man could feel making love. When she climaxed a second time, he felt her go weak and braced her hips with his hands. Then he stood. "You are so lovely."

She nuzzled into his neck. "I'm yours."

For now, he thought miserably.

Clay went to pick her up to put her on the bed, but Bailey stayed his hands. "No, it's my turn." She knew, since it had been a while, he wouldn't last, but he'd kill himself trying to satisfy her again. She also wanted the closeness to his body that this would give her. She slipped off his shirt and ran her hands over his chest, searching the hollows, claiming each and every muscle with a feather-light touch. Then she grazed his nipples with her tongue and he jerked into her. "Bailey, love."

She flirted with the waistband of his jeans before she un-snapped them. She tantalized the zipper before rasping it down. When she knelt, and oh-so-slowly drew the denims and briefs off, he swore. "Bai-ley . . ."

He was violently aroused. She kissed his penis, licked it, and he fell onto the bed. "Ah, good," she murmured, "now I can have my fill."

"Jesus, I'm going to go off . . . arrgh . . ."

It didn't take very long. He came in a rush of feeling, call-ing her name, holding her head, arching into her mouth.

When his breathing evened out, he drew her up and fell back onto the bed with her. She sprawled over his chest. He stared up at her and she was shocked to find his face was a mask of . . . pain. "Clay, what—what's wrong?"

The expression fled. He brushed her hair back and kissed her. "What could be wrong after that? Do you have any idea how much I love you?" he asked.

"Yes. As much as I love you." She tried to lighten the mood by nibbling on his ear. "I'm not done, you know."

He threw back his head and laughed. "Well then, we'll have to attend to that." He flipped her over.

This time it was very fast and a little rough. Actually, his lovemaking had a desperate quality to it, she thought after it was over and they laid together in a tangle of limbs, sheets, and sweat.

She was running her hand through the dark blond hair on his chest, when he said, "I want you to know that, other than having Jon, this is—has been—the most precious thing that's ever happened to me."

"Making love?"

"Hmm. With you. Nothing will ever come close."

She tugged playfully on a tuft of hair. "Well, no woman will come close, I'll tell you that."

He grabbed her hand and fisted his around it. "I hope not. After what I have to tell you."

"Clay, I—"

"No, Bailey, we have to talk. Now. It can't wait any longer."

She tried to pull away. "I don't want to do this."

"You don't have any choice. But let's get dressed first; it'll be easier then."

She grabbed the sheet and pulled it up to her chest. "No, I don't want to get dressed. I'm staying here, like this."

"All right."

Since she was lying flat on her back, her head on the pillow, he braced his arms on either side of her and stared down at her with grim eyes. "You're not responsible for Taz's death, sweetheart."

Bailey shook her head, sending inky locks all over the pillow. "I don't want to talk about Taz."

"You have to."

She pushed on his chest. "Let me up."

He kept her where she was with force. "No. Look at me."

Finally she did.

"You're not responsible for Taz's death. Because I am."

Her actions stilled. "What do you mean?"

He drew in a breath as if he needed it to speak. "When Mazie threatened you and you stormed out of ESCAPE, I drove up to Rochester."

"Rochester?"

"To the high school Taz attended."

"How could you know where Taz was relocated, where she went to school?"

"You let it slip you were leaving for Rochester, when I got you on the cell to tell you about Guardian's funding."

"Oh my God." Awareness—dark and accusing—was dawning.

"I found out where she lived and where she went to school, with the help of my college roommate. He's a PI." Clay stared at her. "He's the one who found out you met with Taz that first time."

"You had me followed?"

"Just that once."

"God, we joked about your ability to find people's addresses.

Your PI friend followed me first, then you set him on Taz."

"I told him I needed her located, yes. I went to see her."

Bailey bit her lip. "What did you tell her?"

"That Mazie had threatened you. That we were married."

"And she told you where Mazie was because of that?"

"Not until I told her you were pregnant."

"Oh, no." Her stomach plummeted when she remembered Taz's words one night on the Internet.

You got kids?

Yes. I wish I had them. It's the only thing I really want. What was it like being pregnant?

I loved it. It was the most meaningful thing—that and breastfeeding—that I'd ever done.

It's a miracle.

A gift from God.

Clay was talking. "I don't know why she came back here, Bailey."

"I do. You don't turn on your home girls. After she snitched, Taz had time to think about it. She came back to warn them." Tears welled in her eyes. "And Mazie shot her because kids don't leave gangs."

"You're probably right. I'm so sorry this happened."

"You're sorry."

"Yes."

She studied him, still dazed by what he'd told her. "Will you let me up now?"

"Why?"

"You were right earlier, I need to get dressed."

The silence in the room as they both put their clothes on was deafening. Bailey could barely contain the emotion she felt bubbling inside her, straining to get out. Still without saying anything, she went downstairs. He followed.

In the living room, she turned to face him and wrapped her arms around her waist. "I don't know what to say."

"Tell me how you're feeling."

"Stunned, shocked . . . sad, I guess."

"What are you going to do now?"

"Do?"

"About us? What does this mean for us?"

For a minute she felt panicky. Then she forced herself to stay calm. Now, she had to depend on herself. "I don't know." He came toward her and she held her hand up. "Don't. Stay away."

He waited a minute before he said, "For now, or for good?"

"I don't know." She sounded like an idiot, but she couldn't take this in, couldn't wrap her brain around what he'd done.

"Can you forgive me?"

"I can't answer these questions." Desperate to get out of there, she looked around for her coat, spotted it on a chair. She put it on, and headed for the door. When she reached the foyer, she turned to him and had to swallow hard at the utter desolation on his classic face. "Do you think we can make it with this between us, Clay?"

"I honestly don't know. But I'd like to try." He nodded to her stomach. "We have a baby to consider."

Her hand crept to her waist. "I know. I need time. I have to think this through."

His brandy-colored eyes flickered with something that resembled her earlier panic. "Can you stay here and do it?"

She shook her head. "I have to get away from you."

He looked like she'd slapped him, this man she loved, this man she'd just given herself to without reservation. Her husband, the father of her child. But, he'd betrayed her. Still . . .

She went back to him, stood on her toes and hugged him. "I love you, Clay," she said grasping on to his neck, choking out the words. "I really do. I just don't know if that's enough now."

He held her in a grip so tight her ribs hurt. Finally he said, "Don't leave me, please."

"I have to." She drew back, tears coursing down her cheeks.

His eyes were red-rimmed and his face was wet. "I'm sorry."

"I know you are." She turned away and said, without facing him, "I'll be in touch."

⟨ TWENTY-TWO

BARD COLLEGE WAS a hundred acres of sprawling hills perched right on the edge of the Hudson River. Today, on this crisp Saturday in mid-November, the leaves had fallen and it was cold, but the sun was out, kissing the water, warming those who walked around campus. Winter was coming late to New York this year, and Clay was glad. He wasn't sure he could battle the elements and still keep his own demons at bay.

He found the campus café where he and Jon had agreed to meet. He'd only told his son he needed to talk to him. It was time to tell Jon what he'd done, and face the disappointment in *his* eyes too. Bailey's accusing stare and hurt words still haunted him . . .

I love you, Clay . . . I just don't know if that's enough now.

Clay had waited a week, to see if she'd change her mind, or discover what she was feeling, or find out whatever the hell she had to find out. But she hadn't called him. Consequently, his mood alternated between utter despair and a biting anger that she could give up on all they had together. That she could let him go.

He watched Jon enter the café. He wore a hooded Bard sweatshirt and jeans, his dark blond hair disheveled. He reminded Clay of what he himself had looked like in college.

The place was not crowded for lunch, thank goodness. Clay stood when Jon reached the table and gave him a bear hug. Drawing back, Jon smiled. At least they were back to displays of affection, which had gone by the wayside the last few years.

After they both sat, his son studied him. "You okay, Dad?"

Clay opened his mouth to say he was fine—typical parent answer—but sank back into his chair. "No, Jon, I'm not."

"Something wrong with your job?"

"No."

"Well, it must be big for you to drive up here just for lunch."

That pierced his father's heart, already wounded by his loss of Bailey. Clay swallowed hard; he was keeping the gates closed on his emotions for fear he would drown in them. Any leak might create a flood. "Your comment tells me I need to do more of this."

"Wish you would, Dad." Jon smiled at him. "I like it."

"I'm glad."

Clay had gotten drinks for them from the food line and sipped his coffee morosely.

Jon scowled. "Dad? What it is?" His whole body stiffened. "Oh, my God, you're not sick, are you?"

"No, no, I'm not sick. I have to tell you something, and I'm . . ." Clay sighed "I'm afraid it will diminish your opinion of me again."

"Just tell me, okay? You're scaring me."

"I married Bailey O'Neil almost three weeks ago. She's pregnant."

"Holy shit." Jon looked down at Clay's hands, where his wedding ring rested. He wondered if Bailey was still wearing hers. "Is that why you married her?"

"No, son, it's not. I'm crazy in love with her. I have been for a long time. I finally got her committed to this relationship, and then she found out she was pregnant. I was thrilled that she agreed to become my wife."

"Then why are you so sad today? Are you afraid this will hurt your career? If you are, I think the days of expecting spic and span politicians are over."

Jon's cynical view made Clay sad. But he had other things to deal with. "No, I'm not afraid of that. Truthfully, I don't give a shit about that right now." Clay drank some coffee. "I'm sad because already I blew it."

"With her?" Clay nodded. "What'd you do?"

"You know she works with gang kids and we quarreled publicly about it."

Jon grinned, making him look younger. "Yeah, she gave you a run for your money. I like her, Dad."

"You would," he said dryly.

"Seriously, she read me the riot act defending you. And her kid . . . Hey!" Jon's brown eyes lit. "I got a stepbrother now! And I'm going to have a half . . . Do you know what you're having?"

How's my girl . . .

He swallowed back the memory. "No."

"I hope it's a girl." Jon watched him. "What happened?"

"Bailey got someone out of a gang and the rest of the posse threatened her for doing it."

"I thought ESCAPE was hidden, like the shelters for battered women."

"It is. They threatened her over the Internet." Jon waited. "I was so worried about her and the baby, I found out where the girl had been placed and went to see her to persuade her to tell me the whereabouts of her gang. She must have panicked and gone to warn them because she ended up back in New York . . . dead."

"Oh my God." Jon's brow furrowed. "Is Bailey safe?"

"Yes, Taz—that was her name—gave me the location of her crib. The police found the leader who was after Bailey, but not in time to save Taz."

"I'm sorry, Dad." Jon toyed at the straw. "Bailey blames you?"

"I don't know. I haven't seen her since last Friday."

Scowling, Jon said, "Aren't you living together?"

"We had plans to, just as soon as we could make our

marriage public. I'd been staying with her during this ordeal, but she booted me out when she discovered what I'd done."

"She okay?"

"Again, I don't know. I haven't seen or talked to her. Our relationship is up in the air. She asked for time to deal with this—what I did behind her back. I've phoned her every day, but she hasn't returned my calls."

"That's why you look like you lost your best friend."

"I have. And it's my fault."

"She'll come around, Dad. She probably just needs time."

"I hope so, Jon."

They got sandwiches from the line and as it had for days, the sight and smell of food turned his stomach. He picked at his Reuben, thinking about the week. When Jon asked about Rory, Clay told him he'd managed to spend some time with the boy, thanks to Aidan. Bailey's brother had set up meetings for them, and accompanied them to the zoo to see the new baboons. The kid had a thousand questions Clay wasn't able to answer, most prominently, why wasn't Clay living with them, if he and his mother were married.

For the rest of the lunch, he and Jon talked about the baby and what Bailey might do. Afterward, Jon took him to his science lab to show him a project he was working on, and over to his dorm room to see his new stereo. Finally, Clay had to leave.

"I'll be in D.C. off and on, Jon, but in New York most of the time because Congress is in recess. When is your Thanksgiving break?"

"I'm done in a week."

"I hope I see a lot of you over the holidays."

"Maybe we could take in a show."

Clay smiled, remembering how he'd had to push to see Jon over the last few years because his son never issued invitations. Some things had changed for the better. He vowed silently to be a good father to Jon, to Rory and the new baby, no matter what.

"I'll look into Broadway tickets. Any play in particular?"

"Maybe *Seussical*?"

Zing, zing. He had to swallow hard.

Jon watched him. "And you know what? I'm gonna have Thanksgiving dinner with you this year."

"You always have it at your mother's."

"I know. So it's time I spent it with you."

Immediately Clay's heart felt lighter. He hugged Jon. "I'd like that."

"Maybe things will be better between you and Bailey by then. It could be the four of us—well four and a half—for the holiday."

God, Clay wanted that. "Maybe." But as he left his son and made his way across campus to the car, the demons returned. "Maybe," he whispered to himself. "But I doubt it."

"IF YOU DON'T go sit down this minute, and put your feet up, I'll fire you." Patrick loomed over the bar when Bailey returned from serving a couple for lunch. His blue eyes were flaming.

Though her back ached, and she was hungry, she jutted out her chin. "If you do, I'll just get another waitress job. The Irish Pub on Fiftieth and Lex, maybe."

He slapped his hand on the surface of the bar. "Son of a bitch. Don't you care about the baby?"

"The doctor told me the baby's fine."

"Whatever you say." He stalked away.

At the mention of the doctor, Bailey bit her lip. Clay should have been at the appointment. She'd almost called him, almost returned his daily messages. But she was still raw, and she did blame him for Taz's death. What was she supposed to do with those feelings? Ignore them, so they could come back at any time and ruin their relationship? No, she knew that wasn't a good idea. So she'd gone to her OB-GYN by herself and cried all the way home because Clay wasn't with her.

She finished serving her last meal and took a stool at the bar. Starving now, she sank onto the last seat by the cash register, near the door, and put her feet up. Her brother came down with a glass of milk and a sandwich, slapped it down in front of her, then started to walk away without saying anything. "Paddy?"

He turned around. "What?"

"I'm sorry. I'll rest more. I'm bitchy, and I shouldn't be taking out my problems on you."

Bracing his hands on the rim of the bar, he sighed heavily. "You're sad and lonely and you miss your husband."

"Guilty as charged." She picked up her sandwich and nibbled at it.

"Go back to him. Wives belong with their husbands."

She caught his underlying tone. "How's it going with Brie?"

"Not good." He shook his head. "She's takin' the kids to Syracuse to her parents' house for Thanksgiving." He ran a hand through his dark hair. It had gotten longer, and she noticed some gray at the temples. "I can't believe I'm not gonna be with my kids on a holiday." His dark eyes were so grim. "That this might be what my life is like."

"Maybe you should go to counseling."

"I hate that stuff."

"You need to compromise if you're gonna get what you need."

"Pot calling the kettle black, little girl?"

"Maybe. I've been thinking about doing the same thing." She closed her eyes and leaned against the wall. "I'm so confused right now."

A pause. She heard the door open, cold air swirl in. "Fuck. You're about to get even more confused."

She opened her eyes. "Huh?"

"Hello, Street Angel. How are you?" She turned to see the smiling face of Eric Lawson.

Damn it, he was about the last person she wanted to see. She dropped her feet to the floor. "Eric, haven't seen you in a while."

The councilman leaned over and gave her a kiss on the cheek. "A condition I'm here to remedy." He sat on the stool next to her. "I called you."

"I know. I called back and left you a message."

"Saying you weren't dating for a while." He smiled, though his dark good looks didn't interest her a bit. "Why is that?"

The hell with it; she was tired of fending off this man. She didn't want to be with him; she missed Clay, and just that peck on her cheek by somebody else made her ill. Besides, she hated this limbo. Still she was reluctant to tell Eric about their marriage. Who knew how he'd use it in his own interests? And since hers and Clay's wedded un-bliss had every earmark of being permanent—God the thought made her stomach do somersaults this time—she knew she shouldn't reveal anything now.

"You okay?" Eric said taking her hand. "You just turned white as a sheet."

"I'm fine." She withdrew her hand. "Look, I've been seeing someone. It's serious between us."

"Really? Who?"

"I'd rather not go into it."

He reached out and took a lock of her hair between his fingers. It was an intimate gesture. "Give me a chance, and I'll make you forget him." He slid his hand to her neck and caressed it. Oh, yuck.

Before she could tell him to back off, the door opened again. She heard, "What the *hell*?" Clay, looking big and beautiful, stalked toward them. "Get your hands off my wife, Lawson."

CLAY WAS SEEING red. He couldn't believe Bailey would actually be spending time with another guy. She was his wife, so he tugged her off the stool and yanked her to his side. Wearing a pair of black slacks and the green shirt of the pub, she looked healthy enough, but her blue eyes were clouded, and her color a bit pale.

Open mouthed, Lawson's brows skyrocketed on his face. "Wife? Are you married, Bailey?"

"She didn't tell you?" His arm tightened on her. This just kept getting worse.

"No, she didn't."

Clay drew back and peered down at her. He hoped she saw the hurt clawing at his insides. "Why didn't you tell him, Bailey?"

"I didn't know if I should let this out, Clay. If it would affect your seat in the Senate."

"Fuck my seat in the Senate."

Lawson snorted. "Can I quote you on that?"

"You can do anything you want, Lawson. Just stay away from my wife."

The potential opponent for Clay's Senate seat shook his head. "You're nailing your own coffin, Wainwright."

"Get out of here."

Lawson arched a cocky brow. "It's a public place."

"*My* place." Paddy had come up to them. "And I'd like you to stop harassing my sister and my favorite brother-in-law."

Lawson shrugged, but stood and ambled out the door, hands in his pockets, whistling.

Bailey faced Clay. "What's he going to do?"

Clay ran a hand through his hair. "Leak it to the press."

"Oh, no." She touched his arm. "I'm sorry."

He turned to her. "Would that be so bad?"

"My cue to leave," Patrick mumbled, and walked down the bar.

"Clay, I'm not ready for . . . I don't know how . . . shit. You're forcing my hand again. I asked for some time to sort this out."

"Well, excuse me for flying off when I saw another man feeling up my wife."

"He wasn't feeling me up." She sounded indignant.

"Whatever."

"I don't like being manipulated. It's so typical of you."

Suddenly exhausted, he sank onto a chair. "Look, I'm sorry. I just reacted."

"What are you doing here, anyway?"

"How can you ask me that?" He brushed his knuckles down her cheek. It felt like down. "I miss my wife." He pressed a hand to her stomach. "My baby." He drew in a breath. "How is she?"

"The doctor says fine."

His heart plummeted. "The doctor? You went to a prenatal appointment without me?"

Her face flushed with guilt. "Yeah, look, I'd made the appointment a while ago. Then I didn't know if I should call you to come."

He swallowed hard and turned to brace his arms on the bar. He scrubbed his hands over his face.

"You look exhausted."

"I am. I can't eat or sleep . . ." He shook his head. "Never mind me, this isn't helping you. I'm sorry I blew it with Lawson. But now we have a problem to deal with."

"I know. You have to put some spin on our marriage politically."

"I'll call Thorn right away."

She shook her head. "This is so us, Clay. Circumstances keep throwing us together when we've decided not to be."

"I never decided that!" He shook his head, feeling the ground slip out from under his feet. "I wasn't aware that you had either."

"I haven't. But we don't have any choice, now. We'll have to live together for show. At least for a little while so you can deal with this publicly." She sighed. "We'd have to do something to explain the baby anyway, so this will fit right in with our original plan."

His heart turned to mush. "Did you find out how far along you are?"

"Just a few weeks. I still don't know which time it happened."

"Early enough so we can fudge the timing." He swallowed hard and took her hand. Turning, he captured her legs between his on the rung of the barstool. "Don't you miss me?"

"Of course I do."

"Can't you forgive me?"

"Yes, but . . ." She looked at him with fathomless eyes filled with hurt. It stunned him, how deep the pain was. "How can I ever trust you again, after what you did? You just take control of everything, regardless of what I say I want."

"I can change; I can win back your trust."

"Maybe, but I'm not sure yet."

Yet. Well, that was good. "All right. However, we have to be living together when I make the announcement of our marriage, or when Lawson does."

"We'll move in together right away. But this isn't a commitment. It isn't a decision. It's just a temporary solution to the problem."

Did she have to keep saying that? "I'll need the ground rules, then," he said tightly, angry and happy at the same time. At least he'd be near her. But he hated her distancing.

"First off, you have three bedrooms in your town house, so we'll live there. I can take one of the spares, Rory can have the other."

He nodded. "I guess that about says it all, then."

"It's the best I can do, Clay."

"No, it's not. But I'll take it for now."

THE NEWS BROKE in *The Daily Sun* the next day before Bailey even got her things to Clay's. He'd been meeting with Thorn all morning, and her brothers helped her move hers and Rory's stuff into Clay's town house.

"Mommy, this is so awesome," Rory said after he'd explored the top floor. "I got my own bathroom."

"You share it with the other spare room." *Her* room, she thought, but didn't want to tackle that issue with Rory.

As her son dug into a box of his belongings, she went to that room, and found her brother there. "How come your things are goin' in here?" Dylan asked as he dropped some bags onto the floor.

"Um, long story."

Liam, usually ready to give people a break, was right behind him with another huge box. "This is crazy, Bay. Are you or are you not in love with him?"

"I am."

Paddy sidled in with a fish tank. "I tried talking some sense into her."

"He's your husband," Liam put in, shaking his head. "I don't understand you two at all."

Exhausted—she hadn't slept last night—she sank onto the bed. "Please guys."

Aidan joined them. "What's up?"

She gave him a help-me look. "They're playing the Spanish Inquisition again."

"They're right, kiddo."

Bailey shook her head and surveyed the four of them.

"Why are you defending him, anyway? None of you even like him."

"He's family now." This from Paddy. Dylan and Liam agreed.

"Besides, what he did, he did to protect you." Again, Paddy took the lead.

Great. Now she had their contingent to deal with.

Exasperated, she said, "Look, it'd be easy to give in. But then what? How can I ever trust Clay to let me make my own decisions? He's a man used to power and control. It was why he went to Rochester. I can't allow him to run my life."

Paddy said, "That's bullshit. If you love him, you can work with him on this."

Aidan jammed his hands into his pockets. "I knew about it, B."

"What?"

"That he went to Rochester. That he put the whole thing into motion."

"*What?* And you didn't tell me?"

"No. What's more, I advised Clay not to tell you. Ever. I knew you'd react like this."

"Damn it, Aidan, I thought I could trust *you*."

Paddy stepped forward. "Bailey, your safety was at stake. I would have done the same thing."

Dylan said, "Me, too."

Liam, of course, agreed.

She lay back into the pillows. "Go away, you guys. I need to rest. Clay's bringing Thorn by. We've got to decide our spin on all this, then we're meeting with a news reporter to give our side of the story."

"We'll finish bringing your things in," Liam told her. "And watch Rory while you rest."

"Thanks." Each of her brothers came to the bed and kissed her. Paddy whispered, "Don't blow this like I did, Bay. I'm miserable. I hate to see you like me."

After they left, she sighed. Her brothers were, by far, the nicest men she knew. Basically moral. Decent. Possessive and controlling, too. But good guys. A lot like Clay.

She closed her eyes thinking about that.

* * *

"SO, MS. O'NEIL, we meet again." Hank Sellers sat in Clay's living room with a tape recorder on. He wore his uniform—jeans and a denim jacket. "Or should I call you Mrs. Wainwright?"

"Bailey will do." She hesitated. "I'm not taking the Wainwright name." But she leaned into Clay. At least he got to be close to her again because of this ruse. He relished the weight of her body next to his.

"I understand." The reporter grinned. "The feminist voters will love you."

She smiled. Clay could see her struggling to make this right for him, and he appreciated it. Thorn had briefed her on the thrust of the interview; she'd made astute observations and promised to be totally cooperative.

"So, how did the Street Angel and the senator get together?"

Briefly Clay outlined their initial meetings. "Despite all that, we liked each other. Right away."

Sellers studied his notes. "You gave me an interview after you'd met him, Bailey. As I recall, it was pretty negative."

The interview was after she slept with me, Clay thought. Wouldn't that make great headlines?

Again, Bailey touched his arm and left her hand there. "If you recall further, I said nothing derogatory in that interview about my husband. I only attacked his views on stopping youth gang crime."

"Let's talk about that issue. How will you reconcile that battle now that you're married?"

"There's no battle to fight anymore," Bailey said succinctly. "I'm no longer working at ESCAPE."

"This have anything to do with that girl who got killed? Was she one of yours?"

"Yes, to both answers." Tears came to Bailey's eyes.

"I prefer you don't ask her any questions about that, Hank," Clay said, covering her hand with his. "It's still pretty raw."

"Yeah, sorry."

"And although it will come out that she's the Street Angel, if we could keep her connection to Tazmania Gomez quiet, I'd appreciate it. For her safety."

He nodded. "So, Senator, was the secrecy about your marriage for her protection only?"

Nothing to do but be honest. "Partly." He gave Sellers a we're-buddies look. "Hank, Bailey and I were sworn enemies. We fell in love. But the differences between us remained. We had no idea where we were going with a relationship. We wanted it quiet until we decided how to handle that angle as well as how to keep the Street Angel's identity a secret. Once the press found out who she was, she would be in too much danger."

"And now that you've left ESCAPE, that reason no longer exists."

"Right."

"What are you going to do with your life now, Bailey?"

"I don't know yet."

He studied them with a reporter's shrewdness. "How long you been married?"

"A few weeks. We weren't ready to tell the world yet." Clay sighed. "When Lawson found out last night, we had no choice but to let people know."

"Sounds plausible. So, tell me, are there fireworks?"

Clay opened his mouth to answer, but Bailey gave Sellers a flirty smile. "Isn't that a little personal, Hank?"

Throwing back his head, the reporter laughed. "I didn't mean it that way. I mean with your differing views."

"We try not to discuss those at home."

They talked some more, and finally Clay said, "I think it's time to end this, Hank. I trust you've got enough information."

"Yeah, compared to Lawson's interview, this is the real deal. One more question, though, for Bailey. Are you going to vote for your husband in the next election?"

She didn't miss a beat. "Who knows what next November will bring." She grinned up at Clay, and her gaze was full of promise. "He's working on me. But I'm still undecided."

About a lot of things.

"Can I quote you on that?"

"Of course. Clay and I aren't going to lie to the public."

"Will your fence-sitting hurt his career?"

Real distress shone on Bailey's face. She gripped Clay's hand. "Oh, I hope not."

Clay slid his arm around her. "I love my wife for who she is, Hank. She has a strong will and her own identity. If the voters can't handle that, then so be it."

"Actually," Sellers said, "I think the voters will love it."

"THANKS FOR DOING the interview today. You had Sellers eating out of your hand." Clay stood in the doorway of *her* bedroom, dressed in boxers and a white T-shirt, ready for bed.

Bailey's hormones went on red alert and the rush was so strong she was taken aback by it. "You're welcome." She was couched in the soft comfort of the bed, wearing her own boxers and T-shirt. His looked better. A lot better, revealing a roadmap of muscles on his chest, trim hips, and great legs. "Thanks for taking over with Rory tonight. He was bouncing all over the place with excitement about being here. I can't believe I had that nap and am still exhausted."

"I enjoy taking care of Rory. We were making plans for a playroom in the basement. He's a creative kid."

She scowled. "Clay, be careful, don't let him get too attached to this place." As an afterthought, she added, "Or to you."

His hand gripped the doorjamb. "God forbid."

She cocked her head.

"Let me say something. I love Rory like he was my own. Even if we *don't make it*, as you keep pounding into my head, I'm maintaining a relationship with him. So will Jon, I expect."

Something about his tone. "Are you mad at me?"

"Well . . . yes." He ran a hand through his hair, disheveling it beautifully. He looked like an angry Greek God. "I listened to us tell Sellers all those things today. Things that were true. We gravitated toward each other, though we knew it wasn't for the best. We fell in love despite the odds. I want you to work out your misgivings, even if it *seems* impossible."

"It's not something I can just *do*, Clay. It has to happen."

"Fuck."

"Damn it. I caved in on everything, every single thing, until you violated my trust so completely it got somebody killed."

He froze. "Oh, my God. You do blame me. You kept telling me it wasn't my fault . . . but you didn't really believe that."

She closed her eyes. "I'm so tired, I don't know what I'm saying. I blame myself, too, if it's any consolation."

"It isn't."

"Clay . . ." Rory called out from his room.

"I'll go," she said starting to get out of bed.

"No, I'll go. As you said, I might not have many more chances to do this."

He stalked off, leaving Bailey stumped. *He* was angry? Shit.

CLAY SAT NEXT to Bailey at a small table in the back of the Build-a-Bear store. Jon had come home from college for Thanksgiving break and had insisted they take Rory here.

Studying the setup, Clay smiled. "This is a great place." Excited squeals of children, the direction of staff, and lots of giggling surrounded them.

"I know." She rubbed her wedding band. She did that a lot, unconsciously, Clay thought. "I always wanted to bring Rory here, but it's so expensive."

He shrugged. "Jon's treat. He insisted."

"He's as generous as you are."

Biting back his impatience, he vowed not to get angry with her again. "I wish you'd let me take care of you financially." He leaned over and squeezed her hand. "I hate your working at the pub."

She held on tight. "I know you do. Please, let's not fight. I hate that. It's hard enough with this distance between us."

"We won't fight. I just worry about you and the baby."

"I promise I'm taking care of myself. You can come to the next checkup and see for yourself."

He smiled weakly. She was blooming physically and had that ethereal glow that pregnant women got. He wondered briefly if she had other things pregnant woman were rumored to have. Like increased libido. If so, he wasn't privy to it. "It's a date, love." He didn't let go of her hand.

Rory raced over to them and skidded to a halt. "Mommy,

look." He held the furry outer shell of a bear. "Jon says we stuff it over there; he's gonna help me."

"I know."

"I love Jon." He threw his arms around Clay. "You too, Clay."

Clay let go of Bailey's hand and hung on to her son. How on earth would he ever give up this child if Bailey couldn't, in the end, trust him?

"Dad, you okay?" Jon had come over to them.

"I'm fine."

Pulling away, Rory looked up at Jon then back at Clay. "He calls you Dad."

"Yes, he's my son."

"Can I . . ." He looked to Bailey. "Can I call Clay Dad, too?"

Jon blinked. "I think that's a great idea."

Clay tugged Rory close again. "Is that what you want, buddy?"

"Uh-huh."

He glanced at Bailey. She was scowling. "Let's talk about this later." She stood and nodded to the other side of the store. "I think I see some Jeter clothes over there. Let's go look."

When she left, Jon took her chair. "What's the matter with her?"

He'd briefly filled Jon in on the events of the week. "She's still not sure if we're going to make it, Jon."

"She moved in."

"It was necessary because Lawson found out."

Jon's brows raised. "Sounds crazy to me."

"This whole relationship has been. So why am I surprised at this turn of events?"

"Jonnnnnnnnnnnnnnn . . ." the screech came from Rory as he ran back to them. "I found Jeter's uniform." He looked to Clay. "Jon likes Jeter as much as we do."

"More," Jon teased, ruffling Rory's hair.

"Nuh-uh."

"Come on, kid, let's go stuff that bear." Hand-in-hand, they walked off.

Bailey sat down. "Clay, I—"

"Let's not talk about it. Let's just enjoy the kids."

"All right."

Later, though, when they got home, the subject of their distance had to be resurrected. Uncomfortable, Clay nonetheless informed his son of the circumstances. He'd waited till Bailey left him and his son alone. "Jon, Rory's got your room." Though he hadn't stayed there much, Clay insisted Jon have his own space in the town house.

"Really? Why doesn't he use the spare one?"

"Bailey's in there."

"Oh, Dad." He looked so old, understanding of the significance of that statement. "It's all right. I can bunk with Rory. It'll be fun."

"For you."

Jon patted him on the back. "Hang in there."

Dinner was fun with the boys. Bailey had taken a nap and then cooked a great meal. Afterward, they played junior monopoly.

At bedtime, things got awkward again. The kids went to watch a video in *their* room, though Rory rarely needed that to go to sleep anymore; Clay and Bailey were downstairs, sitting on the couch, watching TV. Her head rested on his shoulder, and he could smell its lemony scent. Feel her curves against him.

She yawned and straightened. "I'm tired. I'm going up."

"All right."

"Did Jon say anything about the room?"

"No, he understands how things are between us. He's twenty, Bailey. Almost a man."

"I know this is hard for you."

His laugh was rueful. "Is that a pun?"

She chuckled. "I'm sorry about no sex, Clay."

"Sorry enough to come upstairs and make love with your husband?"

She looked torn.

"Damn it, Bailey, what would it hurt? We made love initially when we weren't committed. Would it really make a difference if we took some solace in each other now?"

"It might sway me. Make me forget everything that's between us."

He leaned over and brushed his lips against hers. "Would that be so bad?"

She clung to his shirt. "Clay, please."

"Please what? Kiss you? Touch you? Make you scream with pleasure?"

She drew away. "I won't be seduced into this."

He sucked in a heavy breath. "I see." He stood, hard and hurting, inside and out. "Then I won't force unwanted attentions on you."

"Don't be mad."

He shook his head. "I'm not mad, Bailey. I'm hurt and hungry for you. That's way past being mad."

~ TWENTY-THREE

THE EXTERIOR OF ESCAPE seemed different today. Standing out front, tugging her scarf around her against the cold, Bailey studied the house: its brick front was a bit worn, but the grounds were well kept and guarded by high shrubs. No one would ever expect to find an anti-gang organization inside. She braced herself as she climbed the steps. Bailey hadn't been back since Taz had died three weeks ago. But it was time to visit her friends and officially resign.

Not that she had a choice now. Hank Sellers' article in *The Village Voice* had revealed her identity, as had Lawson's sensationalizing interview. Now as the wife of a senator, Bailey had no privacy. She would be forced to let go of ESCAPE, even if she didn't want to. Which she did. She was done here, with this baby of hers, whom she'd conceived, nurtured, and brought to adolescence. Someone else could see it through college into adulthood. The notion formed a lump in her throat as she entered the building.

Sounds and smells and sights greeted her from the

offices—the hum of computers, the ringing of phones, the bark of conversation . . .

"Fuck it, Joey. If you don't do it right this time, I'm gonna report you."

"To who, God?"

"You are a hardheaded son of a bitch. I wish Bailey was here to keep you in line."

"As if." She spoke from the doorway, where she watched the men square off.

Both guys turned. Rob strode right over to hug her, then Joe took his turn. To him she said, "What'd you do, Joe?"

"Nothin'."

"He's inherited your unorthodox tendencies. Now I gotta worry about him."

She frowned. "Be safe, Joe."

He cocked his head. "Odd advice from the Street Angel."

"The Street Angel is no more."

Rob leaned against the desk and crossed his arms over his chest. "We read the articles."

"ESCAPE's still safe, isn't it?" she said, just to reassure herself.

"Yeah. Nobody knows where we are. We're thinking about moving again, anyway."

Suze came to the door. Behind her was Father Tim. "Thought we heard your voice. Mrs. Senator."

"Spare me. I hate the publicity."

"How are you going to live in that fishbowl, girl?" Suze asked.

"I don't know if I am."

Natale grunted. Rob cocked his head. Father Tim said, "What does that mean? The article made you look lovey-dovey."

As it should have. Clay had had his hands all over her. And afterward he'd wanted to make love to his wife. She didn't blame him. And he was right, it probably didn't matter. This time, though, she was trying to do what was best for them. "Things aren't as they appear. We have to pretend life is just grand for his career, but long-term, who knows?"

"I'm glad to hear that," Natale mumbled.

"What do you mean?"

"He's a politician. Need I say more?"

"He's honest, Joe."

"Is he?"

"Yes."

Angrily, Joe jammed his hands into his pockets. "I think somebody snitched on Taz. I think your senator found her and went up there."

She would not betray her husband. "It wasn't Clay."

"Then putting you in jail, and persecuting you for ten years, as well as his right-wing opinions, are enough for me. You're better off without him."

The thought made her go weak, especially after the past few days. Clay had squelched his resentment and been kind and patient with her. He'd forced her to rest, cooked dinner, and played with Rory. Right now, he and Jon were spending the day with her son—just one big happy family.

"Earth to Bailey." This from Suze.

"Sorry. Listen, I came in to show you all I was doing better."

"You look great," Rob said.

"I feel good."

"Emotionally, too?" Father Tim asked.

"I'm still sad. And guilty. But I'm better."

He didn't look convinced.

"I also wanted to say good-bye."

"Good-bye? You're still going ahead with Guardian, aren't you?" Suze asked with uncharacteristic emotion in her voice. "You're going to retire the Street Angel and run the shelter."

"No, I'm done with any kind of gang intervention."

"That wasn't the plan, Bay."

"I know. That was before . . ." She looked around. "I didn't do such a good job anyway, Suze."

Amid protests, she went to her office to clean out her things. The others got back to work and Suze left. Father Tim, however, appeared at her doorway. "Need some help? You shouldn't be lifting anything."

"That would be great." She nodded to her bookshelf. "Those books need to be packed and addressed. I'm having everything shipped to Clay's house."

"It's not your house, too?"

"No."

Carefully she put pictures in the boxes. There was one of her and Suze when they opened ESCAPE. Rob and Joe when they joined the organization. On the walls were matted and framed posters of bits of letters they'd received from gang kids who'd they'd gotten out and were now living productive lives. She bit her lip at some of the messages: *I couldn't have done it without you . . . You saved my life . . . I have a daughter now because of you guys . . .*

She coughed to clear her throat of the emotion and left the posters where they were. Instead she packed pens, notebooks, personal pictures.

As they worked, Tim said, "You can talk to me about it. I won't tell anybody."

Looking over at him, she shook her head. "There's not much to say."

"Except that you lied to Rob and Joe." His gaze was knowing and full of compassion.

She tried to slough it off. "You can hear my confession."

"Talk to me."

Taking in a deep breath, she continued to pack. "I had to protect Clay."

"And defend him like a supportive wife."

"I meant what I said about this marriage not being made in heaven."

"I know you did."

She shrugged. "He betrayed my trust."

"To protect you."

A big metal dish she used for candy clattered to the floor. She sank onto her chair and scrubbed her hands over her face. "He's so used to being in control, Tim. He says he'll let me do my own thing, then when push comes to shove, he takes over. With disastrous results, this time."

Tim crossed the room and knelt down in front of her. He took her hands. "This is a problem that can be worked out."

"Not necessarily."

"If you love him enough."

Bailey couldn't answer.

"You took vows, in good times and bad times. That's important to remember."

"Are you telling me to stay with my husband—like a good Catholic priest?"

"I'm telling you to follow your heart and work out your problems—like a friend would."

"I love him, so much. I want to get past all this . . ."

He kissed her forehead. "Let's get coffee. Talk this out."

"All right. Then I have somewhere else to go." She stared at him. "Could you come with me?"

"To hell and back, if you need me."

"Well, this place is close."

BECAUSE SHE WAS sixteen and had confessed to a crime for a plea down, Mazie Lennon was in Lancaster State Prison on the outskirts of New York. Because it was the night before Thanksgiving, and Bailey was with a priest, out of curiosity the guard told them, Mazie agreed to see them.

Bailey sat in the visitors' room, forcing herself not to react. But the smell of sweat and desperation, the clanking of bars, and the occasional bark of a guard, catapulted her back to her own days in prison.

Finally, a blond girl was led into the area; she swaggered over to a chair behind a plastic shield, her orange coveralls revealing a tall lanky build. So this was Mazie Lennon. Bailey got up and went to sit across from her, on the other side of the shield. Up close, Bailey could see several piercings, and an all-too-familiar look on her face. It was one the hard-core inmates had worn when Bailey was in prison. "Who the fuck are you?" the girl asked with a sneer.

"I'm the Street Angel."

Mazie threw back her head and laughed—an ugly, maniacal sound. "Looks like I got the last laugh, don't it, chickie?"

"You think killing Taz was funny?" Even Bailey, used to the amoral nature of gang kids, was stunned.

"Yeah, it was a blast. You shoulda seen her choking down the barrel of my gun." She tossed back her hair, snapped her gum. "'Course she wasn't so pretty after I got through with her."

Bailey felt her stomach churn. "I have a question to ask."

"Why'd I do it?"

"No, I know the answer to that one."

Pressing her hands against the glass, Mazie got as close as she could. "Good. Pass it along to your buddies. Nobody gets out of a gang."

"I want to know why she came back? Did she tell you?"

"Who the fuck cares? She never was no Einstein. And she always had a stupid soft streak. She had to know I was gunnin' for her." She laughed at her pun.

Bailey shook her head. "I just don't get it."

"What's there to get? You lost, lady. You ain't gonna get nowhere with your outfit. Gangs are family and we stay together."

"Or you kill each other."

"Damn straight."

"How could you murder a part of your family?" Bailey choked on her words and tears burned her eyes. "How could you murder your friend?"

"You don't turn on your homies, plain and simple."

"I see."

"And it's your fault, sister, for tryin' to get her out."

Bailey stared hard at the girl before her. Her eyes were crazed, her face contorted with the purest hate Bailey had ever seen. "No, Mazie, it wasn't my fault." Or Clay's, she realized with meteoric impact. "It was yours. You pulled the trigger."

Mazie leaped up and started pounding on the glass and yelling. "You fuckin' cunt. It's your fault. You and that goddamn ESCAPE." She used other expletives that resounded in the near-empty visiting area.

Father Tim came running from across the room where he'd been watching Bailey, and the guard went for Mazie. When she was restrained, she yelled, "Go away, Angel."

Bailey backed up but nailed Mazie with a hard glare. "I will. One thing, though, Mazie; think about this. You *do* get out of a gang. Either organizations like ESCAPE can help you leave safely, or you can end up here, without your posse. Taz chose the first way, but you wouldn't let her go. Ironically, *that* got *you* out of the gang."

* * *

CLAY SAT IN the rocker, holding a sleeping Rory to his chest when the front door opened. Bailey was late getting home, but there had been a message on the machine saying she'd been held up.

"Hi," she said coming into the foyer. She nodded to her son. "What's going on?"

"He got sick at the zoo." Clay kissed his head, smelling the shampoo and soap from the bath they'd managed to wrangle him into. "Poor little guy."

"Oh, dear. Did he throw up?"

"All over Jon."

"No."

"I think my son got carried away with having a little brother. Gave him too much junk when I was on my cell phone."

"I'm sorry." She crossed to them and smoothed down Rory's hair. Up close, he could see the fatigue in her eyes and a slump to her usually sturdy shoulders.

"You look tired."

"I am."

He waited. He wouldn't ask about her day. He suspected she went to ESCAPE, but she had to tell him things on her own. He was done pushing. "Did you eat?"

"Uh-huh. With Father Tim. At a diner."

"Good." He rubbed Rory's back. "I hope he's all right for Thanksgiving dinner tomorrow."

"He will be. This kind of thing just wears him out. It's happened before." She looked around. "Where's Jon?"

"Spending the night at his mother's. She's pissed as hell he's not going to be at her house for dinner tomorrow."

"Just wait until he experiences an O'Neil Thanksgiving. He'll wish he was with Karen."

"I highly doubt it." Clay stood, holding tight to Rory. "I'll put him down."

"Want me to fix you a drink?"

"That'd be nice. I'd like a shower, too. I'm a little worse for wear."

"Go on up. Put him to bed." She cocked her head at him. "Thanks for taking such good care of him, Clay."

"I'd do anything for Rory." He leaned over, and still holding her son, kissed her nose. "And for you."

Reaching out, she grasped on to Clay's shoulders, though it was awkward with Rory between them. "That got us into this situation, didn't it?"

"I guess."

He took Rory upstairs, put him down, and sat on the side of the bed for a moment. He wondered if this was the last Thanksgiving he'd spend with the boy—and his mother—or the first. A situation which, he knew now, was out of his control. He'd learned, through this whole ordeal, that a lot of things were beyond his power to make them happen, no matter how hard he fought to orchestrate everything. "I love you, champ."

Rory stirred, but stayed asleep. Clay got up, crossed to his room, and went directly to the bathroom and turned on the shower. He stripped off his jeans and sweatshirt and stepped into scalding water. It should be cold, he guessed, given his body's reaction to his wife. When she'd leaned over, her shirt gaped a bit to reveal the top of breasts swelling with her pregnancy, and he'd gotten stunningly hard. Bracing his hands on the tile, he glanced down. He probably should take care of this himself, before he saw her again, but he didn't want to. "Damn it," he said to his pecker. "I want my wife to take care of you."

He sighed and turned the faucet to cold. But it was more than sex he wanted from his wife. He wanted her commitment to him, and her trust. She had to believe in him. Maybe it would come and maybe it wouldn't. Tonight, he didn't feel particularly hopeful. Over the past week, she'd become more independent, more sure of herself. She'd been kind and polite to him, but only when she was sleepy did she turn to him.

Her brothers, on the other hand, were downright friendly. They even teased him now about getting movie stars' addresses. And they joked about forming a support group for overprotective men, with him and Paddy heading the pack. Funny, the turnaround. Problem was, like Rory, if he lost Bailey now, he'd lose her brothers, too.

Stepping out of the shower, Clay dried off, then wrapped a

towel around his waist. In deference to having Bailey and Rory here, he slept in boxers. He headed to his room to drag some on.

And stopped dead in his tracks. He swallowed hard as he stared across the room.

"Here's your scotch," Bailey said. From his bed. With his sheets wrapped around her. Wearing nothing else, from the looks of it.

"My what?"

"Your drink." She shook back unbound hair that splayed everywhere. Its darkness against her creamy shoulders sent streaks of lust through him. So much for a cold shower.

"What are you doing, honey?"

Lifting her chin, she met his gaze unflinchingly. "Waiting for my husband to make love to me."

He felt his eyes sting. "Why?"

"Didn't you know that pregnant women want to make love twice, maybe three times as often as those who aren't?"

God, his body didn't need to hear that. "Uh, no, I didn't know those exact statistics."

She lazed back into the pillows. "Come get your drink, Senator." And then—holy mother of God—she tipped the glass and poured some of the liquid onto her chest.

He groaned out loud, and crossed to her.

Setting the glass on the sideboard, she took his hand and tugged him down. He sat on the edge of the mattress. She cupped his neck and pulled him to her chest. She smelled like the liquor. He nosed into her, but drew back. "Bailey, love, what . . ." He had to take a breath. "What does this mean? Is it just sex?"

"Nope. Been there, done that." She grasped his hand and brought it to her heart. "It means I want to be your wife, in every sense of the word. It means I'm staying with you, and working out our differences. It means Rory can call you Daddy, Jon can have his room back, and my brothers get to pick on you the rest of your life."

He was speechless, stunned, mystified. Finally he managed to say, "I'll try, Bailey, really I will, to let you run your life."

"You'd better, big guy. Or there'll be lots and lots of those fireworks Sellers asked about." She gave him a sexy grin. "But lots of the other kind, too."

"Sounds good to me." He frowned. "Tell me what brought this on."

She sighed. "I went to see Mazie Lennon today at Lancaster State Prison."

"You *what*?"

Her eyes narrowed.

"Okay, but honey, *Lancaster*?"

"I asked Father Tim to go with me. See, I can be circumspect."

"What happened with Mazie? Why'd you even go?"

"I don't know exactly. I had to see her and ask her about Taz."

His heart constricted. "Did she say it was my fault?"

"No, she said it was mine."

"It's not."

"I realize that, Clay. And it isn't *yours,* either. It was Mazie Lennon's fault that Taz died. And Taz's too. For trusting a brutal, amoral, violent young girl." She kissed his hand.

He drew in a deep breath. "I guess you're right." He watched her. "And for the other?"

"The other?"

"Trusting me."

Her face sobered. "We'll work on that. Father Tim says we'll build up the trust little by little by working together to solve our problems and compromising. We'll probably fight, but . . ." She grinned, a mischievous sexy grin that belonged to the Bailey he first met and fell in love with. ". . . we can spend a lot of time making up."

"Father Tim said that?"

"Not in so many words." She drew his hand to her breast. "So, you wanna practice the making-up part?"

He laughed. "That I do, darlin'."

"I do, too. Now touch me all over and make me scream."

"My pleasure, love."

She yanked at the towel around his waist. "Hmm. Mine, too."

EPILOGUE

The Village Voice

CINDERELLA AND HER PRINCE—
A RETROSPECT IN PICTURES

Hank Sellers

It was two years ago that this newspaper interviewed the then-Senator Wainwright and his bride, Ms. Bailey O'Neil. News of their marriage shocked political circles when it broke in the papers around Thanksgiving. Though no one would know it now, there was a long-standing grudge between the two of them, fought out in papers like ours. Today, as the pictures below show, is the rest of the story.

Picture and Caption #1:
The Second Lady ready to enter the Senate Chamber where she'll address the members in support of Chuck Stewart's new bill on special school programs for at-risk kids.

Picture and Caption #2:
Ms. O'Neil face-to-face with Republican conservative
Tom Carter, at a Task Force on Juvenile Crime and Anti-
Gang measures, which she's headed for nearly eight
months.

Picture and Caption #3:
Ms. O'Neil and Vice President Wainwright relaxing at their
cottage in upstate New York. With them are the O'Neil
brothers: Patrick and his wife, Brie; Liam to the left; Dylan
and Aidan, off to the right with two unidentified redheads.

Picture and Caption #4:
Jon Wainwright and Rory O'Neil Wainwright, the vice
president's sons, frolicking with their dog, Hower (short
for Eisenhower) on the White House lawn.

Picture and Caption #5:
Clay Wainwright, holding his sixteen-month-old daughter,
Angel, while Mom signs autographs after an impassioned
speech to NOW about role models and mentoring programs for troubled girls.

Picture and Caption #6:
Vice President Wainwright and Ms. O'Neil, toasting at the
ball given to raise money for organizations like her old
stomping ground, ESCAPE. Inside scoop: Rumor is, that's
club soda in the Second Lady's hands. This paper has it on
a good source the couple is expecting another child.

And that, folks, is how this Cinderella story ends: happily
ever after.

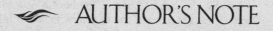 # AUTHOR'S NOTE

In writing this manuscript, an interesting thing happened to me. From the very first chapter, the hero and heroine simply would not do what I had planned for them. As you can tell from reading the book, Bailey and Clay are both strong-minded and often very stubborn; they made their own way through the story. Consequently, I never really knew, until I wrote each scene, what was going to happen. In the long run, it was a delightful ride, though like a roller coaster, it was scary not knowing what was around every bend. I trusted them, though, and was pleased with their choices.

Theirs is a story about two diverse people who, despite the odds, fall in love. I believe in the power of that emotion to overcome any odds—personality differences, background incongruity, life choices. I also believe that people make mistakes and most anything can be forgiven. However, it's not always smooth sailing, and even in the end, people have to work on their relationships the rest of their lives. I'm sure Bailey and Clay will do this.

Another value explored in this book is the power of family.

All of Bailey's brothers jumped right off the page for me. I didn't know they'd be such a big part of the story, and have so much influence over her. What I really loved about them was that, though they disagreed with her and bullied her at times, they were unequivocally there to support her. I'm not surprised at this familial bond, however, as I come from a family of three older sisters and a younger brother, whom I love as much as Bailey loves Aidan, Liam, Dylan and Patrick.

Finally, the central issue of the book—how to stop youth gangs—was not an easy one to deal with. What *is* best—legal intervention or social work? As Bailey and Clay fought heatedly over this issue, I began to see both sides. As they realized, because of the very dire consequences of their actions, that there was no single solution to stopping youth gangs, I agreed. Though the book doesn't give any answers, it does explore the problem and offers various alternatives to this important issue.

As always, I love to hear from readers. Email me at kshayweb@rochester.rr.com, and visit my website at www.kathrynshay.com. I can also be reached by snail mail at P.O. Box 24288, Rochester, New York, 14624.

Kathryn Shay

Turn the page for a special preview of
Kathryn Shay's next novel

CONFLICT OF INTEREST

Coming soon from Berkley Sensation!

WHEN REESE BISHOP approached the front door of his ex-wife's chic condo, and it swung open revealing her young lover, Reese felt like he always did when he encountered Tyler Sloan—old!

"Sloan," Reese said tightly.

"Hey, Reese." Damn, the guy was always so nice, it was hard to dislike him. "Is Kaitlyn expecting you?"

"No." And she wasn't going to be happy, he thought, gripping the newspaper he held in his hand. "She's here, isn't she?"

"In the shower." Tyler shrugged into a casual, unconstructed jacket. His hair askew, his clothing rumpled, it was obvious how he'd spent the night. "Go on inside." When Reese hesitated, Tyler gave him a questioning look. "Want me to tell her you're here?"

"No, I'll be fine. I'll wait downstairs until she's done."

As he watched the other man trundle down the slate walkway in the warm April sunshine, Reese sighed. It came as no surprise that Kate had a younger man in her life. Though she was forty-five and had never been drop-dead gorgeous, there was something vibrant about her—in the snap of her dark eyes, in the glow of her complexion. Hell, even her rich, mink-colored hair shimmered. Men had never been able to stop staring at her. He'd been smitten himself, the first time he laid eyes on her in law school at Yale. But that had been a lifetime ago. Now, when he thought about the past, he remembered only the fights and the searing pain of their permanent split. It had ripped him apart.

Reese stepped into the condo and closed the door. Most everything was white in her house—walls, carpet, leather furniture. The stark décor was accented by black and white prints which decorated the walls, black geometric-shaped pillows, black vases sprouting white flowers. So different from the warm wood and earth tone furnishings of the home they bought just before Sofie was born. A sprawling cedar-sided farmhouse just on the outskirts of town, they'd lovingly restored every single room. Some of the work they'd contracted out, but they'd done much of the renovation themselves, which had made the place *theirs*.

He was examining a photo when he heard her speak behind him and turned. "Ty? Is that you? Did you bring back that buff bod to—" She broke off when she entered the room and found Reese.

For some reason, her sexy tease irritated him. And so there was a clip in his voice when he said, "Sorry my *bod* doesn't appeal to you anymore."

Her dark eyes fired at his retort. "What are you doing here?"

"I need to talk to you. Sloan let me in."

Rubbing the towel on wet hair, she shook her head. Wrapped up in a red satiny robe, even her dishabille was attractive. *Damn her*. Though he hated her for what she'd done to their marriage, and worse, had lost respect for her as a person, the physical spark between them had never quite been doused. "Look, Reese, I don't have time for you this morning."

"Well, make time, sweetheart."

Her whole body tightened. "Oh, my God, is something wrong with Sofie?"

He softened his tone. "Not the last time I spoke with her. Our daughter's fine. Well, as fine as a sixteen-year-old can be living a hundred miles away from her parents in that private school."

The cool façade, the one Kate adopted with him routinely now, replaced the worried mother. "Then can't this wait? My day's packed. I'm running late already."

"It can't wait. And you may have to alter your schedule."

"Really Reese." She hated being told what to do and always needed to be in control. Then again, so did he. The combination had—surprisingly—worked well for them for almost fifteen years.

He handed the newspaper to her. "You won't be in any hurry to get to the courthouse after you see this." His heart beat faster. He still couldn't believe what he'd read in this morning's *Herald*.

She dropped the towel onto the floor; he remembered how much she cluttered things up.

My messiness is part of me, love.

You're lazy, Katie, admit it.

However, at the time, since the towel she'd dropped bared her luscious body to him, and she'd plastered the whole length of her against him, he didn't care that she could be such a slob. He'd taken her against the wall, if he remembered correctly.

Ruthlessly, he shoved the reminiscence back into the compartment where it belonged. "Read the headlines." He'd memorized them. *Longshore Federal Correctional Institute Inmate Dies of Drug Overdose*. And beneath it, *Local judge and lawyer blamed in suicide note*.

Kate's hands gripped the paper. "Not us," she whispered.

He fought hard not to be moved by her vulnerability. "Yes, us. A woman we defended years ago, Anna Bingham."

"Tell me. My glasses are upstairs and I haven't put in my contacts."

He eased the paper from her hands. "We defended her on credit card fraud." Which wasn't the kind of case they usually represented at the law firm they'd shared, but they'd taken on a lot of pro bono that year and needed more paying clients. "She was running a dot com scam and got caught. She ended up in a federal prison camp." The level of incarceration for white collar crime.

"Longshore's not a prison camp. It's high security."

"Apparently, she did her time, got out, and repeated her offenses. Twice. She was sent to New Jersey six months ago."

"Read me what it says about us."

"This is her suicide note. 'I had an affair with Reese Bishop during my trial. When his wife found out, they didn't do enough to keep me out of jail, and are responsible for my downslide after that. Now, I'm in for ten years. I can't handle the bars, the cell, the other inmates. I don't want to live.'"

Kate's entire body stiffened. Her dark eyes lost their hot chocolate warmth and turned frosty. "I see. Is it true? Did you have an affair with Anna Bingham?"

"No, I didn't. It's all a lie. You know we didn't act unethically because of some ridiculous allegation that I screwed her and you wanted her out of the way."

"You could have told her I knew."

"Accusations again, Kate?"

"Well," she said in her best judge voice, "It wouldn't be the first time, now would it?"

Reese stared at the woman he once loved to distraction, unable to believe she could still drive him crazy. "You forget, darling, I was provoked."

Her face turned ashen but she recouped, quickly. "There's blame on both sides, Reese."

Slowly folding the paper, he pulled himself up to his six foot plus height. She was five seven, so he had an advantage. "Could we for once try to be civil to each other? This is going to cause havoc in both our jobs. We have to put our animosity aside."

Crossing her arms over her chest, she tossed her head back. Her hair had started to dry, and without the blower to tame it, the thick locks were curling around her face. These days she wore it straight or in a severe knot at her neck. He preferred the wild tangle it used to be. "Give me a minute to put some clothes on. And call my assistant. Then we can talk this out."

He merely nodded.

"There's coffee. Tyler made it."

"Of course," he muttered. "Tyler—the incarnation of Mr. Wonderful." God, he hated that talking doll who quipped all the things an ideal man should say.

With one last flinty look, Kate headed out the door and up the stairs. Reese drew in a heavy breath. She made him crazy *and* reduced him to spouting nasty comments. Hell, he couldn't think clearly around her now.

Not that he ever could, he reminded himself as he found her all-white, sterile kitchen and grabbed for the pot of coffee her lover had brewed. From the day he met Kaitlyn Renado, his life had been a roller coaster. Only after their divorce, had it evened out.

One broken heart was a small price to pay for being off that ride.

TWO HOURS LATER, in her sunny breakfast nook, Kate sat across from her ex-husband and tried to study the file before her. She and Reese had had a phone conference with their attorneys, who planned to talk to the police regarding the investigation into Bingham's death, then contact the prison to see what they could find out. Because it was Friday, they weren't sure how far they'd get today.

Meanwhile, they gave Kate and Reese some tasks. The first step was to scrutinize the law office's file on Anna Bingham. They each had a copy of it, thanks to Reese's efficient secretary, Yolanda, who used to be her secretary, too. The woman had mothered them both when they started their firm and hired her. Kate and Reese, having been motherless for years, had loved it. She stared down at the file, blocking the nostalgic memory, shutting out the sight of Reese, wishing she could shut him out of her life completely.

It had been five years since their divorce and, thank God, she'd gotten over him. For the first year or so, she cried at night because of what happened those last few months, but gradually she'd begun to heal. The following two years included days and weeks when she didn't think about him at all. Eventually, she'd managed to free herself of feelings for him. But at times like these, when she came face-to-face with him, or especially when what had happened in the past reared its ugly head, she hurt like hell. Thank God no one except her dearest friend, Jillian Jenkins, knew how being with her ex could still affect her. Tyler had some stupid male insecurity about Reese, so Kate never admitted to him how hard it was to have contact with Reese, nor how much their split had hurt. Only Jillian was privy to how losing the only man Kate had ever really loved and the horrible way they treated each other at the end, could still cut her heart to ribbons.

Damn it. She had to concentrate on the matter at hand. She could work on this until one P.M., then she had to take her afternoon cases. Family court judges heard an average of fifty to sixty cases a day and had no room for absenteeism. That she'd shuffled her load to someone else this morning didn't sit right with her. But she had no choice. They had to get to the bottom of this mess.

She sneaked a peek at Reese; he was due in court, too, for a pre-trial hearing at three. He wore a beautiful pin-striped suit but had removed his jacket and tie and rolled up his sleeves. His dark hair fell onto his forehead, which was tanned. He'd probably spent some vacation time in the Caribbean, his favorite place now, with his own private beach bunny. Absently, he rolled a pen between his hands, something he often did when he was thinking. For a brief minute, she remembered what those hands felt like on her bare skin.

Really good.

Her cell phone rang, dragging her from her memories. Reese scowled at it, but said nothing as she picked it up from the table. "Hello."

"Hey, gorgeous. I was just calling to see how it went with the ex." Tyler's voice pitched sexily low. "And protecting what's mine."

"I'm at home, and Reese is still here. Something's happened." Briefly she explained, in case he saw the paper.

"Kaitlyn, honey, I'm so sorry."

"I'll call you when I have more information."

Reese glanced over when she clicked off. "Lover boy checking up on you?"

"He's concerned." Her eyes narrowed. "Does your little sweet thing know yet?"

"Not yet." He closed the file and held it up. "I don't see anything here, do you?"

She shook her head. "It's pretty cut and dried. Bingham came to our firm ten years ago, and we defended her for fraud. She was guilty as hell. Only your expertise got her a self-surrender at Danbury, and a stint of sixteen months with time off for good behavior. You also set her up with the prison advocate guy to help her through the process."

Frowning, he sat back in the chair. "I wonder why she didn't come back to us when she got in trouble again."

Kate's jaw clenched.

He noticed. "What?"

"Nothing. Unless what she says is true."

"Fuck it, Kate. If you're not going to believe me, no one else will. We won't have a shot in hell of coming off innocent if my own partner-at-the-time doesn't stand behind me."

He was right. She hated when he was right. "I know. Swear to God you're not lying in this. If you are, it's okay. Just tell me. We'll go from there."

His mouth turned up in a begrudging grin. It had been one of many private things between them, for big and little testimonials. . . . Swear to God you like this dress and aren't just saying you do . . . Swear to God you don't think I was wrong in that case . . . Swear to God you love me more than anything.

"I swear to God," he said, his tone sincere. "I never had an affair with Anna Bingham." A slash of scarlet appeared on his high cheekbones. "I strayed *once,* and you know why."

Kate's own face burned. She remembered the day she caught her husband of fourteen years cheating on her. His car had been parked in front of the other woman's building, in the middle of the day, for all to see. It was almost as if he was flaunting his indiscretion. Jillian had driven past the vehicle and called Kate. Raw from their prolonged emotional distance and the yelling matches which broke out routinely, she'd gone over to the house and been confronted with Malibu Barbie in a skimpy robe at the door. Kate had barged through the entrance and stalked right upstairs. Reese had been naked, smoking a cigarette in bed.

"All right," she finally managed. "I'll believe that."

"You don't sound convinced." His voice was still tight. "Again, if you aren't. . . ."

"No, I am." She bent back the corner of the file and felt that old vulnerability to Reese, and only to Reese, flood through her. "Truthfully, I was shocked that you went to someone else. Regardless of what happened, we'd always been enough for each other."

Removing his glasses, he braced his arms on the table. They were muscular and strong, sprinkled with dark hair. "You were enough for me, Kate. Maybe too much." He sighed, suddenly seeming weary. "It was the other stuff."

Her heartbeat went at a clip. "You mean you did it to punish me?"

"No. I did it to stop the pain."

"Did it? Stop the pain?"

"Some." He scrubbed a hand over his face.

She shook her head. "This is old ground."

"I know." Again, he held up the file. "Resurrected because of Anna Bingham, I guess."

"Let's bury it back where it belongs."

"Agreed. So, we're square I didn't do what she accuses?"

"We're square. But hell, Reese, how are we going to prove it? Come out from under it all? This kind of scandal could ruin both of us."

"You got that right. My credibility as a lawyer will be shot. If people believe I behaved unethically, I'll be lucky to hold onto the clients I have, let alone bring in new business."

"And I'll be called before the Judicial Conduct Commission. A judge can't have her ethics questioned like this."

"No sense in panicking," he said gruffly.

"I agree. We have to just plow through it all until we find the answers."

And just like in the past that they were trying to ignore, they centered each other.

"We'll do what the lawyers said," he went on. "Now that we've scrutinized the file, we'll look at the trial transcript. And I already have Yolanda downloading any information from the Internet on Anna Bingham. There's some reason this woman lied about us in her suicide note, and we'll find it. I promise."

In the past, he'd made promises he was unable to keep.

She only hoped to God this time his words held quarter.

Kate didn't know if she could handle losing her beloved profession. It was all she had left after Reese divorced her and their daughter stopped talking to her.

SOFIE BISHOP SLID to the floor of her closet and buried her face in her hands. The nightmares she was having sucked and kept her up until five this morning. She'd zonked after lunch, missing classes. Her stomach hurt and even her skin burned. The hole she was digging herself in was deep and she couldn't climb out.

For a minute she considered calling her father. But he'd rush up here like a knight in shining armor and a) force her to go home with him or b) make promises to her he couldn't keep.

Go home. What a flamin' joke. She didn't have a home anymore. Not since the big D. Not since her mother turned her back on the most wonderful man in the world, forcing him to hook up with some bimbo. Now the illustrious judge had a young lover, an ult pad, and a new life. No room there for a daughter who hated her guts.

Well, fuck her. Sofie crawled over to a box on the floor, opened it and pulled out a reefer. She lit it, sucked in the mellow pleasure, and after two more puffs could finally breathe again. Nope, Sofie wouldn't call her parents. She'd have to drag herself out of this pit all by herself. And she would. Much as she hated to admit it, she had her mother's grit. She'd survive and probably be a success in life.

And probably, despite what everybody else thought, she'd be as unhappy as Kaitlyn Renado was. Her mother hid it well from the world, but Sofie knew the real truth about the woman who gave her birth.

From award-winning author
KATHRYN SHAY

On the Line
0-425-19710-7

When investigator Eve Woodward comes to
Hidden Cover looking for clues in an arson case, she
uncovers something completely unexpected—a
handsome fire chief and a burning attraction.

Trust in Me
0-425-18884-1

As teenagers, they were called the Outlaws.
Now these six friends will find that yesterday's
heartaches are part of the journey to
tomorrow's hopes.

Promises to Keep
0-425-18574-5

A high-school principal resents the new
crisis counselor assigned to her school.
But Joe Stonehouse is really an undercover
Secret Service agent. Will the truth temper the
attraction that threatens to set them both on fire?

B066

BERKLEY SENSATION
COMING IN OCTOBER 2005